Availa
fro
Sp

The Man Behind the Cop
by Janice Kay Johnson
&
The Single Dad's Virgin Wife
by Susan Crosby

Baby Makes Three
by Molly O'Keefe
&
Healing the Cowboy's Heart
by Judy Duarte

Her Miracle Man
by Karen Sandler
&
No Place Like Home
by Margaret Watson

The Prince's Cowgirl Bride
by Brenda Harlen

The Boss's Christmas Proposal
by Allison Leigh

The Bride with No Name
by Marie Ferrarella

The Dad Next Door
by CJ Carmichael

BABY MAKES THREE

Alice stared at the black truck that stopped in front of her.

One guy got out, holding a droopy bouquet of yellow flowers. One guy, whose amble towards her was painfully, heartbreakingly familiar.

She used to love his size, love how it made her feel small and safe. He'd wrap those strong arms around her and she'd feel protected from the world, from herself. It hurt too much to remember that.

"Hello, Alice."

"Gabe." Her voice croaked. Why couldn't she be stronger when she spoke to her ex-husband? "What are you doing here?"

"I need you," he said. "Alice. I built the inn. It's gorgeous."

The inn. The home they'd dreamed of. And yet another thing that had been stripped from her when he'd walked out the door. She didn't need to be reminded of how much she'd lost. She got to her feet.

"I need a chef, Alice. I am desperate. And from the looks of things, so are you."

He held out the roses. She ignored them.

Not ever again with this man. She'd worked too hard to forget the past. There was nothing he could say that would convince her to reunite with him – even only professionally. Nothing.

HEALING THE COWBOY'S HEART

Their gazes met and locked.

Sexual awareness flared in all its heat and glory, stirring up something more powerful than words. Seeing that was making Matt forget the shackles of guilt he hadn't been able to shake.

For a moment, he almost felt whole again – as if that accident had never happened.

He knew he ought to say something, but he didn't want her to get the wrong idea and think that they were actually creating some kind of friendship or bond.

Tori was too attractive.

Too appealing.

And pretending otherwise was only going to mess with his mind.

First published in Great Britain 2009
Harlequin Mills & Boon Limited,
Eton House, 18-24 Paradise Road, Richmond, Surrey TW9 1SR

Baby Makes Three © Molly Fader 2007
Healing the Cowboy's Heart © Judy Duarte 2008
(Original title: *In Love With the Bronc Rider*)

ISBN: 978 0 263 87642 0

23-1009

Harlequin Mills & Boon policy is to use papers that are natural, renewable
and recyclable products and made from wood grown in sustainable
forests. The logging and manufacturing processes conform to the legal
environmental regulations of the country of origin.

Printed and bound in Spain
by Litografia Rosés S.A., Barcelona

BABY MAKES THREE

BY
MOLLY O'KEEFE

HEALING THE COWBOY'S HEART

BY
JUDY DUARTE

 MILLS & BOON®

BABY MAKES THREE

BY
MOLLY O'KEEFE

Molly O'Keefe has written eleven books for the Superromance, Flipside and Duets lines. When she isn't writing happily ever after she can usually be found in the park acting as referee between her beleaguered border collie and her one-year-old son. She lives in Toronto, Canada, with her husband, son, dog and the largest heap of dirty laundry in North America.

To Aunt Cherie and Uncle Earl
Sometimes, with family, you just get lucky.
And we are very lucky.

CHAPTER ONE

OUT OF THE CORNER of his eye, Gabe Mitchell saw his father, Patrick, spit a mouthful of seaweed-wrapped tofu into his napkin like a five-year-old.

Gabe kicked him under the table, appalled but envious.

"So?" Melissa-something-or-other, the chef responsible for the foul-tasting vegan spa cuisine, asked. "Was I right, or what?"

"Or what," Patrick muttered, balling his napkin up beside his plate.

"You were right," Gabe said and pushed his own mouthful of bitter mush into his cheek away from his taste buds. "This is really something."

"Well?" She smiled broadly like a cat with her eye on the canary. "When do I start?"

Patrick laughed, but quickly coughed to cover it, so Gabe didn't bother kicking him again.

He managed to swallow the mess in his mouth, took a huge sip of the unsweetened berry smoothie to wash it down and was appalled to discover she'd somehow made berries taste bad, too.

He'd interviewed and auditioned five chefs and

this one really was the bottom of a very dark, very deep barrel.

"Well—" he smiled and lied through his teeth "—I have a few more interviews this week, so I will have to get back to you."

The girl looked disappointed and a little mean-spirited, which wasn't going to help her get the job. "You know," she said, "it's not going to be easy to find someone willing to live out here in the middle of nowhere."

"I understand that," he said graciously, even though it was getting hard not to throw her out on her scrawny butt.

"And it's a brand-new inn." She shrugged. "It's not like you have the credentials to get a—"

"Well, then." He stood up and interrupted the little shit's defeating diatribe before she got to the part about how he was ugly and his father dressed him funny. "Why don't you gather your equipment and I'll call you if—"

"And that's another thing." Now she was really getting snotty. What was it about vegans, he wondered, that made them so touchy? "Your kitchen is a disaster—"

"You know how building projects can be." Patrick stood, his silver hair and dashing smile gleaming in the sunlight. "One minute shambles, the next state of the art."

"You must be in the shambles part," Melissa said.

"Very true, but I can guarantee within the week state-of-the-art." His blue eyes twinkled as though he was letting Melissa in on a secret. It was times such as these that Gabe fully realized the compliment people gave him when they said he was a chip off the old block.

Patrick stepped to the side of Melissa and held out his arm toward the kitchen as though he were ushering her toward dinner, rather than away from a job interview she'd bombed.

Gabe sat with a smile. Dad was going to handle this one. *Great. Because I am out of niceties.*

"Tell me, Melissa, how did you get that tofu to stay together like that? In a tidy little bundle," Patrick asked as they walked toward the kitchen.

Melissa blushed and launched into a speech on the magic of toothpicks.

God save me from novice chefs.

The swinging door to the kitchen swung open, revealing his nowhere-near-completed kitchen, and then swung shut behind his father giving the oblivious woman the heave-ho.

Gotta hand it to the guy, sixty-seven years old and he still has it.

Silence filled the room, from the cathedral ceiling to the fresh pine wood floors. The table and two chairs sat like an island in the middle of the vast, sun-splashed room.

He felt as though he was in the eye of the storm. If he left this room he'd be buffeted, torn apart by gale-force winds, deadlines, loose ends and a chefless kitchen.

"You're too nice," Patrick said, stepping back into the room.

"You told me to always be polite to women," Gabe said.

"Not when they are trying to poison you."

Patrick lowered himself into the chair he'd vacated and crossed his arms over his flannel-covered barrel chest. "She was worse than the other five chefs you've talked to."

The seaweed-wrapped tofu on his plate seemed to mock Gabe, so he threw his napkin over it and pushed it away. At loose ends, he crossed his arms behind his head and stared out his wall of windows at his view of the Hudson River Valley.

The view was stunning. Gorgeous. Greens and grays and clouds like angels filling the slate-blue sky. He banked on that view to bring in the guests to his Riverview Inn, but he'd been hoping for a little more from the kitchen.

The Hudson River snaked its way through the corner of his property, and out the window, he could see the skeleton frame of the elaborate gazebo being built. The elaborate gazebo where, in two and a half months, there was going to be a very important wedding.

The mother of the bride had called out of the blue three days ago, needing an emergency site and had found him on the Web. And she'd been e-mailing every day to talk about the menu and he'd managed to put her off, telling her he needed guest numbers before he could put together a menu and a budget.

If they lost that wedding…well, he'd have to hope there was a manager's job open at McDonald's or that he could sell enough of his blood, or hair, or semen or whatever it took to get him out of the black hole of debt he'd be in.

All of the building was going according to plan. There had been a minor glitch with the plumber, however Max, his brother and begrudging but incredibly skilled general contractor, had sorted it out early and they were right back on track.

"Getting the chef was supposed to be the easy part, wasn't it?" Patrick asked. "I thought you had those hotshot friends of yours in New York City."

Gabe rolled his eyes at his father. Anyone who didn't know the difference between a fuse box and a circuit breaker was a hotshot to him. And it wasn't a compliment.

"They decided to stay in New York City," he said. All three of his top choices, which had forced him into this hideous interview process.

Fifteen years in the restaurant business working his way up from waiter to bartender to sommelier. He had been the manager of the best restaurant in Albany for four years and finally owner of his own Zagat-rated bar and grill in Manhattan for the past five years and this is what he'd come to.

Seaweed-wrapped tofu.

"I can't believe this is so hard," he muttered.

Patrick grinned.

"I open in a month and I've got no chef. No kitchen staff whatsoever."

Patrick chuckled.

"What the hell are you laughing at, Dad? I'm in serious trouble here."

"Your mother would say this—"

Icy anger exploded in his exhausted brain. "What is this recent fascination with Mom? She's been gone for years, I don't care what she'd say."

His cruel words echoed through the empty room. He rubbed his face, weary and ashamed of himself. "I'm sorry, Dad. I've got so much going on, I just don't want—"

"I understand, son." The heavy clap of his father's hand on his shoulder nearly had him crumbling into a heap. "But not everything can be charmed or finessed. Sometimes it takes work—"

"I work." Again, anger rose to the surface. "I work hard, Dad."

"Oh, son." Patrick's voice was rough. "I know you do. But you've worked hard at making it all look easy. I've never seen a construction job go as smooth as this one has. You've got every lawyer, teamster and backhoe operator eating out of the palm of your hand."

"You think that's easy?" Gabe arched an eyebrow at his father.

"I know better than that. I've watched you work that gray in your hair and I've watched you work through the night for this place and I'm proud of you."

Oh, Jesus, he was going to cry in his seaweed.

"But sometimes you have to make hard choices. Swallow your pride and beg and compromise and ask for favors. You have to fight, which is something you don't like to do."

That was true, he couldn't actually say he *fought* for things. Fighting implied arguments and standoffs and a possibility of losing.

Losing wasn't really his style.

He worked hard, he made the right contacts, he treated his friends well and his rivals better. He ensured things would go his way—which was a far cry from having them fall in his lap. But it was also a far cry from compromising or swallowing his pride or fighting.

The very idea gave Gabe the chills.

"You saying I should fight for Melissa?" He jerked his head at the door the vegan chef had left through.

"No." Patrick's bushy eyebrows lifted. "God, no. But I'm saying you should fight for the right chef."

"What're we fighting for?" Max, Gabe's older brother stomped into the room, brushing sawdust from the chest and arms of his navy fleece onto the floor. "Did I miss lunch?"

"Not really," Patrick said. "And we haven't actually started any fight, so cool your jets."

Max pulled one of the chairs from the stacks on tables in the corner, unclipped his tool belt and slung it over the back of the chair before sitting.

As the family expert on fighting, Max had made battles his life mission. And not just physically, though the bend in his nose attested to a few bar brawls and the scar on his neck from a bullet that got too close told the truth better than this new version of his brother, who, since being shot, acted as though he'd never relished a good confrontation.

Yep, Max knew how to fight, for all the good it did him.

"Well, from the look on Gabe's face, I guess we still don't have a chef," Max said, sliding his sunglasses into the neck of his shirt.

"No," Gabe growled. "We don't."

Now Max, his beloved brother, his best friend, stretched his arms over his head and laughed. "Never seen you have so much trouble, Gabe."

"I am so glad that my whole family is getting such pleasure out of this. Need I remind you that if this doesn't work, we're all homeless. You should show a little concern about what's going on."

"It's just a building," Max said.

Gabe couldn't agree less, but he kept his mouth shut. Going toe to toe with his brother, while satisfying on so many levels, wouldn't get him a chef.

"I'm going to go make us some lunch." Patrick stood and Max groaned. "Keep complaining and you can do it," he said over his shoulder and disappeared into the kitchen.

"Cheese sandwiches. Again," Max groused.

"It's better than what we had, trust me."

"What happened?"

"Ah, she fed us terrible food and then said I was crazy for trying to build an inn in the middle of nowhere and get a chef to come out here for little pay in a half-finished kitchen. Basically, what all the chefs have said to me."

Gabe paused, then gathered the courage to ask the question that had been keeping him up nights.

"Do you think they're right? Is it nuts to expect a high-caliber chef to come way out here and put their career on the line and their life on hold to see if this place takes off?"

Max tipped his head back and howled, the sound reverberating through the room, echoing off the vaulted ceiling. "Brother, I've been telling you this was nuts for over a year. Don't tell me you're starting to agree now!"

Gabe smiled. He was discouraged, sure. Tired as all hell, without a doubt. Frustrated and getting close to psychotic about his chefless state, absolutely. But his Riverview Inn was going to be a success.

He'd work himself into the hospital, into his grave to make sure of it.

He had been dreaming of this inn for ten years.

"It's not like I've got no credentials." He scowled, hating that Melissa had gotten under his skin and that he still felt the need to justify his dream. "I worked my way up to manager in the restaurant in Albany. And I owned one of the top ten restaurants in New York City for five years. I've had reporters and writers calling me for months wanting to do interviews. The restaurant reviewer for *Bon Appetit* wanted to come out and see the property before we even got started."

"All the more reason to get yourself a great chef."

"Who?" He rubbed his hands over his face.

"Call Alice," Max said matter-of-factly, as though Alice was on speed dial or something.

Gabe's heart chugged and sputtered.

He couldn't breathe for a minute. It'd been so long since someone had said her name out loud. *Alice*.

"Who?" he asked through a dry throat. Gabe knew, of course. How many Alices could one guy know? But, surely his brother, his best friend, had not pulled *Alice* from the past and suggested she was the solution to his problems.

"Don't be stupid." Max slapped him on the back. "The whole idea of this place started with her—"

"No, it didn't." Gabe felt compelled to resist the whole suggestion. *Alice* had never, ever been the solution to a problem. She was the genesis of trouble, the spring from which any disaster in his life emerged.

Max shook his head and Gabe noticed the silver in his brother's temples had spread to pepper his whole head and sprouted in his dark beard. This place was aging them both. "We open in a month and you want to act like a five-year-old?" Max asked.

"No, of course not. But my ex-wife isn't going to help things here."

"She's an amazing chef." Max licked his lips. "I can't tell you the number of times I've woken up in a cold sweat thinking of that duck thing she made with the cherries."

Gabe worried at the cut along his thumb with his other thumb and tried not to remember all the times in the past five years he'd woken in a cold sweat thinking of Alice.

"Gabe." Max laid a hand on Gabe's shoulder. "Be smart."

"Last I heard she was a superstar," Gabe said. He tried to relax the muscles of his back, his arms that had gone tight at the mention of Alice. He tried to calm his heart. "She wouldn't be interested."

"When was the last you heard?"

It's not as though she'd stayed in touch after that first year when they'd divvied up all the things they'd gathered and collected—the antiques from upstate, their kitchen, their friends. "About four years ago."

"Well, maybe she'll know of someone. She can at least point you in the right direction."

Gabe groaned. "I hate it when you're right," he muttered.

"Well, I'd think you'd be used to it by now." Max laughed. "I think I'll skip lunch and get back to work." He grabbed his tool belt. "The gazebo should be done by tomorrow."

"What's the status on the cottages?" Gabe asked.

"You'll have to ask Dad." Max shrugged his broad shoulders and cinched the tool belt around his waist, over his faded and torn jeans. "As far as I know he just had some roofing and a little electrical to finish on the last one."

Gabe's affection and gratitude toward his brother and dad caught him right in the throat. The Riverview Inn with its cottages, stone-and-beam lodge and gazebo and walking trails and gardens had been his dream, the goal of his entire working life. But he never, ever would have been able to accomplish it without his family.

"Max, I know I don't say it enough, but thank you. I—"

Max predictably held up a hand. "You can thank me by providing me with some decent chow. It's not too much to ask."

He took his sunglasses from the neck of his fleece and slid them on, looking dangerous, like the cop he'd been and not at all like the brother Gabe knew.

"Oh, I almost forgot," Max said, poised to leave. "Sheriff Ginley has got two more kids."

"Can either of them cook?"

Max shrugged. "I think one of them got fired from McDonald's."

"Great, he can be our chef."

"I don't think Sheriff Ginley would smile upon a juvenile delinquent with such easy access to knives."

The after-school work program for kids who got in trouble in Athens, the small town north of the inn, had been Max's idea, but Gabe had to admit, the labor was handy, and he hoped they were doing some good for the kids. "They can help you with the grounds."

"That's what I figured." Max smiled wickedly and left, his heavy-booted footsteps thudding through the nearly empty room.

Gabe sighed and let his head fall back. He stared up at the elaborate cedar joists in the ceiling, imagined them with the delicate white Christmas lights he planned on winding around them.

The ceiling would look like the night sky dotted with stars.

It had been one of Alice's ideas.

He and Alice used to talk about opening a place out of the city. A place on a bluff. He'd talked about cottages and fireplaces and she'd talked about organic ingredients and local produce. They'd been a team then, she the chef, he the consummate host, producer and manager. He'd felt invincible in those early days with Alice by his side.

But then the problems came and Alice got more and more distant, more and more sad with every trip to the doctor, every failed effort that ended in blood and tears and— Well, he'd never felt so helpless in his life.

"Lunch, boys!" Dad called from the kitchen the way he had since their mom walked out on them more than thirty years ago.

Gabe smiled and stood.

Nothing to do but eat a cheese sandwich and get to work. His dream wasn't going to build itself.

THE HANGOVER POUNDED behind Alice's eyes. Her fingers shook, so she set down the knife before she diced up her finger along with the tomatoes.

"I'm taking a break," she told Trudy, who worked across from her at the long stainless steel prep table

Trudy's black eyes were concerned. "That's your second break since you've been here and it's only three."

"Smoker's rights," Alice croaked and grabbed a mug from the drying rack by the industrial washer and filled it with the swill Johnny O's called coffee.

"You don't smoke," Trudy pointed out, trying to be helpful and failing miserably. "If Darnell comes back here, what am I supposed to tell him?"

"That he can fire me." Alice slid her sunglasses from her coat hanging by the door and used her hips to push out into the bright afternoon.

Even with her dark glasses on, the sunshine felt like razor wire against her eyeballs, so after she collapsed onto the bench that had been set up by the Dumpsters for staff, she just shut her eyes against the sun.

The hangover, the sleeplessness, this mindless menial job that paid her part of the mortgage, it all weighed her down like sandbags attached to her neck.

Tonight no drinking, she swore.

She couldn't change the fact that she'd fallen from chef and owner of Zinnia's to head line chef at one of the three Johnny O's franchises in Albany. That damage was already done and she'd come to grips with it.

But she could control the drinking.

A small voice reminded her that she made that promise almost every night.

Sometimes she wanted to punch the small voice, but instead she breathed deep of the slightly putrid air and tried to get Zen about the whole situation. She took a sip of her coffee, and listened to the sound of traffic.

The parking lot was pretty empty, but soon the hungry folks of Albany would be getting off work and looking for a sunny patio and drink specials and a lot of them would head to Johnny O's. The kitchen would be loud and on fire for about eight hours and in those eight hours, while arranging plates of pasta and fire-baked pizzas and grilling steaks and fish specials, she would forget all the reasons she had to drink.

Maybe she'd help the cleaning staff tonight. Work herself into a good exhaustion so she wouldn't need the red wine to relax.

She tilted her face up to the sun and stretched out her feet, pleased with her plan.

A black truck, mud splattered and beat-up, pulled in to the lot and parked directly across from her. She thought about heading back inside, or at least opening the door and yelling to warn Trudy customers were arriving and the kitchen was on demand. But Trudy had been in the business as long as she had and could handle cooking for a truckload of guys.

But only one guy got out.

One guy, holding a droopy bouquet of yellow roses.

One guy, whose slow amble toward her was painfully, heartbreakingly familiar.

Coffee sloshed onto her pants, so she set the cup down on the bench and clenched her suddenly shaking hands together.

Spots swam in front of her eyes and her head felt light and full, like a balloon about to pop.

The man was tall and lean, so handsome still it made her heart hurt.

He stopped right in front of her and pushed his sunglasses up onto his head, displacing his dark blond hair. The sun was behind him and he seemed so big. She used to love his size, love how it made her feel small and safe. He'd wrap those strong arms around her and she felt protected from the world, from herself.

He smiled like a man who knew all the tastiest things about her.

That smile was his trademark. He could disarm an angry patron at four feet with the strength of his charming smile. He could woo frigid reviewers, disgruntled suppliers…his ex-wife.

"Hello, Alice." He held out the roses but she couldn't get her hands to lift and take them.

She left her shades on, so shattered by Gabe's sudden appearance in front of her, as if the past five years hadn't happened.

"Gabe." Her voice croaked again and she nearly cringed.

He took a deep breath, in through his nose, no doubt hoping for a bit more welcome from her, some reaction other than the stoic front that was all she had these days.

His hand holding the roses fell back to his side.

"What are you doing here?" she asked. She sounded accusatory and mean, like a stranger who had never known him at all.

And she felt that way. It was why, in part, the marriage had ended. Despite the late-night talks, the dreams of building a business together, the sex that held them together longer than they should have been, in the end, when things got bad, they really never knew each other at all.

"I could ask you the same thing." His eyes swept the bench, the back door to Johnny O's. The Dumpsters.

Suddenly, the reality of her life hammered home like a nail in her coffin. She worked shifts at a chain restaurant and was hungover at three on a Friday afternoon.

Oh, how the mighty have fallen, she thought bitterly, hating herself with a vehemence she usually saved for her dark drunken hours.

"I work here," she said, battling her embarrassment with the sharp tilt of her head.

He nodded and watched her, his blue eyes cataloging the differences the five years between them had made. And behind her sunglasses, she did the same.

Gabe Mitchell was still devilishly easy on the eyes.

He'd always had her number. One sideways look from him, one tiny grin and she'd trip over her hormones to get into his arms. There was just something about the man and, she surmised after taking in his faded jeans and the black T-shirt with the rip at the collar, the work boots and his general all-around sexiness, there still was something about him.

But, she reminded herself, underneath that lovely candy coating beat one cold, cold heart. She'd learned it the hard way, and she still hadn't recovered from the frost burn her five-year marriage had given her.

Call it fear of commitment, call it intimacy issues, whatever it was, Gabe had it bad. And watching him walk away from her and their marriage had nearly killed her.

"You look good," Gabe said and it was such a lie, such an attempt to sweet-talk her, that she laughed. "You do," he protested.

"Save the charm for someone else, Gabe." Finally she pushed her shades up onto her head and looked her ex-husband in the eye. "I told you I never wanted to see you again."

CHAPTER TWO

"AND—" HIS SMILE SEEMED a little brittle around the edges "—I think we both know you didn't mean it."

She arched her eyebrows in response. Oh, she'd meant it all right.

"What do you want, Gabe?"

"A guy can't visit an old friend?"

She laughed outright. At him. At them. At this stupid little dance.

"Gabe, we were never friends." The lie slipped off her tongue easily. It was better to pretend they had never been friends than to dwell on those memories, to give in to the sudden swell of feelings his presence stirred in her belly. "What. Do. You. Want?"

He ran his fingers through his too-long hair and scowled at her, the fierce look that always warned her he was running out of patience.

Good, she thought, *get mad and leave like you always do.*

She scowled back. She'd never been overly gracious—she was too busy for that—but in her time with Gabe she'd learned to be polite.

But not anymore. There was no one in her life to be polite to, so she had no practice.

And she wasn't about to apologize. Not to him.

"I need you," he said and she fought to keep herself from choking on a sound of disbelief.

"Gabe Mitchell at my door, begging." She shivered dramatically. "Hell is getting colder."

"Alice." He sighed. "This isn't easy for me. You know that. But I need you. Bad."

His low tone hit her in the stomach and snaked down to her sex, which bloomed in sudden heat. Too familiar, those words. Too reminiscent of those nights together, when they'd needed each other so much, good sense got burned to ash.

"I really can't imagine why," she said, crossing one leg over another, and her arms came across her chest, giving him every signal to stop, to say goodbye and walk away.

But he didn't and she wondered what was truly at stake here. The Gabe she knew did not fight and he never begged.

"I built the inn," he said softly. "The one we always talked about."

It was a slap. A punch in her gut. Her eyes burned from the pain and shock of it. How dare he? He'd walked away with her pride, her self-respect, her dreams of a family and now this.

She wanted to scream, just tilt her head back and howl at the pain and injustice of it all.

The inn. The home they'd dreamed of. He'd built

it while she worked shifts grilling grade B steak and making nachos.

She let out a slow breath, emptying her body of air, so maybe the shell she was would just blow away on the wind.

"Good for you," she managed to say through frozen lips and got to her feet. "I need to go."

He stopped her, not by touching her—good God wouldn't that be a disaster—but by getting in her way with his oversize body.

"It's gorgeous, Alice, you should see it. I named it the Riverview Inn and it's right on a bluff with the Hudson snaking through the property. You can see the river from the dining room."

A mean anger seeped into her, culled from her crappy job, her hangover, her ruined life…even from the Dumpster. She didn't need to be reminded of how much she'd lost and she really didn't need to be brought face-to-face with how well Gabe had done.

"Like I said—" she didn't spare the sarcasm "—bully for you. I'll tell all my friends." She ducked by him.

"I need a chef, Alice."

She stopped midstride, snagged for a second on a splinter of hope. Of joy.

Then she jerked herself free and laughed, but refused to meet his earnest blue eyes. Was this real? Was this some kind of trick? A lie? Were the few remaining friends in her life setting up some elaborate intervention?

"Me? Oh, man, you must be in some dire straits if you are coming to me—"

"I am. I am desperate. And—" he inclined his head to the Dumpster, the plaza parking lot "—from the look of things…so are you."

The bravado and sunglasses didn't work. He saw right through her and it fueled her bitter anger.

"I'm fine," she said, stubbornly clinging to her illusions. "I need to get back to work."

"I want to talk to you about this, Alice. It's a win-win for both of us."

"Ah, Gabe Mitchell of the silver tongue. Everything is a win-win until it all goes to shit. No." She shook her head, suddenly desperate to get away from him and his magnetic force that always spun her in circles. "I won't be your chef."

She walked around him, careful not to get too close, not to touch him, or smell him, or feel the heat from his arm.

"I know where you live, Alice," he said, going for a joke, trying to be charming. "Look, I just want to talk. If you decide after we talk that it's not for you, fine. That's totally fine. But maybe you know someone—"

"I don't."

"Alice." He sighed that sigh that weighed on her, that, during their marriage, had filled the distance between them and pushed them further apart. The sigh that said, "Don't be difficult."

"I don't," she insisted. "I don't know anyone who would want to live out there."

"Except you?" Gabe said.

"Not anymore," she lied. "My break is over. I have to go."

"I want to talk. Can I meet you at home?" He caught himself. "At your house?"

Painful sympathy leaped in her. He'd loved their house, had craved a home, some place solid to retreat to at the end of the day. He'd finished the basement and hung pictures and shelves and repaired the bad plumbing like a man in love. And in the divorce he'd given it to her, shoved the lovely Tudor away like a friend who'd betrayed him.

"The locks are changed," she said.

"I'm sure they are, but I'll bet you a drive out to the inn that you still keep the key under that ceramic frog you bought in Mexico." He smiled, that crooked half grin. Charm and bonhomie oozing off him and she wanted to tell him no matter how well he thought he knew her, he didn't.

But the key *was* under the frog.

"Suit yourself, Gabe," she told him. "But my answer won't change."

"Alice—"

He held out the roses and she ignored them. She hit the door and didn't look back. She could feel him, the touch of his gaze even through the steel door, through her clothes, through her skin right to the heart of her.

Nope, she shook her head. Not again. Not ever again with that man. She'd worked too hard to forget the past. She'd worked too hard to stop the pain, to cauterize the wounds he'd left in her.

There was nothing he could say that would convince her. Nothing.

"WELL," Gabe said, tossing the bouquet into the Dumpster. "That went well."

He shook off the strange sensation in his stomach, brought on by the begging he'd had to do just to get her to listen to him.

Dad would be proud, he thought and the thought actually made him feel better.

He still couldn't manage to wrap his head around the fact that she worked at Johnny O's. Last he'd heard, her restaurant, Zinnia or Begonia or something, had gotten a high Zagat rating and someone had approached her about doing a cookbook.

He looked at the neon lights of the cookie-cutter restaurant she'd escaped into and smiled.

This had to bode well for him. She must be dying to get out of this place. He just had to figure out what kind of offer would make her see things his way.

First things first, he'd stop by the house, take stock of her kitchen, run for groceries and have some food waiting for her. Tomato soup and grilled-cheese on sourdough bread, her favorite. Followed up by mint Oreos—another favorite. Maybe he'd get the Beaujolais she loved, set up some candles…

A seduction. He smiled thinking about it, even when something primitive leaped in his gut. It was weird, but he'd set up a sexless chef seduction of his ex-wife.

Whatever it took.

He headed to his truck, climbed in and on auto-pilot wound his way through Albany to the lower east side. By rote he turned left on Mulberry, right on Pape and pulled in to the driveway of 312.

He took a deep breath, bracing himself.

Empty houses with dark windows disturbed him, ruffled those memories of being a boy and wondering if, when he went downstairs, she would finally be there. If this morning, after all the others, would be the one when the kitchen would be warm, the lights on, the smell of coffee and bacon in the air, and Mom would be sitting at the table. She'd tell him it all had been a mistake and she wouldn't be leaving, ever again.

Stupid, he told himself. *Ancient history. Like my marriage. It's just a house. It's not mine anymore.*

Finally he looked up at the two-story Tudor—with its big backyard—where they'd planned to start their family. The magnolia tree out front was in full bloom, carpeting the lawn in thick creamy pink and white petals.

Her herb garden looked a little overrun with chives and she must have finally decided that per-ennials weren't worth the hassle. Otherwise the house looked amazing.

Sunlight glittered off the leaded windows and he tried not to remember how he'd jumped on the house, probably paying too much. But it hadn't mattered at the time—the house was meant to be theirs.

And it had been a happy home for a year.

His neck went hot and his fingers tingled. He

forced himself to fold the feelings up and shove them back in the box from which they'd sprung.

Don't care, he told himself ruthlessly, hardening his heart. He let himself go cold, pushing those memories away with the ones of his mother until his heart rate returned to normal, his fingers stopped tingling.

It's just a building. Not my home.

He got out of the truck and bounded up the slate walkway.

He lifted the blue frog with the bulging eyes that sat on her porch and—as expected—there was the key. But he couldn't pick it up. His body didn't obey the messages from his brain. His body wanted to run.

"Hey, man? You need something?" Gabe whirled to find a good-looking, tall...kid. Really. Couldn't have been older than twenty-six. He stood in the open doorway, a backpack slung over his shoulder.

"Hi," Gabe started to say. "No. Well, yes. Actually."

"You selling something?" The kid pointed to the sign Alice had hand printed and posted on the mailbox: No Salesmen, No Flyers, No Religious Fanatics. This Means You.

He smiled, typical Alice.

"No," he told the kid. "I'm not selling anything. My name is Gabe and I—"

"You're the dude in the pictures." The guy smiled and held out his hand. "You look good, keeping in shape."

Gabe was knocked off stride but managed to shake his hand anyway. "Thanks. Um...I'm sorry, who are you?" *And what pictures?*

"Charlie, I'm Alice's roommate."

Roommate? Gabe's mouth fell open.

"No, no, man, not like that." The kid laughed. "Though I did try at the beginning but she pretty much let me know that wasn't going to be happening. I just pay rent and live in the basement."

"Why does she need a roommate?" he asked.

Charlie shrugged. "Why does anyone need a roommate? Money, I guess. It's not for the company that's for sure. I barely see her anymore. She used to make me dinner." He whistled through his teeth. "Best food I ever had."

Gabe's head reeled, but he saw the sugar he needed to sweeten the deal. Alice needed money, it was the only way his incredibly private ex-wife would ever rent out part of her home and, horrors, share her kitchen with some kid who no doubt scarfed down freeze-dried noodles and Lucky Charms by the boatload.

Perhaps it wouldn't be so hard to convince her—working at Johnny O's, renting out the basement. He only needed to push down her pride and get her to see what an opportunity he had for her.

"She *is* a great chef," Gabe said. "Look, Charlie. If you don't mind, I was hoping to come in and wait for Alice to get home. I am supposed to have a business meeting with her."

"Sure, no problem." Charlie stepped out onto the porch, leaving the heavy wooden storm door open. "Don't touch her booze, though. She gets crazy if you drink her stuff."

Gabe nodded, suddenly speechless as Charlie walked by dragging with him Alice's scent from the house. Roses and lemon swirled out around him, reminding him of the smell of her blue-black curls spread out across the pillows of their marriage bed, the damp nape of her neck after a shower.

"See you around," Charlie said and took off on a bike.

Gabe lifted his hand in a halfhearted farewell.

Suddenly, the narrow hallway leading back to the living room with its big picture windows looked a mile long.

The brass key in his hand—a standard house key, identical to the one he'd carried on his key chain for years—weighed a thousand pounds.

Need a chef. Need a chef. Need a chef.

He wished it didn't require going into that house.

He took a deep breath, buffered himself against the ghosts inside and stormed the gates. Immediately he was caught short by the familiarity of their home.

The foyer still had the cut-glass vase filled with overblown pink roses in it—she'd always loved putting it there—and the walls were adorned with their photos. Black-and-white shots from their various trips. Those were the pictures Charlie had referred to. Gabe was in some of them, standing next to the Vietnamese fisherman and the Mexican grandmother who made the best tortillas he'd ever tasted.

What is she doing with these still on the wall? He wondered. He'd emptied all his frames of her, his wallet and photo albums. Looking at his apartment, you'd never guess he'd been married. Looking at her house, you'd never guess she'd been divorced.

He stalked through the house and turned right toward the kitchen, resisting the urge to check out the family room and the back lawn.

More roses sat on the kitchen table. These were fresh, bright yellow buds still.

The kitchen was spotless. Their expensive renovation still looked modern and elegant, such a reflection of his wife.

Ex-wife. Ex.

An image—one of the few to have survived the war between him and Alice—came and went like smoke in sunshine.

The memory was of a random night—a Wednesday or something in March—when nothing special was happening. Alice had come home late from shutting down the restaurant and he'd woken up while she showered. He'd waited for her in this kitchen, dark but for the bright panels of moonlight that lay over the furniture like a sheet. She'd walked in wearing a pair of boxer shorts and nothing else.

She'd smelled sweet and clean. Powdery. Her hair a dark slick down her back. Her lithe body taut and graceful, her skin rosy and fresh.

"You're better than sleep," she'd said to him, pressing a kiss to the side of his neck, just south of his ear. He'd touched her back, found those dimples at the base of her spine that he'd loved with dizzying devotion.

And then they'd made slow, sleepy lazy love.

It surprised him at odd times when it seemed as though his Alice years had happened to someone else. When he thought he'd finally managed to put it all behind him.

But looking at his former kitchen, the memory ambushed him, rocked him on his heels and had him struggling for breath that didn't taste of his ex-wife.

He tore open the maple cabinets, as if he could tear that stubborn memory out of his brain. But in cabinet after cabinet he only found empty shelves. Which was not at all like her. She used to say that having an empty pantry made her nervous. If there wasn't pasta, garlic and olive oil on hand at all times she wouldn't be able to sleep at night.

Something in his gut twinged. Remorse? Worry?

No, couldn't be. He was divorced. Papers, signed by both of them, exonerated him from worry and remorse.

But his gut still twinged.

He pulled open the cabinet above the fridge only to find it fully stocked with high-end liquor.

No need for the Beaujolais.

Another cabinet over the chopping block was filled with freeze-dried noodles and cereal.

Charlie's small stake in the kitchen.

Something warm and fluffy brushed up against his ankles and he looked down to find Felix, their French cat. Another thing she'd gotten in the divorce.

"Bonjour, Felix," he said with great affection. The gray-and-white cat wasn't really French—he was south-side Albany Dumpster—but they considered him so due to his love of anchovies, olives and lemon juice.

Gabe opened the fridge and found enough anchovies and expensive olives soaked in lemon juice to keep the cat happy for aeons.

He pulled out a slick, silver fish and fed it to the purring cat. "What's happening here, Felix?" he asked, stroking the cat's ears.

During their last big fight, Alice had told him that she would be better off without him. Happier. And he'd jumped at his chance for freedom, relieved to be away from the torture they constantly inflicted on each other.

But, as he looked around the home that hadn't changed since he'd left, he wondered if this empty kitchen was really better.

Is this happy?

He stopped those thoughts before they went any further. That cold part of himself that didn't care about her happiness, that only cared about creating the life he needed, the dream that had helped him survive their divorce, slid over him, protecting him from any reality he didn't want to see.

SHE STUCK AROUND way after her shift, even went so far as to contemplate sleeping in the front corner booth in order to avoid Gabe.

Maybe he's left, she thought hopefully. She longed for her home, her couch. Her scotch.

Her promise not to drink had evaporated in the heat of Gabe's smile. She needed a drink after today. She'd barked at Trudy—who only ever tried to be kind to her, even when she was a nag—she'd burned her hand and screwed up two tables of food. And now, as penance, she mopped the tiled floor around the stainless steel prep table as if her life depended on it.

Maybe I should not be a chef, she considered. Maybe she could get into the cleaning profession. Work in one of those big high-rises after hours.

She imagined going back to her home and telling Gabe that she couldn't be his chef because she was making a career change.

She almost laughed thinking about it.

"Alice?" Darnell poked his head out of the back office that adjoined the main prep area. "Can I speak to you a minute?"

She set the mop back in the bucket and propped it against the wall, making sure it wouldn't slip, and stepped into the minuscule manager's office.

"Go ahead and shut the door," Darnell said from behind the cluttered desk. She had to move boxes of recipe and conduct manuals out of the way in order to shut the door that, as long as she'd been here, had never been shut.

She guessed Trudy had tattled. Again.

"Have a seat." He gestured to the one folding chair beneath the giant white board with the schedule on it. She had to move a stack of staff uniforms in order to sit.

"If you wanted me to clean your office, Darnell, you could have just asked." She thought it was a joke, but Darnell didn't laugh. His brown eyes behind the wire-rimmed glasses were stern and a little sad.

Maybe she'd have to up the apology to Trudy.

She could buy drinks for the whole staff after work sometime. That should put her back in everyone's good graces.

"What are you doing cleaning the kitchen?" he asked. "Did you, by chance, not notice the staff we have for that?"

"I was just helping out," she said. "I'm a team player."

His mouth dropped open in astonishment for a brief moment, and then he sat back, his chair creaking. "I can only guess you're kidding."

She sighed, pulled off her hairnet and yanked out the clasp that held her hair back. She scratched at her scalp. If she was going to get lectured, she was going to do it in some comfort.

"Do you want to be a chef here?" Darnell asked.

No. "Of course."

"Is that why you show up late, take too many coffee breaks—"

"Everybody does that."

"And order your coworkers around?"

"No, I just do that for fun."

"Trudy doesn't think it's fun," he said through pursed, white lips. "I don't understand why you pick on her. She's the nicest—"

That's why Alice picked on her. Nice made her feel mean. Kindness hurt. "I'll apologize—"

Darnell leaned forward on his desk. "I hired you based on your reputation and the few amazing meals I had at Zinnia." Her gut clenched at the name of her failed restaurant, her baby, her reason for living after

Gabe and she ended. "I thought you'd make this franchise something special."

Her mouth fell open and she grabbed a recipe manual from the stack at her knee. "I cook from a manual, Darnell. It's against corporate policy to do something special."

"But you haven't even tried, have you? We have nightly specials and I gave you carte blanche."

"Right, and I've—"

"Served the same thing for two weeks, despite the fact that no one orders it. Our customers don't like duck, Alice. But those ribs you made two months ago were amazing, and you served them for two days. That's it. It's like you don't want to succeed."

Darnell watched her expectantly and Alice dropped her eyes to the recipe manual. She didn't want sympathy. She didn't want to talk about her problems. She wanted to work, pay off the outrageous amount of money she owed the bank and annoy Trudy. That's it.

And drink. Dear God. I need a drink.

"Alice, I don't know the whole story behind what happened at Zinnia—"

"I'll talk to Trudy and I'll put the ribs back up on the specials board." She stood, stared at Darnell with tired eyes. "I have to be back here tomorrow for—"

"No." Darnell shook his head. "You don't."

She slumped.

"You're fired."

ALICE'S CAR rolled slowly down Pape and she could see the dim lights, the shadow of someone moving through her kitchen window. She knew it wasn't Charlie.

He's still here, she thought and hit the garage-door opener on her dashboard. An itchy anger chugged through her bloodstream like a drug, making her head spin.

Gabe was the last thing she needed tonight.

The heavy white door lifted and she drove into the parking spot between the empty freezers and the golf clubs Gabe had left. She tried to gather whatever resources were left in her tired, drink-craving, jobless body.

After the day she'd had, there weren't many left. Gabe reentering her life dredged up feelings she'd been managing, longings she'd been subduing.

But tonight those feelings were here in force, like weights on her heart.

I wish I wasn't alone.

I wish I had a family.

And *he* was in there with dim lights and probably tomato soup, something she lost the taste for after he left.

She chewed her beleaguered thumbnail and watched the door between the garage and kitchen as though it might open and Gabe would come running out throwing knives at her car. Not that she was scared of him, just scared of what they were when they were together.

"I don't need anything," she whispered her oft-repeated mantra that eventually got her through the worst days. "There is nothing I want."

But the fates had conspired tonight. Her mort-
gages—both of them—were due at the end of the
week and she had only enough money to cover one.

Am I too old to sell my body? she wondered. But
that was a bit drastic, even for her.

She felt raw and panicked, like a trapped animal.
Gabe was going to make her an offer she couldn't
refuse and she wanted to punish him for it. She
wanted him to pay for coming back here and rubbing
his success in her face.

She wanted to pick the scabs between them,
scratch at old wounds.

I want to fight. Alice smiled, feeling feral. *And
there's nothing in this world that Gabe hates more
than a fight.*

She opened the door between the garage and the
kitchen and Gabe looked up at her from the bread he
sliced at her kitchen table. He was too handsome for
words in this light.

"You're still here," she said, unbuttoning her dirty
chef's whites. "You make yourself at home?"

His smile dimmed a bit, no doubt startled by her
biting sarcasm. She came out swinging, hoping to get
a few licks in before he made her that offer and she
had to take it.

"Did you take the tour?" she asked, throwing the
dirty jacket on the table. "Visit the baby's room?"

His eyes turned to stone. His smile became a
grimace.

"Alice." There was that sigh again. It told her,
better than words, better than failed doctor's appoint-

ments, better than divorce papers, that he was disappointed in her.

And immediately she regretted wanting to fight over this. A fight she never won.

"Alice, there was no baby."

CHAPTER THREE

"FOR YOU," she said, her eyes narrowed like a cat backed into a corner. "That's the problem, isn't it?"

He didn't want to deal with this Alice, the Alice from the end of their marriage. He'd take her cool sarcasm, her judgment and disdain over this Alice—the Alice who wanted to talk about things.

He didn't like this Alice.

"There were no babies, period."

Every fiber in his body, his gut, told him to walk out the door. He didn't have it in him to go another round over this.

She still wallowed in their old misery, he could see it in her black eyes. The miscarriages were all fresh. Real.

"I don't want to talk about this," he said, pushing away the bread. "I'm not here for that."

Her laughter sounded like ice breaking. "Really? And here I thought you finally wanted to sit down and talk—" She pretended to be surprised when he stood.

"This isn't going to work." He slammed the serrated knife onto the small cutting board. "Coming here was a mistake." He grabbed his keys and headed for the front door.

"Ah, the infamous Gabe Mitchell cold shoulder as he heads for the door. How I have missed that." Her sarcasm raked him and suddenly he couldn't get out of there fast enough.

He put his hand on the doorknob and at the same time, she tentatively touched his elbow and a spark of electricity shot up his arm.

"No. Stop. Please, Gabe." Her tone held a certain honesty that he couldn't walk away from. He could walk away from her anger and sarcasm, her lies and evasions. But when she was vulnerable—he just couldn't walk away.

He stopped, his shoulders hunched as if to protect himself. He noticed and immediately straightened.

"I'm—" He could hear her swallow around the words. "I'm sorry. I...forget I said anything."

He weighed the cost of turning around. Of sitting back at that kitchen table, the one from her grandmother.

He needed a chef and she was the best.

He turned and looked right into her liquid black eyes. "No more talk about the marriage or the miscarriages." He shook his head. "It's counterproductive. For both of us."

She huffed a little laugh and licked her lips. "Okay. You're right."

He sat down in the midst of the awkward silence that breathed between them, but he was satisfied that the past wouldn't leap out at him anymore, ambushing his plans for the inn.

"You want something to drink?" she asked, heading for the cabinet above the fridge. She stood on tiptoe and pulled down a bottle of red wine.

And, despite himself, he watched her move. Her pale skin glowed in the half light. She'd lost some of the lush curvy weight she'd carried in happier days. Her arms were muscled from the hard work of running a kitchen, but the rest of her was a whipcord.

She looked as if she'd missed too many meals. She looked tough.

"I thought you might be hungry," he said. She hadn't even glanced at the stove even though he knew she could smell the tomato soup.

"I ate at work," she said and he didn't force the issue. He'd bet the inn she was lying.

"Wine?" she asked, holding up a bottle.

"I'd love some." He forced himself to be warm to her, cordial. Due to years of practice, he could slip into gracious without batting an eye. It was a suit he donned when he needed it. "I've got Oreos."

That made her smile, and the tension in the room cracked and he could breathe again.

"I met your roommate," Gabe said, watching her uncork the bottle like a professional. "Nice guy."

He tried to steer the conversation toward her situation, remind them both, no matter how unsavory, they needed each other.

"He's clean and pays the rent on time."

"Sounds like the proper arrangement. How was work?"

"Why don't we just cut to the chase here, Gabe."

She popped the cork, poured a perfect four ounces in each glass, grabbed a cookie from the package on the table, then retreated across the kitchen. She hoisted herself onto the counter, sitting in the shadows. He could only see the gleam of her skin, the shine of her eyes and her shaking hands as she lifted her glass to her mouth and drank like a woman in need.

Again, his gut told him to get out of that kitchen, away from the quicksand of Alice's pain.

"Go ahead, Gabe," she said. "Give me your pitch."

He rubbed his face, wondering how he'd ended up here, of all places.

"Having second thoughts?" she asked, her voice a sarcastic coo from the darkness by the stove. "Wondering if your ex-wife might be drinking a bit too much? Thinking maybe she's just a little too much trouble?"

"Yep," he told her point-blank. She poured herself another glass, not even trying to assuage his fears.

"Well, you had to be pretty damn desperate to come find me. So unless things have changed since this afternoon, you're still pretty damn desperate, right?"

He nodded.

"Let me tell you, drunk or not, I'm still the best chef you know. So, give me your pitch."

"I can't ask you to do this if you're...not stable."

"I'm plenty stable, Gabe. I just drink too much

after work. I drink too much so I can live in this house and not go crazy."

He understood that all too well, but it wasn't enough. He couldn't jeopardize the Riverview Inn with a bad decision, and Alice could be a very bad decision.

"But Zinnia? What happened there?"

"I didn't realize I was applying for a job. You came to me."

"Yeah, I came to you in a parking lot at Johnny O's. You're the best chef I know, but something's happened to you and I think I need to know before I make you an offer."

"I'll worry about me, you worry about your inn." She stared unflinchingly into his eyes and he knew from years of hard experience that he wouldn't get any more from her.

"I could leave," he said, a warning he knew he really couldn't follow through on.

"You have before," she said. "But I think you're too desperate to walk out that door and—" her smile was wan "—I'm too desperate to let you. Tell me what the job is."

Honesty again, when he'd least expected it, and as usual when she was real with him, he couldn't refuse.

"The position is executive chef at Riverview Inn. Opening day is May 1."

She choked on her Oreo. "That's a month away. Cutting it close, don't you think?"

"No one knows that better than me right now." He smiled ruefully. "As bad as that sounds it's actually worse. I have the Crimpson wedding in June and—"

"Crimpson? Crimpson frozen foods?" she asked and he nodded. "Well, that's quite a feather in your cap."

"Right, so it's pretty important that the event be flawless."

"Two months?" she asked. She leaned over the stove and waved the scent of the soup up to her nose. "Opening day in four weeks and a wedding in eight?"

"After the event you can walk away," he told her. "And I imagine it would be best if you did."

She dipped her pinkie in the red liquid and touched it to her tongue. "I imagine it would, too." She hopped down from the counter and opened the cupboard to the left of the gas stove. She sprinkled the soup with balsamic vinegar and a couple of twists from the black-pepper grinder and tasted again. She nodded, so he guessed it was better.

"Staff?" she asked.

Gabe didn't answer and her black eyes pinned him to the wall. "Staff?" she repeated.

"A young guy with some excellent past experience." Gabe watched the wine in his glass instead of meeting her eyes and hoped that kid who'd been fired from McDonald's could be trusted around knives and headstrong chefs.

"I'll need more," she said.

"You going to take the job?"

"Not so fast," she said, pulling down the kosher salt from the cupboard and giving the soup a few hefty pinches. "What are you going to pay me?"

He braced himself. "Twenty—"

"Nope."

"You'll only be there two months."

"I won't be there at all for twenty grand."

"Okay." He sighed, having expected that. His budget for a far less experienced chef was forty grand for the year. He was blowing everything on this gamble—he'd have to take money from the landscaping funds to pay another chef when she left. "Thirty. For two months' work, I won't give you more."

She tasted the soup again, nodded definitively and took it off the burner.

"Are you going to have any?" Gabe asked, gesturing to the heavy pot.

"Nope. And I won't go to your inn for thirty grand, either."

"Thirty-five and some shares in the place."

Her eyes burned fever bright. He knew what shares represented. Income. Success. And after two months she wouldn't have to work for it.

It would help, maybe after they split ways again. Make it so she wouldn't have to work at a terrible job or share her house with a stranger.

"You know it's a good deal. I've never had a restaurant not turn a profit."

She rubbed her forehead and he knew he had her. It was just a matter of sealing the deal.

"It would be a fresh start, Al."

Her nickname warmed the air.

"It hardly seems fresh." She laughed. "You're my ex-husband and this is an old plan of ours. It feels like trouble."

"I couldn't agree more." He laughed, too. "But you'd have total run of the kitchen."

She scoffed. "Right."

"I'm serious, I'll be very busy—"

"Getting in my way." She looked at him for a brief moment and all the problems in their relationship— the fights and clashing egos—for some reason, in this room with the wine, he felt…nostalgic for them. Those nights when he made her so mad she threw things at him, broke plates against the floor and ruined meals with her temper. The long days when he wouldn't talk to her, giving her a silent treatment so cold and deep that the only way to thaw both of them…

She cleared her throat, seeming uncomfortable, as if she'd been thinking the same thing. "I'll do it."

Gabe felt both jubilant and wary. *Is this the right thing? Am I making a deal with the devil?* "I'm so glad."

"But—" she held up a finger "—I'm out of there the second that wedding is over and I run the kitchen. Not you."

He nodded, stood and held out his hand.

"I'm serious, Gabe. I won't have you trying to take things over. You hired me to be executive chef—"

"I promise." He put his hand on his chest and bowed his head slightly. "I absolutely promise to stay out of your way as long as you promise to try to be a team player. My dad and Max—"

"Your dad and Max are there?" she asked, bright joy filtering through the dark clouds on her face.

"They are and they'll be very glad to see you."

She smiled and held out her hand. "I can be a team player."

"And I can stay out of your way."

They shook on it and Gabe had to wonder who was going to break their promise first.

PATRICK MITCHELL watched his oldest son walk away whistling.

Whistling! And after the bomb Gabe had just laid on them, watching him whistle was akin to watching him hit himself in the head with a ball-peen hammer.

"Alice?" Patrick, incredulous, turned to his youngest son. "Max? Alice was your idea?"

Max ignored him, or pretended to, and poured more eggshell paint in the trays. He practiced being oblivious as though there was a contest.

"Son." Patrick tried again as Max dipped his roller in the paint and began applying their last coat on the last wall of the kitchen. "I leave you alone with him for ten minutes and this is what you do? Are you trying to ruin this inn?"

"He needed a chef." Max shrugged, but there was a smile on his lips. "Alice is a chef."

Patrick nodded. "She is, sure. But she's also pure trouble for that boy."

"I thought you liked Alice," Max said.

"I do. I love her like a daughter but they are trouble for each other and she is the last thing your brother needs."

"Please." Max looked at him out of the corner of his eye, but still that devil's smile was on his lips. If the situation weren't so dire, Patrick would be happy to see Alice. "They're grown-ups. They can make it work. At least we'll eat well while she's here. I'm about a week away from liver failure after eating your cooking for the past few months."

Patrick's mouth dropped open. "Where did I go wrong?" He pretended to be upset, when really these past few months had been the happiest of his life. This teasing was their old shtick. Kept them from ever having to address anything head-on—such as emotion. Such as the past. "I'm supposed to be growing senile on a porch somewhere with grand-kids on my knee. Not working manual labor for one son and roommates with the other."

"Right, because living with my dad is exactly what I want to be doing," Max said without heat, and Patrick yearned, absolutely longed, to ask his boy what had happened to him. What was wrong. What was still hurting him so badly from the shooting last year that sent him into this tailspin. It wasn't as though he was that different—the scar on his neck was new, sure. But he still laughed. He still made every effort to get the best of his brother. But it was as though he did those things because he was supposed to, not because he wanted to. Something had happened to leach the joy out of his boy, and he wanted to know what that was.

But if he asked, Max would probably fall on the floor in heart failure or shock. The Mitchell men didn't ask probing questions.

So, they worked, the way they always did, instead

of saying the important things. And Patrick hoped that whatever Max needed he was getting in some way.

The back door to the kitchen opened, letting in a warm breeze and a shaft of bright spring sunlight.

A woman stood in the doorway but it wasn't Alice. The woman didn't give off the kinetic energy that had surrounded his daughter-in-law.

Ex-daughter-in-law.

"Excuse me?" she said, stepping from the bright doorway into the kitchen. The door shut behind her and her features emerged from silhouette. "I'm looking for the chef." She had a pretty smile that turned her plain face into something quite lovely.

"She's not here," Max said.

And his dumb son watched the paint dry in front of him rather than look at the pretty girl to his left.

Patrick despaired for the boy, he really did.

"She's supposed to be here Monday," Max said. He darted a quick look her way, then returned to the careful application of a second coat of pale cream paint on a pale cream wall, as though failure could blow up the building.

"Maybe there's something we could do for you?" Patrick asked, stepping into the breach.

"Well, is Gabe—"

"Hello?" Gabe ducked his head out of the small office he'd built off the kitchen. "Hi!" He caught sight of the woman and Patrick knew his eldest son would appreciate how she appeared plain but somehow interesting all the same. True to form, Gabe smiled, the old charmer, and shook the woman's hand. "I'm Gabe."

Patrick shot Max a look that said, "That's how you do it, nincompoop." Max just rolled his eyes.

"I'm Daphne from Athens Organics. We talked briefly on the phone yesterday. I was hoping to meet with your chef about being a supplier for your kitchen."

"Of course," Gabe said, "My chef isn't here yet, but I'm so glad you stopped by. Come on into my office." He opened the door for her and she smiled girlishly and Max rolled his eyes again.

Silence filled the kitchen after Gabe shut the office door. Patrick watched his son paint and Max ignored him.

"You're a virgin, aren't you?" Patrick asked.

"Shut up, Dad."

"It's the only thing that explains why you're such an idiot around women."

"I'm not an idiot, I'm just not…Gabe. And that's fine by me." He smiled, that sharp, wicked smile from the corner of his mouth. It made Patrick feel as though the boy he remembered with the temper and the laugh that could light up a room was still in there somewhere. "And it's pretty okay by the women I have sex with, too."

"Thank God."

Max laughed, sort of. And Patrick's heart leaped.

Now, he wondered. *Is now the right time?* The letter he'd been carrying in the front chest pocket of his work shirt felt like deadweight against his chest. At night, it sat on his bedside table and glowed with a life of its own.

He couldn't sleep. He didn't eat. He took a

hundred bathroom breaks a day so he could sit down and reread the words he'd memorized.

The office door opened and Gabe and Daphne stepped back into the kitchen. Her color was high and her smile ready as they shook hands. Gabe walked her out the door to her car.

"Maybe he's going to start working on those grandkids you want," Max said, nodding in the direction his brother had gone. "It's about time, the guy's been thinking about a family since he could walk."

I just want them to know love. To know love like I knew it, is that so hard? Patrick wondered. *So impossible?*

The subject of love was a sore one among the Mitchell men. Had been since Iris walked out on them thirty years ago.

Not that he was counting.

"You know—" he dipped his paintbrush into the can of paint he'd set on the top step of the ladder and watched Max for a reaction "—when you lost your mother—"

"Dad." Max practically growled the word. "What is this new fascination with Mom? You haven't mentioned her in years and now every time I turn around you're bringing her up."

"Maybe it's because I'm living with her son, who is just as moody and muleheaded as she was."

Max fell silent. Any reminder of being like his mother could turn him off like a light switch.

"When you lost her—"

"You make it sound like she died!" Max cried,

finally setting the roller down. "Or like we misplaced her somewhere. She left. She walked away. I don't want to talk about her. If you want to reminisce about the past, talk to Gabe."

Gabe had given him the same reaction every time he tried talking about Iris. Patrick couldn't blame them—Iris had walked away from them, which, as Gabe had told him, was worse than if she'd died.

She didn't want us, Dad. She didn't want any of us, he'd said.

It wasn't true—entirely. She had wanted them, but there had been things happening that the boys were too young to understand or remember. They didn't understand why Patrick didn't just get over it. Over her.

He'd held out a thin ribbon of hope that maybe, just maybe Iris would realize she'd made a mistake and she'd forgive his. Ignore his foolish anger and pride. For years he'd held on to that ribbon. Two weeks ago she'd finally picked up her end.

CHAPTER FOUR

MONDAY MORNING Alice opened the kitchen door of the Riverview Inn and stepped into a dream. Her dream.

Doubt, second thoughts, worry that she'd somehow screw this up the way she'd screwed up Zinnia, had plagued her for the past three days, since taking the job. Uncertainty had dogged her as she drove down from Albany. But now, as she set down her bag and tried to catch her breath, worry vanished.

This kitchen was hers. Meant to be hers. It was as if Gabe had opened her head and pulled out the daydreams and plans she'd been accumulating over the years.

A south-facing window overlooking a brilliant green forest filled the room with sunshine. The pale cream walls seemed to glow in the clear morning light and the appliances sparkled, clean and unused.

Racks of pots hung from the ceiling. She reached up and carefully knocked the saucepan into a sauté pan and reflected light scattered across the far wall.

It was the most beautiful kind of chandelier.

A stainless steel table filled the bottom portion of

the L-shaped room beside two big glass-front refrigerators.

In a place that was often busy and loud and filled with a sort of graceful chaos, the silence of the downtimes seemed almost healing.

A kitchen at rest, a kitchen such as this one, was a beautiful thing. A place of peace.

She ran her hand along the chopping block sitting next to the stove. The same monster slab of oak, easily ten inches thick, used to sit in their house. It had come from Gabe's mother whose parents had been Polish butchers. Thousands of pigs had been bled on that wood, thousands of cabbages had been chopped, thousands of perogies had been rolled and formed there. Alice wanted to climb on top of it and dance.

This kitchen even smelled like a fresh start.

I will stop drinking, she promised. *I will not waste this chance.* She made the promise even as the remainder of last night's wine throbbed in her skull. *I will swallow my resentment and try very hard not to fight with my ex-husband.*

"Hey," Gabe said from behind her as if her promise had conjured him. She couldn't quite face him yet. Things in her were shaken loose by the beauty of the place, by her earnest desire to deserve this fresh start.

"Executive chef," she said, opening a door to find a small closet, lined with shelves, ready for spices and root vegetables, maple syrup and vinegars, "reporting for duty."

"What do you think?" he asked and she finally

had to look at him. For an instant she wanted to shield her eyes from the radiant brightness of him. He was clean and fresh in a wrinkled white shirt and khaki pants, his blond hair mussed by his hands, his face tanned from working outside.

He looked like a lifeguard. A Swiss Alps ski-rescue guy. He just needed the dog.

She felt small in comparison, dark and mean, dressed in black because it didn't require her to think to coordinate.

"Alice?" he said, breaking in to her ugly comparisons. He ducked his head to look into her eyes and smiled. "What do you think? Recognize it?"

She realized, belatedly, that the kitchen wasn't a coincidence. She'd told him a million times what a kitchen should look like according to her. She'd sketched the floor plan on the bare skin of his back over and over again.

"It's amazing," she said, her joy in finding her dream brought to life turning to cold resentment. Of course he would take this for himself, too. "You know that."

"I practically have the floor plan tattooed on my back." He grinned and the reminder of their intimacies, casually uttered out loud, chilled her to the bone. "When the time came to design the kitchen, I just remembered everything you taught me."

It was a compliment, probably a sincere one, but she didn't want compliments.

This is not mine, she told herself, ripping the dream from her clenched fists. *I am hired help. I am a bit player.* She had no business coveting the butcher's block, imagining years of early mornings in this kitchen, planning menus.

There is nothing I want, she reminded herself. *There is nothing I need.*

She forced cold distance into her head and her heart and when she looked at the beautiful kitchen, the chandelier of pots and pans, she just saw *things.* Inanimate objects that had no relationship to her, that cost her nothing and only represented a way to get out of debt and move on with her life.

They were tools. That's all. Gabe, this kitchen, the whole inn, they were a means to an end.

"I think we better get to work if you want to open in a month," she said, cold as ice.

"But did you see the view?" Gabe pointed to the window. "Come on, we can have coffee and take a walk around the grounds. We have a capacity of one hundred guests between the cottages and the lodge, which we're hoping—"

"No." She shook her head. "I just want to work, Gabe. That's all."

For a moment she thought he might ask her what was wrong. Instead, true to form, he nodded in that definitive way that always indicated he was biting his tongue. "Okay. Come on into the office and we'll talk—"

"Get your hands off me!" someone yelled, and both Gabe and Alice whirled to the doorway leading to the dining room. They stood like deer in headlights while the swinging door banged open and Max and a teenage boy plowed into the kitchen. "Didn't you hear what I said!" The kid, practically drowning in oversize black clothes, yelled.

"Yep. And I'm not touching you."

"Good, don't start."

Alice nearly stepped back, as though the kid were a rabid dog.

"Here he is," Max said and from the corner of her eye she saw Gabe's mouth fall open.

"You're kidding me," he said.

"Nope." Max shook his head. "This is Cameron."

"Cut that out, man," Cameron said, jerking himself away from Max. "The name is Chaz."

"Chaz makes you sound like an idiot," Max said. "Your name is Cameron."

"Hi, Max," Alice said, pleased to see her former brother-in-law. The best things about Gabe were his brother and father, both as emotionally retarded as Gabe, but at least they didn't try to pretend otherwise.

"Hey, Alice," Max said with a quick grin. "Good to see you."

"Good to see you, too." She meant it. "How you keeping?"

"Starving," he said. "We've been living on toast and freeze-dried noodles around here."

Alice shuddered and Max's grin stretched into a smile. He looked thin, painfully so, and wounded in some dark way, as if all the intensity that had illumi-nated him was banked, burning out.

"What the hell am I doing here, man?" Cameron, or whatever his name was, asked. "This is an after-school program."

"Not when you've got a day off school. Then it's an all-day program." Max answered.

"This your love-child you never told us about?" Alice asked Max, falling into their old give-and-take.

"This dude ain't my father," Cameron answered for him.

"Gabe didn't tell you?" Max asked, his dark eyebrows hitting his hairline, and Alice suddenly felt a serious lack of information.

"Tell me what?" She crossed her arms over her chest, just in case Gabe misinterpreted her tone as happy.

It took a moment, but Gabe finally issued a response. He looked at her, put on his game face and said, "He's your staff."

"Bullshit!" the kid yelled.

Alice laughed. "I'm with him."

Gabe winced and remained silent, which could mean only one thing. Alice's mouth fell open. "You're kidding."

He shook his head.

"You're kidding." She turned to Max, who only shrugged.

She finally focused on the kid, whose eyes met hers briefly. "I got nothing to kid about," he said, looking as unhappy as she felt.

She shook her head. "I can work alone until I get proper staff."

"Okay," Max said, opening the swing door behind him. "Let's go back to stacking that wood."

"This is bullshit!" The kid hollered as Max led him into the dining room.

Gabe's silence worried her, actually set small stones atwirl in her stomach. "What aren't you telling me, Gabe?"

"There's no money for staff unless you take a pay cut," he said point-blank. "Not until the next check comes in from the Crimpsons."

"When will that be?" She asked, disbelieving.

"Two weeks."

"Even if that kid was Cordon Bleu trained, I couldn't pull together the menu for this wedding with one staff member!"

"I know." He rubbed his forehead. "We open in a month and I've already got some reservations and am running an Internet spring promotion, so I should get more. I can make this work. We can use the money—"

She laughed, listening to him rob from Peter to pay Paul.

"You think this is funny?" he asked, his blue eyes dangerously clouded over.

"A little, yeah."

"Great. Wonderful attitude from my chef."

"You hired a chef, Gabe. Not a cheerleader. If you're screwing up—"

Her comment must have lit his dormant temper because he bristled. "I'm not screwing up. You're the one doing two months' work for the price of what I had earmarked for a yearly chef's salary."

She shrugged. "You should have gotten a beginner chef."

"No, you should have been reasonable."

"Ah, I thought I recognized that voice."

Patrick Mitchell's loud voice boomed through the kitchen, stalling their argument as he stepped in from the outside. His red flannel shirt matched his ruddy cheeks and it was as if the sun had come out from behind clouds. Indomitably cheerful, that was Patrick, and she was inordinately glad to see him.

"There's only one person Gabe actually fights with," Patrick said and held out his thick burly arms. Alice allowed herself to be hugged, the sensation odd but pleasant enough since it didn't last too long.

When was the last time someone touched me? she wondered. Even casually. That awkward embarrassing kiss from Charlie months ago, when she'd been so lonely and sad and drunk that she'd let him touch her.

She didn't know when she lost the capacity for casual touch, when any sort of physical affection, no matter how benign, made her ache.

"How is my favorite former daughter-in-law?" Patrick asked, his blue eyes twinkling.

Some of the tension from locking horns with Gabe fell away and she smiled, even patted Patrick's grizzled cheek.

"Don't tell me he's got you working here, too?" she asked.

"Slave labor." Patrick shook his head, always one for teasing. "At least now we'll have decent chow."

"Don't be too sure, Dad," Gabe said, leaning

against the doorjamb of his office. "She may have decided she doesn't like the terms."

"Always trying to make it my fault, aren't you, Gabe."

"If the shoe—"

"Wonderful!" Patrick rubbed his hands together. "If you don't mind, Max and I are just going to pull up some chairs and watch you two duke it out for the next few months. That way no work will get done." His eyes flicked from her to Gabe, who, chagrined by his father's reverse chastisement, looked down at his shoes.

"I told Max this was going to be trouble," Patrick said and she could feel his direct gaze on her face.

She'd only been here minutes and already things were going wrong.

"I can make it work," Gabe said, resolute. "It won't be a problem."

"For you," she said.

"You, either," Gabe insisted, his tone hard, his smile sharp. "I will make it work."

She nodded, wondering why she felt so small. So dark and ill-tempered. He was the one who had lied, who had told her he had staff. She shouldn't feel bad because she was making him hold up his end of the bargain.

"You always do," she said. He did. He could make gold out of hay without making it look hard.

"Ah, that's how children should play," Patrick said. "Nice."

"Don't you have some work to do, Dad?" Gabe asked.

"I'm going to hook up your fancy dishwasher," he said, pointing to the far corner of the room where a dishwasher sat, with its tube and wire guts spread out across the floor.

He winked at Alice and vanished behind the equipment.

"Let's get to work," she said and pushed past Gabe into his minuscule office. "I've got some ideas for menus."

GABE HAD PREPARED himself for the worst. He was fortified by too much caffeine, and ready to do battle with Alice over kitchen operations. But, surprisingly, there was no battle. It didn't take long for them to ease into their old routine. They were rusty at first, but the one thing they'd always shared— well, two things—was that they were both perfectionists. Fortunately they both had the same idea of what perfect was.

"All right—" Alice looked down at her notebook "—breakfast buffets at the beginning. You have some kind of waitstaff, or do you expect me to do that?" She glanced at him from beneath her lashes and her eyes, black as night, twinkled just a little more than they had before, and he sighed.

"I've got staff."

"Juvenile delinquents?" She was having too much fun with this at his expense. "Cameron going to be your front-of-house staff? He'll be a real hit with guests."

"You're hilarious. No, I've got it taken care of. Keep going—" He pointed at her list, though he had all the pertinent details of their conversation locked in his head. His years as a waiter had honed his memory.

"Two options for lunch. Two options for dinner, including a vegetarian pasta, and three desserts." She tapped her pencil on the pad. "Are there going to be kids?" she asked but she didn't look up. He wondered how long that open emotional sore of hers was going to still bleed.

"There are no reservations with children yet. I'll let you know when there are.

"Great." She took a deep breath, her thin shoulders lifting under her black blouse. "Then I can make up something kid friendly."

"I'm missing some equipment," he told her. "Food processor, blender, some larger roasting pans. If you want to write up a list I'll go see what I can find."

"I brought what I'll need," she said, still staring at the pad of paper. "It's in my car."

"Always prepared." He repeated fondly the motto she used to live by. The woman used to carry a can opener, a bottle opener, a paring knife and curry powder in the glove box of her car.

Camping with her had been like roughing it at the Ritz.

She flashed him a quick smile but never stopped scribbling.

"I'm getting a list of food we're going to need. I can run to Athens today and pick up some stuff," she said, more to herself than him.

"I've found a few organic farms in the area."

"Great. Let me just finish this…"

She still appeared so dramatic, her thinness only adding somehow to the tragic appeal of her.

Daphne of Athens Organics, her wholesome, honest plainness was the exact opposite of his ex-wife. In fact, most of the women he'd dated after the marriage ended could be considered, in one way or another, the exact opposite of Alice.

Which wasn't an accident.

"Now, the organic farmers. What are we looking at?"

"I met with a local farmer yesterday and we have an appointment to tour her farm tomorrow morning." He handed Alice Daphne's card.

"We?" Alice asked and exhaled heavily. "Gabe, you are supposed to be staying out of my way, remember? We shook on it."

"Okay." He nodded and leaned forward in his chair, putting his pencil against the top edge of his blotter, reluctant to look at her. *Why?* he wondered, angry with himself. *It's been five years, I've dated a lot of women and I'm sure she went on her share of dates, too.* But still, it seemed like he might shatter this nice…equilibrium between them.

"You have an appointment," he said. "I…have a date."

He cleared his throat to break the silence.

"You're dating a farmer?" she asked. She blinked at him, unruffled. He couldn't tell if she was kidding with him, which would be like the old Alice. But this new incarnation…she didn't seem to be much for joking.

"Her name is Daphne and she runs the farm."

"So, she's a farmer."

"She runs...yes, she's a farmer."

"You date her in the morning?" she asked.

"It's our first. For coffee." Why he felt compelled to tell her, he wasn't sure. But perhaps it was better to get it all out there, instead of having her be surprised at some point. A surprised Alice was a recipe for the unexpected.

"This should be good," she said, her lips quirked in a grin. She stood, tucked her notebook into her bag.

That's it? he wondered, waiting for her punch line. Her zinger. But none seemed forthcoming and he wondered if maybe he'd braced himself for nothing. Maybe, he realized with a slight relaxing of his shoulders, they could do this—work together, be in each other's lives—like adults.

"You want to show me to my room, or cabin or whatever?" she asked. Her eyes held no secrets. No questions, no suppressed anger and resentment.

He nodded and stood up as well.

We're going to be just fine, he thought and grabbed the key to the smallest cabin that so far was unrented.

THE NEED FOR a drink was stronger than all her promises and wishes. The need to drink was a demon in the back of her throat, in the back of her head, howling and screaming and tearing her apart with temptation.

A date. Of course. Gabe dates. She knew that intellectually. But to have to watch him do it made her feel trapped.

She followed her ex-husband out the back door of the kitchen, around the front of the inn and down a narrow foot-worn path and battled her demon with the cooling calming influence of lists.

Lists of men she'd dated since her divorce.

Marcus, Luke and…

Marcus and Luke. Each for about ten minutes.

That was depressing. Fine. She'd focus on work lists. Things she needed for work.

Well, first on the list was calling Daphne and re-scheduling her appointment. Alice wasn't going to drive up to the farm with Gabe for his *date*. She needed to find a dairy supplier. Meats. Start making stocks, pesto—

"Here you go," Gabe said, opening the door to a cabin. "This is yours until I need to rent it and then I'll move you into the lodge with Dad and Max and myself. Cleaning staff will come by once a week with fresh linens and towels."

The cabin was small, sweet and redolent of the scent of fresh paint and sawdust. The blue and green linens on the white-painted brass bed lifted and waved in the cross breeze between the open east-facing windows and the door.

The cabin was exactly as Gabe had always envisioned for his inn. *His* dream come true. Her throat tightened with uncomfortable emotion.

"Bathroom's through there." He pointed behind the door, then handed her the keys.

She took them, clenching her fingers around the cool metal. *Say something,* she urged herself. *Say something about how well he's done. How perfectly he's brought the dream to life, how glad I am to see this come to fruition. Say something. Anything.*

"Shout if you need anything," Gabe said, then turned and walked away.

She watched him go, the words dead in her throat. Another in a long line of missed opportunities.

UNPACKING HER PERSONAL stuff from the car took an embarrassingly small amount of time. Four chef jackets, two pairs of checkered pants, some regular clothes and clogs.

She shook her head at the meager clothes hanging in the closet, like deflated, lonely people.

Toothbrush, expensive face and hand lotion sat on the glass shelf over the old-fashioned pedestal sink in the bathroom.

She took a look around the cozy cabin that was no doubt made for lovers, for two toothbrushes and closets filled with his-and-her clothes, and shuddered.

I gotta get the hell out of here.

Far more comfortable in the kitchen, she unloaded those indispensable kitchen items from her house. Food processor, standing mixer, her knives, her grandmother's cast iron skillet, roasting pans and recipe box—all handed down in her family like diamond engagement rings were handed down in others.

With nothing else to do but tour the grounds and

constantly come face-to-face with the physical reality of their once-shared dream, she pulled out the Athens Organics card and rescheduled her appointment.

"Well," she said when Daphne asked her for a good time to reschedule. It was five in the afternoon. "I'm free right now. I can be there in a half hour."

"Ahh," Daphne stalled for a moment and Alice wondered if she actually was going to have to piggyback Gabe's coffee date.

Really, she wondered, *was there anything more depressing.*

"That work's great," Daphne finally said. "I also have some information on local butchers and a great recommendation for an organic dairy farm near Coxsackie."

Smart woman, Alice thought, hanging up. *But I'm still not going to like her.*

Alice grabbed her keys and beat a hasty retreat from Riverview Inn.

She flew down the New York interstate then took Highway 12 along the river, past Black Rock and the old Van Loan mansion. Twilight came to the Catskills like a slow bleed of India ink from the east, while the western sky remained light behind the rounded back of the old mountain chain.

It was beautiful country. She'd grown up here— her parents were only a hundred miles away from where Gabe had built the inn.

Alice rolled down the window and let the cool air hit her cheek, slide into the open neck of her blouse.

She was tired, hungry but, she was honest enough to admit it…excited. Excited about filling the back of her car with herbs and organic potatoes and radishes. Excited about waking up early tomorrow, putting on a pot of coffee and getting to work.

Excited about organic dairy suppliers, mint pesto, incoming guests…all of it. She was excited about life again. She'd lived in such a small dark place for so long, constantly trying to fill up the emptiness in herself with empty things—work she didn't care about, wine that didn't help her forget. But this opportunity…she felt flushed with ideas.

She cranked the wheel left, nearly missing the turnoff to the farm. Another quarter mile and she was in front of a lovely white and yellow farmhouse. Dogs ran out from bushes to greet her and she felt, inexplicably, that Athens Organics was going to be a perfect match for her kitchen.

"Hi."

Alice turned to find a young blond girl standing at her window. She was about five.

For one second, one naked and vulnerable moment, Alice couldn't breathe.

Alice didn't even have to do the math or work hard to recall the expected due date of her first pregnancy. The information was imprinted on her bones. She knew that her own daughter, stillborn at twenty weeks would be this girl's age.

"Hi," she said and swallowed. "I'm Alice—"

"You're here to see my mom," the girl said. "She's out in the herb field and I'm supposed to take you there." She smiled. Her front tooth was missing, and something purple and sticky was stuck to the side of her face.

"Your mom is Daphne?" Alice asked needlessly, knowing the answer already because fate was just that vindictive.

"Yep." The girl nodded, blond pigtails flapping with her zeal. "I'm Helen."

Alice climbed out of her car on legs that felt weak around the knees. She was used to seeing children, little girls or boys who were the age of her two babies who never made it would be. She was used to talking with them, trying not stare at them too long or touch them at all. And she was quick to leave their company.

She just wasn't used to meeting the children of women Gabe planned to date.

No wonder, she thought cruelly, as those parts of her that had begun to feel full—her joy, excitement and thrill—emptied again in her unrelenting grief. *No wonder he's ready to date the farmer.*

TWO HOURS LATER, won over by Daphne's farm and exhausted by trying to ignore Helen, Alice parked in the area behind the kitchen that was still covered in grass. She leaped out of the car, leaving the herbs and sample produce in the back. She'd return for it after she got dinner made.

It was late already, seven-thirty, so she quickly took stock of what the men had been living on.

Bacon, eggs, pasta. Cream for Patrick's coffee.

Two wizened apples, an inexplicable lime and two industrial-size cans of coffee.

All signs pointed to pasta cabonara. With nothing green in sight. The produce in the back of her car was earmarked for the work in the morning. Besides, vegetable-free was the way the Mitchell men liked their dinners.

She pulled down the new pans, turned the dials on the gas stove, and soon, the smell of bacon and garlic sautéing in olive oil had attracted the men like bees to a picnic.

Gabe came in first, standing in the doorway watching her until her hands felt clumsy, her whole body flushed with awareness.

"Thank God," Max said as he came in, grabbed a beer and headed into the dining room.

"You are a blessing, a real blessing," Patrick said, kissing her cheek and actually succeeding in making Alice blush. "I'll set out the plates." He grabbed the classic white dishes Gabe had picked out.

Soon, it was just the smell of bacon, her, Gabe at the door and the heat of blood in her face that would not go away.

She wondered if he knew that Daphne had a daughter. If he'd done the math and realized that the little girl was the same age theirs would have been.

She doubted it. Not that he knew about the girl, that she was sure of—of course he'd date women who'd proved their love of family, their ability to create one—he just wouldn't have done the math.

"Go sit down," she finally said when she couldn't tolerate his observation anymore. "I'll bring it out."

"About tomorrow morning—"

"I've already gone," she interrupted. "We met this afternoon. She'll be a fantastic supplier and she gave me great sources for organic meats and dairy."

She's a wonderful mother with a funny great kid, I imagine you'll share a long and happy life with a million children running around.

I need a drink.

"You've jumped in with both feet." Gabe smiled. "It's still your first day."

She shrugged. "You hired me to work."

He stepped past her and she could feel him at her back though there was at least five feet between them. "It's good to have you here," he said, his voice that warm dark purr that turned her insides soft. "Max actually laughed like he meant it. Dad nearly fell out of his chair."

She dumped the dried pasta into the boiling water and didn't say anything for fear of saying too much. She put butter in the frying pan, studiously not looking at Gabe, pretending to be casual when it felt as if her head would explode.

Still he didn't leave, he stood at the door like a sentinel.

"Are you going to eat with us?" he asked.

She shook her head, there was only so far a woman could go in a day and she'd hit her limit. "Lots of work to do," she lied.

"I didn't think so," he said, knowing her so well she nearly dropped the cream container right into the sauce.

And finally, just as she thought she might scream from the tension, he left.

CHAPTER FIVE

IT WAS LATE and the demons riding her wouldn't back down. In fact, as Alice tried to deep breathe through her cravings, think of all the things she had in her life that she could screw up by drinking, the demons bit harder into her spine, eating at it until she had no defense against her need.

Her grandmother's recipes had been sorted and resorted; the ones that fit her idea of inn fare had been culled. The dinner dish she'd brought to the cabin from the kitchen was clean and upside down in her small shower.

She'd paced. She'd made lists and notes. She'd called Charlie on her cell phone to check on Felix.

Ten o'clock and it was just her and the demons.

Gabe won't like it. You might lose this job. You might have to go back to the city and find some other job you can't stand. You have an early morning. Lots of work to do.

She watched the moon rise from the small window in her bathroom, cupped her shaking hands under the silver light, let it bathe her face like clean cold water.

There is nothing I want, there is nothing—

"Just something to get me to sleep," she finally whispered to no one, her spine gone, her will devoured by demons.

She stepped out into the cool air of spring in the Catskills, zipped up her maroon fleece and went looking for Max and Patrick, who, she was betting her sanity, would have a bottle somewhere.

The lodge glowed, the windows of the dining room revealing mellow light and a fire in the fire-place. It looked warm, welcoming, a beautiful beacon in the night.

But it was all wasted on her.

Drink. Drink. Drink.

She pulled open the heavy oak doors, leaning with all her weight just so she could slide in and catch the tail end of Patrick's laughter as it reverberated across pine and within cathedral ceilings.

"Swans?" Max snorted. "You've got to be kidding me."

The three of them sat around the fire on brass-studded burgundy leather couches. Patrick and Gabe held tumblers filled with a promising amber liquid. Max had a beer.

"Hi," she said, her eyes on the bottle of Jim Beam on the coffee table next to their feet. The three of them turned to find her in the shadows, each registering varying degrees of pleasure at seeing her.

She concentrated on Patrick and the bottle, though she could feel Gabe there, at the edge of the light, touched by shadows.

"Well, if it isn't our chef." Patrick's big voice boomed. "Come sit. Have a drink."

He pulled himself out of his deep seat and walked over to the wooden bar in the corner to grab her a glass.

Hurry. Hurry. Hurry.

Her hungry eyes followed him until she felt the burning touch of Gabe's gaze on her face.

She turned, met those eyes and saw what she knew would be there. A question. Worry. For him. For her. A profound wish that she wouldn't drink what Patrick poured for her.

She almost laughed.

Patrick poured her a splash of whiskey and gestured to the empty seat beside Max, who toasted her with his beer.

"Good dinner tonight," he said. "Best thing I've eaten in months."

"You're in sad shape if that's the case," she said, forcing herself not to gulp down her drink.

She took a sip, sighed and stretched out her legs, imitating someone having a casual drink, enjoying the moment rather than counting the seconds between sips.

"So?" she said, looking around at the silent, masculine faces. "Are we having a staff meeting? Should Max go get Cameron?"

"Nope, just trying to work out the details for the wedding," Gabe said.

Max, beside her, chuckled before taking another swig of beer.

"Must be good," she said.

"I don't know if you could say good," Gabe cringed. The firelight hit his face, highlighting those things about his features that she'd always loved. His slightly too big nose which was balanced by his hard jawline and his ridiculously long eyelashes, a beautiful surprise on such a masculine face. The small scar on his right cheek from an evening of oysters and too much wine, when he'd gotten over-zealous with the oyster knife.

He turned to her, no doubt sensing her blatant staring, and she buried her face in her tumbler.

"I believe we have a…what's the word?" Patrick asked Gabe.

"Bridezilla," he supplied.

"Right. I believe we have one of those on our hands."

"She wants pink swans," Max interjected. "We have an idiot on our hands."

"You've got to be kidding,' she sputtered, looking to Gabe and Patrick who could only nod and drown their sorrows. "Swans don't come in pink."

"She read that a Saudi Arabian prince had pink swans at his wedding," Gabe said.

"Where do you find them?" she asked. "I mean, if she's ready to pay for—"

"You don't *find* them," Max said, crossing his boots on the table. "You *make* them.'

Patrick leaned over and added more whiskey to his glass. She fought the urge to gulp down the rest of hers and shove her tumbler out for a refill. "You have to dip swans in red dye," he said.

"By hand." Max shook his head. "And guess who's job that would be." He jabbed his thumb at his own chest. "Mine."

She reveled in the warmth of the fire, the drink, the masculine camaraderie that she was always far more comfortable with than whatever it was women did in similar situations.

It was the years in kitchens, working in a male-dominated industry that created this preference. She liked men. And, she really liked these men, Gabe occasionally included.

"Poor Max," she said and patted her former brother-in-law's shoulders.

"We're not doing it," Gabe said, rolling his head as if his neck was stiff. "It can't be good for the swans and I'm not endangering wildlife for the Fish-Stick Princess."

"Maybe you could talk to her," Patrick said, gesturing to her with his tumbler.

"Me?" Alice asked. "Why?"

"Talk reason to her, woman-to-woman." Patrick nodded as if he was on to something. "Your wedding was the loveliest thing I ever saw and so—"

"She's handling the kitchen, Dad," Gabe cut in, but it was too late. It was as if the memory of that flawless September day had plunked itself down on the table amongst them. Her mother's wedding dress. Her father's tears as he handed her to Gabe. Gabe's vows that he'd written himself. Max's speech that had them all laughing so hard they cried.

The kiss in front of all their friends and family

that had felt like a promise. The small bulge of her belly where a new life kicked. A new start. The beginning of all things good and right and wonderful in her life.

She drained her glass and held it out for more.

Patrick dutifully refilled it. "Now," he said, "my wedding to your mother, that was a day for the books."

The room went still. Silent. Like a cathedral or, more appropriately, a tomb.

Gabe turned to stare at his father, his face hard and uncompromising. Carved from ice.

Alice held her breath to see how this particular bomb would detonate. No one ever mentioned Iris. Ever. The few times Alice had tried she'd been shut down so hard and so fast that she slept on the couch to prevent getting frostbite by sleeping next to Gabe.

She'd thought curiosity or concern for these men, alone for too long, had been frozen out of her by her marriage to Gabe. But sitting here now, the familiar refrain billowed in her like white smoke from a wet fire.

Poor guys.

"I'm going to get some work done," Gabe said. He stood, rubbing his free hand over his face and through his hair.

He looked tired. Worn. And she knew he took great pains to never look that way. Keeping the facade in place was paramount to Gabe.

"Maybe you should take a break," she said before she thought better of her concern. "Just relax. You won't do your inn any good if you get sick."

"The girl's got an idea," Patrick said and took a sip.

"You worry about you," Gabe said, throwing her words back in her face. "I'll worry about my inn."

She held up her hands, somehow knowing it would come to this, any effort to reach out on her part would be snubbed.

Gabe stared hard at his father for a minute, which Patrick pretended to ignore, and then he walked away, disappearing into the shadows outside the cheerful light of the fire.

Max snorted into the silence.

"What's wrong?" Alice asked, the temperature in the room still arctic despite the blaze in the oversize fireplace.

"Dad can't leave well enough alone," Max said, and then he stood up and left. Disappearing in the opposite direction from where Gabe had vanished.

Alice finally turned to Patrick, who sat with his head resting on the curved back of the sofa, his hand over the breast pocket of his shirt.

"What's going on here?" Alice asked.

She poured herself more whiskey, since the first two fingerfuls only made the demons silent, it didn't put them away. They were there, breathing and waiting.

"Nothing new."

Alice waited for some elaboration, but of course, true to Mitchell form, none came.

"Do you want to talk about it?" she asked.

He rolled his head sideways, his merry eyes were subdued, dark. "It's about their mother," he finally said.

Alice blinked and leaned back, stunned to her core. "The root?" she asked, using her pet name for Gabe's absentee mother.

"The root?"

"The root of all evil," she said. "The root of all Gabe's intimacy issues, his blind need for a family, his fear of—"

Patrick didn't even say good-night, he just stood, poured another inch of whiskey in his glass and walked into the shadows.

Alice sat there, slack jawed.

Thirty years ago, the woman had left all three men high and dry. Alice couldn't believe Patrick would be offended by her words, though clearly he was.

I should apologize, she thought and drained the last of her whiskey. *He's a good man, been nothing but kind to me despite the divorce. I need allies in this place and Patrick has always been a good ally.*

"Patrick, I'm sorry," she said, but only the creak of the stairs as he climbed them answered her.

The firelight played over the amber liquid in the bottle, the reflection cast waves of light across the floor. The fire was warm, the room empty, there was another four ounces in the bottle…

This was supposed to be a fresh start. She'd planned to wake up early tomorrow, prove to Gabe that she took this seriously. That she was the same old Alice, perfectionist and workaholic.

She was excited about all of that.

"One more drink," she sighed. Alice grabbed the bottle, stretched out her feet and settled in.

THE NEXT MORNING Gabe stood in an empty cold kitchen and felt the past wash over him. When would he learn? He shook his head and put his hand on the cold coffeepot. Expecting more from the women in his life had only led to this moment. This…disappointment.

First his mom and now Alice.

Again.

He should have known by the way she watched the bottle of whiskey last night, her eyes gleaming like a starving dog, chained just out of reach of food.

She'd gotten drunk. She'd gotten drunk and now it was 9:00 a.m., well past the time any chef would be up and working, considering the amount of prep she had to do. Instead she would be hungover and it was only the second day.

Grabbing the keys from the hook he hung them on, he hit the door hard and left the inn.

He tried to be reasonable, to understand her position, how awkward it must be for her to come here surrounded by the Mitchell men. He tried. But failed.

I'm such an idiot! he thought, slamming the door on his old BMW. *I should have listened to my gut and walked away from her when I saw her drinking at her house.* He yanked the wheel and spun out of the parking area, spitting gravel and pulling up grass.

She's too damaged. Too locked in the past. No wonder she lost Zinnia. No wonder we could never work it out, the woman is so absorbed in her own pain she can never see what she's doing to other people.

Like him.

She never saw what she did to him. She hadn't when she was screaming at him during their marriage, and she didn't now. He needed her and she didn't care.

She's gone, he decided, speeding down the turnpike toward Daphne. *When I get back I'll tell her to pack up and hit the road. I can't take this. I don't have to. I'll figure something else out.*

Gabe rolled down the window, hoping the cool morning air would chill him out a little. It didn't work. Resolving to fire her didn't work. Alice, when he was mad at her, lived in his brain and under his skin.

This was his fault. Totally his fault.

To even think of bringing her here had been asking for this.

He pulled a hand through his hair and tried to force her out of his head. He was going on a date after all, no matter how unorthodox. Meeting Daphne with Alice stuck in his head wasn't fair to Daphne or him.

He wondered briefly if it was fair to Alice to fire her when she so clearly needed help. He pushed that thought away. He'd spent too many years trying to help her.

He was done saving Alice from herself.

He turned up the radio, found "Baba O'Reiley" and sang along with The Who tune. He'd managed to push Alice out of his head once, he could do it again.

Starting now.

Twenty minutes later, with her only running circles

in the back of his brain, he pulled up in front of the pretty, white-and-yellow farmhouse and climbed out of his car. A black-and-brown dog charged him, but Daphne, standing in the doorway, called the beast off.

"Hi, Gabe," she said, her smile sweet and girlish in a way that called up masculine things in himself. He wanted to hug her.

"Daphne," he said with a grin.

"Come on in, I've got a pot on." She led the way into her kitchen. His mood recovered, spreading a warm glow around him. Her house was perfect, looking messy and well lived in. The pine floors were worn smooth, the curtains in the window faded by the sun, boots and shoes piled up at the door.

It was exactly what he wanted for his inn. Someday he wanted his great-grandkids leading their respective lovers and friends through the front door that he'd built with his brother and dad.

Just thinking about it gave him chills.

"My meeting with your chef went very well yesterday," Daphne said, looking at him over her shoulder.

There went his good mood, his warm glow dimmed. He couldn't even go on a date to get away from her.

"I gave her some herb samples, all of the lettuce and basil she ordered and the purple potatoes, broccoli and carrots." Daphne pulled two mugs from the whitewashed cupboard, and grabbed the coffee carafe and set it all on the table.

Her smile was effervescent, huge, bright and

warm enough to heat cold rooms. Not at all like Alice's, which seemed broken. Sick.

Stop it! he ordered himself. *Stop thinking about her. There are no comparisons between Alice and Daphne.*

"Cream?" Daphne asked, heading for the fridge.

"No, thanks," he said and she stopped and sat down at the table.

"Me, neither." She glanced at him sideways with a look that seemed young and flirtatious, despite the slight gray in her blond hair, and the wrinkles around her eyes.

Wrinkles and gray hair that he liked, considering he had some of it himself.

"Gets in the way of the caffeine," he said, taking a sip of the brew she'd poured.

"Exactly."

She sat back and suddenly the silence seemed to have an awkward weight and heft. *I don't have time for this,* he thought again, suddenly anxious to get going. *I have those press releases to send out and the Web site to update. I have to fire Alice and find—*

"We're supposed to be relaxing," Daphne said, brushing her braid over her shoulder. "And I think both of us are making lists."

He nodded. "Guilty. The curse of owning your own business."

"The plus side is we can make up for whatever work we're not doing right now later. So—" she took a deep breath "—let's stop making lists and act like normal people."

"Normal people…" He narrowed his eyes. "I can't quite remember how they act."

She laughed, the sound husky and deep, and it made him smile. He did have time for this, because if he didn't make time to date, to meet nice women over coffee, he'd end up like his dad and brother. He'd end up living with them forever.

"Your chef, Alice? She's an intense woman," Daphne said. "Striking. She seems very sad."

Well, talking about his ex-wife wasn't really what he had in mind.

"She's complicated," he said and took a sip of coffee. Telling Daphne that Alice was his ex-wife seemed a bit precipitous since she wouldn't be around much longer.

"Hey, Mom—" A miniature version of Daphne— complete with the long white-blond braid and bright green galoshes—came running up the stairs from the basement.

"Hey, Helen." Daphne opened her arm and the young girl hugged her mother's side. "What's up?"

"Matt's coming over. His mom has to go to the store."

"Okay. You guys can help me in the greenhouse."

Helen turned up her nose and Daphne kissed it. "You might have a day off kindergarten, but I still have to work," she said. "You two help me out in the greenhouse and I'll take you for ice cream in town."

Helen nodded, the deal struck, then ran back downstairs.

Gabe felt his heart expand, fill like a balloon until it threatened to lift him off his chair.

Family. His pulse seemed to chant it for him.

"My daughter," Daphne said needlessly. "Her father and I divorced about three years ago."

Gabe nodded and looked around, noticing the things he'd missed before. The drawings on the fridge. The kids' cereal on the counter. The Barbie book bag set up by the door.

A family. Right here.

He looked at Daphne with new eyes. His heart so full in his chest he could barely breathe.

"Do you like kids?" she asked.

Gabe nodded. "Yes," he said. "I've always wanted kids."

THE HEADACHE FROM her too-short night and too much whiskey had been muted to a dull throb. The coffee helped. The cooking helped more. Alice's kitchen was warm—a chicken, three lemons, a bay leaf, onion, carrots and celery boiled away in a huge pot on the stove, creating stock she would freeze for later use. The crisp sweet smell of mint wafted from her food processor as she added a little more sugar to her mint and walnut pesto.

The dairy farm she'd visited at dawn had already delivered the cream and milk and some of the owner's early attempts at cheese. The ricotta was good. Not great, but okay.

She took another sip of coffee, and tried to encourage that small fire of happiness that was back in her belly. If she could just stay in this kitchen all day and never talk to Gabe or—

"Pack your bags."

She whirled to find him in the doorway, angry and bristling as if he'd heard her thoughts.

"I want you gone," he said.

CHAPTER SIX

IF ALICE WAS SURPRISED, she hid it well. Her face was empty, composed. Her eyebrows slightly arched as if to say "excuse me?" The cup of coffee in her hand steady.

"I'm not kidding," Gabe said as coldly as possible. He bit his tongue against what he really wanted to say: *I need to be free of you. I can't get on with my life with you here.* "I want you out."

"Why?" she finally asked, setting down her cup as though it might break in her hand. "What's happened?"

"It doesn't matter. This isn't going to work."

"I think I deserve an explanation," she said. Her anger fueled his, especially since she didn't have any right to hers.

"What time did you finally get out of bed today?" he asked. She opened her mouth but he didn't want to hear what she had to say. He knew the truth. He'd always known it and he was a fool to try to convince himself this situation could go a different way. "How late did you stay up drinking last night? It was Monday for crying out loud. Your first day and you decide to get drunk?"

"Gabe—"

He shook his head, feeling oddly emotional. As if a great boulder of pain and anger was bearing down on him. "I was an idiot to think this was going to work."

"I don't understand what's going on here." The white flesh of her neck flushed slightly pink and he nearly relished that small sign of her involvement. Her caring. Her goddamn interest in what was happening. "You're firing me?"

"Yes."

"Why?"

Because you're a drunk. You're unstable. "Because this is my home," he said instead, surprising himself with the honesty. His body was hot and he couldn't control it, couldn't calm himself. His throat hurt from not yelling. "Mine. I made it. You can't have this one. You can't take this one from me. Or ruin it."

They both blinked while his words rocked the very foundation of the building.

"You think that's what I want to do?" she asked, so composed, except for her hands, which trembled before she pressed them against her apron. Her lips were white.

"I don't think you want to, but you will."

She looked away for a moment, blinking, and he wondered if he'd gone too far. Compassion for this woman he used to love with an all-consuming force welled up in him, slow like black tar.

But he refused to give in to it. The Riverview, his sanity, his home—it was all at stake now.

Alice didn't know why she didn't open her mouth and tell him the truth. Why she, in fact, didn't scream the truth from the rooftops and rub his face in his wrong conclusions and allegations.

Because he's right. Part of her agreed with him. *I am a failure. Everything I touch turns to mud.*

She brushed her hands of mint and turned to leave. She'd have her bags packed and be back in Albany with a glass of wine before the real pain set in.

"We went to the dairy farm outside of Coxsackie," Max said from the door to the dining room, where he'd been standing for God knows how long. The blush and emotion she'd been able to barely control flooded her and she put her hand on the chopping block for balance because her head felt light. Her body too awkward. "She wanted to go early to see the first milking."

"Max," she started to stay, ready to tell him she didn't need defending.

"You were going to let him think the worst," he said, not looking at her.

He sauntered to the coffeepot and smirked at Gabe, practically egging him into a fight. Max loved to catch Gabe flat-footed and from her ex-husband's openmouthed, slack-jawed look of surprise, she had to guess Max won this round.

She'd been defended. The truth was out and all it took was one look at Gabe's face to realize it didn't matter.

He wanted her gone, drunk or not, working or not.

Gabe shut his mouth, shook his head and seemed

to gather himself. She could read him like a book. He still didn't want her here, but now he had no reason to fire her.

She fumbled with the ties on her apron.

He was right—this was a mistake. For both of them. If this failed, if she screwed this up…it would hurt. More than what she felt right now. If she cared more…if she worked longer with these beautiful foods, in this beautiful room and then had to leave…the pain would magnify. Double and triple over.

Max poured himself a coffee. "Stop being an ass," he told his brother and slapped Gabe on the back before heading outside. Alice wished fervently she could join him.

"Why didn't you say something?" Gabe asked.

"I thought I was supposed to be running the kitchen. You weren't going to interfere," she managed to say, when what she wanted to say was, "You're right. What's the point of defending myself against the truth."

"But I accused you—"

"Of what? Drinking too much?" She shrugged. "I did. I do."

He licked his lips, his gaze so steady, so rock solid that she ached from the pressure. Nothing about her was rock solid. Nothing was steady. She was a house of cards and there was a fire beneath her.

"But you could have told me what your plans were. I don't think it's—"

She let out some of the steam building in her, vented it on him. "Considering—" her voice dripped with sarcasm "—your date this morning with the young mother, I didn't want to bother you with details like milk."

He rocked back on his heels. "Young mother?" His incredulous laughter felt like acid against her skin and heart. "You have got to get over this. I am sorry about the miscarriages, but that's years ago."

It's right now, she wanted to howl. *It's every minute I'm not a mother.*

They both took deep breaths until the tension in the air dissipated, something they'd learned to do the hard way in the last few months they were together.

"This isn't about Daphne," Gabe said, his voice soft. "And it's not about our marriage."

"And it's not about me drinking. So what is it, Gabe? What do you really need from me right now that I'm not giving you?"

"I need a commitment," he said plainly. "You're my chef, you're a cornerstone for my business, and you've got me so nervous right now that I'm ready to do it myself."

"Tomato soup from a can and grilled-cheese sandwiches? The bride will love that." She mocked him, mocked the meal he used to make for her that once brought her such joy.

He winced, then rubbed his hands through his hair, putting the blond waves on end. The mask he wore—the I-can-do-it-all Gabe Mitchell mask—fell away for just a moment and she could see him. The real him—small and nervous and sleepless inside the suit of professionalism he wore—behind the smoke and mirrors.

The great and powerful Oz was at the end of his rope.

She trembled on the edge of something, on the edge of her solitary existence, on the edge of her combined failures that she wore like armor to prevent herself from risking too much again.

She tried to remember how she'd once been, when she'd taken risks, when she'd loved her life and her work, when collaborating with Gabe had been as exhilarating as making love to him.

Give a little, Alice. Give a tiny bit. Offer something that he doesn't have to fight for.

"Look, I can handle prep and cook for your guests. But I need some help for that wedding by the end of this month." Her voice was gruff, her compromise hidden and buried beneath her begrudging tone.

Gabe blinked, then blinked again. "I can find you help before then. I've got feelers—"

"I'm telling you, you don't need to. I can handle it—just not the wedding."

"That's a lot of work," he said. "I'm expecting twenty guests in May and I'm still taking reservations."

She shot him a *puh-leeze* look. She'd handled more than that as a sous chef with laryngitis and a broken oven.

"All that work? Really?" he asked.

She nodded. "It's not like there is anything else to do," she said. And work would keep her mind off other things. Like booze. Like Zinnia. Like failed marriages and her ex-husband dating.

"Okay," Gabe said. "I can hire—"

"I'll hire someone," she interrupted, "from my salary for a larger percentage of ownership." The words toppled out of her mouth willy-nilly and awkward. She had very little experience with compromise.

She managed a quick look at Gabe to see if his response was favorable.

"Oh, shut your mouth," she said, exasperated by his shocked expression. "Let's both be reasonable."

"Those are great terms," he said and stuck out his hand.

She slid her hand into his giant paw and quickly tried to remove it, but he gripped her, his thick callused fingers closing in around hers.

"Al." Her nickname again and the room shrank, the space between them was too small. She could feel his heat and his breath against her face. "Please stop drinking."

She shook her head. She should and she would. But it wouldn't be because of he'd told her to do it. "No. What I do on my time is my business."

"I can't—"

"I've committed, Gabe." She finally looked right into his eyes, the brilliant blue that could burn her or freeze her, that could bring her to life or shut her down in a hundred different ways. Belatedly she realized what she'd done. She'd tied her fortune to a man who could destroy her—again.

"You won't get any more from me," she told him and somehow they both understood that it wasn't only work they talked about. His hand was hot in hers. The callus on his thumb seemed suddenly personal, the proof of his labor too much for her to witness.

"Alice, about Daphne—"

She jerked her hand away.

"I have a lot of work to do." She turned from him, retying the strings of her apron.

"Me, too," he murmured. She heard him go into his office and shut the door.

The breath she hadn't realized she'd been holding leaked out of her, and she nearly sagged.

A business card appeared under her nose and, startled, she jerked upright. Max, the damn sneak stood there, his expression unreadable. "Sheriff in town runs an AA meeting out of the station on Sunday nights," he said.

"I'm not an alcoholic," she said.

He shrugged. "Not really my business," he said, "but if you want to talk to him tell him I gave you his number."

"Max." She tried to laugh. "I don't need the card."

But he just stood there, so different from Gabe yet at the core of both of them lay the same stubborn compassion that ran them both ragged in different ways.

Once upon a time Max had wanted to save the world and all Gabe had wanted was to save was his own family.

She sighed and took the card knowing Max would stand there all day if she didn't.

A WEEK LATER, Alice checked her watch and decided an afternoon coffee break was in order.

Coffee, she decided, *some fresh air and I'll think about those potatoes that need to be dealt with.*

The sun sat in the crook of the western mountains and the property was a dramatically different world than the one she'd greeted at dawn this morning. The fog had burned off, the cacophony of springtime insects that had seemed so loud this morning were gone, replaced by the sound of Max and his gang of street thugs clearing brush.

A week after her compromise with Gabe and she was seriously regretting her decision to do all the prep herself. Not that she'd ever admit that to Gabe, who'd been staying out of her way, even as he watched her like a hawk, waiting, she was sure, for her to screw up.

So she worked and pretended he wasn't there, though she felt him at her back so much that when she slept she could feel him there, curled against her the way he had when they were married.

She woke up every morning, turned on and annoyed. And it only got worse throughout the day.

But all of this watching and ignoring had to come to an end. She had a menu coming together that she needed to be sampled and she didn't have any details on the wedding. Numbers. Themes. Money.

Sooner or later they were actually going to have to work together. But until then it was best they avoided talking to each other. He called up things in her that she hated, emotions that were ugly and petty.

In the meantime, she was up to her sore elbows in work. She'd forgotten how hard it was building a kitchen from scratch. There were deliveries to put away: heavy bags of onions and potatoes from Athens Organics; sides of beef that she preferred to butcher herself, which was no easy task.

And then there was the constant boiling, baking, basting and freezing of stocks, marinades and flavored oils. She fell into bed at the end of every day too tired to even think of drinking and woke up every morning sore to the bottom of her feet but her mind already working on the day's chores.

Today it was potatoes. Gnocchi and latke. The huge bag of potatoes sat in the pantry mocking her and her tired biceps.

She wished she had some help, just a little, for the afternoon. But she'd made this bed, she would lie in it. After her break.

She slid on her sunglasses and sat down on the small hill behind the kitchen, flanking the makeshift parking lot, and watched Max herd the kids like they were cattle. Or cats.

"Hey," he said, his voice echoing through the woods as he emerged from the tree line. "Stop slacking, this is our last tree."

He and a girl dragged the shorn trunk of a fallen poplar toward the huge pile of debris they'd gathered in a cleared area next to the lodge.

"We gonna burn this stuff or what?" Cameron appeared from the woods, halfheartedly pulling a limb from the tree behind him. "Because I think that would only be the right way to end this whole thing, you know?"

"No," Max said succinctly, rolling the thick trunk

under some of the brush at the base of the pile. "I don't."

Alice couldn't tell if Max and the kids were a match made in hell or heaven. From the closed-down, locked-up expression on Max's face she bet he wasn't sure, either.

"This huge tree goes down, no one knows. It sits there in the woods, rotting, bugs eating it, animals pooping on it. That's no way for a tree to go," Cameron said and Alice found herself warming up to the kid with his overworked sense of drama. "We gotta burn it. Put it out of its misery."

"Be quiet," Max said and Cameron, after a few more jokes on the tree's behalf, did. Alice was a little surprised at the progress Max had made with the mouthy kid. He wore a hat that kept the hair out of his eyes, and his pants, still too big, were held up by a belt. And he was working.

Maybe now that he was house-trained she could actually work with him in the kitchen. He could run his mouth and peel potatoes at the same time.

"We're not done," Max said, heading back to the forest, and a chorus of groans followed him even though the kids didn't. "Let's go," he said. "Anything you're doing right now is better than what you'd be doing in juvie."

That shut up some of them, Cameron included, and they started after Max.

"Max," she called, pushing herself to her feet. "Can I borrow Cameron for the day?" she asked.

Max looked at her, then at Cameron, who made a

face as though she'd asked him to run around naked, and finally shrugged. "If you want him."

"Hey! I'm not some slave you can trade whenever you feel like it!" Cameron cried and Alice was starting to realize the kid had a good-size brain to go with that mouth.

"It's easier than what you're doing," she said.

"I'm there," Cameron said quickly, and stepped out of line to head her way.

"Good luck," Max called over his shoulder. "If he gives you trouble, send him out to me."

"Will do," she yelled back.

Cameron came to stand in front of her, his face scratched and dirty and his eyes on his shoes.

"You gonna give me trouble?" she asked and he shrugged.

I can't ask for more honesty than that.

"Well," she said, as she led him inside. "It's time for you to meet your new best friend—a potato peeler."

He groaned, but he followed.

GABE CLOSED his e-mail and sat back with a grin. Four more guests thanks to his Internet promotion, plus Bridezilla had capitulated on the swans—thank God—and had promised him final guest-list numbers by the beginning of next week. Though he wouldn't hold his breath for that, so far the guest list had swelled and receded at least five times.

She'd decided on a band rather than the quartet, and the singer had e-mailed him their requirements, which weren't too bad.

With blue marker in hand he turned to update his wall-size calendar.

Someone knocked at his office door. It could only be Alice since his father and brother didn't believe in things such as closed doors and polite knocks.

"Come on in," he said. They'd been walking careful circles around each other for the past week and a half—smiling politely and staying out of each other's way. But he'd been watching her and if she was drinking, it didn't show. The woman was a chef possessed. And he couldn't be more relieved.

"Gabe," she said from the doorway, her voice cool and stark, letting him know she was here for business. He nearly rolled his eyes. Alice always wore her intentions on her sleeve and the tone of her voice let everyone know what her next move was.

She thought she was going to put his feet to the fire right now. As a partner and chef she thought she had that right.

And, he considered, she probably did.

He grunted while writing in the Andersons and Pursators on the third weekend in August. They would share the five-bedroom cabin closest to the lodge.

"Earth to Gabe," she said, annoyed, and he finally turned, capping his pen.

He shook his head with a laugh. "Sorry. A lot's going on."

"Right, well, me, too." Her tone was all business and he didn't want to fight. Not anymore. They needed to work together. He just needed to figure out how to get them from here to there in as little amount of time as possible. "I wanted to talk about a few things with you," she said, still in the doorway.

Sunlight streamed in behind her and lit the black hair escaping the bun she always wore while she worked, turning the runaway strands red.

In the week and a half she'd been here she'd managed to get some color on her face, her lips were pink, and she'd lost some of the fragile tragic look she'd had when he'd first seen her behind Johnny O's.

"You look good," he said, putting her off stride, which had been his intention. "Healthy."

Her fingers darted to her hair and she turned her face to the side for the shortest second, a small uncontrolled moment of womanly self-consciousness. The gesture pinged through him, turning his compliment into a double-edged sword that sliced though his gut.

"Thanks," she finally said.

He nodded and looked away, his throat dry. But the tension around her was eradicated. Compliments were the best way to disarm a person, always worked. "What did you need?" he asked.

"Information about this wedding. I've got some sample menus, but I don't know anything about the event."

"I have a conference call with them at the beginning of next week." He glanced at the calendar behind him and quickly wrote the time of the call into his busy work week. "I'm supposed to get final numbers and details then. Why don't you join me."

"On the call?" she asked, clearly surprised.

"Sure." He shrugged. She'd compromised with

him, the least he could do was try to make her job easier. His life got much easier by having her deal directly with Bridezilla and her flesh-eating mother rather than through him.

Brilliant, really, why didn't I think of this earlier?

"It'll be easier for everyone," he said. "I'm probably going to need some of your ideas on decorations—"

She smiled.

"Are you laughing at me?" he asked, knowing she was. This moment of ease, of light conversation was too nice to give up.

"You're great with leather and black-and-white photography," she said, summing up the decor of every apartment and restaurant he'd ever owned. "I would imagine wedding receptions will be a bit beyond you."

"You have better ideas?"

"About a million," she said, her dark eyes gleaming.

God, she's pretty when she's happy.

And it had been so long since he'd seen her happy.

The skin along his arms and chest twitched with the sudden urge to hold her.

"See—" he got swept up in their sudden chemistry "—I knew you were the right person to bring in on this."

That might have gone too far. His silver tongue had led him astray and what he'd said was too close to a lie. They both knew he didn't choose to bring her, they'd both been too desperate for anything else. The color faded slightly from her face.

"I'm happy to help out," she said and the air

between them changed again, turned cold. Her lush mouth compressed to a thin line.

"Thank you, Alice. The call is on Monday, late afternoon."

A huge crash from the kitchen made her whirl in the doorway and he braced himself for some minor emergency. Some five-hundred-dollar stand-up mixer perhaps, or another two-hundred-dollar hospital visit for his brother who tended to get over-confident around saws.

"Cameron?" Alice cried. "You all right?"

"Fine," the disembodied voice of the kid Gabe barely remembered yelled back, clearly disgusted.

"Cameron?" he asked. "You changed your mind about having the kid help out?" He was surprised on a number of fronts. The kid had enough attitude to light up New York State, and Alice, since the last miscarriage and the failed in vitro procedures, had gone way out of her way to avoid children of all ages.

Maybe she's healing, he thought, his stomach twisting with hope and sadness, a chronic sensation left over from his marriage. *Maybe she's finally letting go.*

"Just for today," she said. She turned back toward him, her lips fighting a smile. "He knocked over the bucket of potato peels. He's covered head to foot."

He laughed. "Beats hauling wood with Max."

"That's what I told him."

"So, when do you want to dazzle me with your menus?"

"Well, with Cameron taking some of the load

off today, I think I could pull it together for tomorrow night, Friday. I know we discussed things already, but I had to tweak the duck and so far I haven't found any good—"

"I trust you, Alice," he said, shocking both of them. "You don't have to defend your decisions. Max, Dad and I will be ready to be dazzled tomorrow night."

She eyed him suspiciously. "This is not the Gabe Mitchell I know. The Gabe Mitchell who likes—"

"Gabe Mitchell is busy," he said. "He's busy and tired and he knows, very well, how good you are."

Another compliment. Wasn't he full of them today? This one had slipped out unbidden. Caught him unprepared. The truth was, he had intended to ride her the entire time she was here. Since her latest compromise, however, she'd been on point and he could rest easy. It was a gift, almost, one he wasn't sure didn't tick, about to blow up in his face.

"Thanks,' she said. "Again."

"I, ah…need to get to work."

"Right." She pushed herself off the doorway. "Gabe, what I said last week, about Daphne—"

"Don't worry," he said quickly, heat scorching his neck. This was the apology he'd thought he wanted, but now he'd rather continue with this comfortable unsaid truce between them. He didn't want to discuss his love life with his ex-wife, not when things were going so well. "It's forgotten."

"I was out of line," she said, pressing on, as she always did when he wanted her to stop. "It's none of my business and she's a lovely woman."

"Yes, she is. Thanks for the apology." He hoped she'd leave it at that, that she wouldn't ruin this fragile equilibrium.

He glanced at her, lit by sun, her chef whites unbuttoned, revealing a green shirt underneath. She smiled, awkward and sad, a different version of the bristly woman she'd become over the years with him.

She looked like the twenty-four-year-old he'd met ten years ago. Sweet and smart with the devil in her eyes and the corner of her mouth.

And his whole body, all of it, reacted, leaned toward her with the old desire.

He didn't need this. He didn't need a reminder of the good times, of the woman he'd loved rather than the woman he'd grown to hate.

She was beautiful, she was an asset, and she couldn't leave soon enough.

CHAPTER SEVEN

THE ENVELOPE PATRICK had just signed for burned in his hand. He wondered if he would be branded, his palm black with the words *to my husband.*

It had been three weeks since the first letter and a week and half since he'd mailed his response, via the lawyer. A week and half of checking the horizon for the black sedan bringing another letter from her. A week and half of eating better food that tasted like dirt and sat like stones in his stomach. A week and a half of wondering if he could ever change his sons' minds.

"Who was that?" Max asked, arriving silently from nowhere, to suddenly be at his side. Patrick watched the car brake at the end of the gravel road, then turn left toward the two-lane highway that would take it to the interstate.

"No one," Patrick said, shoving the envelope into his back pocket. "Letter from my lawyer."

"Everything okay?" Max asked and Patrick could feel his son's police officer gaze searching him for clues.

"Fine, just some information about investments."

"My inheritance?" Max asked and took a slug from the bottle of water he held.

"Sure," he said, distracted. "I better get back to work. I'm finishing electrical on the gazebo today so the Fish-Stick Princess can have her pink twinkle lights."

Max lifted his plastic bottle in farewell and headed off for the forest and his trail blazing.

Patrick nearly ran to the gazebo, the warm wind at his back pushing him toward the freshly built structure with the view of the Catskills and the Hudson.

He stood on the concrete slab he'd poured and leveled himself and ripped open the envelope.

You're not giving me the truth, Pat. I could always tell. Does Gabe still take after you, so eager to smooth away the bad stuff?

When you say the boys are coming around to the idea, does that mean they are actually allowing you to talk about me? Or does Max simply walk away? You always were a silver-tongued man, Pat. But I can tell from what you're not saying that my boys don't want to see me.

Patrick raked his upper lip with his teeth, guilt over the decision he'd made years ago forcing its way through the righteous anger and all his good intentions.

I didn't argue with you, Pat, when you told me to stay away. Both times. And I couldn't blame you. I know what I was and it's why I left. I believed you and the boys were better without me, without my problems. But I sent you the signed divorce papers and you never signed them. Why isn't this marriage over, Pat? If you hate me so much? Why aren't we free of each other?

He nearly laughed. As if a piece of paper could make them free. God had joined them. Walking away or signing legal documents had nothing to do with it.

I've done what you asked. Twice. It's broken my heart a thousand times a day, but I agreed with you. I left, I forfeited any rights I might have claimed. You were their father, raising them in my place. I bowed to your wishes and I have not been in touch with any of you for over twenty-five years.

But things are changed now, Pat. Things are different. I need to see you. I need to see my sons.

It won't be for long and they don't even need to know who I am. Please, Pat. My husband. I want to come home to you.

His knees buckled and he sat on the wooden railing. He lifted his face to the wind; the smell of the river and pine blew up from the valley, but it did not dry his tears.

Iris was coming home.

ALICE SCRATCHED her nose on the sleeve of her chef jacket since her hands were covered in slime and chicken meat from the carcass she was tearing apart. The broth was already cooling in the fridge, to be put to use tomorrow night for the menu rollout. This meat would be put to use in the Thai stir-fry she craved for dinner. The clock above the stove told her she had about two hours before she needed to get that stir-fry cooking.

The door at her elbow swung open and she whirled, startled, splattering Patrick with chicken juice.

"Oh, no, Patrick." She grabbed the dish towel that was tucked into the waist of her apron and handed it to him by the smallest corner she could. "I'm so sorry."

"Don't worry." He smiled, then wiped at his flannel shirt and, oddly, his eyes. "I should know better than to sneak up on a woman murdering a chicken."

She laughed and picked up the leg she'd stripped meat from. "It's for a good cause, I promise."

"Have you seen either of my boys, preferably Gabe?"

"Not for hours, sorry." She noticed, as he seemed to take great efforts not to look directly at her, that his eyes were red. If he were any other person and not a Mitchell man, she'd think he had been weeping.

"Patrick." She dropped the chicken and wiped her own hands. "Are you okay?"

"You bet." Patrick's smile was wide and, to the uninitiated, believable. But she'd spent years with this man's offspring, translating the many smiles to mean any number of things, and this smile tried just a shade too hard.

She knew better than to call him on it, however, so, as she had in her marriage, she approached the topic sideways.

"I'm glad you stopped in," she said. "I am so sorry about the first night I was here. I should not have said anything about Iris and my apology was almost as hideous as what I said. I've felt bad about it for two weeks, but I just haven't had a chance to find you and say something."

The smile twitched and she knew that whatever was making this man's eyes red had something to do with Iris.

"I was a little out of sorts," she continued. "Being back with—"

"Would Gabe and Max have been better off with their mother?" Patrick asked suddenly and Alice was rocked back on her heels. "I mean, not instead of me, but if she had been in the picture, would my boys have benefited?"

"Of course," she said cautiously after a moment. "I mean, only if she wanted to be there. If she was there and didn't want to be, well, then they were certainly better off with just a father who adored them."

"Really?" he asked, white and stricken, and Alice felt trapped. "If she had wanted to come back—"

"But she didn't come back," she raced to say. "She left and no one heard from her again."

Patrick went white and stared at his hands, at his thumb as it worried a cut on his palm.

Alice didn't know what to think with this uncharacteristically insecure man in front of her.

She should say something, do something, to bring the regular Patrick back, but she didn't have that power. His vulnerability called out to her and she could only stand there and bleed silent sympathy.

"She left, walked away without a word. Like none of us mattered," he said. "What was I supposed to do?"

"Exactly what you did," she said, tense and uncomfortable. There were a lot of things wrong with her ex-husband that could no doubt be traced back to being raised by a single father—by this single father who spent so much time pretending everything was fine—without the influence of a mother, but she could hardly say that to Patrick now.

He nodded slowly. "Right," he said, his nod gaining speed and, as though he'd never left, the assured Patrick was back pink cheeked and smiling. "You're right, sweetie." He gave her a loud smacking kiss on the cheek. "Don't worry about the other night," he said. "We were all a little out of sorts. We'll try it again tonight, without the arguments."

She knew, of course, what he was referring to. They'd sit in front of the fire and share a drink, but she couldn't do that. She'd committed. Like it or not. She'd stocked the kitchen, built a menu, worked herself to the bone from dawn until dusk without killing her ex-husband or taking a drink.

All good things.

"I'm sorry, Patrick." She winced. "I am going to be so busy the next few weeks. Tomorrow night I'm rolling out my menu and on Monday I've got my first call with Bridezilla."

"Too bad. Don't let my son run you ragged."

"Not likely," she quipped because she knew he'd like it and, as she'd expected, he laughed on his way out the door. The kitchen fell silent as if he'd never been there.

Wary of the lingering chicken grease, she wiped a stray black curl from her forehead with her wrist and went back to work. What had brought on Patrick's mood? Hopefully it was over and they could all not talk about things such as regrets and what-ifs and second chances.

CAMERON MANAGED to get all the way through the potatoes the first day and had started on the carrots. The next morning Alice had woken up, her hands sore, her lower back in knots, and realized she needed about a million cloves of garlic peeled—on top of putting together the menu—and Cameron was just the man for the job.

"You sure?" Max asked while they both glared at the coffee machine, waiting for it to finish hissing and puffing. "He's working out?"

"Well, he hasn't cut himself or me. And as long as I don't actually listen to him talk all day it seems to work out." She shrugged. "I need the help and he's doing okay."

"Enough said." Max filled his travel coffee mug,

even though the machine wasn't done, and Alice stuck her mug under the stream of coffee running onto the burner.

"I'll send him your way when he arrives," Max said and disappeared out the door.

"Send who where?" Gabe's rusty voice asked from the dining-room door. She turned only to find him, hair standing on end and blurry eyed, propped up against the door frame.

"You look like crap," she said and pulled out the mug she'd noticed was his favorite, despite the chip in the lip.

"Ah, is it any wonder we couldn't make it work?" he asked without any heat and she found herself smiling at this morning version of Gabe. He'd always looked like a little boy in the morning, someone in desperate need of coffee, a doughnut and a long cuddle.

She'd enjoyed being the one to cuddle him, kissing his forehead and warming her cold feet against his thighs until his brain fully clicked into gear.

The memory wrapped around her like a cozy blanket.

"I had this dream last night that I was being chased by pink swans," he said, gratefully accepting the coffee she'd poured for him.

"Stress dreams, you need a break," she said.

He nodded and slurped from his mug.

"Did your dad find you yesterday?" she asked. "Just before dinner, he was looking for you."

"He found me." His voice changed. Cold Gabe

stood before her, his blurry eyes gone, his easy morning repartee frozen out of him.

Is he okay? What did he want? What's going on with your mother? Did you listen to him or freeze him out like you are me right now?

All of that and dozens of other questions burned at her lips, but she dammed them. The lessons of her marriage were ingrained and impossible to forget.

"Good," she said and turned to her notebook of lists. "Have a good day."

She was too tired, sore and preoccupied to do anything else.

CAMERON ARRIVED sullen and filthy just after three.

"Good God," she cried. "What happened to you?"

"You and those potatoes," he shot back, tossing his greasy brown hair over his eyes.

"Well, didn't you shower last night? Or this morning?" She noticed he wore the same baggy black T-shirt with the anarchy symbol across the front. She doubted he even knew what it meant. She wondered what his home must be like if a kid could wander around covered in dirt for two days.

"It wouldn't matter if I was outside dragging trees around," he said.

"Well, you're not. You're in my kitchen. Let's get you cleaned up." She grabbed the bar of lava soap that had the power to remove the smell of garlic from hands and shoved him toward the employee bathrooms. "Lose the shirt and I'll find you something else to wear."

"I'm not wearing your clothes." He sneered at her tomato-red Henley that she had put on for dramatic flair underneath her chef whites.

She nearly laughed at herself now.

"I'll find you something," she promised and nudged him into the bathroom.

Ten minutes later he emerged, soaking wet and shirtless. He looked embarrassed standing in the doorway, his thin arms crossed over his concave chest, two inches of his underwear visible at the top of his ratty blue jeans.

Poor kid, she thought, nearly smiling. But she didn't because intuition told her that would just kill the fifteen-year-old. Instead she chucked her smallest, oldest chef jacket and pants at him.

He caught them and vanished, doing a strange side step into the bathroom before turning around. She just managed to see the purple-and-yellow bruise on his shoulder blade before the door slammed shut, the sound louder than her strangled gasp.

She knew most of the kids in Max's program were from troubled homes, but seeing the proof of it was shocking. Searing.

For a brief period of time after the divorce, she went to a support group called Mother's Without Babies. The name alone should have warned her of the craziness to be found amongst those women. But one thing they all shared was a profound horror, a gnawing sadness that there were parents in the world who would hurt their children. Children the women in that group would have died for.

And she felt the same primal rage, looking at the shut bathroom door, as she had sitting in that group, her grief still so raw she couldn't look at children on the street.

The door swung open and Cameron stood there, hair dripping, clothes a little too big, but surprisingly not too bad since he was tall for his age.

"What happened to your back?" she asked point-blank.

"Nothing."

"Your dad or—"

His face twisted in disdain. "Please," he scoffed.

"He didn't hit you?"

"Nah." Cameron shook his head. "I think I did it two days ago hauling wood."

She watched him, having years of experience with the excuses created by prep chefs and wait-resses and dishwashers. She was pretty good at spotting a lie. And all her radar told her Cameron wasn't lying.

"No one hit you?"

He shook his head. "No one even notices me," he said. "Now, what disgusting thing am I supposed to do today."

She set him up at the chopping block with the cloves of garlic and explained how to deskin them.

"I'm gonna stink!" he protested.

"It's not as if you smell like roses right now."

"Who wants to smell like roses?"

"It's an expression." The small tiny curve in the corner of his mouth told her he was giving her a hard time and she had to fight herself from ruffling his hair.

"Get to work," she joked and set up her own station of chopping the garlic he peeled.

She had about two hours before she needed to get to work on the menu rollout. She'd already set the table in the dining room, putting a little effort into the flowers and candles, letting Gabe see how it should be done, rather than the tiny bud vases and two votives he usually used.

"So, like, how'd you become a cook?" Cameron asked.

"Chef," she corrected, just to give him a hard time.

"Right, whatever." He rolled his eyes at her and she couldn't remember the last time she'd had this much fun with her staff. Torturing Trudy had been fun for her, but it wasn't a reciprocal thing. "How'd you become a *chef?*"

"I went to school for it," she said, smashing the garlic with the flat of her knife and then dicing it into tiny pieces. She'd preserve it in oil, perfect shortcut for soups, stews and quick sautés.

"Why?"

She took a deep breath and considered her answer to a question no one had ever asked her. "I guess I've always wanted to be a chef. My grandmother and father were chefs and I spent a lot of time in the kitchen with them. I always really loved it."

He grunted, his eyes narrowed over the garlic clove in his pink hands.

"What do you want to do?" she asked.

"Pro basketball player," he answered quickly.

"Oh really?" she asked, again fighting the grin. "You got game?"

"I'm tall." He shrugged.

"It might take more than that," she said.

"Maybe you can show me how to cook something and I'll see if I like that."

She blinked, taken aback. An apprentice. A fifteen-year-old juvenile-delinquent apprentice.

Stranger things had happened, she guessed.

"Okay," she said, "but you need to tell me what you got in trouble for."

"Max didn't tell you?" He asked.

"Max doesn't talk much. I don't know if you noticed."

Cameron grinned and went back to his peeling. "I missed a lot of school," he said. "Truancy or something."

"Why'd you miss school?"

He shrugged again, his face carved of stone. Her years with Gabe had taught her not to push against people made of stone. She knew she wouldn't get any more from him.

"All right," she said. "When we finish this we can start work on the menu I've put together for the inn. Tonight we're trying it out."

The boy's muddy-brown eyes, usually downcast and sullen, sparkled with sudden interest and Alice felt an answering spark in her breast.

"Cool," he said and went to work double time. "Hey," he said after a moment. "Where are your kids?"

Her stomach fell to the floor. "Why…" She swallowed. "Why do you think I have kids."

"Because that's what adults do. They have kids. Don't they?"

"Not me." She smashed the flat of her knife down on the butcher block. "I don't have any."

"Too bad," he said as if it weren't devastating, as if his words, so casual and friendly, didn't lay waste to her. "You'd be good at it."

CHAPTER EIGHT

IT WAS PERFECT, the slow spin of satisfaction in her chest told her that. The bubble of joy in her throat confirmed it. Appetizer portions of the lunch menu and dinner salads sat, beautifully plated, ready to be served.

"All right, Cameron," she said—and because they'd worked hard together and he'd listened and only dropped one sandwich, which he ate, and because he seemed to really enjoy himself—she put her hand on his shoulder and gave it a squeeze. "Let's show 'em."

She grabbed three of the plates and left him with two. "You remember your lines?" She asked, turning backward to face him and opening the door with her butt.

"Spinach salad," he murmured, rehearsing. "Grapefruit vinegar—"

"Vinaigrette," she corrected.

"Grapefruit vinaigrette, blue cheese, egg and pine nuts."

"Not bad." She smiled at him and they stepped into the dark dining room.

The table she'd prepared was a small island of

glittering light in the shadowed room. The three men sitting there looked up at her with expectation and happiness on their faces.

It was what every chef wanted to see when they stepped from kitchen to dining room. It was like being wrapped in a warm embrace, a victorious hug.

I love it, she thought, her throat choked with sudden pride. *I love it so much.*

She set down her first dish in front of Gabe because it was one of his favorites. "Grilled salmon salad with miso dressing," she said. "You have to share."

He grinned at her, his fork already poised to eat.

"Ham and white cheddar panini with sweet maple mustard." She set the plate down in front of Max, who groaned as if there were women performing sex acts on him.

"Thai chicken stir-fry," she said, placing the bowl under Patrick's eager nose. "With soba noodles."

She turned toward Cameron. In this light with everyone looking at him, the kid seemed suddenly so young. So vulnerable. Her heart hiccupped with pride and the old longing she had gazing at any child.

"Spinach salad," he said, placing the salad next to Max. The candle glow revealed his sudden nerves, his naked glance at Max who, she realized, was probably more of a father figure than Cameron had ever had.

She stepped back out of sight and wiped her suddenly wet eyes on the sleeve of her jacket.

"It's got a bunch of stuff in it I can't remember,"

the boy admitted, looking toward her in the shadows apologetically.

"Looks good, kid," Max said and Cameron's chest puffed up. "Looks real good."

Cameron set down the carrot-ginger soup. "Enjoy," he said with an awkward little bow and came to stand at her side.

"We'll be back with the dinner entrées," she said and left the table of men as they began to eat.

"Oh dear God," Patrick sighed. "That's good."

"So's this," Max said. "Hey, get your fork away, I'm not done."

"You've done a great job, Alice," Gabe's voice floated through the dark room to wind around her. "Thank you."

"You're welcome." She slung her arm around Cameron's shoulder. "Great job," she whispered near his ear and quickly, briefly, his arm came across her waist in a sudden tight squeeze and then vanished.

Pride, relief, excitement, all combined in her, lifted her off her feet with a sensation that was unfamiliar.

I'm happy, she realized. *For the first time in five years, I'm happy.*

"WHY'D YOU LEAVE HER?" Max asked, using his finger to wipe up the last of the sour cherry sauce that had covered the duck.

Gabe pushed away from the table, too full to even answer.

"Yeah?" Patrick asked. "A woman who cooks like that and is—"

"Shut up," Gabe finally managed to say, though his command lacked enough heat to actually get them to stop talking.

Every single dish had been perfect. Max even ate the vegetarian pasta. Gabe needed to go back into the kitchen and tell Alice how good it had all been, but he didn't. He would, he told himself. In a minute. At the moment he needed to just sit here and marvel at the total fruition of all their plans.

Tonight it was as if they'd never split up. As if they'd gone seamlessly from that bedroom on Pape, sketching out their plans for this place to this moment, with the solid walls around them and the delicious food still perfuming the air.

Right now, with the sound of Alice's laughter creeping under the kitchen door, it was as if the bad stuff had never happened.

And that was dangerous.

"Alice was the right woman for the job," Max said. "It sure would be nice to get a little appreciation for having come up with that."

"Thank you," Patrick said and swung his eyes over to Gabe. "And you two seem to be behaving yourselves."

"We haven't killed each other, if that's what you mean."

"Good food and no bodies." Max burped and stretched out his legs. "That's win-win."

His father's eyes didn't leave Gabe's face and he could practically read his thoughts. It would be better if they were fighting, and his father knew it. Gabe felt the pull of what had been good about them. He wanted to go into that kitchen and wrap his arms around her, kiss her just below the ear in that place that she loved, the way he once would have.

"I'm okay, Dad," he said. "It's all okay."

Patrick watched him a few minutes longer as if knowing he wasn't telling the whole truth before finally standing to gather the plates as he went.

"I'm going to go help them do the dishes."

"Yeah." Max stood, too. "I better get Cameron home since he missed the bus to help out."

"He's a good kid," Patrick said as they walked away from the island of light.

Gabe stared at the ceiling and wondered why, with everything going so well, so according to plan, he felt as though the ground beneath his feet was quicksand and he was in terrible danger of losing his balance.

IT WAS THE SCHEDULED late-afternoon Monday conference call and Alice's notebook was filled with the Crimpsons' wedding demands, which she'd tried to organize into lists and pages according to days. But as the call progressed and the demands kept coming, her attempts to organize it had fallen apart. Now she simply doodled pictures of a giant lizard wearing a veil, eating a woman. Chuckling, she sketched a little chef hat on the woman and showed it to Gabe, who laughed silently.

"We're sending you the boat we want filled with sushi," Gloria Crimpson, mother of Bridezilla screamed, clearly not understanding the basic function of speakerphones.

Alice stopped doodling.

"Boat?" She mouthed to Gabe in the silence of the office. "Did she say boat?"

"What kind of boat are we talking about?" Gabe asked, reading Alice's fears.

"It's a small rowboat."

"You want a rowboat filled with sushi?" Alice asked, just to clarify.

"Won't that be fantastic?" Savanah Crimpson said. "I mean, since we decided on a nautical theme…"

Alice threw her notebook in the air and sat back in her chair. "When?" she mouthed to Gabe. "When did we decide on a nautical theme?"

Gabe put his finger to his smiling lips and she wanted to kill three people—the Fish-Stick Queen, the progeny and her ex-husband who seemed to be delighting in this.

"We look forward to getting the rowboat. We need to know the final numbers so we can figure out just how much sushi we're going to need."

The numbers. The all-important numbers. A muscle twitched below Gabe's eye and Alice felt her own stress level start screaming for the roof. If the numbers were huge, the small hold they had on things would be blown and they'd need many more staff and tighter deadlines on food and—

"We've cut our guest list," Savanah said, an unheard-before iron edge to her voice.

"Sweetheart," Gloria wheedled. "We're still discussing this."

"No, Mom, we aren't." Gabe's eyebrows lifted and Alice crossed her fingers that perhaps the previously spineless bride had managed to remember she walked upright. "Our numbers are ninety-five."

Gabe's arms shot up in the air and Alice flopped back in her chair, a weary rag doll of relief. Ninety-five they could do. Easily.

The tension on the other end of the line was crushing and Alice was grateful when Gabe went to work with his charm.

"Savanah, we will put together a beautiful event for you and your guests. Ninety-five people will allow it to be personal and elegant and filled with your personality."

Alice choked on a laugh since the Fish-Stick Princess didn't seem to have a personality and Gabe shot her a control-yourself look.

"Now, when you say nautical theme, are you referring to food and decor?" he asked.

"Well," Savanah said, "since you said there were environmental laws against the pink swans…"

"Nice one," she mouthed to Gabe and he nodded.

"I think yes, maybe some anchors and—"

Alice shuddered.

"Savanah, my partner and I will put together a list of decoration options and a menu with your nautical theme and I will e-mail it to you by the end of the day."

"Tomorrow," Alice piped in, and Gabe scowled.

She shrugged, there was only so much she could do as a one-woman wedding planner.

"Wonderful," Savanah said.

"Gabe," Gloria added, "if the numbers change again, are we—"

"Your numbers have to be final by the end of day tomorrow," Alice chimed in. "I'm ordering food on Wednesday."

Gabe winced and she guessed she hadn't handled that as well as he would have.

"If we had more time," Alice said, "perhaps—"

Gabe slid a thumb across his throat, telling her to stop.

"Well, there isn't more time," Gloria said, her voice frigid. "My daughter—"

"The time frame is perfect. Trust me," Gabe said, leaning over the phone and pushing Alice out of the way. "We will put together a beautiful event."

A beautiful, small, quick event. Alice wondered if the Fish-Stick Princess was knocked up.

"We'll be coming in a week early," Gloria said. "With guests arriving two days before the wedding."

"We already have been getting reservations," Gabe said. "As I said when you contacted me, Gloria, there is no need to worry. You just need to check your e-mail and show up."

Everyone hung up and Alice and Gabe sat in the quiet of his office, staring at the phone.

"She's pregnant, isn't she?" she asked.

"Six months. She was going to elope, but her mom talked her into a quickie wedding."

"Can't have a Fish-Stick Bastard?"

Gabe laughed then fell silent. She could guess what was going through his mind—the same things that were going through hers.

"Anchors?" she asked, incredulous.

"What else says nautical?"

"We could trap some seagulls and have them crap all over—"

"Funny," he said, sitting back. "But not helpful."

She picked up her pencil and tapped it against the notebook.

"We could dress the waiters as pirates," she said, enjoying the look on Gabe's face.

"Dunk tank?" She asked.

"Clearly, there is something about the Crimpson women that makes you a bit giddy," he said. "Other than flooding the place, or hanging anchors from the ceiling, what can we do?"

"Let me sleep on it," she said, stretching.

"Ah, yes, the famous Alice 'it came to me in a dream' solution." He wasn't mocking her, his eyes were warm and his body relaxed. She realized that she hadn't seen him this comfortable around her in years.

"Hey, it saved your ass a few times," she said. "Remember that corporate—"

"Of course," he groaned. "Of course. And if I remember correctly, I thanked you, quite handsomely, for that."

As soon as he said it, Alice felt her face get hot, a flush built across her chest and up her face to her hairline. He'd surprised her with a trip to Mexico, an all-inclusive resort, and they'd lain on the beach and drunk fruity drinks and made love for a week straight.

It was the first time she'd gotten pregnant. The only time without the help of doctors. She'd miscarried at twenty weeks, just after their wedding.

"I'm starving," Gabe said, standing so fast his chair spun out and hit the wall behind him. She looked up at him, watched the nervous energy radiate off him like radioactive rays. He remembered, too, and it made him uncomfortable.

His discomfort with their history used to make her angry. It made her want to fight and wound him for his coldness, for his uncaring heart. But with the years came a new understanding of the man.

He wasn't cold. He was scared.

Not my problem, she thought, trying to control her wayward heart, which melted at this new understanding of her ex-husband. *It's not my job to fix this man anymore. I was never good at it anyway.*

"Ham sandwich?" she asked, knowing his weaknesses.

"With white cheddar?"

"Like I'd put together a ham sandwich with anything else," she scoffed, and led him from the office into her kitchen, where, as always, things were in balance.

She never let her kitchen get messed up with personal things. It was bad chi…or whatever.

Even the bad memory of Gabe trying to fire her almost two weeks ago had been replaced by the rolling out of the inn menu with Cameron's enthusiastic help.

In her kitchen she and Gabe could discuss work, be friendly, laugh, even, as though the past were not between them. But nothing too personal, nothing too painful, nothing that would sully this beautiful room where she spent all her days—those topics were strictly off-limits.

He pulled up the stool where Cameron had been camped out for the past three days.

"So how are things working with the kid?" Gabe asked, leaning against the counter. "Max said you haven't kicked him out of the kitchen yet."

Alice pulled the ingredients for the ham sandwiches out of the fridge then slid open the big heavy drawer she was using as a breadbasket and grabbed the baguette Cameron had attempted to bake yesterday. Tasted fine. Looked terrible.

"Pretty well," she said. "He's very keen. He did a great job Friday night."

"I couldn't believe it when he came out those doors carrying plates with you. He didn't even look like the same kid."

"Well, pulling his hair back helped."

"That's great, Alice. I mean great that you found a little help—"

"I don't know how much he's helping," she said, grinning at him over her shoulder. But the arrangement was good for both of them, her and Cameron. He filled the room with empty chatter that saved her from thinking too much, and he listened to her when she explained something, which made her feel as though she was contributing to something besides the destruction of her liver. He'd learned how to hold a knife confidently and how to check when duck was done or when carrot-ginger soup needed more salt.

She got to watch the pallid sullen look around his eyes vanish and his gray complexion turn pink.

Another patient healed by her kitchen.

"Well, it's got to be a good thing for him," Gabe said, plucking a slice of cheese from the stack she'd cut. "The kid doesn't have any positive role models, that's for sure."

"What's his story?" she asked, spreading maple mustard on the misshapen slices of bread. "He says his folks don't care about him, but I can't tell if that's just him being a teenager or if it's real."

"I'm pretty sure it's real. The mom's gone, the dad drinks." He shrugged. "They live way out in the country and if his dad is too drunk to get Cameron to school he misses school, which is what landed him in trouble. I don't think he's in danger of going to juvie. I think they want to remove him from his home."

Her heart sank for Cameron. "The kid is bright, he should have a shot at school."

"I know."

Silence reigned and soon it became too heavy. Sunset was about a half hour away and the shadows were growing long in the kitchen. It was her favorite time of day, quiet and special.

And somehow, either by his quiet or the feel of

his gaze on her back, she knew in her bones Gabe was remembering that and it created a hushed intimacy between them. Two weeks before, the truce wouldn't have been there.

Her spacious healing kitchen was becoming smaller with every breath.

But there was nothing to stop the rush of good memories, the little sweet details they remembered about each other. Her favorite time of day. The way he liked his ham sandwiches. Five years ago she'd do this for him and place the sandwich in front of him with a kiss and he'd pat her bottom every time she was in reach and it would be a good thing. And right now, in her kitchen at her favorite time of day she missed that closeness with a physical pain.

And frankly it scared the bejesus out of her. She felt a little naked without her anger. Defenseless without her resentment.

"Lettuce?" she asked needlessly, as if she hadn't made him a thousand ham sandwiches, but she needed to put the distance between them. Needed to pretend she didn't remember him as well as she did, to pretend her life truly had gone on without him.

"God, no." He pretended to shudder.

She slid the plate across the butcher's block toward him and leaned against the counter with her own sandwich. "So," she said, "the nautical food is easy. Lobster tail and filet?"

He shook his head, turning up his nose. "How many weddings have you been to with that on the menu?" he asked. "And frankly, my serving staff isn't that plentiful, or well trained for table service."

She nodded, he was right.

"How about stations?" he asked. "You know we have the sushi boat and perhaps some oysters and we could have another station with paella?"

"And a grill station with fish, and we've got to have a meat option." She grabbed his wavelength. "We could do portobello mushrooms for the vegetarians."

"Excellent. Some cheese and crudités—"

"And dessert," she said, smiling. "Done and done."

"You're going to need some trained chefs to handle those stations," he said. "And I don't—"

"I'll ask my folks." Her father was trained, her mother was simply an excellent cook. They couldn't ask for better. "They'll think it's a hoot."

"A hoot?" Gabe swallowed audibly and she smiled at him.

"They've forgiven you for knocking up their only daughter."

"You sure? Because those Christmases at their house were pretty chilly."

"Right." She laughed. "The way they showered you with gifts and that homemade eggnog only you loved? Yeah, they hated you." After her folks had gotten over the initial whirlwind of her and Gabe meeting, falling in love, falling in bed, getting pregnant and getting married, they'd done their part and fallen for Gabe in a big way. The divorce had hit them pretty hard.

"They'd love to help you out," she said. "And they're cheap."

"Perfect. How quick can you get me a budget?" he asked.

"Tomorrow."

"Sounds good." He nodded at her, his smile electric, and she faced it head-on before it got too uncomfortable. She wished he were a stranger. But then they wouldn't work together this well. Every situation had its own catch-22.

"Can I ask you a question?"

"Sure," she said, "I can't guarantee I'll answer it."

"What happened with Zinnia?" He put down his sandwich and watched her.

She avoided his eyes. There was nothing wrong with talking about it, she tried to convince herself, but it still wasn't easy to open her mouth and let the words come out. "Bad management on my part," she said. "I'm a good chef but a lousy businesswoman."

"Was it because of the drinking?" he asked.

She shook her head. She couldn't even pretend to be angry for some reason. Her kitchen took all the heat out of her, plucked her righteous indignation away like a feather. "I wasn't drinking that much then." The words stuck in her throat like a fishbone. She hadn't told anyone this, largely because no one really cared to ask. Restaurants failed all the time; no one except Gabe would understand that hers shouldn't have. "I just trusted the wrong people. I was so used to working with you." She smiled at him briefly, looking through her lashes at his solemn expression that he never realized was more attractive than all his grins. "I didn't watch my manager closely enough, or my accountant, for that matter. We bled money, and by the time I realized it, my accountant was gone and my manager had gotten a new job and I was left with a lot of debt."

"I can't imagine how hard that must have been," he said, his voice and the look in his eyes a loving stroke to her pride. This was the man who had listened to all of her dreams, stroked away those early tears before they were both flooded. This was the man who bolstered her when she was down, made her rest when she was weary and told her, every day, how special she was.

She busied herself wrapping the bread and putting it away so she wouldn't do something stupid such as reach out for him.

What happened? part of her howled. Where did that man go? She'd forgotten about him, lost him in the years that followed their string of tragedies.

"It was hard," she said. Stupidly, tears burned behind her eyes and she would have sworn she'd cried all she could for Zinnia. "The divorce and losing the restaurant—" She took a deep breath, mortified when it shuddered in her chest. "It was a pretty powerful one-two punch."

On top of the miscarriages, she didn't add, because he'd leave and suddenly she didn't want that. She hadn't just lost her husband in the divorce, she'd lost her very best friend. Her partner. A person who understood her inside and out.

And right now, in her warm and beautiful kitchen, she missed him. She missed Gabe, her husband, best friend and partner. The scrape of his stool against the terra-cotta tiles was like a low growl.

She could feel him—in her skin and along her nerve endings—approaching her.

"Hey," he whispered and she looked up to find him a breath away from her.

His hand brushed her arm, pushed back the black hair that had slipped from her bun. "I'm so sorry," he said.

She swallowed, unable to speak, unable to breathe because there was no air in the room.

Her eyes met his and the heat in those beautiful familiar blue depths melted her bones, her resolve, her better sense. So when he put his arms around her, she collapsed willingly into his chest, finding that familiar place under his chin to rest her head.

She slid her arms around his back as though the past five years hadn't happened, as though she still had the right to his touch, his long strong embraces.

She closed her eyes and, with a sweet piercing ache, she let her body be reminded of his.

"Alice," he murmured and she looked up, knowing how far away his mouth would be, knowing the stormy depths of those eyes and knowing that what she'd see there—confusion and desire—was the same thing he'd see in hers.

"This is a mistake," he breathed across her lips.

"I know."

But they did it any way. Slowly, like magnets across a small space, their lips found each other's. She sighed at the touch, at his remembered taste, and he pulled her closer still while their kiss remained careful, chaste.

The sound of the outside doorknob turning shattered the reverent cocoon of her kitchen, and Alice hurled herself away from Gabe.

She expected Max or Patrick to walk in and she put cool hands over her hot face.

What would she say to them?

What would Gabe say?

With trembling hands and pounding heart she packaged up the homemade ham.

The outside door stuck and finally pushed open to reveal, not her ex-in-laws, but Daphne and Helen bathed in the gorgeous light of sunset.

GABE WAS RARELY CAUGHT speechless. Almost never since the divorce. But looking at Daphne and Helen in that doorway, while his body still screamed for Alice, literally struck him dumb.

"Hi," Daphne said, her wide eyes taking it all in.

"Hello, ladies," he finally said, forcing a smile.

"You told us to come watch the sunset here," Helen reminded him, unaware of the treacherous adult undercurrents swirling around the kitchen. "You said this was the best place in the world for that. So we're here." She hopped forward in her bright pink galoshes and Gabe's heart staggered and paused.

Right. Date two with Daphne. A sunset hike to the Hudson. Yesterday that had seemed like a good idea, but watching Alice from the corner of his eye blanche and brace herself momentarily against the fridge, he cursed himself.

"Is this a bad time?" Daphne asked, her face bland but her eyes piercing. She was no fool and wasn't about to be played like one.

He did not know what to do. How to make this right. He glanced at Alice, searching for some clue, some hint of how to not hurt her.

Hurt her? he suddenly thought. *She's my ex-wife and we made a mistake. There's no hurt here. There's just a mistake.*

That justification seemed right. How could they be hurt if days ago they were screaming at each other? They'd gotten caught up in working together. That's all. Talking about Zinnia and the divorce in a darkened warm kitchen had allowed them to forget for one brief moment that the past was best left in the past. That's all.

"No," he finally said, pushing Alice and the disaster of that kiss away. "This is a perfect time." He took a deep breath, willing Alice to understand what he so clearly knew to be the truth. The kiss was a onetime mistake. "You good?" he asked Alice. "I mean for the budgets?"

"No problem," she said, her head buried in the fridge. "Have a good time."

He smiled at Daphne, held out his hands and ushered them back out the door. "Let's go for a walk," he said, hoping he'd done the right thing but feeling Alice at his back like a burning fire.

CHAPTER NINE

"HEY, RUN ON AHEAD, Helen, and see if you can find me some river rocks for the porch," Daphne said. The words weren't even totally out of her mouth before Helen was just a flash of pink and blond ponytail behind the bend in the river.

Uh-oh, Gabe thought, carefully pulling the fronds from the center stem of a fern leaf he'd plucked to keep his hands busy. His stomach churned in knots. There were words, explanations to Daphne, to Alice, to all of them knocking at his teeth and he worried that if he opened his mouth, he might say something dumb such as, "I kissed my ex-wife because I like her. I like her but she's like poison to me."

He worried that if he opened his mouth he'd turn to this wonderful woman and say, "I am so confused."

Not exactly the right thing to say on a date.

"Gabe, I don't know what's going on with your chef, but we interrupted something tonight and I think—"

"Alice is my ex-wife."

There. I said it.

He felt some of the knots loosen in his stomach.

Her mouth hung open for a second, then shut as she digested what he'd said. "Are you in the process of getting back together?" she asked.

"We are in the process of—" He stopped, unsure. "Working together."

"That's all? Because it didn't look like you were just working together. And that's fine." She held out her hands as if she had given up any interest she had in the situation and he didn't want that. He wanted her interest. He liked her, he really did. She was a potential future while Alice was and would always be the past.

Gabe grabbed her hand and stopped walking, turning her to face him.

"As a rule," she said, crossing her arms over her chest, her gray eyes shooting out sparks, "I don't date men who are still in love with their ex-wives."

He nearly laughed. Still in love with Alice? Good God, he hoped he wasn't that dumb. "I am not still in love with Alice. She's had a rough go of it lately and tonight she finally talked about it." He took a deep breath. "Things got emotional on both sides, but there is nothing going on with her. I swear it."

Daphne studied him, the intelligence in her eyes made him uncomfortable, as if she could see truth that he didn't.

"Why did you split up?" she asked.

"Why does anyone split up?" he asked, as if all couples, in some deep place, shared the same reasons.

"My husband and I wanted different things," she

said. "He thought living a simple life out on a farm was what he wanted. Two years in he changed his mind." She shrugged. "I figure I should have seen it coming."

He shook his head. "Alice and I wanted the same things." *Family. Home. A tribe of our own.* "We just couldn't give it to each other."

He tossed the frond. "I needed a chef and she needed a job and it seemed like it could work."

"It's not?" Daphne asked.

He stepped forward, away from her eyes, tired of being questioned for the truth. "No, it is. It's working out fine." *Better than fine, it's like the dream we had a million years ago. Better even than that.* Kisses at dusk, troubled kids working out their problems in the kitchen, weddings being planned—there was nothing he could ask for that would be better. Except…if his chef wasn't Alice. If his blood didn't hum for his ex-wife. If it was another woman with whom these two months could actually build into something more. Then it would be perfect. There was no chance of that with Alice. "I should have been prepared for that as much as I was prepared for it not working out."

"What was the thing you couldn't give each other?" Daphne asked.

His throat was tight. Thick. And he didn't know where this emotion had sprung from. "Children," he finally managed to say.

"What happened? Was she—"

"I'll tell you, Daphne. Someday. Just not today." When Alice wasn't here. He could tell Daphne was dissatisfied by that answer. She was a good woman who deserved more, but that was as much as he could give her.

Alice would kill him if she knew he was talking with Daphne about the things he could never to talk to her about.

They continued walking, the sound of Helen ahead of them like a lighthouse in a dark night. And just when he'd controlled the unruly ends of his emotions, Daphne slipped her hand in his, her fingers brushed his, and her grip, true and firm, a warm surprise, held him strong.

ALICE CLOSED HER EYES behind her sunglasses and rested her head against the tree at her back. It was nearly 3:00 p.m. and she could not muster any enthusiasm for baking. None.

Chocolate turned her stomach, the smell of lemons made her gag, everything was too bright and looked too rich. She didn't want to touch food. Or smell it.

She took a sip of coffee and her stomach nearly rebelled.

The demons had run her ragged last night.

And she was paying the price today.

At some point in the middle of that bottle of wine she'd realized what had gone wrong; her mantra had changed over the last two weeks. She'd gone—subtly and in small steps—from not wanting anything, to wanting everything. It had started with the kitchen, and the food, and Cameron. Then she'd started wanting to make more decisions, she wanted to impress her ex-husband, Max and Patrick. She wanted everything she touched to be perfect, yet two weeks ago she'd been grilling grade-B steak at a chain restaurant so she would never want anything. So that she couldn't long for perfection.

She'd kissed Gabe last night. She'd kissed him because she wanted him. And there's no telling where that would lead. Sex? Wanting to try again? Try again to have a baby? Try again to be a family?

Those were ridiculous notions, suicidal. She couldn't survive another go-around with Gabe even if she wanted it—which she didn't. And, more to the point, it was very obvious from the way he walked away from her last night that he didn't want it.

So what am I doing? She wondered. *Why am I feeling so crappy?*

This morning she practiced her old mantra, the one that made it possible for her to wake up in the morning and not weep for all that she couldn't have.

There is nothing I want.

There is nothing I need.

"Hey, Alice!" Cameron jogged up the small hill to where she sat overlooking the parking lot and the trailhead Max had so carefully made. "I looked for you in the kitchen," he said. He looked like a puppy, floppy brown hair and an overeager smile.

"I'm not there," she said, managing to surprise herself with the flatness in her voice, the harsh edge to her words.

"Yeah." The overeager smile fled. "I figured."

He watched her for a minute, the look in his eyes slowly changing, slowly reverting to the hard, who-gives-a-shit kid he'd been over a week ago, and she hated that she had so much influence over him. That what she said or did mattered so much.

I want to be alone, she thought. *I just want to be alone.*

"What's the matter with you?" he asked, his sneer creeping back onto his mouth.

She didn't answer. She didn't *have* an answer. Heartsick and stupid? Foolish and hungover? Tired and battered? Kissed and forgotten.

"You're working with Max today," she said instead.

"But—"

Oh, God. The wounded look in his eyes shattered her and she had to look away.

"You said we were working on desserts."

"Well, it's complicated." She pushed herself to her feet. "It's better if I do it by myself."

She walked by him, the ground uneven, and she stumbled slightly. "You're drunk," he snapped and his tone froze her. Such vivid loathing was something she only heard in her own voice.

Cameron ran away, down the hill, across the parking lot and onto the trail, probably toward Max. She figured it was for the best.

She swallowed the last of her coffee, hoping it would wash away the taste of self-loathing and headed back to her kitchen.

The door swung open before she put her hand on the knob and she stepped out of the way as Gabe came storming out. He stopped, just shy of touching her.

"I was looking for you," he said. "I wanted—"

"It was a mistake," she said, glad for her sunglasses so he couldn't see her eyes. "It won't happen again."

"But—"

Ice filled her veins and she understood why Gabe froze her out so much. It felt good to feel nothing.

To not be responsible for someone else's pain.

"You get your wish, Gabe. We'll never talk about it again. I won't wallow and you can pretend it didn't happen. And in a month and a half you'll never have to see me again."

He swallowed, his strong throat flexing and relaxing. Her belly coiled with tension of all sorts. She took a step away, hoping distance would help her breathe, would help her body relax, but it didn't. She could still feel him there, just out of touch.

"I wanted to tell you we're having a staff meeting this afternoon," he said finally.

She didn't even feel embarrassed, she was that cold.

"Fine," she said and blew past him.

"OUR FIRST GUESTS arrive on Thursday," Gabe said, looking out at his staff, which included his dad, brother, ex-wife and four women and three men who'd answered his ad to help clean and serve food to the guests

"We have two couples coming from Canada, Joy Pinter from *Bon Appetit* and Marcus Schlein from *New York Magazine*." His hired staff paid attention, but his chef seemed wildly distracted. Alice stared at him, or rather through him, as if he wasn't here, as if he was just a voice from the heavens. The breeze that blew from her was icy cold and that worried him. It worried him that she looked more like the woman he'd met behind Johnny O's than the woman who drew funny pictures of giant lizards for his amusement, than the woman he'd kissed last night.

He'd awoken this morning like an amputee searching for a missing limb, patting down the side of the bed he'd never stopped thinking of as hers. He'd dreamed of her with him, in his bed, her slight snores, the way she mumbled kitchen lists, the sweet swell of her backside pressed into the cradle of his hips, the smell and feel of her hair across his pillow, because she'd always slept better close to him.

He'd tried to forget the dream, but his chest and arms felt the phantom shape of her against him, no matter how much he tried to think of Daphne.

Oh, man, this is a mess.

A mess made worse by his father mooning around like some teenager for a woman who'd left him to raise two small boys by himself over thirty years ago. Gabe knew Dad wanted to talk about it, but what the hell was he supposed to do? She'd left and Gabe wasn't about to start talking about her now as if she'd never been gone at all.

His stomach was in knots, his head ached, and his hand, which had been held by Daphne, burned as much as his lips, which longed to kiss Alice.

Such a mess. A disastrous mess.

A little more than a month, that's all they had to get through. Then the wedding would be over and Alice would be gone. It didn't matter that this was the most important month of his career.

"I've written all their arrival and departure dates, the cottages they will be staying at and any dietary concerns they have." He handed out the papers he'd copied, and his staff, except for his family, looked at it.

"Is everyone ready for this?" he barked. "Opening weekend, we have two huge magazines—"

"We're ready, Gabe. Relax," Max said, and turned to Alice. "Have you seen Cameron today?"

"Yeah, about three," she said, folding up the paper without even reading it, which meant she didn't know one of the couples from Canada was vegetarian with a milk allergy.

Wonderful. Great. This is going to go so well.

"I sent him to you," she said and stood as if they were done.

"He didn't come to me," Max said. "Why didn't you let me know your change of plans?"

"I didn't know I had to." Her voice was lifeless as she walked away.

"Alice," Gabe called, trying to keep his temper in check. "Joy and Marcus will want to interview you."

"Fine."

He took a deep breath. "It would mean a lot if you'd pretend to be human rather than a—"

"I said *fine*," she repeated.

He stared at the ceiling and counted to twenty.

"What happened to her?" Max asked. "One minute she and Cameron are thick as thieves and the next she's…like that."

Gabe knew of course. He'd kissed her. He'd kissed her and then gone on a date with another woman.

"I'll fix it," he said and Patrick laughed.

"What?" he snapped at his father.

"There you go again, thinking you can finesse everything," he said.

"I'm not finessing anything. Alice is angry with me and I'm going to fix it."

"How?"

"I don't know how!" he snapped. *I never knew how. I still don't. I can't fix her.* "I'll think of something."

"When your mother was mad at me she would only get madder if I tried to bring her flowers. I always had to—"

"I can't handle this," Gabe said to his brother. Max nodded and held a hand up at hip level. *I got it,* that gesture said, and Gabe thanked his lucky stars that Max was here.

"Has Mom been in touch with you, Dad?" Max asked when Gabe would have told his dad for the hundredth time to shut up. "Is that what all this is about?"

Patrick didn't say anything, his blue eyes said it all, and Gabe fell back in his chair, as though he'd been blown down by a stiff wind.

Mom had contacted Dad.

He couldn't even get his head around it. After he'd realized that Mom wasn't on a vacation, that making her pancakes that got cold every morning wasn't going to lure her back into their lives, he'd forced himself to think of her as dead.

But here she was, brought back to life.

"What does she want?" Max asked.

"To see you," Patrick whispered.

"Forget it," Gabe said, trying to get his legs under him. "We don't want to see her."

"I know," Patrick said.

"What the hell is wrong with you, Dad?" Gabe asked, finding a vent for all of his pent-up anger and confusion. "She left us. She left you thirty years ago and never came back and now you're acting like some lovesick kid? I don't get it."

"Me, neither," Max agreed in a much quieter voice.

Patrick finally looked up, his eyes wet but burning with some dark emotion that made both Gabe and Max lean away or risk being scorched by his gaze.

"You don't get to pick who you love," he said. He looked right at Gabe, right into his heart. "Do you, son?"

"You're wrong," Gabe said, feeling a soothing cold wave of anger cover him. "You can control that, you can control yourself."

Patrick laughed at him. "You're doing a great job of that son. Wanting to want Daphne while you've got your wife—"

"She's my ex-wife, Dad."

"Paper doesn't change things, Gabe."

"Wait, wait." Max held up his hands. "Are you saying you still love Mom, Dad?" Max asked, looking as baffled as Gabe felt. "After all these years, after never hearing from—"

"She's your mother," Patrick said. "She's my wife."

"No," Gabe said, standing. "She isn't, she hasn't been for years. We don't want to see her."

He walked away, furious. Furious with his father, with Alice, with his long-gone mother and with himself.

How am I going to fix this? he wondered, his head spinning. *How do I make all of this right?*

DURING THE LAST DAYS of their marriage Gabe had loved to tell Alice she was a glutton for punishment. He used to say she could teach self-flagellation to a monk. It was tiring, he told her, living with a woman so happy to wallow in her misery.

Sitting in her car outside Athens Organics she realized Gabe was right.

What the hell is wrong with me? she wondered, ignoring the dog that sat, panting outside her open car window. This is high-school stalker stuff.

She had a list of things she needed considering the two vegetarian Canadians coming this weekend, but she could have called in the order and had it delivered, allowing her to never see Daphne's and Helen's pretty, wide-eyed happy faces ever again.

But no—she shook her head—*I had to be sick about it.*

She realized how stupid this was and quickly put the car in Reverse to leave before she was seen. But she looked out her side window and saw Helen standing with the dog and Daphne behind her.

"Hi," Daphne said, shielding her eyes from the setting sun. "Did you need something?"

Therapy? Electroshock therapy? A friend? "Mushrooms," Alice finally said, putting the car in Park and turning off the ignition.

"Do you want to get out of the car?" she asked carefully, as though she knew what kind of mental case Alice really was.

Is it written on my face? Alice wondered.

"We're having smoothies," Helen said. "After-school snack. You want one?"

She nodded numbly as Helen's sweet voice sent arrows through her.

"Or a glass of wine," Daphne offered. "You look like you might need something stronger than blueberries and bananas."

Alice wiped her mouth with hands that shook and knew that at any moment she could be crying or screaming.

This is what working with Gabe had brought her to. She'd stopped feeling this way, she'd numbed the pain with alcohol and work she didn't care about. And now here it was all over again.

"I just need to pick up a few things for opening weekend." She took the list from the passenger's seat and opened the car door.

"Okay," Daphne said diplomatically, her eyes scanning the list. "We've got it all. I can just run down…" Daphne paused, her eyes flickering to her daughter then to Alice and, in that moment, that brief gap, Alice knew Gabe, who would never talk to her, had talked to Daphne about the babies.

The betrayal tore the breath from her body and she leaned against her car, suddenly feeling a million years old, everything about her too tired to keep pretending.

"Helen, can you go down to the hothouse and give Dan this list and ask him to bring the stuff up to the house?" Daphne asked, sending her daughter away with a pat on the bottom.

The dog barked and took off for the fields after Helen, startling some bird nesting in the trees by the house. Daphne stared at Alice and she stared back, wondering what had possessed her to come here. And more important, what was possessing her to stay.

"Gabe said there is nothing between you," Daphne said.

Alice nearly laughed. "Nothing good," she said. "You don't need to worry."

Daphne smiled, but it was grim. "He said the reason you split up was because you wanted the same things but couldn't give it to each other."

"He was chatty," Alice said through clenched teeth.

"I had some questions, seeing as how he is supposed to be dating me." Daphne crossed her arms over her chest. "Would you agree with him? You couldn't give each other what you both wanted?"

"That about sums it up."

"That doesn't sound like a good enough reason to spilt up," she said. Alice rocked back, angered at this woman's presumption, angered that it was the same way she had felt at the beginning of the end, as though there should have been something they could do to save themselves. Then she'd learned better.

"Trust me," she said, getting her bearings. Maybe this was why she'd come here, to put it all into words, to sort out the reasons and track the fall of their marriage to someone who didn't have front-row seats.

Or to start a fight.

She wasn't sure yet.

"It was plenty good enough," she said. "We were young and headstrong and in the end we just couldn't give a shit."

Daphne smiled, warmer this time. "Now you sound like a divorced woman."

"Great," Alice said, not sure if she should laugh or cry. "I'd hate to get the vocabulary wrong."

"Are you here to tell me all the things wrong with Gabe?" Daphne tilted her head, her braid falling over her shoulder like a rope.

God, wouldn't that be nice, Alice thought. *Give the woman a little map to the dangers ahead.* But she shook her head. "He's a good guy," she said, surprising herself. Warmth bloomed in her chest as her heart was bombarded by memories of better days, when he was the best guy. "One of the best."

Daphne's eyes narrowed again and Alice wondered if she was giving away too much of herself. If this woman could see through all the years to the twenty-four-year-old woman who had loved Gabe so wholeheartedly.

Do I still? she wondered, hollow and scared. *Is that what's so wrong with me?*

"Gabe said you couldn't have children. I'm sorry," Daphne said. "What—"

"Two second-trimester miscarriages, thousands of dollars in doctor bills, a load of disappointment and no babies." The words poured out of her, like water from an upended pitcher. She couldn't control them or stop them and didn't want to.

She stared at the blazing ball of the setting sun until the tears that burned in her eyes turned to water and slid away.

How can this be so easy? She wondered. For years she'd held this stuff in, refused to discuss it except to punish Gabe who never wanted to talk about it. And now that it was gone…she felt taller. As if she'd grown in the last few minutes.

Her mom had told her she needed to embrace group counseling, let it heal her, and at the time she'd wanted to tell everyone to leave her alone. But, now, this felt good.

"The doctors said for me to carry a baby to full term I would need to be on bed rest from about three months on and even that wasn't a guarantee. And I just…" she shook her head. "We couldn't afford it. I didn't believe it." The pain of the truth, that she might have caused her own tragedy, sliced through her over and over again. "And in the end it didn't matter. The last miscarriage did us in."

She stared at the sun for a long time, until her face got hot, her body, freed of all of its bitter underpinnings relaxed into something else, something less brittle, something human.

Blinking, she turned to face Daphne. "I'm not sure why I said any of that."

Daphne smiled. "I'm a stranger on a bus."

"A stranger dating my ex-husband."

"Do you want me to stop?" she asked, eyebrows raised.

Yes. Yes. I do. Until I'm gone. Until I can't see.

"Of course not," Alice said. "We split up five years ago. There's nothing between us."

Nothing. No marriage. No house. No family.

"How about that glass of wine?" Daphne asked.

"Just one," she said, ready to sit down with the devil for a drink. "I'm driving."

CHAPTER TEN

GABE POURED HIMSELF some peach smoothie from the silver pitcher and placed it back into its dish of ice. The silver pitchers had been Alice's idea.

Another one of her great ideas.

Like the fresh frittata and the cinnamon rolls and the Swiss muesli in the silver bowl beside the pitcher.

He should tell her, of course, walk right over to where she sat at the corner table waiting for him and Marcus from *New York Magazine* for the first of their interviews. It was Sunday, the last day of the opening weekend and in a few hours all the guests would be gone, giving them time to prepare for the next arrivals.

Saying those words, compliments, empty or not, used to be so easy for him. A way to grease the wheels and keep things running smoothly between him and anyone he worked with.

He watched her drink from her coffee cup, brush the dark hair from the side of her face and he knew she was hungover. Had been the whole week. But it didn't stop her from working. She worked like a woman possessed, which was great for him.

So why do I feel so bad?

She's doing everything I need her to do. She's got a month left and then she's gone and she can self-destruct on her own time.

He knew part of it was guilt. A part of this situation had been brought on by him. By the kiss and Daphne. He understood that. But Alice had been blaming him for all the mistakes, all of her hurt feelings almost the entire time he'd known her.

How much more responsibility could he take?

"Gabe?" Lori Zinger and her husband, Ian, one of the Canadian couples, stood beside him dressed for a morning hike.

"Hi, guys. Everything okay?" Gabe asked, tearing his thoughts and gaze from Alice.

"Wonderful," Lori said emphatically. "We just wanted to let you know that we're going to come back later in the summer with some other friends. This place is such a find!"

Gabe smiled and asked them to just write the dates down and he'd give them a return-visitors' discount.

"Another reason to love the Riverview," Ian said, grabbing a cinnamon roll as he walked out the door.

Gabe picked up one of the carafes of coffee and his own smoothie, then walked over to where Alice sat, shielding her eyes from the morning sun.

"Hi," he said, pouring more coffee into her mug.

"Thanks," she muttered.

"Food looks great."

"People seem to like it," she said and took a sip of coffee.

"One of the Canadian couples is coming back later in the summer."

"That's good news for you."

Every word between them was coated in acid, and compliments weren't making it better. Maybe reminding her of their partnership, of the investment she had in this place, would return this tin woman, this robot, into something familiar.

"The drawing for the decorations was approved by the Crimpsons."

She nodded as if she couldn't care less.

He took a deep breath and tried to remember what his father said about how sometimes things couldn't be finessed, that sometimes he had to beg.

"You ready for the interview?"

She shrugged and he felt the banked fires of his temper flare. He sat down opposite her and leaned in, wanting to shake her, to rattle her until she cared, just a little bit, about what these interviews meant to him.

He opened his mouth to tell her how much he needed her on her game right now. That she could go back to being a ghost, to blaming him for everything, to drinking away her life—

"You can't fix this, Gabe," she said, her eyes bone dry and burning. "We already tried."

His anger sizzled and died in a shroud of white smoke. Her pain spoke to his—the confusion, the weariness of the fight in her voice and eyes—spoke to all those matching emotions in him.

And it seemed, even in this, in their defeat, they were joined.

"I take everything too personally and you…do, too." She rubbed her forehead. "You just don't know it. Or don't show it. Or…" She smiled, a shaky, trembling thing that tore at his guts. "I don't know anymore, Gabe. I only know…you can't fix us."

Him, of course, it was supposed to be up to him.

"I'm not responsible for this, Alice."

"Of course not, Gabe." She reached out and touched his hand, a small incendiary touch, and then her hands were tucked back in her lap while his flesh burned. He flexed his fingers to shake off the feeling. "You are only responsible when things go right."

"That's not fair," he protested, but he knew if his father were sitting here he'd be nodding his head in agreement.

"There's not much about any of this that's fair."

"Is it because of Monday night? After the conference call?" he asked, the words *when we kissed* lodged in his throat, the memory of it stuck in his head. Not so much the dry touch of her lips to his but the feel, the beautiful remembered feel, of his *wife* in his arms. He'd never realized how much he missed the perfect fit of her head under his chin until she was back there.

It was why he didn't want to talk about it. He could tell in the way she didn't meet his gaze, it was why she didn't want to talk about it, either.

"Is it because of Daphne?"

She sighed and shook her head. "It's me Gabe. It's—" She looked up at the ceiling, her elegant neck arched, the pale white of her skin pulsing with her heartbeat. He felt the same pulse in his body.

He wanted to push these feelings away, the smoky tendrils of connection, of understanding and of caring that still lingered around his heart, tying him to her. He wanted them gone so he could get on with his life.

"Every time I want more—" she swallowed, her voice a rasp "—every time I reach out for something I don't have…" She shook her head and tried to laugh and he nearly cringed at the heartbreaking rattle. "I'm just reminded of how much better it is to not want anything."

"What did you want that night in the kitchen?" he asked and the air between them was still. She didn't move, didn't blink. His heart didn't beat. His lungs didn't work.

What answer do I want? What am I doing even asking this?

He felt himself pushed toward the edge of some cliff. A cliff he'd gone over once before and had no business flirting with again.

"You, obviously." Her voice was a sigh and his heart thudded painfully in his chest. "I think I wanted what we had. Before everything went so wrong. Working together just reminded me of the good times."

"But I could never make you happy," he told her, repeating his bare-bones reason for leaving the marriage. His failure that haunted him and drove him away.

"It shouldn't have been your job," she said. "And I think we both expected it."

These were words they'd never spoken. The truth they'd hidden behind fights and anger and slammed doors.

"I just want you to be happy." He said, turned and came out with this suppressed wish. "That's all I've ever wanted."

"That's all I've ever wanted for you," she whispered. Her eyes were on his, the beautiful obsidian gaze, and he felt himself fall over that cliff again. Back into feeling something for this woman. "And I wish, so much, that I was the person who could make you happy, Gabe."

He sat back in his chair, a hole in his chest with a cold wind blowing through it.

"Alice!"

"Marcus!" Her face lit up, her eyes sparkled, and for a moment she was the Alice of a week ago, before the kiss, the Alice before the miscarriages. The wind whistling though his chest blew colder when he realized they were the same Alice. Happy Alice. Glowing Alice. Infectious and laughing. Alice in love.

Marcus hugged her, his hands trailing across her back. Alice grinned up at him.

"God," he said. "How long has it been?"

"Five years," she said.

"You look good." The way he said it made Gabe's ears perk up. As though she looked *good* good. Jealousy, unwanted and stupid, gripped him.

"Never thought I'd see you here," Marcus continued, gesturing at the cathedral ceilings. "I thought you were a bright lights kind of girl."

Ha! Gabe thought. *That's how well you know her.*

"A girl can't live in the city forever." She

smiled. "Look at you, hotshot reviewer for *New York Magazine*."

"Well, you're partially to thank. You urged me to apply."

Alice smiled and assured him he would have found his way to New York City eventually.

Gabe let their words wash over him while he made every effort to shake the inappropriate jealousy. Was this how Alice felt when he left with Daphne? Even as he wondered, he knew she must have felt worse.

He suddenly was torn between smart and stupid, right and wrong, what he wanted and what he should want.

He missed Alice in love. He missed being the man to make her light up. And while he knew those days were behind him, he hated being the person responsible for taking the light out of her eyes.

He let the truth of what he needed to do sink in. He didn't expect it to make her happy again, but he'd at least be taking responsibility for the one thing he could control.

They were still connected, by the past, by their marriage, by whatever lingering feelings had survived the carpet bombing of the divorce and, while she was here, he needed to respect that.

He took a deep breath. As soon as the interview was over he'd call Daphne.

ALICE PULLED the frozen cinnamon rolls from the freezer to thaw and proof on the counter overnight. Most of the guests were leaving tonight, but Joy

Pinter from *Bon Appetit* was staying one more day in order to get a tour of the grounds from Gabe.

And Alice had noticed that Joy seemed to like her espresso hazelnut cinnamon rolls.

Max walked in the side door, looking every inch the cop he'd once been—stone-faced, straight backed and exuding a general displeasure, a disappointment directed right at her.

Guilt leaped in the pit of her stomach. She'd handled the Cameron thing all wrong, and if she were less of a wimp, she'd actually deal with it. She'd ask to bring him back to the kitchen. She could take it, she was tough. The conversation with Gabe this morning had actually moved some of her baggage so she could deal with other people. Such as Cameron.

"Cameron's been arrested," Max said and the cinnamon rolls fell from her hands to clatter on the floor.

"What?" she asked, her hands and feet numb.

"They've sentenced him to the group home in Coxsackie." Max flexed his shoulders as though being around her made him uncomfortable and she realized that she wasn't a wimp—she was a coward, and the one who suffered was Cameron. "I thought you'd want to know," he said and turned for the door, as though he couldn't quite get out of her kitchen fast enough.

She wiped her face with a shaky hand. "What can I do, Max?"

"It's a little late to do anything."

She grabbed his arm, held him in place. "What

can I do to make it right?" She shook her head. "I...God. I was so wrong to treat him that way."

Max watched her for a long time weighing, she was sure, her sincerity. "Well, we can't get him out. But you could visit."

An idea sprang up in the back of her head, one she might pay for in the long run but that was the nature of doing the right thing.

"All right." she picked up the cinnamon rolls. Scanned the counter and her mental to do list and figured she had three hours before she needed to be back. She untied her apron and set it on the chopping block. "You have time to drive up there?" she asked Max, and his lips lifted in the smallest smile.

"That's my girl," he said and Alice nearly crumbled. He didn't know how wrong he was.

FORTY-FIVE MINUTES later they pulled up to an old white farmhouse surrounded by modern outbuildings. One looked big enough to be a gymnasium and the other looked as if it might be dorms.

Alice didn't know what she expected, but a group of kids playing basketball in the parking lot wasn't quite it.

"It's a school," Max said. "School and dorms and treatment facility."

"Treatment for what?" she asked, watching the kids, who all wore khaki pants and white shirts and couldn't have been older than fourteen, scramble for the ball. A tall boy with short hair grabbed the ball and tossed it toward the basket, missing spectacularly.

"Alcohol and drugs," Max said, parking the car and turning off the ignition. "Let's go. We need to talk to the director before we can talk to Cameron."

"You think this will work?"

"I'm not sure. They often have work-release programs, but usually not so far away."

"If he just had a car, he could get to school."

"I know. Let's go see what we can do."

Alice had stones in her stomach. She knew she wasn't totally responsible for this, but she couldn't help feeling that her sudden change in the way she'd treated Cameron had led him here.

Max waved at the faculty member working the basketball game, and the tall kid with the short hair stopped running and watched them.

It was Cameron, hardly recognizable without his long hair and filthy, oversize clothes. Alice waved but he just watched her walk by.

The director was a kind man, unassuming but with two huge dragon tattoos up his arms. Alice explained her plan to hire Cameron in her kitchen and asked if it was okay. He wholeheartedly approved.

"He'll need a ride back and forth after class," he said. "We don't have the staff to provide a chauffeur all the way out to the inn."

"We'll be able to work it out," Max said. "Don't worry."

"Worrying is my job, Max." The director laughed and gave Alice an empty classroom to use to talk to Cameron and then sent the secretary out to pull him from the game.

Alice waited in the room, looking at drawings of dogs and horses and mountains and homes that had been tacked on the walls.

She couldn't help the flutter of nerves, the kick of worry that he'd yell at her, or refuse to see her. That she wouldn't have a chance to try to make things right. It had been over a week since she'd seen him and it felt like a month.

The door banged open and Cameron stood there, fresh faced and angry in properly fitting clothes.

The mother instinct in her that had survived her efforts to drown it for the past five years sighed. *What a good-looking boy.*

"What do you want?" he asked, his face twisted in an ugly sneer.

"To apologize," she said. "Come in."

He hesitated for a moment, then stepped inside, the door sliding shut behind him. He watched her, offering her nothing, and she almost smiled, recognizing his behavior and his need to protect himself from her.

She had a Cameron inside of her—a small girl, petulant and hurt and scared. And she'd been letting her run things for far too long.

"I'm sorry you got arrested," she said.

"I didn't." Cameron shrugged. "The school sent these people to my house and they brought me here."

"Do you like it here?"

He shrugged. "I get to go to class and play basketball."

"Sounds good."

"What are you doing here?"

"I wanted to apologize for the way I acted last week."

"Apologies from drunks don't mean anything," he snapped and she felt as if she'd been blasted right between the eyes with shards of glass.

"Okay…" She sighed and steeled herself for his venom because she deserved it. "How about a job?"

He looked at her, made a rude noise and looked away, but quickly looked back at her. "What are you talking about?"

"We have a wedding coming up in a month and I need help in the kitchen."

"Peeling potatoes?" His eyes narrowed and she nearly smiled. He was so transparent, as she figured she had been this morning with Gabe. Wishing so much that she was different. That he was. That they could make it work between them, in some alternative universe.

She nodded. "Among other things. I'll pay you well enough that, when you turn sixteen, Max will go with you to buy a used car so you can get to school."

His mouth fell open and his shoulders slumped and for a moment she saw his eyes turn bright with a sudden flood of tears.

She could feel the hope and longing roll off him and slam into her chest. Breath was thick in her throat, her chest felt tight, but in a good way, as though she couldn't hold in all the things she felt for him. How glad she was she could help him. Gabe probably wouldn't approve of her hiring Cameron with part of her salary, but he had left it up to her. And this was her choice.

Wanting more for Cameron felt good. She'd start there, maybe, and work toward getting more for herself.

"No," he said, surprising the hell out of her.

"No? Why?"

He chewed on his lip and crossed his arms over his chest, revealing a sudden strength she'd hadn't expected. "I've had enough of drunks," he said. "I'm here now. My dad can't—" he stopped, his voice cracked, and Alice's heart, which she'd been sure had been broken and rubbed into the dust, clenched and tore. "I won't work for you if you're drinking," he said.

"I'm not drinking anymore," she said. The words, like birds startled from a tree, were a surprise. But she realized that if Gabe couldn't make her happy, she needed to do it herself, and not drinking was square one.

"Since when?" he asked, doubtful, probably having heard similar words from his father.

She swallowed her pride, a thick ball of it that did not go down easy. "Since right now."

Alice stepped toward him and he watched her sideways as she put out her hand to shake on the offer, sealing his chance at school and a future and her promise to stop drinking and work on being happy, on her own.

"I want to work the grill," he said, jerking his chin up.

"Not on your life."

"No potatoes."

She winced. "Sorry. There will be potatoes."

"A car?"

"A Max-approved car." She nodded, her hand still hovering in the space between them.

"All right," he said, his hand slapping hers so hard her palm stung. "You're on."

She bit back a gleeful bark, a strange crow of joy, and shook his hand. "We'll pick you up tomorrow."

CHAPTER ELEVEN

GABE HAD ENDED his share of relationships. Probably more than his share. More like his share, Alice's share and probably Max's share, too, since Max and Alice didn't seem to believe in ending things when they needed to be ended.

Even so, with all that practice, with his "it's not you it's me" speech refined to an art form, spending Wednesday evening telling Daphne that he couldn't see her anymore didn't go quite as he had planned.

She braced herself on one of the posts in the gazebo and laughed until tears rolled down her cheeks.

"Oh, I'm sorry." She sighed. "I am. This is just—" She started to laugh again and Gabe crossed his arms over his chest and waited, impatiently, for Daphne to act reasonably.

"Oh, this is perfect. Just my luck, you know?" Daphne pulled a tissue from her dark blue barn jacket and wiped her eyes. "My first time back out in the dating scene and I get involved with a guy who isn't over his ex-wife."

"This has nothing to do with Alice," he lied. Too many things right now were tied to Alice. Breaking up with Daphne, the success of his inn, his dreams, his thoughts. He felt a resentment churn into the feelings he still had for Alice, the desire he felt when she touched him, when he saw her bent over the chopping block, the sun in her hair. "We are only working together."

Daphne tilted her head at him as though he were some misguided teenager. "Gabe, it's fine if you don't want to tell me the truth. I understand that. You and Alice have a right to your privacy, but you have to at least be honest with yourself."

"I am," he said, but he could tell she didn't believe it, and frankly, neither did he. "It's a proximity thing," he finally admitted. "She'll be gone in a month and my life will get back to normal. We just—" He kicked a rock on the worn path. "She's got this gravitational pull that I get sucked into every time I'm around."

"Then why fight it?" Daphne put her hand on his arm and with that touch and its total lack of electricity and heat he knew that even if Alice weren't here it would never work with Daphne. "Gabe, if my ex came back, nothing in my life would change. Helen would probably be happier, but I don't feel anything for him. I don't hate him, I don't still love him, nothing. He has no gravitational pull."

"You're lucky."

"No." Daphne's voice had bite and she grabbed him to face her. "You idiot. You're lucky and you don't get it. What I felt for Jake is gone. Vanished. Because it wasn't real. If you really love someone, really love them, those feelings may change but they don't go away."

The truth in her words rattled around in his head, stirred things up in his chest.

"We don't work," he whispered. "Outside of sex and the restaurant business, we've never worked."

"Then you're not trying," she said, patting his cheek. "Start with the sex and work out from there."

THROUGH THE WINDOW over the stove Alice surreptitiously watched Daphne leave.

"What are you doing?" Cameron asked, a sneak catching another sneak.

"I'm spying on Gabe," she said as Gabe slammed the driver's-side door of Daphne's beat-up truck and she drove out of the parking area.

"Aren't you an adult?" Cameron asked.

"Sometimes," Alice answered, ducking out of the way when Gabe started walking toward the kitchen. "Keep going on those pots," she said and Cameron scowled, hating his temporary job as dishwasher.

She whirled to the far work counter where she'd stacked the material she'd ordered for the Crimpson wedding, grabbed it and hit the door to the dining room running before Gabe entered the kitchen.

She was being a child, she knew that, spying on the guy and then leaving so she wouldn't have to talk to him for fear of what she might say.

Their conversation four days ago haunted her. A thousand times since those moments of naked honesty she'd wanted to turn to him and ask him, Why now?

Why couldn't they have spoken that way while married? When they'd both so clearly needed it.

"Alice?"

Crap. He'd followed.

"Hi, Gabe," she said, setting the bundles of blue silk on a nearby table. "What's up?" She pretended to check the bundles, keeping her back to him, but his silence compelled her to turn. "Did Daphne—"

Looking at him, her words stopped, hung suspended in her throat. He was a man ravaged, dark eyed and stormy. Barely contained anger mixed with a desire they'd both been suppressing rolled off him like heat from a banked fire.

They'd been skirting this moment, pretending this heat between them wasn't happening.

Apparently, Gabe was no longer pretending.

Her treacherous body longed for this reckoning.

"Drop off the spinach?" She finished the question, her voice weak.

He shook his head, coming farther into the room until he stood next to her. His silence was like another person in the room, a person sucking in all the air, taking up all the space.

"How did the tour with Joy go on Monday?" She asked, playing with the hemmed edge of silk like an inspector.

"Fine." His voice was that low rumble of thunder, like a faraway storm gathering strength.

"You and Marcus sure seemed friendly," he said, sounding like a jealous ex-husband. Alice lifted her head, aware of a sudden change. A rise in temperature.

"We dated." His eyes flared. "It was brief," she said, moving from stroking the edges of the cloth to unfolding it, as though more industry on her part would help her breathe, or would speed up this conversation, so she could see where it would go.

"When?"

"After the divorce before he got the full-time job and moved to the city."

She handed him one edge of the material, the indigo edge that matched his eyes at this moment. "Take this," she said, unable to stand next to him, feeling the heat of him, smelling the spicy and warm scent of him—that had nothing to do with soap or fabric softener and had everything to do with him— and talk of the other people in their lives.

She stepped away, holding the silver edge of the cloth and it unfurled into a watercolor banner six feet long and ranging from indigo to violet, to royal blue and down the radiant spectrum.

"Pretty, isn't it?" she asked, to fill the room with some sound other than the odd pounding of her heart.

What do you want?

What are you doing here?

"Beautiful," he said. Again the distant thunder and she looked up at him, caught his eye and knew it wasn't the cloth he'd been talking about.

"Marcus asked me to meet him in the city for dinner some night," she said, throwing it between them like a shield, but it landed like a gauntlet and his hands fisted the fragile fabric.

"Are you going to?"

She shrugged. "Depends." These were the words she'd been scared of saying. These were the stupid steps toward ruin.

"On what?"

"On what Daphne was doing here."

There. She'd said it. She couldn't take the words back. They couldn't pretend the pink elephant that breathed desire in the middle of the room wasn't there.

"I broke it off."

"Why?"

"Same reason you're not going to dinner with Marcus."

The air crackled and hissed and practically smelled of sex. Six feet away from him and she knew he was hard, just as he'd know she was wet.

Oh, I love it. She loved him this way. Loved and hated him.

"Why's that?" she asked, cocking her head and playing her part, devastating though it would be.

He pulled on the fabric and stepped toward her, reeling her in and chasing her down, and she let it happen. She wanted it. Waited for it. Then there it was.

His lips, moist and hot against hers. This kiss wasn't tentative or careful, it was pained and angry. It was the unleashing of a thousand repressed kisses, a hundred long nights and dozens of mornings wishing he was there.

He wrapped her up in his arms and the silk, held her so close she couldn't move and she wouldn't have if she could.

"You're ruining my life," he said against her

mouth, before biting her lips aggressively, the way she loved. His words stung, particularly since he was such a part of the rebuilding efforts of her life. But thought dried up and blew away as the temperature between their bodies flared.

She arched her hips against his, felt the ridge of his sex beneath his jeans and her body turned to mercury against his.

"What are we doing?" she asked as he pushed her against the table. "What—"

"I don't care," he muttered against her throat, his hand sliding up her thigh to her hips. "I don't want to stop."

Yes. Right. No stopping. She opened her legs and he stepped between them, their dance as familiar as if they'd done this yesterday. His hands fisted in her hair and she sucked on the skin of his throat, used her teeth on his ear and every groan, every sigh and hiss from their lips threw gasoline on the fire between them.

The uncomfortable clearing of a throat behind Gabe didn't stop them. Barely slowed them down.

"For God's sake, son, you're in the dining room!" Patrick's hoarse bark doused them like ice water and Gabe stepped away, his hand on her elbow. She rose from the table and turned to pick up the banner, blushing like a sixteen-year-old, but she couldn't move, thanks to being wrapped up in the silk. She struggled her way free.

"Hi…Dad." Gabe said, smiling. They'd been caught making out by his father and Gabe was smiling.

Which, despite her general embarrassment and

confusion, made her smile, then, oddly enough, laugh. Gabe watched her sideways and his lips twitched before he laughed, too. Patrick watched them as though he'd stumbled down the rabbit hole.

"You two are nuts!" Patrick said. "You always have been."

"That explains a lot," Gabe murmured, bending to help her pick up the material.

"You better know what you're doing, Gabe," Patrick said. "Because I remember what you were like the last time you guys wrecked each other, and I don't want to see you that way again." Patrick left, muttering and stomping his way to the kitchen.

That sobered Alice and she searched Gabe's handsome face for some twitch of emotion. "What were you like?" she asked, their faces so close she felt his warm breath on her cheek.

"A mess," he said and swallowed. "I loved you, Alice. I wanted to make it work."

His words flayed her, paralyzed her. Tears trembled on her eyelashes and she wiped them away before they fell.

"I can't..." He sighed. "I can't go through that again. This—" his hand swirled between them "—whatever this is between us, it's not a second chance. I can't survive a second chance, not if it's going to fail."

"Me, neither," she said.

Neither one of them asked why it would have to fail, though the words nearly leaped from her mouth.

"So?" His eyes bored into hers. "What was that?"

he asked, referring to their kiss and near-tabletop lovemaking.

"It was good, Gabe." She smiled and stroked his cheek. "Maybe it's better to say goodbye this way, to end our relationship like this rather than the way we did five years ago."

"You mean the plate fight?"

"We did some damage." She nodded. "But I think what we had deserves better than that." She got lost in the depths of Gabe's eyes, lost there among the swirl of affection and memory of desire, just barely contained.

"I need—" He covered her hand with his, the rough skin on his palms sending sparks through her body.

Me.

Us.

To get naked. To kiss you. To love you.

"I need some time to think."

She pulled her hand free of his. Part of her hurt knowing that she was so toxic, such a risk, that involvement—even only physical—was not something anyone took lightly. But part of her understood and appreciated the chance to think. "And I need time to hang these silks."

The cool air blowing between them vanquished the last of the fire they'd built with their bodies.

"You need help?" he asked.

"I do, but that's why your dad was here. He volunteered to help me get the lighting up and ready."

"I'll send him back in." He tucked his hands in the pockets of his worn jeans and spoke louder in a near yell. "I'm sure he and Max are listening on the other side of the door."

"We can barely hear you!" Max yelled through the kitchen door, confirming Gabe's words. "You need to speak up!"

Alice felt emotion pulse through her body, longing and gratitude and regret that she no longer had a permanent place with these men.

"Bye," she whispered with a smile she knew would seem sad, but she couldn't pretend otherwise.

"Bye." He nodded, turned and left her alone with silk the color of his eyes ruined with her tears.

SHE AND PATRICK stayed up late building frames for the material. He'd been persistent with his questions, which she knew were born of concern, but she dodged them as best she could.

"I don't want to see you two hurt again," he said.

"Me, neither." She bent the thin light strips of pine in an effort to make the silk billow like waves. But all the wood did was crack. She swore and removed the splintered wood from the frame.

"Are you still in love?" he asked and Alice hung her head backward, examining the ceiling so she wouldn't have to look at her ex-father-in-law's knowing face.

"In love?" she asked the ceiling. "I don't know. I still love him. I think he still loves me, but that doesn't mean things will work," she said. "We loved each other last time, too."

Patrick grunted and hammered the finishing nails

into the left corner of the six-foot structure. "I loved his mother," he said.

She sighed in relief. Finally the heat was off her and Gabe.

"I loved her so much that when she left I hated her."

"I know that feeling," she said, having experienced it for a number of years.

"I loved her so much that I hated her and I wanted her punished."

"Sounds familiar."

"So when she asked to come back I said no."

"That's about—" She looked up at him, her stomach in her knees. "What?"

"She asked to come back, twice. Well, three times."

"When?" she whispered.

"Three months after she left, then a year after that and now."

Her head reeled, she sat hard on her butt. "Do the boys know?"

"They know she's been in touch recently," he said and shook his head. "But not about her earlier letters."

"What?" She hardly knew what questions to ask, where to start. "Why?"

"Why?" He took a deep breath and let it out slowly. "Because I was a fool. Because I was scared. Because I was angry. Because, the truth was, life got easier without her. With just us."

I'm scared, her heart spoke. *I'm scared of Gabe breaking me all over again.* And she'd spent much of the last decade being angry.

God, I've wasted so much time.

"What are you going to do?" she asked him.

"What *can* I do? She wants to see them and the boys will barely even talk about her." He shrugged. "I don't want anyone to be hurt."

"What about you? What do you want?"

"I want my family together." His voice cracked and he hammered at the frame as if it were an animal trying to eat him.

"You should do it. Tell her to come here," she said, bold and gutsy because she'd be long gone. "Gabe and Max need to deal with what their mom did to them. They need to hash it out or forgive her or scream at her or whatever. But everyone pretending there's not this giant mom-size hole in their lives is getting a little ridiculous."

Patrick stared at her, then tipped his head back and laughed. "Right, and where will you be during World War Three?"

"Behind locked doors in Albany," she said with a smile.

Patrick set down his hammer, pushing himself up with much groaning and creaking knees. "You know," he said, "there are other holes in Gabe's life. Watching the two of you pretend that you don't still feel things for each other has been pretty ridiculous."

"Well—" she felt a blush ignite her neck "—obviously we've stopped pretending."

"I'm not talking about sex." Patrick helped her to her feet and patted her shoulder. "I'm talking about the love that's running you two ragged."

Emotion surfaced and bobbed in her throat and

she busied herself stacking the lightweight frames and supplies along the west window. "It's too hard," she said. "It's too hard to go back."

Patrick's eyes were liquid with compassion. Suddenly, she saw everything he hid behind his smiles and teasing. He was a man with a broken heart, living with one eye on the past.

"That's what I said years ago when my wife wanted to come home," he said, brushing his hands clean of sawdust and memories, "and I've never regretted anything more."

PATRICK'S WORDS haunted Alice as she grabbed her flashlight and fleece jacket and headed back to her cabin. The heavy shadow of the Catskills made an already dark night even darker and not even the glimmer of a star broke up the ebony velvet of the sky. The moon was hidden behind trees and clouds.

Without the flashlight, Alice literally could not see her hand in front of her face.

She tripped over a tree root and barely caught herself before landing on her stomach in the dirt.

Such a difference from her illuminated and neon existence in the city and stranger still that she didn't miss that life, her car or her house. She did miss Felix, but really that was all.

Which didn't bode well for her return to it.

Her flashlight illuminated the front of her cottage, the closed door, the chair she'd placed on the small stoop.

Gabe sitting in that chair.

She stumbled again, her thumb hitting the button on the flashlight and the slice of light it provided vanished.

The night breathed.

"Gabe?" she whispered. He didn't answer but she heard the scuff of his shoe against the concrete, could feel him a few feet away. "What are you doing here?"

"Thinking."

Her heart tripped, and her skin, forgotten and cold, sang while it flooded with heat. Her eyes adjusted to the shadows and her body sensed his in the darkness.

"And?" she whispered, taking the small step up to stand near him.

"And I'm done thinking."

CHAPTER TWELVE

HE REACHED OUT of the black night and folded her into his arms. His lips, despite the dark, unerringly found hers and all the confused desire between them fused into something new, different.

Dangerous.

She dropped the flashlight and wrapped her arms around him, tugged at the blond curls at the back of his neck and did all she could to climb into his skin.

He peeled the fleece from her shoulders and where the cool air should have chilled her he warmed her, lighting fires under her flesh. He cupped her shoulders, laced his fingers through her hair, kissed her neck. Her ear. Her lips again.

She groaned, pulling him closer, tighter. And he picked her up, her feet dangling over the ground, and spun her so her back hit the outside wall of the cottage.

"I've dreamed of this for so long," he muttered, yanking at the hem of her shirt and sliding his hand along her spine, up to her neck, then he held her still, immobilized as he devoured her mouth.

"Me, too." She sighed when he released her. She didn't bother with his shirt. Years of celibacy, years of remembering this man and his particular brand of fire, the way he could make her loose and crazy with just a look, made her bold and she reached for his belt.

With her fingers clumsy, her brain fevered, memory saved her. There were no years between them. No fights.

Just this.

His buckle clanged open and she undid the zipper, sliding her hand in between warm cotton and hot flesh. He gasped, groaned and shoved her against the wall. His chest hard against her, his lips open on her neck.

He bit her. She squeezed him, then he laughed— the devil's laugh—and the fire in her belly, across her skin, buried in her sex blazed hotter.

The contention in their marriage had seeped into their bedroom and sex had become a game of control between them. By the end, neither one of them gave themselves freely.

"This," he murmured against her skin, his breath tickling her ear and lighting her up. "This was something we always got right." He yanked open the top of her pants, the button flying off into the night. And his fingers, rough and big and so familiar, brushed her skin, the curve of her belly, the scar of the emergency C-section, the damp curls between her legs. Then he stopped.

She groaned and arched into him, mindless and needy.

"Alice?" It was a sultry question. A tease.

She threw her head back against the building and moaned. "You okay?" he asked.

"Come on," she groaned, reaching into his pants, but he knocked her hand away. This would be one-sided teasing and she melted farther into him.

"Come on, what?" he asked, licking at her neck.

She lifted her head, found the glitter of his eyes in the dark and focused on him.

She didn't know what he could see in her eyes, what the dark hid or revealed, but her feelings, she knew, were there out in the open. And she didn't care.

"Touch me."

"Where?"

"Inside."

Her husband's thick fingers eased into her and she saw stars on a starless night. The world spun and fell apart and Alice held him to her as hard as she could.

He slid his arms under her legs and pulled away from the wall, taking her with him, the scrape of his belt against her inner thigh a delicious torment.

Hurry, her heart pounded, her lungs chugged, her heart screamed.

"Hurry," he groaned against her throat when they got to the door.

She reached behind her and opened it so they could stumble in and fall across the bed. She bounced, then his body covered her like a blanket.

He didn't bother removing her clothes, and she could care less about his. She used her feet to push his pants to his knees and he yanked hers off one leg and put his knee on the bed, slid his hands around her hips, lifting her slightly.

"Stop," she said, putting her hand to his chest.

"What?" His eyes were wide-eyed and panicked.

She slid her knee up and pushed him over, climbing on top of him.

"You made me beg," she said, pressing small light sweet kisses against his neck, down his throat.

He groaned, reached for her and she slapped his hands away.

"Now it's your turn," she whispered in his ear.

GABE ROLLED HIS HEAD to look at the open window that was letting in all the cold air. Alice's body, pressed naked against his on top of the covers, was covered in goose bumps.

I should get up and close that, he thought. *Or we should get under the covers. Something.*

But moving—any movement—required herculean effort. And it might make Alice move away and, frankly, nothing was quite worth that. Not yet. Even cold and pressed against him, he didn't want her to move.

They had a limited number of these moments and he planned on making them last as long as possible.

And he did not plan on examining those feelings any further.

"Hey." Her voice was a raspy croak and he smiled hearing it.

"Hey."

"It's cold."

"Yep."

He felt her swallow against his chest. She turned her head and her chin dug into his ribs. He knew she was looking at him. "Do you want to stay?"

He stared at the ceiling, at the pine wainscoting that had cost him a fortune but had made the cabins something truly special.

"Gabe?"

He was a careful man, he took calculated risks and he never—well, not since getting involved with her the first time—made a move without weighing the costs.

What would I lose staying?

What would I gain leaving?

His head was too stupefied, too blurred by orgasm, to do the math.

"I'm freezing," Alice said, her voice getting a little harder, her chin digging a little deeper. "So, if you're staying let's get under the blankets."

He lifted his head and smiled. "You always were good at the postcoital conversation."

She grinned and rolled away and he got infinitely colder.

Better go, his head said. *Better get out of here before things get worse. Messier. Because they always do with her.*

But she pulled down the duvet and in the shadows he could see the delicious curve of her breast, the swell of her hip and the scar bisecting her belly into top and bottom.

She would have been the mother of my children.

Thoughts of those babies, the boy and girl, who had been born too early, who were so small, the size of his palm, with their perfect eyelashes and paper-thin toenails. The babies he'd carried to Alice and they'd baptized with their tears before letting the nurses take away, while Alice screamed in her bed, had been banished long ago to places in his head he refused to visit. Doing so made living possible. Made recovering and getting on with his life easier.

But what was the cost? The rogue thought surfaced, from places unknown. *What was the cost of doing that?*

"Gabe?" she whispered, her hand fluttering awkwardly over that scar. "What's—"

He sat up, leaned forward, wrapped one arm around her thin yet strong back and pressed his lips to that scar, felt the small ridge under his tongue.

She gasped, dropped the blanket and put her hands in his hair, hugging his head to her belly.

He jerked the blankets down and pulled her into the warm envelope of the bed, his lips traveling from belly to breast, his tiredness forgotten, his reasons for leaving vanished.

"Gabe? What's—"

"No talking," he said, taking refuge in the sex they shared, like he always had. He wrapped his hands around her wrists, holding them against the bed and loved her the only way left to him.

"I'VE GOT A LOT of work to do," Gabe said the following Saturday while he and Alice waited for her parents to arrive. "Really, there's the gutter situation on cabin five and I really should return Mrs. Crimpson's e-mail about the—"

"I told you," Alice interrupted with a laugh. Gabe's insecurity was actually pretty endearing right now, drunk as she was on sex and coffee. "You don't have to be here when my parents arrive. I can show them around myself and we don't need you for the meeting about what stations they'll staff at the wedding reception."

"I know." But he didn't leave.

"So, go ahead and get your work done." She bumped his hip with hers.

She was torn, as she had been for the week since Gabe had appeared up on her porch in the dark. Her heart sang some kind of crazy tune these days.

Nonstop.

While she taught Cameron how to ice a wedding cake, while she revised the menu every week, while she and Patrick worked on the wedding decorations. While she and Gabe made love. While they ate, while they worked side by side, while they debated East Coast cuisine versus West Coast. While they lay in bed, silent, curled around each other.

While she knew it was all going to end after the Crimpson wedding.

But her heart, stupidly, kept right on singing.

"You don't want to look like a coward?" she asked.

"I'm not a coward and—" he crossed his arms over his chest "—I'm not scared of your dad."

She laughed because her father was a scary man. A giant in their industry and a physical bear of a guy.

Ten years ago, when she and Gabe had told him they were getting married and having a baby, her dad had taken Gabe outside for a little chat. Gabe had returned white-faced and calling him sir.

This would be the first time Gabe had seen them since the divorce.

"They won't blame you, Gabe," she said. "My parents understand better than most how hard I can be on a relationship."

Gabe slid an arm around her waist and pressed a kiss on her forehead.

But didn't say a word.

Alice wasn't stupid. So she kept her mouth shut but wished fervently that the Crimpsons would push the wedding back a few months. A year perhaps. Just until she and Gabe finished this long goodbye.

At the sight of her parents' old Volvo chugging up the gravel driveway Gabe dropped his arm and stepped away as if she were on fire.

But not fast enough for her dad. Michael saw the embrace through the driver's-side window and scowled.

"Hi, honey!" Her mom, Janice, a tiny elfish woman with hands of steel from years of kneading homemade dough, leaped from the passenger's-side and jogged around the car to fold Alice in a hard hug. "Oh, look at you, sweetie. You look so good." Janice pulled back and cupped Alice's face in her hands. "A little lipstick wouldn't kill you," she whispered.

"Good to see you too, Mom." Alice laughed, accustomed to her mother.

"Quite a place you've got here," Michael said, stepping out of the car and standing to tower over Gabe. Dad had a beard and a belly and at least five inches on Gabe's six-foot frame.

"Thank you, sir." Gabe said, like a schoolkid.

Michael's lip curled. "I told you ten years ago to call me Mike," he said and held out a giant paw for Gabe to shake. "Offer still stands."

Gabe sighed and shook his hand.

"Would you like a tour?" Gabe asked.

"We'd love one," Janice said and stepped over to kiss Gabe's cheek. "It's good to see you again."

Alice could tell he was surprised by their affection, surprised and moved. But it probably wouldn't last if her folks knew about this new relationship between them. So, Alice stepped in before her mom started asking questions and grabbed her dad's arm.

"Let's start with the kitchen," she said, pulling them into movement. "Cameron is my assistant, Dad. And I'm warning you, he's a kid, so go out of your way to be nice."

"Am I that scary?" he asked.

"Yes," Gabe answered from behind them and everyone laughed.

AN HOUR LATER Alice and Janice walked arm in arm toward the gazebo, while her dad and Gabe unloaded the half-barrel barbecue from the back of the Volvo.

"So?" Janice asked. "It looks like things are going well."

Alice nodded but did not meet her mother's eyes.

"When is your contract up?"

"Three weeks."

"Have you found a replacement?"

She'd been ignoring that little issue. "Not yet. I've put out some feelers."

They stepped into the gazebo and Alice let go of her mom to go watch the Hudson flow by, wishing the questions her mother was bound to ask, had been asking with her eyes since setting foot on the property, would flow on by, too.

"Why are you lying, Alice?"

And no such luck.

"I've just been busy." Alice held her breath to see if her mom would accept that lame answer.

"What are you doing, sweetie?" Janice asked, sliding an arm over Alice's shoulders. She didn't have to clarify Alice knew what her mother meant. *What are you doing with Gabe? What are you doing with your life?*

"I don't know, Mom." She sighed. "I know it's a bad idea, but if you could see how different Gabe is right now. How different both of us are—"

"I'd see how it's okay for you to be involved with your ex-husband again?"

"You'd see how it's impossible not to be involved with him again."

"Just be careful. Find a replacement so that when things go bad—"

"Maybe they won't go bad," she whispered her stupid wish, words she only sighed against Gabe's chest in the dead of night with his sleeping breath in her ear.

"Oh, Alice." Janice pressed her lips to Alice's head and Alice closed her eyes. Her mom didn't need to say anything else; the words unsaid, blew through her, right into her foolish heart.

Things always went bad with Gabe.

MICHAEL HELPED Alice with dinner, working the grill and putting a twist on her filet that earned raves out in the dining room.

"You want to replace me when my contract here is over?" she asked over the mouth of her water bottle when the last dessert had been plated and served and the dishwasher chugged away in the background.

Dad tipped back his head and laughed, swirling the red wine in his glass, before draining it. "Your mother would kill me."

She watched him swallow and waited for the demons to stir, but they remained silent, unmoved by the fruity noir her dad drank.

"I'm retired so she can have me paint the house and work in her garden," he said. He poured more wine into his glass and gestured with the bottle toward her.

"No, thanks," she said.

"That kid you got working here—"

"Cameron?" She smiled, remembering how Cameron had taken one look at her dad and all but ran from the room.

"He's got talent," Dad said. "Real talent."

"I think so, too. He's a good kid."

"Things working out for him at that group home?"

"Seem to be. He's only been there a week."

"Reminds me of Max."

"He reminds all of us of Max."

Gabe and Janice came in from the dining room laughing about something, but when Gabe saw the wine bottle, his laughter faded. His eyes darted to her, and when she lifted her bottle of water, he physically relaxed.

She wasn't offended, oddly. She understood the situation from his perspective now that she was sober and was grateful that he'd taken a risk on the wreck she'd been.

"You ready, sweetheart?" Janice asked, taking the wineglass from her husband's hand. "We need to get on the road now, if I'm driving."

"Oh, you're driving," Dad said.

"You can stay here," Gabe offered for the tenth time. "We've got lots of room."

"No, we need to head home," Janice said and the four of them walked out the kitchen door into the cool moonlight.

Alice longed to wrap her arm around Gabe's waist as they watched her folks get into the Volvo, her father fumbling with the seat controls so he could actually sit in the passenger's seat without eating his knees. Mom rolled her eyes and turned on the engine, the headlights taking slices out of the night. When the car turned and headed up the road, Gabe, as if he could read her mind, slid his arms around her shoulders, pulling her back against his chest.

"Your dad wants to kill me," he muttered into her hair.

"No, he doesn't," she said, resting her bottom in the cradle of his hips.

"He's always wanted to kill me. But your mom sure did go out of her way with Max."

"I thought she was going to give him a haircut there for a minute."

"Well, the guy could use it. He looks like he's been living in the bush."

They stood, loosely embracing, watching the tail-lights fade into the ebony dark.

"Is Max okay?" she asked.

"He's better than he was."

"What happened to him?"

"After he was shot in the line of duty and got out of the hospital, he quit the force and came out here. Dad and I have tried to talk about it but he insists he's fine."

"He's not," Alice said. She tilted her head back and kissed his cheek. "It never occurred to you to push him a little harder? Try a little more?"

"Good God, no. He'd probably shoot me if I tried." Gabe pressed kisses along her neck, slowly making his way to that spot on her collarbone that turned her to jelly.

"You know what I'd like to talk about?" he asked.

She laughed, pressing her back against him not as playfully this time. "I can imagine."

"You weren't drinking tonight," he said. He rested his lips against her neck and the kisses stopped.

She shook her head, plucking at his fingers where they clasped her belly.

"Is it hard?" he murmured.

"Not drinking?"

He nodded against her neck.

"No," she said truthfully, surprised that she hadn't even been thinking about it. "I'm too busy, too preoccupied, too—" She stopped, caution suddenly making an appearance. She had been about to say happy, but that felt like some kind of declaration and that would spoil what was between them, scare him off like a deer on the side of the road.

This was supposed to be goodbye. They'd agreed on that.

"Good," he said and went back to kissing her neck. He stepped forward, pushing her with his body away from the lodge toward her cabin, which had, over the past week, become their cabin.

"I deserve a reward or something," she said.

"Oh," he chuckled against her skin, sending goose bumps along her body. "I'll reward you."

CHAPTER THIRTEEN

"So?" Patrick asked, watching his son ignore him, pretending to focus on the men unloading the tables, chairs, dishes and linens they were renting for the wedding in two weeks. The sun had set and the men hustled to get the van unloaded before it became full dark.

"So what?" Gabe asked. "We're putting it in the gazebo, guys," he said to the men taking the tables out of the truck. They grunted and crossed the lawn toward the shelter.

"I hope Max got enough tarps," Gabe said, as if that was what they were discussing.

"Gabe," Patrick slapped a hand on his son's shoulder, wanting to shake him until he saw sense. "You're avoiding the issue."

"What issue?" Max asked, approaching them from the kitchen door.

"I don't know. Dad's got issues," Gabe told his brother, and Patrick looked heavenward for patience.

"Alice!" Patrick cried. "Alice is the issue. And what you've been doing in her cabin every night."

Gabe and Max shared a wry look.

"If I have to explain it to you…" Gabe said.

"Don't be smart with me, kid." Patrick growled in frustration. "I'm still your dad." Gabe's smart-ass grin faded. "You're headed for trouble and pretending like nothing is going on."

"Nothing is going on," Gabe said. "Thanks, guys." He shook the hands of the movers, and Patrick and his two boys watched the truck drive off. Gabe bent to pick up one of the boxes of linens, but Patrick, tired of this silence they maintained, this fear they were all cursed with, grabbed Gabe's arm and turned him to face him.

"Talk to me, son. Don't pretend like this is no big deal."

Gabe sighed. "Dad, it's…temporary. It's what's happening right now."

"What about after the wedding? When she's supposed to go?"

Gabe betrayed himself by looking at his hand for a split second and Patrick wanted to rejoice. *He is human after all.* "Then she goes home," he murmured. "This isn't a second chance."

"Why?" Max asked. "I mean, why isn't it?"

"You, too?" Gabe asked, shooting his brother a killing look. "I didn't know you two were so interested in my love life."

"You love her," Max said and Patrick nodded. "She loves you, it's so obvious Cameron asked me about it."

"That doesn't change anything," Gabe said.

Why am I protecting them? Patrick wondered. *What's the damn point?*

"Because you're a coward," Max said.

"Oh!" Gabe hooted. "And you're so brave? Why the hell are you here, Max?"

"Not what we're talking about, Gabe."

"No, God forbid we talk about what's wrong with you. We should just let you go wild in the woods and never ask what happened last year."

Yes! This was good. This was healthy, this is what real families did, they talked about things. They hammered out the hard stuff. He and his boys didn't need to be afraid of this, they could do it. Talk like men.

"Is it because you can't have kids with her?" Max asked. "There are other ways to create a family."

Gabe's fists clenched and Patrick watched his sons start to square off as though they were sixteen again. He didn't get in the way.

"You're ruining this second chance you've been given."

"What do you know about second chances?" Gabe asked. "Or family for that matter. You fight and fight and fight until there's no one left in the room."

Okay, maybe they were going a bit too far.

"Boys—" He held up his hands between them, but they shouldered him out of the way.

"I know I'd kill for a second chance with a woman like Alice. And you're throwing her away like you don't care."

Patrick's heart spasmed and ached for Max, his young son with the hidden wounds.

"Maybe I don't care! Maybe she doesn't. Maybe this is none of your damn business."

Gabe was in Max's face, a breath away from shoving him and Max, who loved a good knock-down, drag-out fight, stepped back, put his hands up.

"You're right," Max conceded and headed out toward the forest and whatever waited for him in the dark.

Patrick let out the breath he'd been holding. In the end the Mitchell way always won out. Avoid. Don't talk. Run.

Patrick saw what he'd done here, how the way he'd lied to his sons, waited too long to tell them that their mother had left and then, in an effort to make the wounds heal faster, he'd pretended she'd never been there at all. Now both of his sons were doing it. Pretending they didn't even hear the drumbeat coming ever closer.

Gabe rubbed his hands over his face. "We're saying goodbye," he murmured. "That's all, it's what we agreed. We're ending our marriage the right way."

"By pretending it didn't end?" Patrick was seeing him with new eyes.

"No," Gabe said, cold steel in his blue eyes, "I will never forget that it ended."

"Is it because she can't have children?" Patrick asked. "You could adopt."

"When I brought it up before—" Gabe shook his head. "You should have seen her. It was like she couldn't stop crying. And then she couldn't stop screaming at me."

"But you're older. Wiser."

"We're just not meant to be together long-term. Let it go, Dad. There's too much between us to make it work."

"Like it would work better with someone you don't feel as much for?"

"Maybe."

Patrick stared at him slack jawed. "Your mom really did a number on you, didn't she?"

"I don't even think about her, Dad. I stopped years ago. She had nothing to do with this."

It broke Patrick's heart that his son couldn't see the truth of what he was doing—pushing away a good woman before he got hurt again. It was the same thing he'd done when Iris had asked to come home. He'd eliminated every chance that they might work, on the off chance they wouldn't. It was even worse that his wife wasn't here to see what she'd done to her boys with her middle-of-the-night abandonment of them.

She should see this, he thought, fuming.

Gabe bent to grab a box, ending the conversation, and Patrick, muttering under his breath, bent to help him.

"Gabe?" Alice said and both men looked up as if there'd been a gunshot. Patrick tried to discern whether she'd heard his son's callous words, but it was too dark, the light coming out from the kitchen door behind her too bright.

She doesn't deserve this, Patrick decided. Not Alice and not Iris. They didn't deserve to be so ignored, no matter what happened.

"Come in," she said, her voice merry and full of secrets. If she'd heard, she didn't reveal it. "I have something to show you."

GABE'S SKIN CRAWLED. It crawled and itched, his muscles twitched, his brain hurt. The question he asked himself every day, every moment, dogged his footsteps as he walked into the dining room.

What am I doing?

The promise he made every night walking to her cottage, his blood on fire for her. The promise he made every night, when she curled up next to him echoed his question.

This will be the last time.

The dining room was dark, the last of the fading light making shadows across the ceiling and floor. There were things hanging from the rafters and he realized Alice had finished the decorations.

"Close your eyes." Her voice came out of the darkness like the loving hand of the wife she'd been.

Sad and torn and worried about the future, he did as she asked.

He heard the flip of a switch and light bloomed behind his eyelids.

"Open them," she said and his eyes opened to a surreal water landscape. The silks covered the ceiling, blowing slightly with the ceiling fans she'd turned on, undulated like waves across the wooden beams. Long cords hung down among the silks and ended in old round Christmas-tree lights of the clear variety, and among the waves and the half dark, they looked like bubbles all across the ceiling, at different lengths and different intensities.

He took a slow turn, admiring her vision, her work, and wishing all the while that things were different.

"I could put up a few anchors if you think it would be better," she said and he realized she'd taken his silence for disapproval.

"Not on your life," he said, he couldn't look at her, not yet. "It's amazing, Alice. Really beautiful."

She sidled up to him, wrapping her arm around his waist and he felt so guilty for his words out in the yard, his callous, deliberate misunderstanding of what was between them that he stepped away, making it seem as though he wasn't quite done looking around.

"I'm sort of hoping she wants a disco ball," Alice said. "Then it would really look like we were underwater."

Gabe laughed and worked at getting himself back in check. Back on point. He watched her from the corner of his eye as she stared at her work, a satisfied smile on her lips. So beautiful, so different from the woman he'd hired.

But, history repeats itself. And their's was bloody and painful. He didn't need any more lessons in how incompatible they were when the going got tough. In these times—easy and happy and hard at work— they could survive, help each other. But any moment things could go wrong and then the truth of their marriage would win out.

Right?

He couldn't gamble that it would be different. There was too much at stake.

Gabe felt as if his skin were falling off in great strips, his back, his chest were naked, his heart pounded under muscle and bone, flinching from the cold air.

I want a family. I want children. Grandchildren. I want to watch my dad teaching my kids how to sand wood, and watch Max showing them the differences between red and white oak. I want babies and the terrible twos and driving lessons and failed science tests. I want it all.

And I can't have it with her.

"I can take it down in the morning," she said. "I just wanted to make sure it would all work before it's too late." She pulled her ever-present notebook out of her back pocket. "We've got one week before the family arrives and two weeks before everyone else arrives and we start the rehearsal dinner and wedding activities."

It was the time line, the hourglass running out of sand, and he felt as if he were in a race. Love her, love her as much as he could before she left. Touch her and kiss her and hold her close because in two weeks it was over.

"My folks will come in that last week and we'll get all our prep done. We can—"

He knocked the notebook out of her hands and hauled her into his arms. The pins fell out of her hair at the rough touch of his fingers and her arms were hard and fast around him as if she, too, understood it was all coming to an end.

She swung up in his arms as if pushed by some force and he was led out of the lodge by something outside of himself. Their clothes fell off and they never stopped kissing.

He felt his heart gathering itself, beating faster toward something. Something dark and stupid and foolish.

This is the last time.

The thought pounded in his brain as he kissed her throat.

I can't do this anymore.

The truth screamed through his blood as his hands cupped her hips, her waist, the light swell of her breast.

Gotta slow down, he realized. Everything felt too out of control—her breath against his chest, her hands on his body, the growling sighs from the back of her throat. It all felt as though it spun too fast toward oblivion.

Slow down.

He lowered her back onto the bed. Pushed away her hands when she reached for him. He crawled down her body, ignoring her efforts to pull him up.

"Ask me," he said, seeking distance in these games of control and contrition that they excelled at. He kissed her belly, blew cool air across the damp curls at the apex of her thighs.

"No, Gabe."

He chuckled, glad she played her part with such skill.

"Ask me, Alice." He kissed her thigh, traced that

sweet tendon at her hip with his tongue. "You're going to have to ask me."

Her hands, strong and cool, framed his face and forced him to look up at her, her black eyes gleaming in the dark. "Love me, Gabe. Like it was in the beginning."

His heart exploded in painful joyous memories of two people in love, looking at each other while they kissed, while they orgasmed, two people so naked in their need for each other that there was no need for games.

Two people, unwounded, free from scars, with no idea that loving would be so painful.

He shook his head, dislodging her hands. He couldn't do it.

"Please," she sighed. "Please, Gabe. No games. Not tonight."

He couldn't move, torn between staying and leaving. Loving her his way or hers.

In his silence and inaction, she took over.

"Shh," she whispered, sitting up. "It's okay, Gabe. It's just me." She brushed the hair back from his face and smiled crookedly into his eyes. "Just us." She kissed him, pushed him onto his back and he allowed it to happen even though he knew where it would end— the destruction of the barriers he kept around himself, the removal of the cushions he kept on the sharp corners of things that could hurt him all over again.

I love her.

I love her and I can't be with her.

"Just this," she breathed into his ear, peppering his

face with small kisses, his lips with tiny bites. She held his hand, put it to her face, looked into his eyes.

And loved him.

ALICE TURNED her head, stared out the window at the sky turning gray and pink, and fought back tears when she heard Gabe stand up and start to get dressed.

She wished she could be more surprised, summon up some stunned outrage that he could love her and leave her this way.

But she wasn't surprised.

She'd known the moment was coming when he stared, heartbroken, into her face as they made love. As he'd kissed her as if it were the last time.

Grief and anger warred in her. Maybe if she hadn't pushed the issue, forced him to truly make love to her. Maybe if she'd waited. Maybe if he wasn't such a coward.

There were so many maybes.

"I need to go," he said.

"You haven't slept," she said, as if he'd say, "You're right, scoot over," and climb back in with her rather than do what she knew he was about to do.

"Too much work to do." He shot her a grin over his shoulder that struck sorrow in her heart. The man she'd made love to, looked in the eye while he came, had left the building, and this Gabe, this slick, uncaring man, was about to end it all. "I'm not sure how much time we're going to have in the next little while."

She sat up.

"So, if we can't—"

"Turn around, Gabe." Her voice was iron again and he stiffened, hesitated, but finally turned to face her. She'd known this moment was coming since this affair started, but when she'd overheard Gabe and Patrick talking tonight, she knew it was coming sooner, rather than later.

Sooner as in right now.

"I would adopt," she murmured. She was older, wiser, more adept at reality, at understanding that not being able to have children did not make her less of a person. Adoption sounded like a good idea, if it meant she could build a family with this man.

He didn't say anything for a moment, he simply gaped at her, thunderstruck, and she rushed to fill the silence. "I heard you talking to your dad. And you're right. This is supposed to be goodbye, but—" She swallowed, looked down quickly at the edge of the sheet she pleated in her hands. "But I don't want it to be."

"We don't work," he whispered. "Remember?"

She shook her head. "Not as well as I used to." She tried to smile, but in the end she just stared at him, willing him to reveal himself to her—his true self, not this man of obstinance and fear. "You can't tell me you haven't been thinking about it."

"About what exactly?" he asked.

"About trying again. About second chances." She took a deep breath. "About regrets."

"Sure," he said honestly. "But I've also been thinking about the fights. And the tears. And how we went out of our way to hurt each other. I've been thinking about how you said you were tired of being disappointed in me. That I wasn't the man you thought I was."

Echoes from their fights and those words, meant to hurt, had scarred him. Three months ago she would have been delighted to know she'd managed to affect him in some way. But now, watching him gather himself to leave her again, she wished desperately that she'd never said such hurtful things.

"But it feels so different right now, doesn't it?" she asked. "If we could just sit down and talk about how we feel about the miscarriages—"

He jerked on his shirt and shoved his feet into his boots, muttering under his breath. She'd pushed him too far.

I should have kept my mouth shut. This was too much. Too fast. He can't handle all this.

"What are you doing?" She grabbed his arms, fighting for her life. "Why are you running?"

"I'm not running, I just have to go."

"What did I say?" she asked, feeling panicked and hurt.

"We can't get over the past—"

"Right," she cried. "Not if you don't talk about it. Sit down and we can talk—"

"I don't want to talk about anything!" he yelled, pulling her hands off his arms. "This isn't a second chance. It's goodbye. Like we agreed."

He looked at her with frozen eyes, his face glacial. His heart unreachable. She sat back on the bed, cold. Alone.

"Go," she said. "Get out."

He left without another word.

HE WENT TO HIS ROOM, stripping off the clothes that smelled of her. Of sex. Of two people doing stupid things, and fell exhausted across his bed. His eyes shut briefly and he saw those babies. His children. He felt them in his hands, their still chests and cold skin.

He gouged his fists in his eyes, trying to shove those images away. Push them out of his head.

He didn't want to talk about them. Think about them. And being with Alice again, talking about adoption. Regrets. Jesus, how much did a guy have to take?

Everything hurt—his body, his head. He rubbed at his chest, where it felt as if something sat on him, crushing him. He struggled for breath.

It hurt. It hurt worse than the first time, when he'd been so anxious to leave. This time he could have stayed, could have climbed back into bed with her and talked about adoption.

He sat up.

It was best this way. They'd be busy, then she'd be gone and life could return to some sort of equilibrium. He could concentrate on those things that were important to him now. He couldn't go back to those failed dreams, sifting through the ashes of what they'd once had to see what could be reused. It would only be a matter of time before the fighting started again, over something else.

He put his hands to his eyes again, feeling them burn beneath his fingers. But a baby…

He shook his head and stood. It was dawn and since there was no way he could sleep now he figured he might as well get to work.

PATRICK SAT BACK from the table and studied the objects of his downfall. His hemlock and poison asp. They looked like mere pen and paper, lined up square against each other waiting for him to set in motion what could be the worst mistake he'd ever made.

He took another sip of the fine scotch that seemed suited to this moment of big decisions and strong emotion. A swig for the soon to be executed.

He tilted his head back, felt the burn of the fine liquor in his belly and allowed himself to wonder for the very last time if this was the right thing to do.

She'd been sick in some way. He knew that. There was something dark that lived in her that he couldn't touch all those years ago. A demon that had run him ragged and he was inviting it back.

He sucked back the last of the booze, picked up the pen and scrawled:

Come. We'll be waiting.

He threw down the pen, folded the paper, crammed it into an envelope, not stopping when he tore the paper and crinkled the envelope. He licked the seal, put the return address in the corner so she'd know where he was, so she wouldn't have to go through their lawyer. He called his lawyer and left a message to have someone come and pick up the letter first thing in the morning.

"Done," he said, his heart thundering around his chest like some jackrabbit. For good or bad it was done.

CHAPTER FOURTEEN

ALICE MADE every effort to take this second breakup in stride. To convince herself she'd been wrong, that Gabe, with his fear of intimacy and abandonment issues, was right.

This was better. Really. It was better being alone in that bed, for the past three nights.

But these few weeks with him back in her arms had scattered the previous five years like birds, as if they'd never happened. His empty side of the bed was a gaping wound all over again.

And despite her efforts, she wasn't convinced that it was better feeling as if she couldn't breathe every time they were in the same room. Or that it was better waiting with pounding heart and cold hands for him to enter the room so she could pretend he wasn't there.

"Hey," Cameron said over her shoulder, while she worked mindlessly on a bowl of egg whites. "Is that supposed to be meringue?"

She looked down to see egg whites the consistency of library glue around her fork.

Disgusted with herself, she threw the bowl down on the counter.

"You…okay?" Cameron asked just as Gabe walked in the door, crossed the corner of the kitchen as if no one was there and slammed the door of his office shut.

She and Cameron watched and flinched at the noise.

"What's with him?" Cameron asked and Alice, sad and sick of being sad, swore. Like a sailor. A sailor who only knew swearwords.

Cameron's eyebrows skyrocketed.

"Sorry," she muttered. "I'm just…frustrated."

"Is it the wedding?" he asked. "I mean, because we're behind on the prep or something?" He was so worried that he might have something to do with what was wrong that her heart went out to him.

Six weeks ago this faith, this pressure he put on her—to be at least a participant in this relationship, to give him the smallest crumbs of affection and loyalty—would have sent her running for the door. Right now she wanted to hug him. She wanted to promise that nothing else would hurt him.

As much as that was a lie.

"Not at all," she assured him. "We're ahead of schedule. The families arrive in five days and all we need to do is figure out what to serve them the first night they're here."

He nodded, fidgeting slightly with the tie on his apron.

"Did you have an idea?"

"Well, I've been looking at your books, you know…" He pointed to her shelf of cookbooks and grabbed her old family one, grease spattered and dirty. "I like this one." He flipped to the grilled rabbit stuffed with parma ham and herbs.

"Rabbit?"

"Max said it tastes like chicken. We could serve it with this." He turned the page to the delicious springtime risotto.

"Yeah, but rabbit?"

"It's probably a dumb idea." Defeated, he shut the book and started to put it back on the shelf.

It might very well be the least appropriate meal to greet them with, she thought. Time intensive and hard work for just the two of them. Heavy and oddly paired and—

What did it matter? she wondered suddenly. In the long run the Crimpsons would forget that meal, but Cameron would never forget the chance to put this meal together.

Sometimes the greater good, the real payoff was hidden behind compromise, lost among the wrong priorities.

Alice braced herself against the counter as the new reality of her life settled in around her.

Look at me, she thought. *Look at me with this boy. Before I came here I never would have sacrificed something for his feelings. Oh my God, three nights ago I told Gabe I would adopt.*

She put her hand to her forehead. When did this happen?

She'd been focused so hard on Gabe, on making them work, that she'd missed what was truly important. She was over the past. Well, maybe not over, but getting over it. Those children didn't haunt her. Adoption sounded like a good idea, it still did, with or without Gabe. She wanted a family and was ready to get it, find it. Beg, borrow and steal it.

She was sober. Working.

She was happy.

"Rabbit it is." She nodded, grabbing the cookbook. "I'm going to need you to call our butcher and get this set up for fourteen people. And we're going to need a lesson in risotto."

He looked at her, slack jawed. "You sure? I mean, I could screw it up—"

"Yep, but that's how you learn."

Cameron took a deep breath and took the book. "Can I work the grill?"

"Not on your life."

Gabe opened the office door and stormed out into the dining room, again pretending the two of them weren't there.

She saw him with new eyes, and while it hurt, while her whole body hurt from the force with which she wished they could work it out, she knew they wouldn't, not until he got where she was.

Pretending the past never happened didn't make it go away. His mother leaving, the babies dying, the marriage falling apart, they all ate away at him and he'd never let anyone close again until he figured it out.

She watched him go and felt her heart strain after him.

"You know what my dad taught me?" Cameron asked.

"I can't even imagine," she said, trying to pull herself together.

"You can't make someone love you," he said. His eyes were far too old, too all seeing for a boy his age. "I tried and tried," he said, and shrugged.

I love Gabe, she realized. *I always will, but there's nothing more I can do.*

Alice sighed and before Cameron could flinch or run away she hugged him. Hard.

"I'm so glad you're here," she said. "I'm glad I met you."

Awkwardly, carefully, Cameron hugged her back.

ALICE LOADED the herbs and vegetables needed for Cameron's meal into the backseat of her car. She'd come here, to Athens Organics, on a two-part mission. Get veggies. Apologize to Daphne.

But it wasn't as easy as she'd thought it would be.

It wasn't as though there was a Hallmark card dedicated to this kind of thing.

Sorry my ex-husband dumped you to date me, only to dump me, too.

Too bad we fell for the same intimacyphobe, wanna chat?

"How are the wedding plans going?" Daphne asked, brushing the dirt off her hands onto the seat of her jeans.

"So far so good." Alice shielded her eyes with her hand so she could better see Daphne, gauging if the woman was furious or not. So far it didn't seem so. "But that usually means we're missing something."

"Wedding?" Helen asked, looking up from what seemed to be an intricate sketch she was drawing in the dirt with her shoe. "What wedding?"

"At the inn," Alice said, smiling at the little girl. Maybe coming here had a three-part goal. Apologize. Get food. Test acceptance of the past, by standing in the company of this little girl who would be the age of her own daughter.

And so far, judging by how badly she wanted to straighten Helen's ponytail and squeeze her, she was doing okay.

"Can we go?" Helen asked her mom.

"Sorry, sweetie, but—"

"Of course," Alice interjected, surprising everyone, most of all herself. She had no business inviting people to the wedding. But she wasn't really going to let that stop her. She could handle the Fish-Stick Princess on behalf of this little girl.

"Are you sure that's okay?" Daphne asked.

"Why not," Alice said, tapping into this new attitude of hers. She felt breezy and fluid, expansive and loving. Toward everyone.

"I've never been to a wedding!" Helen cried. "Will we dance?"

"Absolutely!"

"Will there be flowers?"

"They're being delivered and planted right now."

"Mommy! Mommy! Can we go? Can we?" She grabbed her mother's hand and nearly knocked her off balance with her hopping and leaping.

"We can stop by," she said in a stern voice. "We can see how the inn looks and then we'll leave."

"We can dance?"

"One dance."

It was enough for Helen, who went spinning off into the backyard.

Daphne eyed her sideways, and Alice smiled. "It will be fine. There are other kids invited and I'll double-check with the bride."

"That's not what I'm worried about," Daphne said. "You're a different woman today than you were the last time I saw you. I take it things with you and Gabe worked out?"

Alice's heart spasmed and gushed hot blood, proving she wasn't as okay with their breakup as she wanted to pretend. She swallowed back the sudden pain and shook her head. "Nope," she said. "We crashed and burned, like we always do."

"So? What's with this happy version of the bitter chef?"

She smiled at the description and was glad the bitterness was gone.

"I realized I can't change him. He's got to do it himself. So, I took the energy I was throwing his way and used it to make myself happy."

"And it's working?"

"Most of the time." Alice was again blindsided by a swell of feelings for Gabe. "I wish things were different, but—" She took a shaky breath and Daphne touched her arm, forestalling her.

"Good for you."

Alice laughed. "Well, we'll see about that. But I'm serious about you two coming to the wedding. I swear, they won't even notice."

"Well." Daphne looked out after her daughter who was showing one of the farm employees a spectacular twirl. "I don't think I could keep her away." They both laughed and it felt so good to do it that Alice nearly wept.

Jeez, I'm emotional, she thought, and got into her car before she cried like a baby in front of Daphne.

GABE WAS MAD. He was mad at the landscapers who had showed up late and were taking their time planting the flowers around the property and managed to destroy the grass in front of cottage four.

But mostly he was mad at Max.

"Go away," he said for perhaps the twentieth time.

"Gabe, I'm telling you, we've got to talk about this."

"We already did." Gabe stepped away and bent to reposition the orange, yellow and red daylilies that were going to be planted around the gazebo.

"Jesus, you're stubborn."

Gabe swung incredulous eyes up at his brother. "Hello, pot," he muttered.

"Dad is acting different. Something has happened."

"Dad has been acting different all spring. We figured it out—Mom contacted him. That's it."

"Yeah, but have you noticed that he stopped talking about her? And he's walking around whistling—"

"He realized we were right and that it's better to just leave it alone." He decided to go see how the flower beds around the entrance to the lodge were doing, hoping his brother would give up and head back to his cave in the woods, or wherever he'd been spending most of his time.

But Max grabbed him and the anger that was simmering in Gabe's bloodstream boiled over.

"What the hell is wrong with you?" Gabe snapped, knocking Max's hands loose. "Dad's better, he's not moping around like some teenager. Leave it alone."

Max blinked at him. "You're like one of those birds that keeps his head in the sand all the time. Don't you wonder why he's acting better? Do you think it just magically happened? And what about Alice? Why's she—"

Gabe took off again, he didn't want to listen to this. He didn't have to. It was his inn. "You're fired," he said. "Go bother someone else."

Max stepped out in front of him and Gabe, who knew he'd never win a fistfight with Max—hadn't since he was seven—decided he didn't care.

He punched his brother right in the face. Max staggered back and Gabe, his hand on fire and his anger only growing, stalked past him.

Max tackled him from behind. Gabe landed on the ground with an *"ufff!"* and possibly a cracked rib. Max rolled him over and sat on him, using his knees to hold Gabe's hands down.

"Dirty trick!" Gabe hollered, bucking up only to be shoved back down by his bigger former-cop brother.

"Yeah, well, you deserve it."

"Get the hell off me."

"No."

Gabe bucked and twisted and managed to get one solid punch to his brother's stomach, knocked him off balance and rolled over him, digging his elbows into Max's sides, rubbing his face in the dirt. But victory was short and soon Max had him pinned.

"Mom left on a Tuesday," he said and Gabe scrambled to get free, but Max grabbed his leg and pulled him back. "She kissed us good-night, remember? She sat on your bed and told us a joke about a penguin and a chicken.

"Shut up."

"We went downstairs that morning and we sat in our places and we waited for what seemed like hours—"

"Max, I'm serious." Something was cracking in his chest, that rib maybe. His stupid brother, of course, would break his ribs. He tried to rub away the pain. "You are so fired."

"We did that every morning for two weeks. You refused to go to school, remember? You made her pancakes every day and we watched them get cold on the table. Ring any bells in that stupid head?"

"No!"

"You stopped eating and I did whatever you did. Finally Dad begged you to eat something and you said you'd only eat if Mom came back and that's when he told us that she wasn't going to come back. You said 'Never?' And Dad nodded, crying his eyes out and I waited for you to cry. I waited, and I waited, and you just watched Dad, then finally you said, 'Good.'"

Gabe couldn't breathe, the earth wasn't at his back and he was flung into empty space, a free fall into nothing.

"You said *good*." Max shook his head, rolled away from Gabe but he still couldn't stand up. All his bones were broken. The dam shattered and the past swept him up and away. "I couldn't believe it. Dad tried to tell you not to be so angry but you wouldn't hear it. I've never seen you grieve for Mom. Ever."

Gabe lay on the grass and stared up at the sky, the memory as fresh as if she'd left him yesterday.

"I still feel that way," he whispered. "I know he wants us to see her, but—" he shook his head "—I can't."

Max flopped onto his back beside Gabe and neither of them mentioned how odd this was, two grown men lying on a lawn after trying to beat the hell out of each other.

"You know, I've tried and tried to think of why she would leave. Were we bad? Did Dad do something wrong? Was it another man?"

"I don't know. I remember she cried a lot."

"You do?" Gabe asked, stunned. "I don't remember that at all."

Max shrugged. "We were kids, who knows if it's real or not."

"What do you think?" Gabe asked Max. "Do you want to see her?"

Max shrugged. "I kind of want to yell at her. Tell her what she did to us and Dad." They were silent for

a long time. "What happened with Alice?" Max
asked.

Gabe felt that anger well up in him again.
"Nothing." He stood and walked away, wiping the
grass off his pants as he went as if they were
memories that clung so determinedly.

"You never grieved for her, either," Max said. "Or
those babies."

"Shut up, Max."

"You know I'm right."

Gabe broke into a run toward the lodge.

He stepped into the kitchen from the dining room
just as Alice came in the back door, her arms filled
with a box of vegetables.

"Gabe!" Her brow knit with concern. "What
happened to your face?"

He touched the corner of his split and bloodied lip
and winced. "My brother," he said.

"What's wrong?" She slid the box onto the
counter and crossed her arms over her chest. The
kitchen swirled with tension, with everything they
wanted to say and do. He wanted to fold her into his
arms, have her kiss away the pain of his bruises and
at the same time he wanted to bundle her up and send
her home. That dichotomy was tearing him apart.
Tearing apart the whole damn inn.

"Gabe." Her face softened. She knew what he was
going through and had the power to make it better.
But he knew what she wanted. She wanted to repeat
the past, hash it out, pull it into the present and go
on from there.

"Do you have a replacement?" he asked, stone-faced and angry, and she shut down in response.

Stop caring, he wanted to say. *Just give up on us. We're not worth the pain.*

"I'm looking, Gabe," she said as calmly as she could. "Tim Munez called me back yesterday but I've been too busy to get in touch with him."

"Tim would be good."

She bit her lip and nodded, turning back to her vegetables. "I have work to do," she said.

He watched her take the box to the fridge and start putting away her produce. He knew he needed to apologize, he wasn't handling any of this well.

"Alice, I don't mean to be so—"

"I get it, Gabe," she interrupted, throwing spinach into the bottom drawer of the fridge. "Everything will be easier when I'm gone. For both of us."

"Something like that," he said and, with the die cast, he finally turned away, feeling worse than when he'd come in.

CHAPTER FIFTEEN

"IT'S BEAUTIFUL, Gabe." Gloria Crimpson and her heavily pregnant daughter toured the grounds and Gabe listened to her with half an ear. "It's exactly as you promised."

"I'm glad you like it," he murmured. Gloria looked over her pink Chanel-clad shoulder at him. He smiled, trying to reassure her. Trying to get in the game. This was a big day for him and he felt as though he watched it all through a fog he couldn't get clear of.

"David's folks should get here tonight," Savanah said, so in love and so young that the prospect only brought joy to her, despite Gloria's pinched lips pinching farther. "I can't wait to show them the cabins. They are so amazing!"

Gabe wished he could snap out of this funk and revel in the success of everything. But the funk was stubborn and his brother walking around with a shiner and Alice suddenly being Mary Sunshine as if this weren't their last week of seeing each other, as if it didn't matter that she would be leaving soon, didn't help.

"Thank you," he said. "They turned out even better than I had thought, too."

"When do the decorations go up?" Savanah asked. "They looked so beautiful on the sketches."

"The night before," he answered.

"Your chef made them?" she asked and when he nodded she laughed. "That's a talented chef."

You don't know the half of it, he thought, wishing she were here instead of him right now. In the past few days dealing with these women she'd been taking the lead, possessing a sudden sweetness compared to his unabating sour attitude. He'd thought she was different during their brief rekindling—laughing, working hard, loving her work. But this new Alice—welcoming and open and gregarious—he had never seen her. Ever.

His attraction to her doubled and redoubled every time he saw her hug Cameron, or offer the delivery guys coffee and cinnamon rolls. Every time she teased his brother and dad as if they were her own.

She needed to leave. Soon.

"Not judging by last night's meal," Gloria, whose acidic voice, normally loaded to capacity with superiority and judgment, managed to sharpen just a bit more on.

"It was wonderful," Savanah insisted. "I've never had rabbit before."

"I should say not. You weren't raised in the hills."

Gloria kept up her pace across the grounds despite her high heels and narrow skirt. Gabe and Savanah lagged behind momentarily.

"You'll have to excuse my mom," she said, stroking the round mound of her belly. "She's not taking this pregnancy and small nonsociety wedding very well."

"I hadn't noticed." He tried to say it magnanimously but it came out coated in sarcasm.

"Ah." She swiped her long curtain of shiny blond hair over her shoulder like a woman in a shampoo ad. "Our unflappable host finally shows some cracks." She said it with a laugh so Gabe didn't jump to his own defense. He didn't have the energy.

"We tried to book three other small inns along the Hudson and after the second conversation with my mother all three of them backed out." The girl seemed to expect this reaction without any rancor and he found himself watching her, slightly astonished by the reality of the Fish-Stick Princess.

"But not you." She shook her head and whistled. "I resorted to pink swans and sushi boats and you still didn't crumble."

Gabe gaped at her. "You wanted us to back out of the contract?"

She smiled and patted Gabe's shoulder. "David and I always wanted to elope. This wedding is a compromise for my parents and I was trying my best to weasel out of it." She winced comically and Gabe felt some true affection for the surprising Savanah. "Not the most honorable thing, but I couldn't imagine my marriage, the creation of my family, taking place in front of seven hundred people I don't care about."

"I understand," Gabe said as they strolled. "It's a

very personal thing. I hope having your wedding here won't seem like such a bad compromise."

"It won't be. This is so beautiful, I couldn't have even imagined it. I am so grateful you didn't get run off by those pink swans."

He laughed and patted her shoulder. "It takes more than pink swans to chase me off," he said and swallowed.

"I'm glad."

"Savanah!" Gloria shouted from the newly planted rose garden. "What's the problem? Are you okay?"

"I'm fine, Mom." Savanah rolled her eyes and picked up her pace. "You know in the end it only proves something I've learned from my mother."

"What's that?" Gabe asked, matching her stride.

"That I can't control everything. Sometimes you have to embrace what the world puts in your way."

Gabe stopped for a moment, the world slightly tilted under his feet.

"Gabe?" Savanah placed a hand on his arm.

"Sorry." He smiled without much heart, wondering what other surprises were in store for him this week.

ALICE SENT OUT the last of the lamb loins, served with the cucumber riata and fresh tomatoes. Elizabeth, one of the waitstaff, opened the door to the dining room and the sound of laughter came flooding in. The bride's and groom's parents certainly got along, though Alice wasn't surprised. David Barister and his folks, when she'd met them today, seemed

to be truly lovely people. Lovely enough to round off
Gloria Crimpson's sharp edges.

Of course, the bottles of wine they were going
through didn't hurt.

She tossed the pan in the sink and the gamy smell
of cooked lamb and garlic punched her in the face.
She staggered away and tried to breathe fresh air
before she lost her dinner all over the kitchen.

Oh God, she thought, swallowing nausea and bile.
This place is getting to me. I need a vacation.

The phone in Gabe's office rang.

"Cameron?" she said, and her apprentice looked
up from the lemon torte he was setting out to serve
at room temperature. "I'll be right back."

"Okay," he said. "I'm going to play with the
grill," he joked.

Alice threw the towel from her shoulder at him and
went to grab the phone on Gabe's desk by the third ring.

"Riverview Inn, this is Alice."

"Hey, Alice. It's Tim Munez."

"Tim!" The nausea in her stomach tightened into
knots and she sat in Gabe's chair, trying to ignore the
smell of him that wrapped around her like an
embrace. "How are you?"

"Fantastic." Tim said and Alice smiled. He was an
infectiously cheerful man. The two years they'd
shared a kitchen in Albany had been two of the most
fun years of her career. "Really good. How are things
on that mountain?"

"Better every week, Tim." She nearly laughed
at the lie.

"Well, the spread in *New York Magazine* made that place look like heaven on earth."

"It is, Tim. So, have you thought about coming to work here?"

"Yep, and I'd love to do it."

She sighed and melted into the chair, a thousand pounds lifted from her, while another thousand re-settled on her shoulders.

This is it. I'm leaving. It's over.

"But—" Tim said and her muscles reseized.

"But what?"

"I can't come on the date you wanted. I need two more weeks. I'm training my replacement here and it's going a bit slower than planned."

Alice spun and looked at the calendar on the wall behind her and did some quick math. She could do it. She could stay an extra two weeks.

Her heart pounded. It was a curse and a blessing. She was torn right down the middle between wanting to be here and wanting to put this place in her rearview mirror.

"No problem, Tim. We'll see you at the end of June."

"Excellent. I can't wait."

Alice hung up and continued to study the calendar. The wedding weekend was the tenth, which would make Tim's arrival the twenty-fourth, and she would stick around two days and—

She blinked.

Today was the fifth.

Her period was two days late.

As if summoned, the nausea gurgled in her stomach and she raced to the bathroom to throw up.

HOPE, FEAR and dread churned through Alice's brain, eating away at her nerves for the next three days. Every time she went to the bathroom she was sure she would see blood. Sure that her period was only delayed by stress and the fact that she had no appetite whatsoever.

But every time, there was no blood, and hope would replace dread. Then upon thinking about a baby, about miscarrying again, fear would replace hope and the vicious cycle would spin.

I should tell Gabe, she thought as she sugared flowers to place on the wedding cake. She took a purple pansy, dipped it in egg white and sugar and placed it on a wire rack to dry.

I should tell him.

But she didn't.

Another day went by and her period still didn't come. Guests began to arrive. Her parents came in the evenings and helped finish the prep work and it was all background noise, to the constant conversation she had in her head.

I should tell him.

There's no point in telling him if I don't know for sure. Why get him all worked up?

She never bought a pregnancy test—she put it off and put it off.

Another day went by.

Hope was unfettered, a giant bird loose in her body. She stopped drinking coffee.

"Are you kidding?" Max asked as he waited, cup in hand, for the coffee machine to stop brewing one early morning with the sky just beginning to lighten. "No coffee?"

"It's bad for you."

Max scowled at her. "You've lost it."

Find out! she thought. *Just find out for sure.*

But then there were problems with her decorations. In storage a panel of silk tore from its frame and she and Max spent hours repairing it.

"You all right?" he asked while she mended the silk that had torn and he hammered a new nail into the corner joint.

"I'm great." She smiled at him. "Why?"

"You seem a little juiced."

"Juiced?"

"Yeah, like you're on something. And I know it's not coffee."

"Right." She laughed. "I've managed to find the time to start a drug habit."

"I thought maybe it was Gabe. Maybe you fixed things."

Hope, that giant bird on the loose fell like a stone in her stomach. Reality crashed in around her and she couldn't laugh. Her face felt suddenly paralyzed.

I might be pregnant with Gabe's baby. Again. The nightmare might start all over. Again. She rubbed her forehead. What if she told him and he asked her to marry him, then she lost the baby? Again.

She swallowed back a sudden painful sob.

This was a horrific roller coaster she couldn't get off.

It was ludicrous that she could be pregnant after the years, money and procedures dedicated to getting this way. But it was like those women in that counseling group who, years after accepting their fates, ended up knocked up.

When you let go of the obsession, they'd said, laughing and flushed with their unbelievable luck, *it happens.*

She'd sat there and doubted them.

And yet here she was. Poised on this terrible precipice.

Do I want to try this again? Go through all of this again?

But, hope tried to say, what if she took it easy? What if she went on modified bed rest, and was really careful and Gabe could help her?

She shook her head, clearing hope's voice from her brain.

I don't even know for sure, she rationalized.

"Alice?" Max asked. He touched her shoulder and she flinched. "You all right?"

"Yeah." She sighed. "I—" She swallowed and felt the sudden burn of tears. "I'll be right back."

She stood and ran for the bathroom, feeling Max's suspicious gaze on her as she ran.

THIS IS CRAZY, Gabe told himself. *You're crazy. The stress has finally eaten your brain and now you are standing outside your ex-wife's cottage like a stalker.*

Worse, this was his third night out here.

He felt as if the proverbial other shoe was poised

above his head, waiting for him to relax so it could fall and crush him. Alice didn't look good these days and he wondered if she was drinking again. He told himself he was out here, watching her in her cabin to make sure she wasn't. But the truth was, this was the only place he could actually take full breaths of air.

Everything was going fine. The wedding was four days away and the details that he checked and re-checked obsessively so as to keep thoughts of Alice and his mother away seemed straightforward and taken care of.

So what the hell is wrong with me? Why am I here?

Because in his office, his stomach burned as if filled with acid. And in his room, his chest ached and he couldn't sleep.

He watched David and Savanah, day in and day out, young, in love, expecting their first baby, and missing Alice felt like an open wound.

It would be better when she was gone, when she wasn't constantly there reminding him of things they would never have.

But then where will I go to breathe?

"Gabe?"

He whirled away from the cabin he'd been watching only to find Alice on the trail behind him, a plastic grocery-store bag in her hand which, when he looked at it, she tucked behind her back.

"Did you need something?" she asked.

He nearly laughed, nearly fell on his knees under

the force of all the things he wanted. He opened his mouth but only a rattling gasp came out. Silence.

"Gabe?" Her voice was that soft pet, the delicious stroke against his body, and he wanted to pull her into his arms one last time. Banish the demons, the past, the specter of the future.

"Just wanted to make sure everything was going okay," he said. "We've been so busy I never get a chance to see you."

"I know. It's like I blink and three days have passed. But everything seems to be going really well."

"That's making me nervous."

She laughed and the tension in him balled tighter.

"Oh, I forgot to tell you, Tim Munoz has taken the job. He'll be here on the twenty-fourth, so I can stay or—"

"That's fine. Thank you."

He was too abrupt, too close to apologizing, to asking for another chance, another doomed chance.

"Good night," he said and walked away, into the dark.

"Good night, Gabe." Her voice chased him all the way back to the lodge, to his empty cold bed.

THE WORLD CRACKED, opened and then closed again, different now than it had been before Alice looked at the stick. Pregnant.

She tore open the plastic around the second test, downed a glass of water, peed, waited and got the same blue plus sign in the window.

The earth dazzled, sparkled; her small cottage was the epicenter of the universe. Of creation.

She pulled in air that tasted like sugar and salt. Her heart pumped blood through her body, through the small tadpole deep in her belly.

"A baby." She sighed, the words delicious on her tongue, the prospect all she would need to sustain her. For months. Years. Her life.

She put her hand to her mouth to stifle the laughing sobs. The giddy screams of joy and panic. Alice collapsed onto the toilet, slid sideways when she miscalculated and she landed on the floor. She lay back, flung her arms out and laughed at the ceiling.

A baby.

The world was filled with blessings and second chances.

Gabe.

She put her hands to her face, kicked her feet against the wall in a sudden thrilled spasm.

Gabe standing in front of her cabin, looking for the whole world, like a boy lost in a mall. She could give him a second chance, them a second chance. Another shot to make it work.

Tears burned down her face into her mouth, a champagne of hope and wish.

But soon the tiles grew cold against her back and what would be settled around her like a curtain, a screen showing old home movies of their life before the divorce.

She'd tell him she was pregnant and Gabe, honorable and longing for a family, would propose.

She didn't want that marriage. She didn't want him that way, tied to her by this fragile pregnancy. What she wanted them to have had to be real.

Gabe couldn't know. Not yet.

CHAPTER SIXTEEN

"I'VE REQUESTED A few more servers from the catering company in Albany," Gabe said to Alice and the rest of his staff in the kitchen the morning of the rehearsal dinner. Alice barely listened, still blissfully distracted by her pregnancy.

Gabe's confidence in this staff, including Cameron and her folks, was tangible. He treated everyone like a team member and they listened to him like the good boss he was. Affection, a great tidal wave of love for everyone in this room, washed over her, and she bit her lip to keep her eyes from welling with happy tears.

"These people are drinkers and we're going to need the extra hands just to get rid of the bottles and empty glasses," Gabe said. "We don't want it to look like a teamsters' picnic."

"We've added a few heartier appetizers," her father said. "Maybe we can keep the drinkers from getting too drunk too fast."

What a guy, she thought, looking at her dad. She wished she could tell him he was going to be a grandfather, but the past had taught her to keep the joy silent until it was a sure thing.

She looked at Gabe and felt paralyzed by the choice she had to make, the news she was keeping from him. Was it for his own good? Or hers?

"Excellent idea, Michael," Gabe said, and the meeting broke up, everyone heading to their last-minute duties. Alice watched Gabe head to his office and took a step to follow. To say what? To do what? She didn't know, she just knew she wanted to be close to him.

"Can I talk to you for a second?" Max asked, touching her elbow slightly.

"Sure," she said, eager for the distraction. "What's up?"

"Outside," Max said and opened the door for her to step into the beautiful June morning.

Surprised, she walked over to the small hill with the view of the lawn and gazebo, which were getting decked out in fine style.

"What's going on with you?" Max asked, cutting to the chase.

Alice nearly blanched. "What do you mean?"

"I mean, what's going on? You're—" He blew out a breath. "You're happy. Gabe's a wreck. I haven't seen either of you like this since—" He stopped suddenly and Alice could actually see the math in his head, the wheels turning. "Are you pregnant?"

For a moment she was able to pretend she was going to lie about this, that she had the capability to keep a straight face when fireworks were going off in her head. But then she smiled.

Max flung his hands in the air. "That explains it. Gabe's just worried about another miscarriage."

"Gabe doesn't know."

Max's mouth fell open slightly. "You haven't told him? You're pregnant after everything you two went through and you're not telling him?"

"Yet. I'm not telling him *yet*." She stepped closer and considering how right she believed she was, she had no problem standing up to her tough former brother-in-law. "If he and I are going to make it work, he needs to come back to me for me. Not because I'm pregnant and he's trying to do the right thing, or to get his shot at a family. It has to be about us, first and foremost."

Max stared at her a long time, and Alice kept his gaze. "Sounds reasonable. But he's got to know at some point. You can't walk away from him with his baby."

"What if I lose the baby, Max? What then?"

He shook his head, clearly understanding her dilemma. "So, what are you going to do?"

"I am going to…" She took a long breath and let it out. "I'm going to give him another chance to try to make it work without knowing about the baby. If he's still too scared, then I'm going to leave and talk to my doctor and then…" She took another long breath. She really hadn't thought this out very well. "If everything seems good, I'll contact him."

"When?"

"When I think it's right."

"You're going to do it all by yourself?"

"If he's too scared to try to make it work with me before I go, then—" she swallowed "—yes."

He shook his head. "Not acceptable."

"Excuse me?"

"First of all, you shouldn't do all of it alone. Bed rest and doctor's appointments and whatever else you're going to have to do to carry this baby the whole way and, second—" Max's eyes went soft for a moment "—it's Gabe's baby."

Her stomach melted into her feet. "I know, Max. But it would kill me to have him ask me to stay because of a baby. We did that before and it failed miserably. I need to know it's about me. Us. That we could make it together if I lost this baby."

Max didn't blink. He didn't move until finally he nodded, once. Definitively.

"You have two months and if Gabe doesn't hear from you, I'm sending him to you to tell him."

"Max—"

"That's the deal, Alice. He's my brother and if you won't look out for him, I will."

Alice nodded. It was fair. It was ugly and weird, but it was fair. And she truly hoped, in the end, it wouldn't come to that.

"Hey, hey." He pulled her into his arms, a big hard hug that made it difficult to breathe. "Congrats, Alice," he murmured against her hair. "I know how bad you want this. But remember, so does Gabe."

"I know," she whispered. It was the thought that plagued her.

THE REHEARSAL DINNER rolled around and Gabe had asked Alice to play hostess with him, so she kept her chef whites in the closet and pulled out the one dress she'd brought for the event. A black kimono-style dress with an embroidered cherry tree along the side. It skimmed over her body, formfitting but not too tight. She endured, for the sake of fashion, a pair of modest high heels, that made her feet hurt just looking at them.

She kept her hair down, brushed to a blue-black shine and for once, not an unruly curl in sight.

At the last minute, she added the mascara she knew her mother would hound her over and a bit of red lip gloss.

All of which was worth the effort when she walked into the dining room, and Gabe, giving last-minute instructions to the two bartenders working the event, glanced at her then did a quick double take.

Patrick, looking dashing in a suit and tie, whistled. Max, still in his flannel shirt and fleece, looked at her and mouthed, "Tonight."

She scowled at him and joined Gabe at the bar.

"You look beautiful," he said.

"You're not too shabby yourself," she said, straightening the collar on his black shirt. Her hand lingered, touched the plane of his chest, felt the thump of his heart under her hand.

"You okay?" he asked, just barely touching her wrist.

"Yes." She lifted her hand to her forehead. "I am, but I—"

"Hold that thought, Al. We've got mother of the bride at three o'clock, looking mad."

Gabe stepped away to intercept Gloria, and Alice sagged briefly against the bar.

"Club soda, please," she said to the bartender and she avoided Max's pointed look.

The rehearsal dinner passed in a blur. The sea bass was well received, but perhaps not hearty enough to counter all the alcohol the party went through. Alice was called into duty to help various women with safety pins and tissues. She directed a drunk bridesmaid out back with the rest of the smokers and noticed the great-aunt of the bride was sitting alone at one of the dark tables while the speeches got started. She brought the woman a cup of tea just as the sound system screeched and Patrick was called into duty to fix it.

"That's not a good sound," Alice joked, setting the teacup in front of the older woman.

"If that's the only thing that goes wrong, sweetheart," she said, "you'll be laughing. So far this is the most beautiful event I've ever seen."

"Well, there's tomorrow. Things could still go plenty wrong."

She patted Alice's hands. "I'm ninety years old and I've seen a lot of weddings. You have to trust me. You and your husband have done a very nice job."

Alice was about to protest their marital state but she looked up to see Gabe in the shadows, his bright eyes on her, burning her through the darkness, and she couldn't say anything.

AT THREE IN THE MORNING, Gabe shot up in bed, startled out of a fitful sleep by what sounded like a gang of fighting toddlers. He pulled on the dress pants he'd shucked just a few hours ago and slid into his work boots before racing out into the front yard to see what was killing what and making so much noise.

Alice, in sweatpants and a chef jacket, her hair a wild halo around her head, was already there.

"What the hell is that noise?" she asked, peering into the dark, flashlight in hand. "It's freaking me out."

"I don't know," Gabe murmured. He turned toward the tent they'd erected for the ceremony only to see the canvas sides roll as if they were being buffeted by gale-force winds. "But it's in my tent."

They took a few cautious steps in that direction before Max was suddenly with them, in boxer shorts, work boots and a T-shirt.

"You guys making all that noise?" He growled the words, rubbing at his whiskered face.

"It's coons," Patrick said, stomping past them armed with two old hockey sticks, one of which he tossed to Gabe as if he were John Wayne and they were about to fight marauding invaders.

"Raccoons?" Gabe asked. "In my tent?"

They pulled open the front flap to a scene of heart-breaking destruction. Most of the chairs were on their sides, and the topiaries with the fancy bows that had taken hours to tie were toppled over and half eaten.

"Oh, no," Alice cried, and Gabe, furious and exhausted, caught sight of one of the giant mutant raccoons eating a bow and chased it, stick held high, out of the tent.

All along he'd expected something to go wrong. Some miscalculation or dropped detail. He hadn't counted on Mother Nature sending rabid minions to destroy the event he'd sunk way too much time and money into.

Max joined in, clapping and yelling and corralling the animals in a corner so Patrick could chase them out one of the flaps.

Alice screamed. Gabe whirled and found her cornered by one of the animals, using a chair to keep him away from the topiary she was trying to repair.

"There's a whole forest out there!" she cried. "Get. Scat. Shoo."

Gabe charged, wielding his hockey stick like a giant ax, and the raccoon abandoned his campaign, turned tail and ran down the center aisle and out the front of the tent.

In silence Gabe took in the destruction. Half the topiaries were toast. The ribbons were a mess. The chairs were filthy and he'd stepped in raccoon poop. They all had. Raccoon poop was everywhere.

"No." He moaned. "No. This is a disaster."

"We'll get it fixed up, Gabe." Alice said, patting his shoulder. "I'll go put on a pot of coffee and get some rags and hot water."

"I'll come with you," Max said. "We need some trash bags."

"No one will ever know, son," Patrick told him and started righting the folding chairs and picking up what was left of the flower decorations.

BY TEN A.M., moments before the bride walked down the aisle, no one would have believed that hours ago the scene had been chaos. Carnage. The stuff of wedding disaster.

Nope, Gabe thought with satisfaction and a deep exhaustion. *You'd never guess I was picking up raccoon crap in my underwear in the middle of the night.*

Grandmothers were escorted in to Pachelbel's Canon in D and Gabe stifled a yawn under his palm.

"Looks good," Alice said from behind him. He turned, relieved in some deep place to have her next to him. The way he had been all night as they worked side by side until dawn, fixing the tent.

"Well, your idea to spread out the topiaries and scrap the bows altogether certainly made it easier."

"I only suggested it so I wouldn't be on poop patrol," she said. Her hand on his arm burned through the sleeve of his black jacket and the white linen shirt beneath that to his skin, muscle and bone. "Its looks beautiful, Gabe."

Just a touch and he was branded.

"Well, I couldn't have done it without you," he told her, making a point of not looking at her. He could do this. He could tell her the truth and say goodbye as long as he didn't have to say it to her face. "I owe you."

She didn't say anything and her silence forced him to glance at her. Tears trembled on her lashes, turning her dark eyes to obsidian.

"Alice?" he asked, startled by this sudden emotion. "What's—"

She rose on her toes and pressed a wet kiss to his cheek. "You don't owe me anything, but we have to talk."

He shook his head, knowing instinctively what she meant. "There's nothing to say, Alice. You know that. We've—"

"A conversation. That's what you owe me." Something fierce in her wet gaze made him nod his head.

"Okay," he agreed softly as the sweet swell of "Ode to Joy" started. The bride arrived at the tent and the audience gasped, coming to its feet.

THE MUSIC PUMPED and the lights twinkled. Couples danced, bridesmaids kicked off their shoes and Gabe quietly folded in the corner. He rubbed his eyes and wished he could put his head down on the table and sleep for a week.

"Hey, Gabe." A little voice at his elbow made him open his eyes. Helen. He smiled, glad that Alice had invited Daphne and her daughter, because the little girl had twirled nonstop for hours. The bride had noticed her initially and asked her to dance and Helen had leaped around like a jack-in-the-box come to life.

"Hi, sweetie," he said and pulled on her long ponytail. "You look like a princess. Have I told you that?"

"Like a thousand times, but I want to dance." She jumped up and down in her scuffed black patent shoes.

"Then we dance," he said. Luckily, the music changed and the singer crooned an old blues song about love coming at last.

He spun her dramatically and dipped her upside down and sang the words off-key so she'd giggle and hold on tight to the lapels of his jacket.

Finally she laid her head on his shoulder and he held her and swayed a little bit, his heart a puddle in his shoes.

"It's time to take her home," Daphne said at his elbow. "She's out like a light." Daphne looked tired but happy and still elegant in her red dress. She'd caught the eye of one of the ushers and Daphne had been out on the dance floor almost as much as her daughter. "Here," she said, reaching for her.

"I got it," Gabe whispered. "I'll take her to your car. No sense in waking her if we don't have to."

Daphne nodded and led Gabe out the front doors, grabbing her purse and shoes from under one of the tables.

"It was a beautiful night, Gabe," she said, walking to her sedan parked in the employee area behind the kitchen. "You did a great job."

"Well, it was a team effort." He deferred the glory, gladly. "Alice really deserves the kudos."

"She told me about the raccoons," Daphne laughed and shook her head as she unlocked her car. "Unbelievable."

Gabe eased the little girl into her booster seat in the

backseat and it was a testament to her exhaustion that she barely stirred while Daphne clipped her in.

"How is it going with Alice?" Daphne asked, standing up. "If you don't mind me asking."

"It's not. Going, I mean. We never should have tried in the first place."

"I'm sorry to hear that."

He tucked his hands in his pockets and nodded. *Not as sorry as me,* he thought.

She reached up and kissed his cheek. The gesture didn't even register a spark or flutter. Nothing. Daphne stepped away and he could tell in her eyes that she didn't feel anything, either.

"You need to listen when the universe tries to tell you something, I guess," she said. "You and I were meant to be friends."

"Good friends," he agreed and watched as she climbed into her car and drove away.

He wondered what the universe meant for him and Alice. What were they supposed to be?

"Gabe?"

He turned, and Alice, stepping over the small hill behind him, arrived.

He felt solemn. Sad even. His arms were heavy and empty and his chest, where the little girl had slept, cold.

"It seemed like Helen had a good time," she said and they watched the taillights disappear down the road.

He nodded, words clogged in his throat, stuck behind emotions and a sickening lack of courage.

"She's the exact age our daughter would have

been," she said and his eyes slid closed as grief lanced him.

I know.

"I won't ask you to talk about the children we didn't have," she said. "But I need you to know that I love you, Gabe," Alice whispered, her sweet voice tying ribbons around him, wrapping him up. "I am in love with you. I always have been and I probably always will be."

He swallowed and the cowardice bobbed but remained stuck. He kept his eyes on the horizon, like a seasick sailor longing for solid ground.

"I want to stay here." Her voice grew rougher, and he knew that his silence was making her angry, so he finally turned to her. She blazed and burned, casting a light that could keep him warm his entire life if he only would reach for it.

"I want to keep working on this dream." She tilted her head. "On our dream." She searched his face. "Don't you have anything to say?" Tears gathered in her eyes and he felt the same burn in his. This constant echo of emotion between them. Whatever she felt, he did, too. It was exhausting. Destructive.

"What happens when things go wrong, Alice?" he asked, his voice scorched and burned by the heat of his barely contained emotions. "What do we do when the fights start?"

"We're older now, Gabe. We're different. We'll handle it better. Look at today. We were a team today."

He nodded. "Today. But two months ago I tried to fire you because you drank too much. Are you trying to tell me that we've changed that much in two months."

"Yes. I have. I have changed that much." She waited for his answer, no doubt longing for him to finally realize that he'd changed, too. That being back together, that seeing the success of this place had cleared the old cobwebs from his head and he was ready to start a different life as a different person.

But he wasn't. He was the same. And slowly, as he watched her face, he saw her recognize that. His heart shattered when he watched the love in her eyes grow cold, turn to disbelief. Anger.

"I'm sorry," he whispered. "I can't take the risk."

"The risk that we won't have children?" she asked. "That we won't be able to adopt if it comes to that?"

He shook his head, opened his mouth. There was nothing but silence. He didn't know how to say what he felt.

"You can't take the risk of loving me and having me leave," she said. "Like your mom."

A hot tear seared down the side of his face.

"Like my mom, like those babies—" his voice cracked. "Our babies. I can't." He shook his head. 'I wanted them, too, Alice." He finally told her, an avalanche of words accompanied by more hot tears scalding his skin. "I named them when you said we should wait and see what they were like." He closed his eyes, doing his best to shove these memories of Daniel and Chloe—his children—away. He rubbed his hands in his eyes, brushing away the tears. He mentally shook himself, took a deep breath and looked Alice in the face.

"Let's stop pretending that everything is great, Alice. It's not. As a couple you and I are always on the edge of disaster and I can't live like that."

She laughed. "Everyone is on the edge of disaster. Everyone. Love puts you there. You think having a relationship with a woman you don't love is going to keep you safe?"

"Not being in a relationship with you will keep me safe," he told her and watched his words hit home. She practically shrank and he wished he could take them back to spare her this truth, but she wouldn't leave well enough alone.

She stepped backward, nearly tripped, but found her ground.

"You're a fool, Gabe," she said, turned and left.

Fool or not, he needed security, a security they'd never found together. Inside the dining room, the party raged on, his inn a success, his future, for the moment, set.

And he had never in his whole life felt so hollow.

ALICE CURLED UP on her bed, her hands cupped over her stomach as if that could protect her unborn child from all those things that could cause pain. Grief. Bone-deep loss.

She wished, stupidly, despite the rejection that she could do the same for Gabe. But it was impossible.

Grabbing the cell phone off the bedside table, she

wiped her eyes and called her parents. They'd left hours ago but she knew her dad would only be dozing in front of the TV.

"Dad," she said when he answered, sleepy and gruff.

"Hi, sweetie," he said. "Everything okay?"

She bit her lips but the tears came anyway. "No, Dad," she whispered. "I need a favor."

CHAPTER SEVENTEEN

GABE CAME DOWNSTAIRS, braced for Alice. For seeing her, for her cold shoulder and red-rimmed eyes. So when he stepped into the kitchen at dawn, the last thing he expected to see was Michael. Sharpening knives.

"Good morning, Gabe," he said over the vicious *snick-snick* of his chef's blade running along the sharpener.

"Michael." He nodded and took the long way around the giant man with knives toward the coffeepot. "Where's Alice?"

"Albany, by now, I'd imagine."

Hot coffee sloshed over his hand. "She left." It was more statement than question. And Michael nodded, eyeing the edge of his knife, like a pirate about to commit murder.

"Did she say why?"

"No." Michael turned to him. "But she asked me to fill in for the next two weeks and she was crying. Know anything about that?"

Gabe put down the coffeepot with shaking hands. It was over. Done. He didn't have to worry about seeing her again every day, about the constant temptation of knowing she was within reach.

Turning from Michael and the threat of decapitation, Gabe put his hand to his forehead, a helpless moment to get himself under control.

"Thank you, Michael,' he managed to whisper, throwing a quick smile over his shoulder, "for filling in."

Michael slapped his knife down on the butcher's block. "Jesus, you kids are killing each other."

"It's what we've always done best," Gabe said and went into his office in an effort to lose himself in work.

PATRICK DIDN'T even bother going to the gazebo when a driver finally delivered the letter. Patrick ripped it open in the driveway, reading it before the driver was even back in the car.

He'd expected a response right away. Truth be told he'd expected Iris right away. But as every day went by with no Iris and no letter, that hope turned to cement and filled his body.

>Patrick,
>Thank you. Thank you so much. I will be there, but I need time. It's not what you think. But I need a few months. I will be there. Trust me. For once, I will be there.

Patrick scowled, heartbroken and disappointed and angry that he was actually disappointed. He crumpled the letter, unable to save this one. He'd believed her earnest and genuine desire to come here, to make things right. But he should have remembered the way his wife could turn on a dime.

Now, he didn't know what to believe.

GABE STARED BLINDLY at the *Bon Appetit* spread on his desk. A rave review, pictures that made his inn look like something outside of himself, something he'd never seen before. The only reason he recognized it was because he and Alice were standing at the front doors in the first picture.

"Congratulations," Michael said, his backpack over his shoulder, ready to go. "It's a great article. You should get lots of business from it."

Gabe couldn't find the will to respond.

"Tim is going to be an excellent addition here," Michael continued, but he might as well have been speaking French. "He's got a lot of great ideas."

"How is she?" he asked off the conversation topic, but she was the only thing he thought about these days. "Alice. How is she?"

"I won't be your go-between, Gabe. My daughter is an adult. If you want to find out how she is, be an adult and call her." Michael waited for him to say something, but there was nothing to say. Finally he shook his head in disgust and left.

God, Gabe sighed and kicked away from his desk, the contact of his foot against the metal felt good. Violent.

He'd thought things would get better after Alice

left. He would find some clarity. Get back to being himself.

But nothing got better.

The final payment from the Crimpsons, along with a lovely thank-you note and photograph, arrived, followed by two phone calls from women who had been at the wedding and wanted to talk about having an event at the inn.

He didn't know what to promise them. Alice, who had made all the magic possible for the Crimpsons, was gone and the magic was absolutely absent without her.

But he talked to the new clients and made empty promises that sounded good but echoed falsely in his mouth.

Alice was right, he realized as he told these women what they wanted to hear. It's win-win until it all goes to crap.

And it had definitely gone to crap.

"Gabe." Max stood at the door, his forehead creased with concern. "What's wrong? Did you hear from Alice?"

If only. If only he'd heard from her and this ache might leave, this boulder on his chest might be rolled away.

"Did she say something? Are you going to Albany?"

"No!" Gabe yelled, the boulder making him scream. Making him crazy. "She has not called. She's gone. Let's all get on with our lives, okay?"

Max blinked at him, no doubt stunned by this sudden vehemence. "You're doing a hell of job with that," Max said. "Really moving on without her."

"Shut up," Gabe yelled. He stood up from his desk, the chair spinning out behind him to smash into the wall. Gabe shoved his brother out of the door frame, and then gripped the door as hard as he could and hurled it shut. The walls shook from the force.

Blood and anger pounded in his brain. And slamming doors wasn't enough. He kicked the empty cardboard boxes in the corner.

Still not enough.

He picked up the jar of pens on his desk and smashed it against the wall. He swept the desk lamp off, his, the shattering of glass a sweet stroke to his rage.

What is wrong with me?

Why do they always leave?

Why can't I keep the people I love close to me?

He was blind, reckless. Objects found their way against walls, under his feet. Destroyed by his hands. He didn't feel cuts or blood or physical pain.

He felt only grief—a bottomless pit of grief that could no longer be ignored.

PATRICK JUMPED BACK from the office door when it sounded as if a chair had been hurled into it.

He and Max had been standing there for the better part of ten minutes and whatever was going on behind that door was not slowing down.

"He's really going for it," Patrick said. "There can't be much left of that chair."

Max nodded and took a sip from his coffee cup that was filled with scotch. Patrick had one, too. They were preparing themselves for what would happen when Gabe finally stopped destroying his office and opened the door.

"What's going on here?" Tim, the new chef—a nice guy having a really bad first day—asked. He set down the box of kitchen stuff he'd brought in from his car and flinched as Gabe howled from behind the door, sounding like a man who had lost everything.

Which, Patrick supposed, he had.

"Is everything okay?" Tim's eyes were worried behind his dark oblong glasses. He pulled his shirt away from his belly and practically twitched from the tension in his kitchen.

"My son's just working a few things out," Patrick answered over the strains of smashing glass.

"Here," Max said, grabbing a coffee cup from the counter and filling it from the bottle of scotch at his feet. "Welcome to the Riverview Inn."

Tim took the scotch and tossed it back. "I hope it gets better than this," he muttered and they all laughed.

Finally, abruptly the office door opened and his son, shattered and bleeding from a cut on his hand and another one above his eyes, stood there.

Crying.

"Come on, son," Patrick said, feeling the bite of tears in his own eyes. "Let's get you cleaned up."

"It hurts, Dad," he whispered.

"What does, son?"

"Everything."

GABE FELT as if he'd been hit by a truck. As if he had no bones in his body. After his dad bandaged him up,

Max herded all of them to the couches in the dining room. He tried to get all of them to have a drink—his kind of therapy. But Gabe didn't have the taste for it.

Tim, his new chef, sat next to him looking a little shell-shocked.

"It's not usually like this," Gabe said, patting Tim's bent knee.

"Right. Usually there are raccoons running wild," Max said into his own coffee mug.

"Raccoons?" Tim asked.

"He's kidding." Gabe assured him, then decided the truth from here on out would feel better. "Sort of."

Tim took another swig from his mug. And Gabe concentrated on breathing. On his sudden longing for canned tomato soup, Oreos and Alice.

I want Alice.

I just want her back.

"Consider this an initiation, Tim," Patrick said. "The Men's Club of Broken Hearts, Eastern New York Division."

The pain, the guilt and confusion in Gabe's chest coalesced and spun faster, growing bigger. He shifted in his seat, trying to make room for what was happening to him.

Tim smiled, the dimple showing up in his cheek. "I've had a broken heart once or twice."

"The price of admission," Patrick said and Tim laughed.

Max simply watched Gabe from the other couch as if he saw right through him.

"Welcome to the rest of your life," Max said and toasted Gabe.

And just like that Gabe was on his feet. The hurricane in his chest taking over his body. He didn't want this for the rest of his life.

He wanted Alice. Good or bad. Because sadly, there was no good without her anymore.

Maybe she was right. Maybe they were different. Older. Wiser. He just had to trust that, trust what they had.

"I gotta go," he said.

"Where?" Patrick asked.

"Albany."

ARMED WITH canned tomato soup and roses—two dozen of them, pink and lush and nearly overblown, just the way she liked them—he arrived at the house on Pape. It was nearly ten o'clock and he was relieved to see the lights still on on the bottom floor.

The truck was barely parked before he'd leaped out, roses and cans of soup in hand. It had been a little over two weeks, surely her feelings for him couldn't have changed. She'd be mad, sure, angry that it took him so long to get his head out of the sand, but in the end, after he groveled, after he told her all the dreams he'd had for those children who had died, all the dreams he had for the children they now would have, by whatever means, she'd be happy.

He'd talk about his mother, about how he still felt like that kid sitting at the kitchen table waiting for his mom to come home.

He'd tell her that nothing was worth having if she wasn't there to share it. He'd tell her anything she wanted to hear.

It would work, eventually.

It had to—his life depended on it.

But his palms were still sweating and his heart still thudded and he hoped he wouldn't be forced to use the key under the frog.

Surprisingly, the door opened under his light knock and he poked his head into the hallway.

"Charlie?" Alice's voice came from the living room in the back of the house. "Come on in! I'm starved."

He stepped in and walked down the hallway hoping her reaction would be a good one. Surprise, sure. Joy, if he was lucky.

Please let me be lucky.

"I hope you remembered the vinegar because I hate—"

"Ketchup on your fries," he finished her sentence as he stepped into the living room.

She was camped out on the couch, Felix in her lap. The two of them surrounded by magazines, water glasses and McDonald's French fry containers.

And the look on her face was not joy. It was horror, quickly being replaced by rage.

Horror and rage. Not at all what he'd expected.

Felix leaped off her lap to curl around his ankles.

"What are you doing here?" she asked, plucking at the collar of the ratty David Hasselhoff T-shirt she wore when she felt sick and in need of comfort.

"Seeing the patient?" he tried to joke. "The Hoff and French fries—you must not be feeling very good."

"I feel fine. Did Max send you here?"

He laughed. "In a way."

Alice huffed through her nose like a bull about to stampede and hiked herself up farther on the pillows. "Great, and now you're here to do the right thing."

"Well, I think so. I mean. It's— Why are you angry?"

Felix, no doubt sensing the volatile atmosphere, took off.

"Why? Because your being here because you have to be isn't the way I want you. I want you here of your own free will, because you want me. Because life without me sucks."

"It does." He shook his head. "I'm missing something here."

"Yeah, right. Your shot at a family. I get it." She put her feet on the floor and began to stand and Gabe pushed her back against the couch.

"I'm here because I don't want to be like Max. I'm here because my life is terrible without you. Food tastes like dirt. Success feels hollow and the Riverview Inn is empty without you in the kitchen. And yes, I want a family. I thought that was the point."

Alice started to cry, staring at the ceiling as tears rolled down her face. She wiped at them with her T-shirt.

"Alice." He set down the roses and got down on his knees in front of her to touch her, offer whatever comfort he could. She pushed him away. Smacked his hands until he finally sat back. "What am I missing?"

"What happens if something goes wrong, remember? That's what you said. So what if I lose this baby and you're here and you hate—"

"This baby?" he asked, slowly because his brain was imploding.

Finally she looked at him, stared right into his lost soul. "You don't know."

"What don't I know? Exactly."

"You're here on your own? You're here—"

"Because I love you. I'm in love with you and always will be. Now tell me what's going on." He gripped her hands, hard, an anchor in this sudden void he'd been dropped in.

"I'm pregnant."

"You're—" He fell back on his butt. "What?"

"Seven weeks," she said, looking like a princess, regal and above touch. "I'm seven weeks' pregnant."

He was sweating. Buckets. It rolled down his back, flooded his eyes. "Are you…okay?"

"Dr. Johnson says yes. He says I need to rest whenever possible—" She gestured to the couch behind her.

He swallowed. "Are you…happy? I mean to be pregnant again."

"Yes," she said fiercely.

"Are you happy to be pregnant with my baby?" he asked, poised on the edge of a knife.

"I'm not sure yet," she whispered. "You're kind of a jerk."

He bit back the sudden bark of laughter. She needed some groveling and rightfully so.

"Al. You are my life. Baby or no. Family or no. Nothing is good without you. My life is empty. My inn is empty. My dream, our dream, is a shell without you. And I will spend the rest of my life trying to fill your life as you have mine."

"And—"

He laughed, but the sound rattled with tears and emotion. "And I will spend the rest of my life apologizing for being a jerk. Now, before I die of a heart attack, are you happy to be pregnant with my baby?"

She lurched forward, tears magnifying her stunning black eyes, and grabbed his face. "I am so happy to be pregnant with your baby. No matter what happens."

He gripped her hands on his face, holding tight to her, looking right back at her, seeing all their flaws collectively and separately and still wanting to make it work. "You weren't going to tell me?"

"Not until I knew I was out of the woods." She stroked his face carefully, with just her thumb. Tentative. "I didn't want you to be obligated to me. I wanted you to love *me*."

"I do. Oh, you have no idea how much I love you." He pulled her into his arms, across his lap, held her as close as he could, tried to soak her into his skin, through his bones and muscle so they would never be apart.

He pressed his lips to her head, tears fell into her hair and he couldn't stop laughing.

"So, you're happy?" she asked against his neck,

her arms locked around his back. "I mean, you're not mad?"

"Well, you have to explain why Max knew before me but—" he shook his head, stroking her hair away from her beloved face "—no. I'm not mad. I'm nervous. I'm worried. I'm so happy I think I might throw up."

"I've been doing enough of that for both of us," she said, making a face. "I guess we have a lot to talk about, huh?"

"I want you back at the inn," he said. "You won't have to lift a finger. I'll be your personal French fry slave."

"Hmm, sounds good," she said and kissed him.

Her lush familiar beautiful lips pressed to his, her body, changing right under his hands, the future spreading out before them with endless possibility.

They still had things to deal with—but they could handle it. No matter what came their way.

"Sounds like heaven," he said.

* * * * *

Look for the next book in
THE MITCHELLS OF RIVERVIEW INN *mini-series,*
A Man Worth Keeping
by Molly O'Keefe.
Coming in November 2009 from
Mills & Boon® Special Moments™.

HEALING THE
COWBOY'S HEART

BY
JUDY DUARTE

Judy Duarte always knew there was a book inside her, but since English was her least favourite subject in school, she never considered herself a writer. An avid reader who enjoys a happy ending, Judy couldn't shake the dream of creating a book of her own.

Her dream became a reality in March of 2002, with the publication of her first book. Since then she has sold nineteen more novels.

Judy makes her home near the beach in Southern California. When she's not cooped up in her writing cave, she's spending time with her somewhat enormous, but delightfully close, family.

You can contact her at JudyDuarte@sbcglobal.net or through her website, www.judyduarte.com.

IN MEMORY OF:

Mahnita Boyden-Wofford, who went above and beyond the call of duty by taking such good care of her boss, his wife and a slew of kids and grandkids.

"I'm not family," you used to say, "I just work here." But that couldn't have been any further from the truth.

May God bless and keep you until we meet again.

Chapter One

Tori McKenzie slapped her hands on her denim-clad hips and studied the twenty-six-year-old man sitting before her, defiance etched in bold strokes across his handsome face.

She'd taken all she could stand from Matthew Clayton, and even a softie like her was bound to explode sometime. "Are you immune to the feelings of others? You've made the poor cook cry three times this week. And she doesn't deserve it."

The afternoon sun slanting through the window highlighted strands of gold in Matt's uncombed, chestnut-colored hair. If he'd been going for the rugged, sexy look, his tousled locks and unshaven appearance would be enough to cause a flock of buckle bunnies to swoon.

But Tori knew better than that. Matt didn't seem to care about anything these days. Not even his appearance.

If she hadn't been a registered nurse once upon a time and sworn to promote healing, she would have ditched this thankless assignment the moment Granny—Tori's employer and Matt's sweet, elderly mother—had suggested it.

As it was, now she was stuck trying to get through to the stubborn man who refused to let anyone break down the walls he'd put up.

"I just want to be left alone," he said. "Can't you and the cook get that through your pretty little heads?"

Tori wasn't prone to violence, particularly when the target was a man who'd been confined to a wheelchair following a tragic car accident, but she had a growing compulsion to grab him by the scruff of his shirt and shake some sense into him.

Instead she muttered, "A lot you know."

Matt relaxed his rebellious pose, allowing himself to sit easier in that chair than a former rodeo cowboy ought to. "Now, listen here, Red—"

"Don't call me Red." He couldn't know that the childhood taunt still rubbed her the wrong way, and telling him might actually make his mood worse, but her patience had run thin today. "You have no idea how old that nickname has gotten or what negative connotations it holds for me. Call me Tori. Or Ms. McKenzie, if you prefer."

"All right." He crossed his arms over his chest. "Then Miz McKenzie it is. But either way, I'm still not interested in your help or your sympathy. And you can pass that info on to Connie, too. She was hired to cook, and you signed on to clean the house and do laundry—not babysit me. So go peddle your damn TLC elsewhere."

"I have nowhere else to peddle it." And that was the truth. Tori had left her job at the hospital and had no intention of applying for another position elsewhere—at least, not in the near future.

Nor was she ready to provide references and offer any explanations.

She wasn't sure what had gone down in her personnel file after her brother's foolish crime, but she'd been officially reprimanded about it.

And the entire situation had been embarrassing— painfully so.

Someday she'd go back to nursing, she supposed. But right now, she was still licking her wounds.

"Well, I don't need your golly-gee, everything's-turning-up-roses attitude," Matt said. "So why don't you find something else to do and leave me alone?"

"Because I need your help."

His brow furrowed and his right eye twitched. "What do you want *me* to do? Reach something for you? Maybe run out to the barn and saddle a horse so you can go out riding?"

"Actually," she said, "your mother's birthday is coming up in a few weeks. And I need help planning a party."

He blew out a snortlike breath. "I don't *do* parties."

"She's going to be eighty." Tori made her way toward his wheelchair, as though they'd broached some kind of friendship when that couldn't be any further from the truth. "And you and I are going to figure out a way to surprise her."

"Good luck with that. People in town have been trying to plan celebrations behind her back for as long as I can remember, and she always catches wind of it. No one surprises Granny."

"You and I will."

He reached over to the lamp table and took a glass of amber-colored liquid, which could be either melted-down iced tea or whiskey.

She suspected it was the latter, although she couldn't be sure unless she got close enough to catch a whiff of his breath.

"I told you before," he said. "I don't *do* parties."

"And I told *you*, Granny is going to be eighty in a few weeks. That's a very big deal. Do you realize this could be the last birthday party she ever has?"

"Don't say that!" His words came out sharp, abrupt. And his response was the first sign of any tender feelings he might have bottled up with all that grief he'd undoubtedly suppressed.

Good. That meant she was making progress. So she was glad she'd thrown out her ace in the hole—his deep love for and devotion to the woman who'd raised him.

Granny had been a childless widow who was pushing sixty when she adopted Jared, her oldest son. Matt, the youngest, had come next, followed a year later by Greg, whom Tori had never met.

The homeless boys hadn't had any kind of future to look forward to when Granny had opened her heart and her home to them. And as a result, they each loved her unconditionally.

Tori got behind Matt and began to push his wheelchair, just as she'd been pushing him emotionally for the past few minutes, pressing him to do what was best for him.

"What in the hell do you think you're doing?" he asked.

"Taking you outside."

"And *then* what are you planning to do? Push me down the steps?"

"Would you blame me if I did?"

He grunted as though he knew how difficult he could be, how miserable he'd become to anyone who got within five feet of him.

"The foreman had a couple of the ranch hands build a ramp from the mudroom into the yard so that you can get in and out easier." She didn't dare admit that the men had done so at her request.

"What if I don't want to get in and out?" He turned his neck, glancing over his shoulder at her. His gaze locked on hers as she continued taking him where he didn't want to go. "Did you hear what I said? I don't *want* to go outside."

"You don't seem to give a darn about anyone else's feelings around here," she said, catching a whiff of alcohol on his breath. "Why should I care about yours?"

"Because you're a pushy little thing. Did anyone ever tell you that you remind them of a bantam rooster when you get your feathers ruffled?"

"No. But thank you. I do believe that's more accurate than what you called me yesterday."

"You mean carrot top?"

"Carrot tops are green."

"So they are."

She'd been warned that he could be especially surly and ornery when he drank, so she'd have to keep that in mind as she chipped away at his barriers. She might have pushed him too hard today already, but she couldn't very well backpedal now.

In the kitchen she stopped long enough to open the plastic

container in which Connie, the new cook, kept the leftover goodies and sweets she'd made, and Tori grabbed two chocolate chip cookies, handing one to Matt. Then she continued to take him through the mudroom to the back door.

As she began to steer him down the wooden planks the ranch hands had built, the slope and his weight caused the chair to pick up momentum. "Uh-oh."

He grabbed for the top of the wheels with hands that still bore the calluses of a man who'd worked with cattle and horses all his life. His efforts crushed the cookie she'd given him a moment ago. "Dammit, Tori. Are you trying to kill me?"

"Actually, the thought crossed my mind earlier, but I suspect Granny would like to have you around, at least until her birthday." Tori continued along the dirt pathway to the barn.

"Where do you think you're taking me?"

"I have an idea for the party, and I want to get your thoughts on it."

"I don't see why. You seem hell-bent on having your own way no matter what I say."

Actually, she was hoping that the fresh air and sunshine would brighten his mood. That maybe, if he were able to inhale the familiar smells of the ranch, the animals, the alfalfa and oats, he'd remember what he'd liked about life—before the accident had taken all he loved away from him.

Jared had said that Matt had been a rodeo cowboy, that he'd always enjoyed life and had lived it to the fullest. But after the accident that had crushed his legs and killed his fiancée and her young son, Matt no longer cared whether he lived or died. And apparently, that meant he didn't care if he walked again, either.

According to Jared, Matt's doctor had wanted him to start physical therapy, but for some reason he'd chosen not to.

So the nurse in Tori was determined to pull him out of the blue funk he'd slipped into, even if it was the last thing she did.

Sometimes life dealt a sucky blow to people—or sometimes more than that, as it had to her. And a person just had to make the best of it.

She pushed Matt through the open doorway into the barn, where the scent of oats and horse and leather was especially strong. A couple of broodmares and their colts were stabled along the side walls.

"What are we doing in here?" Matt asked.

"Checking out the setting of the party."

"You can't be serious. You want to have a party in the barn?"

"Well, we could at least hide the people in here." She studied the interior. "You have to admit, it limits the amount of decorating we'd need to do if we chose a cowboy theme. Hey, what do you think about hiring a country-western band?"

He scoffed. "And how about pony rides for all the guests? And maybe a piñata filled with candy under the tree in the front yard."

She wondered what his voice actually sounded like without the ever-present surly tone. She really didn't know the real Matt. Only that he'd been a rising star on the rodeo circuit and could no longer compete because of his injuries.

"I'd like to surprise Granny," she said. "And where better than right under her nose? She goes to church each Sunday. We could have everyone arrive after she leaves. We can hide the vehicles, then set up all the food in here. I think we can pull it off."

"If you're dead set on having it at the ranch, why not have it out near the lake?"

"Ooh. That's an even better idea. I'm glad you thought of it." She scanned the barn again. "We can give people a ride on a buckboard to the lake."

"A buckboard? What the hell are you talking about? We don't have a buckboard."

"Maybe we can rent one."

"From where?"

"Hmmm." She put the tip of her index finger into her mouth and lightly bit down on it. Then she cocked her head to the side. "I don't know. But I'm sure you'll think of something. Put that on your list of things to do."

He grimaced, but didn't say no.

"And if we have it by the lake, we'll also need to rent portable potties. You can be in charge of getting those, too."

"Okay, now you're *really* getting out of hand."

A horse whinnied, and Tori turned toward it. "Oh, look. How sweet is that? A mom and its baby."

She made her way to the stall and stroked the mother's velvety nose. She'd always been a city girl, and all of this was new to her. But if she had to give up her old life, at least the new one wasn't completely intolerable.

"Her name is Willow," Matt said. "And she's one of the best cutting horses Granny has."

"She's cute."

"Horses aren't cute."

"I think they are." She turned, leaning her hip against the stall. "Or were you referring to the jackass on the premises? You know, the one who snaps at anyone trying to reach out to him?"

Touché. So she thought he was an ass. That served his purpose.

Instead of conjuring a snappy retort, Matt studied the pesky redhead, with her wild curly hair and eyes that were as green as anything the Emerald Isle had to offer. He could almost imagine her speaking with a bit of the brogue, although there was an intriguing lilt in her voice as it was.

Either way, she promised to be the death of him, but only because he hadn't been able to run her off, like he had Connie, the cook. A part of him felt a bit of remorse at having made Connie cry, but not enough to change his tune.

He wasn't in the mood to socialize and hadn't been since the accident. Why couldn't people just leave him alone?

For that reason he made one last attempt to get Tori off his back. "I heard a rumor about you and want to know if it's true."

She tucked a loose strand of hair behind her ear. "What did you hear?"

He hadn't believed what Jared had said about her background. After all, why would she be stuck out on this ranch, getting a small wage plus room and board, if she had other options?

But his older brother didn't spread tales.

For one guilty moment Matt considered changing course by making up something that would provide some comic relief. But he reminded himself that even though he'd told her to leave him alone, she hadn't been sensitive to his need for privacy. So why should he care about hers?

"I heard that you used to be a nurse," he said. "Before you became a maid."

She stilled to the point that a light breeze might blow her off balance, a reaction that told him what he'd heard was true. And he figured a career change like that hadn't been made on a whim.

Not that there was anything wrong with being a maid. But people didn't usually put aside years of training and education without having a good reason to do so, and it made him wonder just what hers was.

"Why'd you give it up?" he asked. "I would imagine there's always a need for nurses."

She seemed to stew on her answer.

Or maybe she was suffering over it. It was hard to say.

Her stance softened. "Let's just say that there have been a lot of changes in my life."

Apparently so, but it only made Matt all the more curious about her.

"Have you seen the kittens?" she asked, changing the subject.

"No, I haven't." He ought to keep chipping away at her, but then again, he had his own demons and secrets, so maybe he should respect hers.

She turned her back to him, and in spite of his efforts to shun both her and her feminine attributes, he couldn't help watching the sway of her hips as she walked toward an empty stall.

Tori McKenzie was a pretty woman. And even though

Matt had teased her about the color of her hair, it wasn't because he didn't find it attractive.

Cindy Wilson, his fiancée, had paid to have hers dyed that same color, which he suspected was natural in Tori's case.

In fact, Tori reminded him a lot of Cindy, at least in looks. She wasn't nearly as tall, but she was just as pretty. Maybe even more so.

And that was another reason to keep his distance. He didn't need the constant reminder of the woman who'd died. A woman who would still be alive today if it hadn't been for Matt's stubborn streak and competitive spirit.

Not a day went by that Matt didn't blame himself for his fiancée's death—her son's, too. And he'd never be the same man again.

In more ways than one.

Damn, he missed the rodeo.

"The kitties are right over here," Tori said. "Joey told me where to find them. And I've been checking on them each day for him."

Joey was the bookkeeper's nephew, a six-year-old kid who'd had heart surgery a week ago and was now recovering at Jared's ranch.

Matt could hear the sound of friction and shuffling, as Tori moved something away. A box, maybe. Then she stepped out of the shadows and back into plain sight, where she stooped, providing him with a vision of her perfectly rounded backside.

His hormones stirred, letting him know that there was still a healthy young man lurking inside of him. A man capable of feeling again—if he would only allow himself to.

But to be honest? Matt wasn't sure if that was a good thing or not.

Part of him wanted to waste away in an effort to find peace and resolution. Yet he knew that really wasn't going to help. He feared he was stuck with the remorse and grief forever.

A flurry of mews and meows sounded from where Tori was bent, and when she returned, she carried a tiny gray tabby with white markings. Its eyes hadn't been open long.

"This is Boswell," she said.

"You named it?"

"Of course." She placed the kitten against her cheek, allowing the fur to caress her skin. "Why wouldn't I?"

"It's just a barn cat."

She turned the kitten's face to hers and whispered, "Matt makes being a barn kitty sound like a bad thing, Boswell. But you're precious, aren't you?"

Crazy woman. Cindy had been like that, too—a real animal lover.

Tori handed the kitten to Matt, and even though he didn't want to take it from her, he accepted the small ball of fur. It wasn't cute, of course, as she'd claimed. Instead he thought it resembled a baby rat.

He supposed he could understand why she thought differently, though. She was like his mother—at least, in that one respect.

Granny had instantly zeroed in on the potential she'd seen in Matt and his brothers, the possibilities that could take place if they were given some time to grow and a whole lot of nurturing.

Of course, homeless adolescents with big chips on their shoulders weren't at all what most women would call "cute." And they weren't as easy to raise as a kitten was. So Matt knew better than to think Tori was anywhere near as admirable as the woman who'd taken him into her heart and home.

Boswell mewed, although it was actually more like a cry of distress.

"Here." Matt handed the kitten back to Tori. "He wants to be with his mother and his brothers and sisters."

In fact, Matt realized, the mama cat must've been out scrounging for a meal, because it struck him odd that she wasn't whining and carrying on about the loss of one of her babies.

"There are six of these little guys in the litter," Tori said. "Joey is going to take the orange tabby, as well as the gray-and-white one."

"Has anyone considered whether they're males or females? We'll need to know if we place an ad in the paper to give them away."

Tori paused, then turned it over and looked at its belly. "This one's a girl, I guess. So maybe I'd better think of a different name. Boswell isn't very feminine."

Obviously, she figured it was as easy to determine the sex of cats as it was dogs. And Matt knew better.

"Let me take a look at it."

She handed it back, and Matt looked under the tail. "This one's a boy. So the name Boswell shouldn't cause him any trouble with his feline peers."

"It can't be a boy. He doesn't have a…" She paused and their gazes locked.

A smile tugged at Matt's lips. "Oh, yes he does. It's just not as evident as it is on dogs or horses or cattle."

Or on humans.

His grin widened. Damn. When was the last time he'd smiled?

It felt like forever, but he hadn't found anything even remotely entertaining since the hours prior to the accident. And actually, considering the way events had unfolded that day, it had been longer than that.

Either way, a slight frown slid back into place, eliminating any sign of a smile.

Footsteps sounded, and Matt turned to see Lester, the foreman, enter the barn.

"What you got there?" Lester asked, as if he didn't have eyes and couldn't see for himself.

"Tori took a fancy to one of the kittens," Matt told him.

"Oh, yeah?" Lester lifted his hat and raked a hand through his thinning, scrub-brush hair. "How bad of a fancy?"

"What do you mean?" Tori asked.

Lester crossed his arms and shifted his weight to one booted foot. "Bad enough to bottle-feed that little critter for the next couple of weeks?"

Matt knew there wouldn't be any other reason for the foreman to ask. "What happened to the mother?"

"A coyote got a hold of her last night," Lester said. "I'm afraid she's dead."

"Those poor babies." Tori clucked her tongue. "They're too little to make it on their own, so I'll take care of them."

"That's a lot of work," Matt said.

She stiffened and stood as tall as her barely five-foot frame would allow. "Not for me."

Something told Matt that a wise man wouldn't doubt her word. And being a man who prided himself on having good sense, Matt realized he'd better brace himself for more run-ins with Tori.

Because in spite of his wishes to be elsewhere, here he sat, virtually kidnapped by an attractive redhead who didn't take no for an answer.

He watched as Tori returned the kitten to the nest it shared with its brothers and sisters. He'd lucked out when she'd determined the orphaned felines were more in need of her tender loving care than he was. After all, he was getting tired of her interference.

Yet instead of wheeling himself out of the barn and back to the house, he found himself studying her shapely backside. He couldn't help admiring the way the denim stretched across her hips.

Her blouse had pulled away from her waistband and provided a view of the fair skin of her lower back. And in spite of every lick of good sense he'd ever had, he imagined himself walking again, pain-free and without a limp. Imagined moseying closer and...

A jolt of testosterone shimmied through his veins and kicked his pulse up a notch.

Damn. Matt might be temporarily confined to a wheelchair—and more or less resigned to limited mobility.

But there were still parts of him that were in prime working condition.

Chapter Two

Tori sat behind the wheel of the white pickup she'd borrowed from Lester and turned into the long, graveled drive of the Rocking C.

She'd driven into Brighton Valley and stopped at the feed store, where she had purchased a case of formula and two small bottles. She would do whatever it took to make sure those poor orphaned kittens survived, especially the two Joey was planning to keep.

Now she was bumping along the rutted dirt road, kicking up dust and heading toward the house.

She pulled the truck to the side of the barn, where she'd found it, parked and turned off the ignition. Then she grabbed the brown bag filled with her purchases and slid out of the driver's seat.

Eager to gather up the babies and take them inside the house, she went directly to the barn.

Just outside of the stall where the kittens were nested she found an empty box, which Lester must have put it for her to use. She appreciated his thoughtfulness and would be sure to tell him the next time she saw him.

After carrying the box to the place where the orphaned kittens lay crying and squirming, she knelt beside them. There was no way of knowing when the mama cat had fed them last, so she hoped they weren't dehydrated. She'd have to get some milk down them as soon as possible. So she put them into the box and carried them in the house.

Right now their bed was only cardboard. But as soon as she was able, she would find some soft rags to make them comfy. And later she would use a hot water bottle to keep them warm.

By the time she'd gotten into the kitchen, the babies were really rooting around and crying for food, and she had to readjust the bag she'd carried in from the truck while getting a better grip on the box to hold it steady.

She'd purchased two bottles, but could only feed one kitten at a time—unless, of course, she found someone to help.

And she had just the right someone in mind. It wouldn't hurt Matt at all to focus on something other than himself.

As she washed and prepared the bottles with the canned kitten formula, a voice from the doorway interrupted her work.

"I see you're back."

Matthew.

She turned, her gaze zeroing in on him as he sat in that

wheelchair. He was a handsome man, even unshaven and wearing a trademark scowl. And she couldn't squelch an appreciative grin.

Dang. She'd have to stay on her toes around him, so she quickly rallied. "I'm glad you're here. I need an extra pair of hands."

"You're still dead set on feeding them yourself?" he asked.

"I can't let them starve." She glanced over her shoulder at him. "And don't tell me they're just barn cats."

Matt put up his hands in mock surrender. "I wouldn't think of it."

He appeared both boyish and manly in that pose, and something in her heart stirred. Something that had very little to do with sympathy. But she tamped down every bit of sexual attraction as quickly as it rose. She'd come to Brighton Valley to get away from her problems, away from the whispers and knowing looks. So she certainly wasn't going to risk drawing attention to herself here.

She reached into the rag drawer and pulled out a couple of soft pieces for bedding. Then she took an old worn towel and tore it in two. She swaddled the orange tabby, the one Joey had been calling Pumpkin, and handed the squawking bundle, along with a bottle, to Matt.

He took it, then asked, "Why'd you wrap it up?"

"That's how we feed newborn babies. They eat better when they feel secure."

"But these are just…" He didn't finish, and she suspected he was going to say cats.

Still, it pleased her to know that he was being sensitive to her feelings about the value of these tiny creatures who hadn't been asked to be orphaned.

It didn't take long for Pumpkin to figure out what he was supposed to do with the nipple, and he soon began to chow down.

"I'll be damned," Matt said. "That nursing skill of yours seems to come in handy around here."

She stiffened, her heart thumping like dead weight against her chest wall.

Her skills had been coming in handy all right, but that didn't make her feel any better about not working in a hospital setting when she'd been trained to do so.

When Matt had asked her about being a nurse, she'd been taken aback. But not by his question or his natural curiosity about her past. It was the fact that he'd seemed to realize that she hadn't given up nursing because she'd really wanted to.

She wasn't about to confide in him, though. The memories were still too painful, too raw.

If it had been just one ugly secret, instead of two, she might have stuck it out and remained working at the hospital, hoping her brother's drug problem and theft would soon become yesterday's news. But her sister's betrayal had been a devastating blow—and completely unforgivable.

That particular incident had been the final straw, the trigger that made her turn her back on her family, as well as her career.

How could she go to work each day when everyone at the hospital, from the janitors to the chief of staff, had looked at her as though she was guilty by association.

Tori reached for the smallest kitten. It sucked a few draws from the bottle and soon lost interest.

"This one isn't eating," she said, her gaze seeking Matt's. "What do you think is wrong?"

Matt glanced up. Tori, her big green eyes laden with an overabundance of compassion, was looking at him as though he was an expert on cats, which he wasn't. But he'd lived on a working ranch long enough to learn and to accept certain laws of nature.

And, if truth be told, before he'd been lured to the rodeo circuit, he'd harbored a dream of becoming a vet. But other than an aptitude in math and science, he hadn't been that good of a student, so it had been fairly easy to decide against college.

"That's the runt," he said, knowing that the weakest one in the litter usually had an uphill battle to survive. But he knew better than to tell that to Tori. She'd probably get all weepy-eyed, and he didn't want to deal with her tears.

"He's got the cutest white markings on his feet and his nose."

Matt didn't glance her way. He was still of the mindset that at this age, these little critters weren't much different from rats.

"Oh, and look at his tail. I'm going to call him Tippy."

Great. She'd pinned her heart on the one cat in the litter with the least chance of making it.

Damn. Matt opened his mouth to warn her, but instead of popping off with a comment she wouldn't appreciate, he held his tongue and focused on the orange tabby. He almost felt sorry for the poor thing. And not just because it had been orphaned.

To add insult to injury, Pumpkin was a lousy name for a cat. If this kitten pulled through and Matt had anything to say about it, he was going to suggest they call the little critter Rusty or Tiger or something like that.

About the time they'd fed each kitten—or at least, in the case of the runt, given it a try—Granny entered the kitchen.

"What's going on?" she asked.

Tori explained the situation. "I hope you don't mind if I try to bottle-feed these little ones until they can fend for themselves."

"Of course not," Granny said. "Joey would really be upset if anything happened to the two kittens I promised him. And I'd hate to see him brokenhearted."

So would Matt. But as his thoughts were prone to do whenever he laid eyes on Joey, they drifted to Tommy and, subsequently, to the dark, gruesome vision that would remain etched in Matt's mind for the rest of his life.

He would never forget the sight of that little boy slumped in the back seat of the dual-wheeled pickup, his body bent and twisted.

Damn. No matter how hard Matt tried, he couldn't stop the memory from marching through his brain like an enemy battalion on a mission of destruction.

"Just look at you two," Granny said, as she pulled out a chair and sat next to Tori. "You're tending those babies like doting parents, and it's just about the sweetest thing I've ever seen."

Sweet? There wasn't a damn thing sweet about any of

this. Nor was there anything wholesome about the guilt that came barreling down on Matt like two drag racers taking up both lanes of the road and leaving a man with nowhere to turn.

"You know what?" He turned to Tori. "I'm tired. And now that you've got help, I'm going to head back to my room and rest."

"Are you okay?" Tori asked.

No, he wasn't okay. And he doubted that he ever would be again.

"Yeah, I'm fine. Don't worry about me." He was trying to learn how to live with the guilt.

He just dealt with it better when no one was around.

Matt sat in his bedroom trying his damnedest to follow Captain Ahab's relentless quest for Moby Dick, and even though he was nearly three-quarters of the way through the novel and had actually found himself enjoying it, he just couldn't get back into the story.

For the past two days Tori had been drawing him out of his comfort zone, and he was beginning to feel as though she was trying to shove a tablespoon of cod liver oil down his throat.

Jared had asked Matt to stay behind at the Rocking C and keep the books for Granny while Sabrina was gone.

How could Matt say no to that?

But now he was stuck back home with Granny and the hired women who lived in the house—Connie, the cook who couldn't seem to make an edible meal if someone held a gun to her head, and Tori, a maid who looked too damn much like Cindy for comfort. And to make matters worse, neither one of the women could keep their noses out of Matt's business.

Could life be any crueler than that?

He'd managed to scare Connie off with a surly attitude, but Tori wasn't nearly as sensitive.

And if Tori didn't back off...

Well, Matt wasn't sure what he'd do. But he suspected things were going to blow sky-high.

A knock sounded on the door, interrupting his thoughts.

He wasn't up for chatter tonight—or togetherness. He just wanted some time alone.

A second rap convinced him that peace and quiet wasn't ever going to be found on the Rocking C, and he was going to have to get out of here for a while—a *long* while.

He rested the open book in his lap. "Yeah?"

"Dinner's ready," Tori said.

"Thanks," he told her through the closed door. "I'm not up for a family-style meal. I'll fix a plate and then come back in here to eat."

"Don't worry," she said. "I'll bring it to you."

That wasn't quite what he had in mind.

Moments later another knock sounded, and Tori's voice sang out. "Room service."

Matt wasn't in the mood for lighthearted banter, so he hoped she would drop off his meal without saying anything and leave him alone.

"Okay, bring it in," he told her.

As she entered the bedroom, she balanced a tray that held two plates, silverware and glasses of iced tea. "I thought I'd join you for dinner."

He ought to appreciate her presence and her attempts to take the edge off his dark thoughts, but he didn't. Sometimes it actually felt good to stew and wallow in a foul mood.

Of course, at other times, a man didn't have any choice in the matter.

Tori set the tray on the dresser, then made room on the desk for two place settings.

"What makes you think I want company?" he asked.

She turned, lips parting, cheeks flushing—and looking sweeter and prettier than he'd like her to.

"I'm sorry," she said. "It's just that you spend way too much time alone, and I thought—"

"You thought that you'd spread a little Mary Sunshine my way?"

She straightened and stared him down. The fire in those green eyes made her all the more attractive, and he struggled to right an escalating pulse rate that set his hormones on end.

"Your attitude really needs a tune-up," she said.

"Does that mean you're dead set on accepting the challenge?" He watched the billowing wind in her sails fade ever so slightly.

"You're a handsome man, Matt. That hasn't changed. And while Granny insists that all of her boys are smart as a whip, she implied you might be the brightest of all."

So what? he thought. A lot of good any of that did him now.

He'd never ride in the rodeo again; he'd never be able to bring Cindy or Tommy back.

"You have a lot to be grateful for—your life, a loving

and supportive family. Do you have any idea how many people in this world would give anything to have what you fail to see as a real blessing?"

Was she one of them? He couldn't seem to stifle the curiosity. Or the urge to turn the tables and start prying into her past for a change, poking at her pain and disappointment.

That is, if she'd ever had any.

"The life I once had is over," he said, "so you'll have to forgive me for not feeling like I ought to celebrate."

He'd expected some response—either an argument or an apology—yet she didn't offer either one.

As if he hadn't uttered a peep in retaliation, she just pointed to the book in his lap. "What are you reading?"

"Moby Dick." He glanced down at the novel he'd found in the den, a classic he suspected had once belonged to Greg or Jared. "I thought it looked…interesting."

"It is. I read it in high school. I'm not really a fan of literary fiction, but the book was assigned to the entire class, so I didn't have much choice. But it was really good. I'm sure you'll like it."

"Yeah, well, I never read any of the books I was told to read when I was in school. I'd just catch a ride with one of the ranch hands into town and pick up the Cliffs-Notes."

"You got by without reading the actual novels?" Something in her tone suggested that he'd admitted to being an ax murderer.

"I pulled Cs," he said. "There's nothing wrong with that."

She rolled her eyes. "There is when you could have read the books and gotten As or Bs. It's a form of cheating."

"No, it isn't. Besides, I read the CliffsNotes cover to cover."

"You missed out on a lot of great stories you wouldn't have normally read, so you cheated yourself."

He chuffed. "What do you want me to do? Confess to Miss Heinrich so I don't have to face a lifetime of guilt?"

He'd meant the comment to be snide, but the fact was, the guilt he actually carried wasn't likely to ease. And the reason it wouldn't had nothing to do with the hell he used to raise in school or the shortcuts he'd taken in the classes he hadn't liked.

"Well, at least you're reading it now." Tori returned to the task of setting out the plates of food—God only knew what the cook had thrown together tonight. Then she set out glasses of iced tea, silverware and napkins.

"What's for dinner?" he asked.

"It's a chicken and rice casserole."

"You could have fooled me."

Those hands, lightly freckled and neatly manicured, returned to her hips, and she gave him the eagle eye, much like Miss Heinrich used to do whenever it was her turn to watch over the detention room.

"Have you always been a jerk?" Tori asked. "Or is your surly tongue a result of the accident?"

The fact that she'd called him on his attitude didn't sit well with him, especially since he had little excuse. Well, actually, he figured he had a damn good one, but he wasn't about to spill his guts to her.

Besides, she ought to choose her battles.

"You're not the cook," he said, "so why are you getting so riled up?"

"Actually, Connie wasn't feeling well, and I volunteered to fix dinner tonight. So before you complain, you might take a bite."

"I never have cared much for casseroles."

"Do you like chicken?" she asked.

"Yes. If it's fried or barbecued."

"How about rice?"

He shrugged. "It's okay."

"Then give this a try."

"I like seeing the chicken and rice in two separate piles on my plate."

"I'll have to keep that in mind for the future." The spunky redhead got behind his wheelchair and pushed him to the desk, where she'd set a place for each of them.

Matt grumbled a complaint, but he picked up a fork anyway.

"You're acting like a spoiled baby. Maybe I ought to put a bib on you."

He shot her a warning glance. "Try it and you'll be sorry you got within arm's reach." If he got his hands on her—figuratively speaking, of course—he'd…he'd…

Damn. His mind took an unwelcome detour, and the thunder in his surly, empty threat suspended in midair.

Their gazes met and locked.

Sexual awareness, in all its heat and glory, flared, stirring up something more powerful than words. Something that, in spite of all his bluster, all his pain, was vibrant and medicinal, making him forget the shackles of guilt he hadn't been able to shake.

For a moment he almost felt whole again—as if that accident had never happened.

He wondered if it was because Tori reminded him of Cindy, but he quickly tossed that thought aside.

It was true there were similarities—the red hair, green eyes and fair complexion, not to mention that they were both nurturers, warm and loving to a fault.

Yet at this very moment, it was their differences that intrigued him, those things that set Tori apart and made her unique.

She was about six inches shorter than Cindy had been. And she wasn't anywhere near as easygoing and agreeable. She also had a hell of a stubborn streak.

Why else would she continue to stick around Matt when he'd done his best to run her off?

Unable to let his mind wander into forbidden territory, he broke eye contact and studied his plate, which was filled with a hearty helping of chicken and rice casserole, almond-dotted green beans and a golden-brown roll with slab of real butter.

Rather than lift his head and risk meeting her gaze again, he dug in.

To be honest, the casserole wasn't half-bad.

He knew he ought to say something, to thank her or praise the taste, but he'd be damned if he would allow himself to admit it. He didn't want her to get the wrong idea and think that they were actually creating some kind of friendship or bond.

She must have gotten the message, because they ate in silence until he'd cleaned his plate, which should've been proof enough that this dinner had been better than any Connie had made in the past couple of weeks. As far as meals went, Connie hadn't come up with anything to shout about, other than her desserts. Still, the casserole was better than mediocre and a part of him felt pressured to comment.

"Well," Tori said, pushing back the desk chair she'd been using and getting to her feet. "I told Connie I'd clean up the kitchen, too. And I need to feed the babies. They're probably hungry."

He hoped she didn't ask him for help with the kittens again. If she did, he'd have to tell her no.

Tori had him growing softer by the minute, and he couldn't afford to let down his defenses. She was too much like Cindy in all the wrong ways.

Too attractive.

Too appealing.

And when it came to Cindy, Matt had reason to believe that he'd gotten right and wrong mixed up.

Chapter Three

No one could ever accuse Matt of being obedient or backing down from a challenge.

So even though the orthopedic surgeon hadn't exactly given him the green light to get out of the wheelchair, he'd decided to take a shower after dinner anyway.

He'd gotten so sick and tired of those god-awful sponge baths that he'd been more than ready for the real thing. But that didn't mean he was stupid. He'd taken it slow and easy. And he would have quit the moment he'd had any reason to believe he was doing any permanent damage.

Still, standing had hurt like hell, and he'd been pretty shaky on his feet.

A couple of times he nearly slipped and fell, which could have been a real disaster, but he figured the doctor wouldn't have prescribed physical therapy if it wasn't time to stretch his legs.

Of course, he hadn't actually started the therapy yet.

A couple of weeks ago, when Jared had wheeled him into the clinic and was signing him in, Matt had noticed a wall in the waiting room that displayed photographs of all the therapists. While looking them over, he'd recognized Cindy's cousin, Joanne. The two young women had been raised next door to each other and were closer than most sisters.

Matt hadn't known which therapist would be assigned to work with him, but there was no way he'd risk running into the young woman who was undoubtedly still grieving Cindy's loss—and blaming Matt for it.

The last time he'd seen Joanne had been the day of the accident. Matt had gone with Cindy and her son to a Wilson family reunion at the city park. It would have been a tolerable day—and maybe even pleasant—if his competitive nature hadn't blown sky-high.

Cindy's ex-husband, another bronc rider Matt had met on the circuit, had shown up at the park. Dave had been an old neighbor of the Wilsons' and a friend of Cindy's brother, so it wasn't surprising that he would stop by. But things had grown more and more…awkward, not to mention competitive, as the day wore on.

After a while, Cindy had gotten angry at Matt, insisting that they leave before the day was over.

Matt suspected that, even if the accident hadn't happened on the way home, he would have wanted to avoid Joanne. There were several other occasions when Matt had sensed that Joanne was hoping and maybe even encouraging Cindy and Dave to reconcile, even though their divorce had been final before Matt had even entered the picture.

Joanne had given Cindy a goodbye hug, then she'd shot a frown at Matt, letting him know she thought he'd been out of line.

Matt hadn't thought so then.

But after the crash?

Well, there weren't any excuses that he could make—in public or in private—that would make him feel better about what he'd done. None that would hold water anyway.

So there was no way he was going to take a chance on seeing Joanne each time he went to the clinic.

"Let's get out of here," Matt had told his brother.

When Jared had tried to get him to see reason, Matt had reached up and gripped Jared's arm. "I'm not staying. And if you don't want to be embarrassed by my actions, you'll get me the hell out of here. *Now.*"

Apparently, Jared had figured out that Matt meant business, because he'd told the receptionist they'd have to reschedule. Then he opened the office door for Matt, who'd wheeled himself straight to the elevator.

When quizzed on the way back to Jared's ranch, Matt had told his brother he wasn't ready for therapy yet and refused to discuss what was really bothering him. Some things were too painful to talk about, even with family.

Then afterward, each time Jared had badgered him about it, Matt had merely clammed up.

Talking about it would only make it worse. Besides, what could Jared do to make it better?

Not one damn thing.

Now, as Matt wheeled himself out of his private bathroom and toward the bed, he was glad he'd taken the chance and showered this evening. The pounding water on his face and back had felt good, and so had his head after a good scrub with the shampoo. He managed to dry off and slip on a pair of shorts before his legs gave out.

He was thinking long and hard about turning in for the night when a knock sounded at the door.

"Who is it?" he asked, still not wanting to mix or mingle.

"It's Tori."

What now?

Earlier, the pretty redhead had seemed almost as eager to end the meal they'd shared as he'd been. But he sensed something in her voice. Something troubled.

"Come on in," he said.

She entered the door with a towel-wrapped kitten in her arms and concern etched across her brow. In fact, she seemed so worried that she'd obviously failed to realize she was wearing only a nightgown.

Or maybe she didn't think he'd notice, or that he wouldn't speculate she had on very little—if anything—underneath it.

"There's something wrong with Tippy," she said. "And I'm not sure what to do."

Matt had expected the cat to weaken. "He's the runt, Tori. And that means he's got two strikes against him already."

"What do you suggest we do? I don't want him to die."

Matt ought to focus on the cat, but he couldn't help studying Tori, who wore her wild Irish curls hanging loose and free, hair he could envision splayed against a pillowcase.

His pillowcase.

That white cotton gown she had on was the kind a grandma might wear, yet it took on a whole new look on Tori. He shouldn't find it the least bit sexy, but he did.

And so did his hormones, which were whooshing and pumping to life, letting him know that some of the long-forgotten parts of his body were still in their prime, his libido one of them.

Still, he tried to be sensitive to her concerns—a first for him in a long time. "Why don't you look for an eye-dropper. Maybe we can force some milk down him."

There he went again. Throwing out words like *we* and implying some kind of bond when there wasn't one. When there *shouldn't* be.

"Will you hold him while I go and look for one?" she asked, handing the kitten to him.

In spite of his reluctance to get involved, he took it from her.

How the hell was he supposed to tell her no?

After she left the room, he looked the runt over carefully. It seemed perfectly formed, just smaller than the rest. But it was definitely weaker.

If Tippy didn't pull through, and that was becoming more and more possible, he sensed that Tori was going to take it hard. The orphaned critters had become more than barn cats to her, and she seemed to have bonded with each one of them.

Early on, he'd learned to stay detached, which wasn't always easy to do. But a guy sure didn't have to make friends with the four-legged creatures that lived on a ranch or farm. Losing a pet was tough on some people.

That's why Matt never named animals.

Not anymore.

Tori, of course, wasn't of that same mind-set. She'd named each of the kittens, and if truth be told, he figured she was trying to get him to feel that same affection, which he was doing his best to fight.

But he'd even begun to think of the baby cats as Pumpkin, Fur Ball and Boswell. Since neither of the two solid-black kittens in the litter had any markings to distinguish them, it was impossible for him to tell them apart. But Tori seemed to have an innate sense of which one was Stormy and which was Midnight.

"I'm back." She swept into the room, the hem of her gown several inches above her ankles, revealing bare feet.

His gaze traveled from her pretty, cotton-candy-pink toenails to her head. He had to force himself to glance away from her face so that he could look at the bottle full of formula and the eyedropper she was showing him.

"I hope this does the trick," she said.

Well, it certainly could. But there were no guarantees, and he hated to be the one to tell her. Instead he watched her unscrew the top, dip the dropper into the bottle and squeeze the bulb to draw in the milk.

"Okay," she said. "You hold open his mouth, and I'll try to get this down him."

She stood close enough for Matt to catch a hint of her shampoo, something floral. Lilac, maybe? He took another whiff, relishing the scent of woman.

As she stooped over the kitten, the neckline of her

cotton nightgown gaped open, revealing the swell of a perfectly formed breast and the dusky edge of a nipple.

Damn.

"Be careful," she said. "Help me hold his head still."

It wasn't the kitten his hands itched to hold, to touch, to stroke and caress...

She moved to the right, trying to get the dropper into Tippy's mouth, but all Matt could seem to do was watch the scooped neckline swoosh this way and that and catch another glimpse of her breasts, soft and full and begging for a man's hand.

Double damn.

Uncomfortable with the way his thoughts were going, he tried his best to focus on Tippy. Hopefully, the runt would perk up soon.

If this joint feeding venture was dragged out much longer, Matt wasn't sure how much of this his libido could stand.

Still, as her arm brushed his shoulder, jolting him with simmering heat, the scent of lilacs mingled with her peppermint-fresh breath, taunting him.

Did she have any idea what she and her ready-for-bed appearance were doing to him?

Tori studied the eyedropper, wondering how much Tippy had eaten. He was just a little guy, so she didn't want to over-feed him. But she wanted to make sure he got enough, too.

Straightening from where she'd been bent over Matt's lap, she said, "That's probably enough for now, but I'm going to set the alarm every hour and feed him through the night."

She arched and stretched, hoping to work out a kink in her back. As she turned toward Matt, she saw that his eyes were on her and not the kitten.

But he wasn't merely watching her.

There was an intensity in his gaze that nearly took her breath away, jolting her with sexual awareness.

She'd been so worried about Tippy that she'd forgotten she was only wearing a nightgown.

Feeling as unbalanced and self-conscious as a woman who'd just woken up in a window display at a bustling department store, she crossed her arms over her breasts. "I, uh, guess I should have put on a robe."

"No problem." His blue eyes glimmered, male interest burning bright.

He glanced at the lamp that glowed behind her, and she suddenly realized the light had made her gown almost useless.

She shifted her weight to one hip. "You should have said something."

"And lose the best view I've had in ages?" His mouth quirked at one side, and humor glimmered in his eyes.

It pleased her that he found her attractive, in spite of the fact that she ought to be uneasy about that.

But Matt Clayton was one heck of a handsome man.

She could almost imagine him swaggering across the ranch or riding a bucking bronco, one hand on the saddle horn and the other in the air, as the crowd roared their approval.

Yet even sitting here in a wheelchair, his hair damp and mussed, he was breathtakingly male.

His scent, which she'd failed to recognize earlier, was

clean and brisk, a pleasant blend of soap and musk. And with each breath she took, her pulse kicked up a notch.

He hadn't shaved in a while, and the light stubble of his beard gave him a rugged appearance she found far more appealing than she should.

"I'd better take Tippy back to his brothers and sisters," she said, reaching for the kitten.

Matt snagged one of her corkscrew curls, gently pulling it straight, then letting it go. "Is it natural?"

"The curl?" she asked. "Or the color?"

His gaze dropped to her hips, as though he expected the lamplight shining through the cotton material to provide him further proof.

She ought to be annoyed.

Yet instead, she felt a bit naughty and more of a flirt than ever before. "The kids used to call me Strawberry Short-cake when I was a girl. So does that answer your question?"

"For now."

His words and the implication that he'd want further proof someday caused her pulse to first spike, then skitter through her veins, a heated reaction she hadn't expected.

She tried to remind herself that Matthew was her employer's son. And that, while she could no longer be a nurse, she ought to consider him as off-limits as any other patient.

Besides, she didn't need to get involved with anyone right now, especially one with all the baggage she suspected Matt carried. After all, she'd moved from Dallas to Brighton Valley to get away from her own memories, so why take on someone else's?

Still, she suspected that it was good for Matthew to see

himself as a sexual being again. It just might help him to heal, to forget about the past and to move on with his life. And the dedicated nurse who still lived inside of her, the professional who'd once loved her career more than anything in this world, insisted that encouraging Matt to move beyond his pain was a good thing.

But on the other hand, the heated physical response she'd had to his innuendos and the desire simmering in his eyes only served to remind her how long it had been since she'd felt any sexual longing. So she decided the wisest thing for her to do tonight was to excuse herself and get out of the line of fire and temptation.

"Thanks for helping me feed Tippy," she said.

He didn't respond.

Neither did he try to stop her from turning around and walking away, ending things before they had a chance to start.

Early the next morning Matt sequestered himself in the office, a dark-paneled room that was located in the house, just a couple of doors down the hall from his old bedroom.

He had plenty of reasons to hide away from distractions, and Tori was definitely one of them.

Last night, while she'd been in his room, he'd been bombarded with thoughts and desires he'd never expected to experience again.

And he wasn't sure how he felt about that.

His hormones were willing, but common sense urged him to beware.

All during the night he'd heard her alarm go off and knew she was taking care of the kittens, which now resided in her bedroom. But she didn't ask for his help any of those times, and he was grateful for that.

Between the taunting glimpses of her breasts and the desire to get a clearer view of what lay hidden beneath her white cotton gown, he was going to have a hard time keeping his hands and his thoughts to himself.

Still, he couldn't help wondering why she hadn't come looking for him yet.

He glanced at the clock. It was nearly noon. Had she been avoiding him, too?

Probably.

Evading her had been his own game plan, which was why he was in the office.

Sure, he'd agreed to hold down the fort for Sabrina, the bookkeeper, while she was at Jared's ranch helping little Joey recover from surgery. But that had nothing to do with Matt closing the door and demanding privacy this morning when the room was usually open to anyone passing in the hall.

Actually, it had been a good idea to shut himself inside. Without any interruptions, he'd gotten a lot of work done so far.

He'd gone over the books, noting that Sabrina had everything in order. He'd also reconciled the latest bank statement, which hadn't balanced at first. But it hadn't taken him long to figure out why, and he soon had it all squared away.

Next he planned to pay the monthly bills, which he'd pulled from the to-be-paid file and placed in a stack.

Several of the statements had sticky notes on top, which Sabrina had left to remind herself—or in this case,

Matt, who was her temporary replacement—to call and have the companies fax the missing invoices. One he'd gotten that chore taken care of, he studied the to-do list Tori had given him for Granny's party. He'd better check out the prices and availability of portable potties and the damn buckboard she insisted they needed.

He thumbed through the yellow pages in the phone book, then chose a couple of companies he knew were reputable.

As he picked up the telephone to dial the first number, footsteps, heavier than usual, sounded in the hall. They paused before the door, then a soft knock sounded.

Matt looked up from his work. "Yes?"

"It's me," a gravelly, male voice said. "Can I come in?"

The man didn't identify himself, but he didn't need to. It was Lester, the ranch foreman.

"Sure." Matt watched the door swing open and the rangy, fifty-something cowboy walk in.

"I was in town picking up supplies," Lester said, "so I stopped at the post office to get the mail."

"Thanks. I appreciate that."

"Here you go." Lester dropped a stack on the desk. "It's mostly bills, I suspect."

Matt scanned the top envelope, noting the logo of the phone company.

"So how are those kittens doing?" Lester asked.

"I haven't heard Tori crying, so I figure they're still alive."

"That gal sure is a softie," Lester said. "Reminds me of my sister, Irene. She never did see a sick or injured critter she didn't want to nurse back to health."

"There's a runt that isn't doing too well," Matt said. "And, wouldn't you know, that's the one Tori took a liking to."

"That sounds a lot like my sister," Lester said. "Once, when Irene was just a kid, she found two orphaned baby sparrows and brought them home, nest and all. She kept them alive for a day or two, but they both died. And she damn near fell apart. I didn't think she was ever going to stop bawling."

That's what Matt was afraid of. Tori was setting herself up for heartache.

"Well," Lester said, "I'd better get back to work. Hank told me there's a large section of fence that needs to be replaced in the south pasture. I thought I'd better go check it out."

Matt nodded, wishing he could ride with the men and do some good, hard labor. To feel the sun beating on his face and the perspiration gathering on his brow. Sitting in this damn chair was getting old fast.

Lester shut the door behind him, leaving Matt to the phone calls he'd needed to make.

Twenty minutes later he was going to take a break from writing out the checks to pay the monthly bills and head to the kitchen for lunch. But having second thoughts, he decided to wait until everyone else had already eaten.

Okay, so he was still hoping to avoid Tori.

He took the stack of mail Lester had brought, thumbed through it and tossed out the fliers and junk. He made a pile of anything that would interest Granny or that needed her attention, like a newsletter from the Brighton Valley Community Church and a save-the-date notice from the Ladies Aid Society. But when his eyes landed on an envelope addressed to Tori, his interest piqued.

Odd, he thought, as he noted the return address: Sean McKenzie.

Tori's last name was McKenzie, wasn't it?

So who was this guy?

A brother?

A husband?

Under his name, he'd written: In care of Twin Oaks Ranch. Matt had heard about that place before. He'd been roped into helping with a charity event, and the proceeds went there. It was a rehab place of some kind.

Curiosity damn near threatened to burn a hole in Matt's brain.

Apparently, the woman who'd been dead set on prying into his misery and his past had a few secrets of her own. And Matt was determined to learn what they were.

What would it hurt?

Worst case scenario, she'd get mad at him for prying. But what was so bad about that? It might make her back off and leave him alone.

And if it didn't?

Maybe it would toss a bucket of cold water on whatever had been zapping and buzzing between them last night.

Chapter Four

The oldest of three children, Tori supposed it had only been natural for her to fall into the role of a nurturer and to grow up responsible. And that was also one of the reasons she'd chosen to get a degree in nursing.

It had been a perfect career.

As she sprayed window cleaner onto the glass door of the china hutch in the formal dining room at the Rocking C Ranch, she blew out a sigh. Yes, it did seem a little odd to be employed as a maid now.

But it wasn't as though she minded the work.

Over the years she'd taken on a lot of the chores, like cooking and scrubbing and chasing after her younger brother and sister. So she knew what was expected of her.

Not that she'd be working at the Rocking C forever. She'd go back to being a nurse again someday.

She unrolled a length of paper towels from the roll and climbed onto the stepstool so she could reach the top of the glass panels on the door.

No, having a job as a maid hadn't been part of the game plan, but the pay was okay, and Granny provided her room and board. The best part of it all was being able to put plenty of distance between herself, her self-centered siblings and the problems and heartbreak they'd caused her.

As she wiped down the glass until it shined, she heard footsteps as someone sauntered across the hardwood floor. She looked up and watched Lester make his way through the living room and enter the hall with a stack of mail in his hands.

If he had noticed her, she would have acknowledged him or said hello. But he walked with a determined step, intent upon where he was going.

At the office door, he rapped lightly, which caused her to pause and wait to see if he'd be invited in.

The office door had been closed for most of the morning, so she'd assumed Matthew had wanted some privacy and had decided to clean that particular room last. She'd just been waiting for him to come out.

In the meantime, she'd been focusing her attention on some of the special projects she'd planned to do today, such as dusting the bookshelf in the living room, wiping down the shutters and cleaning out the handcrafted oak hutch in the dining room.

Within moments Lester came out of the office, his arms now empty. As he strode out of the house, she wondered what Matthew was doing inside.

Bookwork, she supposed, but whenever Sabrina had

gone over the accounts or paid bills, the door had always remained open.

She knew Matt was struggling with depression after his accident, something Jared had been worried about. So it concerned her whenever he was holed up by himself.

For that reason she climbed down from the stepstool, left her cleaning supplies near the hutch and went to check on him.

As she stood before the door, she knocked lightly.

"What is it?" he asked.

Neither his response nor the snippy tone had been an invitation to enter, but she opted to take it as such and let herself in.

Matt was sitting at the desk, where he'd pushed the tufted leather seat aside to make room for the wheelchair. He appeared busy; there were some files and stacks of paper on the desktop.

But her interest was drawn to the man himself.

He'd showered this morning; she'd known because she'd cleaned his bathroom already. But he hadn't combed his golden-wheat-colored hair. Or maybe he had, but he'd run his fingers through the strands numerous times throughout the morning.

His square-cut jaw seemed to shout defiance, as did the fact that he still hadn't shaved. The light bristle on his cheeks gave him a dark and edgy aura, which appealed to her more than it should have.

His eyes, the color of a field of Texas bluebonnets, provided him with a softness he might not fully appreciate. And when his gaze locked on her, it darn near turned her stomach inside out.

She tucked a loose strand of her hair behind her ear, inadvertently catching a whiff of ammonia from the cleaning product she'd been using, which only served to remind her of her place. She was, after all, just an employee who had no right to gawk at her boss's son.

Yet the sight of Matt stirred something deep inside of her. Something profoundly female and sexual.

She tried to shake off her interest, her momentary attraction, but she probably hadn't been very good at doing so, because Matt leaned back in his wheelchair and crossed his arms, then asked, "Can I help you?"

"I, uh…" Great. Now she was at a loss for words, which rarely happened to her.

Think, Tori. Think.

She cleared her throat. "I was wondering when this room would be available for me to clean."

"It's a big house. Surely you can find somewhere else to be."

"Yes, I suppose I can." Still, her legs didn't move. And neither did her gaze, her perusal of the man.

Even in that chair, Matthew Clayton had a commanding presence.

"Who's Sean McKenzie?" he asked, completely drawing her out of her girlish musing.

Her heart thumped in her chest, and her lips parted. "Why do you want to know?"

He held up a letter addressed to her, in care of the ranch.

She recognized her brother's handwriting and stiffened. Her first thought was to question how Sean would have known where to find her. Then she realized her grandmother must have given him her contact information.

For a moment she wished she hadn't let Gram know where she was, but she couldn't have done that. Someone in the family had to be responsible. And Lord knew the elderly woman couldn't depend upon the other two siblings, the kids who had been coddled until they'd become self-centered and spoiled rotten—and damaged in their own way.

Matt placed the letter on the desktop and pushed it across the polished oak toward Tori.

Her first impulse was to open the envelope and make sure that her grandmother was okay, that an emergency hadn't arisen. But that was good ol' dependable Tori's natural response. And she was determined not to enable the younger McKenzies any more.

No, if his attempt to contact her had anything to do with her grandmother, her brother would have called, not written a letter.

So she took the envelope and slowly tore it up in pieces. Then she stashed the remnants in the pocket of her apron.

Matt watched her carefully, one of his brows arched and indicating surprise or maybe confusion.

"Sean McKenzie is my brother," she said.

Then before he could question her further, before she felt compelled to vent, she turned and walked away, leaving him to stew in his curiosity.

Connie served meat loaf for dinner that night, but by the time Matt got a chance to sit at the table, he'd learned that the ranch hands who'd eaten earlier had used up all the ketchup.

He couldn't fault them for that, he supposed, since

they'd undoubtedly tried to do what he was hoping to do—mask the flavor of baked hamburger that tasted more like cardboard than meat.

Still, he swore under his breath and reached for the bowl that held the potatoes, which didn't look too bad— what was left of them anyway.

Fortunately, there was still a lemon meringue pie left, but only because Connie had hidden it from the hands, who'd eaten earlier. He'd bet that they'd left plenty of meat loaf, though.

How in the hell Connie could make such lousy meals, yet whip up great cakes and cookies, was beyond him.

At least it hadn't taken the new cook very long to realize she had to double and triple her dessert recipes so she didn't have a dinnertime rebellion on her hands.

If she were smart, she'd ask Tori to trade jobs with her more often. That chicken and rice casserole had been one of the best dinners they'd had in a long time. But Matt figured Tori had enough to do around here without taking on more work.

He glanced to his right, where the redhead sat, picking at the food on her plate.

Granny was across the table from him. He could have sworn he'd seen the elderly woman grimace as she choked down her meal. Yet she never said a word to Connie, other than, "Thanks for dinner."

Matt was still hungry, but pushed his plate aside. If he'd been more mobile, he might have helped clear the table. But the damn wheelchair was bulky and difficult enough to move through the house.

He glanced at Tori, watched her scrape the meringue off the top of her pie and dig into the lemon filling.

What was her story?

How had she come to wind up on the ranch?

When he'd finished his second helping of pie, he asked if she wanted to take a walk outside with him this evening. No need to quiz her in front of Granny, which might only make things more awkward than necessary.

She looked up from her plate. "You want to go for a walk? With *me?*"

"Well, you'd be doing the walking," he said. "I'd have to wheel around in this thing."

She bit her bottom lip. What made the question so difficult? Had he been so tough on her that she had to decide whether or not she wanted to be alone with him?

Or was she thinking about the sexual attraction that had ricocheted throughout the office earlier?

Damn. It wasn't as though he was going to make any moves on her. Matt didn't start something he couldn't finish.

Of course, it wasn't as though he *couldn't* finish something with her. In that sense, the wheelchair was just a bit of an inconvenience. If they were stretched out on a bed, he'd…

Hell, he'd put a sated smile on both of their faces.

"Sure," Tori said. "I'd like to take a walk."

"That's a very good idea." Granny pushed her chair back and got to her feet. "You two go on outside while I help Connie with the dishes."

Matt hoped Granny wasn't thinking that he and Tori were tiptoeing around a romance. He knew better than to get involved with anyone again, especially another redhead—and a bossy one at that. But there'd been several questions weighing on his mind.

Questions that demanded answers. Like why she was no longer a nurse. Why she'd shut her brother out of her life.

Matt wouldn't be living at the Rocking C forever. Eventually, he'd heal and get on with his own life—even if he didn't have a clue what he'd do with the rest of it, now that he couldn't be a rodeo cowboy anymore.

Either way, when he decided to ride off into the sunset, he was going to have to feel good about leaving Granny with a cook who didn't know her way around a stove and a woman who'd rather be a maid than utilize a nursing degree.

Something just didn't add up.

Matt maneuvered his wheelchair away from the table, then rolled into the kitchen and out to the service porch, where Tori opened the door for him. As he started down the ramp, she reached for the handles at his back.

"I've got it," he said. Hell, the last time she tried to help, he'd been afraid the chair would barrel down that ramp like a wild bronc out of the chute.

Moments later, when he'd reached the ground safely on his own, she joined him in the yard.

"Where to?" she asked.

He nodded toward the barn, then began to push the wheels of his chair forward.

"I'm afraid I ate more pie than I should have, so it's nice to get outside and walk off some of the calories."

Matt couldn't care less about fresh air and exercise, but he wanted to get her alone. So most any direction would do. "Let's walk along the driveway. That outdoor light at the back of the barn ought to illuminate our way for a while."

"All right." She scanned the horizon. "It's a pretty night."

"Yep." He glanced at the evening sky, where a lovers' moon shone bright, and a jillion tiny stars winked as though they were in on some kind of celestial secret.

As they walked and wheeled along, the sounds and the smells of the ranch soon lulled Matt into an easy mood.

Had it done the same to her?

There was a stretch of pasture to the left, as well as to the right. He remembered the first day the social worker had driven him along this very road and told him she'd found him a new home.

He'd been scared and angry, yet he'd been in awe of the place, too. It was a lot different from the city streets or the small apartment in which he'd lived with his uncle.

"I love this ranch," he said.

"It's easy to see why you would."

He supposed the Rocking C held a certain appeal to a lot of people, especially a boy. In Matt's case, it had been the vast grassy pastures and the animals that had roped his interest first. Then it had been the men who'd taken him under their wing, the self-satisfaction of a hard day in the saddle and the reward of a warm, cozy bed at night.

And before he knew it, he'd found the real key to contentment—a mother's love and a sense of belonging that had always eluded him.

He slid a glance at the pretty redhead who walked beside him. Would she feel better about sharing something personal with him if he opened up a bit first?

Maybe.

"Did Granny ever tell you how she and I first met?" he asked.

Tori slowed and turned, her face bathed in moon-light, interest sparking in her eyes. "No. But I'd like to hear about it."

"When I was about ten, I tried to steal her purse."

"No kidding?"

"Well, it's kind of a long story." He glanced over his shoulder at the house and nodded. "Let's head back before it gets too dark to see."

"Okay."

For a moment he questioned his plan to share the details with a virtual stranger. But then again, it wasn't anything that she couldn't find out by asking Granny.

So he turned the wheelchair around and began to tell Tori what he'd never told anyone. Not even Cindy, the woman he'd planned to marry. "I was a city boy by birth. And I lived in downtown Dallas with my mom until I was nine."

"What about your father?"

"He took off when I was just a baby, so I don't remember him."

"I'm sorry."

He shrugged. "It all worked out for the best, I guess."

Again he questioned the wisdom in spilling his guts, then realized he wasn't telling her any real secrets. "Since it was just us, my mom had to work two jobs to pay the rent, so I learned to fend for myself early on."

Matt had more or less been on his own since he'd been Joey's age. At the time, he hadn't seen anything unusual about it. There were a lot of kids in his neighborhood who'd learned the ropes while on the street.

"Were you close to your mom?" Tori asked.

"Yeah. I suppose so. But she died when I was nine."

"I'm sorry to hear that."

Matt had been, too. But not as sorry as he'd been after moving in with Uncle Vern. "A social worker called my mom's half brother, and when he agreed to take me, I moved to Brighton Valley."

"How did that go?" she asked. "I mean, you eventually moved to the ranch, so I figured it might not have worked out."

"It didn't. I guess you could say we butted heads more often than not. Vern didn't like anyone to cross him, and I wasn't used to having a boss."

"You argued a lot?"

"My uncle had this warped idea that he could beat or starve me into submission." Looking back, Matt supposed that had merely served to help him develop an even tougher hide and spirit.

Tori crossed her arms and shifted her weight to one leg. "That's barbaric."

"Unfortunately, that's also a reality for some kids." Matt raked a hand through his hair. "Anyway, one day, as I was wandering through town and making excuses not to go home, I came upon an ice cream social that was sponsored by the church. I hadn't eaten since the night before, and even then, it hadn't been much. So I was really hungry. I didn't have any money, and the only option I saw was to steal a lady's purse."

"Was it Granny's purse?" Tori asked.

"Yeah, but I didn't know who she was then. I just saw that she had gray hair and was kind of pudgy. So I figured she'd be no match for me in a foot race. But little did I know that Granny was just as tough and cagey as she was loving."

"What did she do?"

"She caught me before I could get ten yards away. And she knew right off the bat that I'd been neglected and mistreated—probably because I was so skinny and was sporting a bruised cheek and a split lip. So, after she bought me all the ice cream I could eat, she reported the abuse. And when authorities investigated my living situation and decided to remove me from my uncle's home, she offered me a place to live on the ranch."

"And you ended up becoming a part of her family."

"Eventually. But it was tough at first. One of the things I'd learned growing up was to protect myself by not caring, by withdrawing. It took her a while, but Granny drew me out of my shell. And before long, the men on the ranch began to show me the way adults ought to treat children."

"That's a nice ending to a sad story," she said.

"Yeah, I guess it is."

Tori studied the man in the wheelchair, appreciating his self-disclosure. Her heart had gone out to the little boy in him, the defiant child who, by Matt's own admission, had learned to protect himself by withdrawing, by pretending not to care about anyone or anything.

Apparently, as an adult, he'd fallen back into that same old pattern when tragedy struck.

She wanted to ask about the woman who'd died, the woman he'd loved. But she thought it was best to wait until it was his idea to tell her.

"Why don't we sit on the porch?" she asked.

"I'd have to park this thing and climb the steps. But that's okay. There's a railing."

"No, it's *not* okay." For some reason she'd completely

forgotten about his limitations, in spite of that darn wheel-chair. "I can't allow you to do something the doctor hasn't said you could do. And I'm sorry for being so thought-less as to even suggest it."

"If you want to sit outside," he said, "get yourself a chair from the porch and bring it here."

"All right." Tori made two trips back and forth, bringing first a wicker rocker, then a small matching side table that bore a ceramic pot holding a citronella candle.

"All we need is a match," she said before dashing into the house to get one.

Minutes later they sat outdoors, the flame flickering on the wick while a sliver of curly smoke snaked into the night sky, promising to fend off any insects that might be lurking nearby.

A horse whinnied in the distance, and crickets chirped near the water trough. It might not seem like a romantic setting to anyone else, but it did to Tori, and she found it surprisingly appealing.

She enjoyed the stillness for a while, the peace.

"So how did *you* meet Granny?" Matt asked, drawing her from her appreciation of the night.

"I was in Brighton Valley, filling out a job application at Caroline's Diner."

Tori didn't think she should mention that Granny, who'd been eating a muffin with a friend and sharing a cup of coffee, had spotted Tori crying her eyes out. If she did, he'd probably ask what had caused her tears. And, if she wanted to be honest, she'd have to admit that she'd realized the owner of the café wanted her to list her previous employers, as well as provide the names and contact numbers for any supervisors she'd had.

She could have lied on the application, she supposed, but dishonesty had always gone against her grain. And if a person didn't have any honor, what did they have left?

"Why did you decide to become a maid rather than a waitress?" he asked.

Actually, Tori would have preferred to be a *nurse*. It's what she'd been trained to do. It's what she loved.

But the betrayal and embarrassment were still so fresh, her feelings so raw, that she wasn't ready to explain herself or to discuss her brother's crime with a potential employer.

Of course, that hadn't seemed to matter when Granny sat beside her and offered a tissue. Moments later the story had just tumbled out, along with a new onslaught of tears. It had seemed a real blessing to have someone sympathize with her heartbreak and disappointment, to understand her need for some R & R.

"Your mother provided a maternal connection I'd been missing for a long time," Tori admitted. "And before I knew it, I began to bare my heart and soul to her, revealing things I'd never expected to tell anyone."

"So when she offered you a job, you took it because she was motherly?"

"I'm not trying to overstep my bounds," she said, hoping he understood. She wasn't attempting to worm her way into his family. "I really don't know why I came out to the Rocking C with her. Maybe because she was so kind. Maybe because she offered me room and board, too. Maybe because I wanted to…"

Be careful, she advised herself. Telling Granny had

been one thing. But sharing the same with Matt was out of the question. He didn't need to know that she'd wanted to get away from her family so she could regroup and become completely independent of them. So she side-stepped the fact altogether and added, "Well, because I wanted to spend some time in the country."

"You obviously know your way around a stove better than Connie," he said. "So why didn't you get her job?"

"Elsie Tuttle, the previous cook, hadn't retired yet, so Granny's only opening was for a housekeeper. And when Connie came along, Elsie had just announced that she was moving in with her daughter in Galveston, so that's the position she was offered."

"Did you ever think about swapping jobs with Connie?" Matt asked.

"Actually, yes. Connie hasn't had much experience as a cook, although she did work in a bakery for a while. But your mother wouldn't hear of it. And I'll be darned if I know why. Sometimes she almost flinches when she looks at some of the dishes Connie puts out on the table. And she usually takes double helpings of dessert, too—just like we all do. But I've never heard her complain."

"I'm afraid it's impossible to second-guess my mother and figure out what her real objective is," Matt said. "And even if some of her plans are far-fetched, her motives always come from the heart."

"Well, obviously, she has her reasons." Tori wasn't sure what they could possibly be, though.

"So why did you give up nursing?" Matt asked.

While she supposed it was natural for him to have posed that question, she pondered her response. The truth wasn't something she wanted to run up a flagpole for all the world to see.

She tucked a strand of hair behind her ear. "Let's just say that it seemed like the right thing to do at the time. I might go back. We'll see." Then she glanced out into the pasture, into the night. "Have you given any more thought to Granny's birthday party?"

If he suspected she was trying her best to avoid any more revelations about herself, he didn't mention it. Instead he said, "No, I haven't given it much thought at all."

"Why not? I'd think that you'd be excited about helping her celebrate."

"I'm happy that she's having a birthday. But the kind of party you're envisioning seems like an awfully big chore."

"It's *not* too much work." She glanced his way, saw him watching her intently, and her voice just naturally lowered, softened. "Not if we share the load."

"Why does this party mean so much to you?" he asked.

"Because Granny trusted me, a virtual stranger to her. And she provided me with a job and a place to live."

"Doc Graham has a lot of pull at the clinic in Wexler," Matt said. "I'd think that working with him would be a lot more fulfilling for you."

Maybe someday, she thought. But not yet. "I'm enjoying a break from nursing right now."

She thought she heard him scoff, but couldn't be sure. Still, she couldn't blame him for not believing her. She'd been in her element whenever one of the hands was injured. Why, just a couple of weeks ago, when Charlie McDougall suffered a gash in his head and refused to see a doctor, she'd actually gotten a lot of satisfaction out of convincing him otherwise. And in spite of her fears for Joey's health, she'd received a rush of personal fulfillment when she'd been able to detect the seriousness of his heart condition and had accompanied him to the hospital for the tests and subsequent surgery.

No, she might be enjoying the break from her younger siblings. But she didn't like being away from nursing.

Was Matt buying into her lie?

She was afraid to steal a glance his way. Instead she gazed at the full moon and the vast array of stars, her mood growing solemn, pensive.

Matt spun his chair a few degrees to the right, facing her full on. "Can I ask you something?"

Her heart skipped a beat, and for a moment she wondered if he was turning the conversation toward something…personal. Something romantic. And she wasn't sure if she'd be flattered or uneasy.

"Sure," she told him. "Ask away."

"Why did you tear up your brother's letter without reading it?"

So much for him leaning toward romance, which would have put her on the spot—whether she was flattered by the idea or not. But the question about her brother took her completely aback.

She slapped at a mosquito that lit on her arm. "I'd rather not discuss it."

"Fair enough." His gaze traveled to the pasture, where a couple of the brood mares grazed.

"Now I have a question for *you*," Tori said.

"I guess turnabout is fair play. Shoot."

"Jared told me that you quit physical therapy. Why? Don't you care whether you walk again or not?"

Matt continued to stare off into distance for a while, as if he hadn't heard her. Or, if he had, that he wasn't sure he wanted to discuss his thoughts or reasons with her.

When she suspected he wasn't going to give her an answer at all, he surprised her. "The first time Jared drove me to physical therapy, I realized that there was someone who worked there that I didn't want to run into. So I refused to take my appointment."

"And so, for some crazy reason, you'd rather risk the chance of not having a full recovery from your injury."

"First of all, the reason wasn't crazy. And second, I'll never be one hundred percent. Not as long as I can't ever ride in another rodeo. So what the hell difference does it make?"

It ought to make a lot of difference, and she struggled to figure out what was really going on in that head of his.

"Who were you trying to avoid?" she asked.

"No one important."

"Was it a woman?" she asked.

"Yeah, but not for the reason you're thinking."

Oh, no? She suspected that the woman had been an old lover. And that their breakup had been messy. Yet something told her that even if she was partially right, there was more to it than that.

"I'll probably have physical therapy someday," he added, "but it'll have to be at another place."

Good. At least they were making progress.

"You mean you'd consider making an appointment in Brighton Valley?"

"Sure, but it's a pretty small town. I doubt if there's a physical therapist there."

Tori studied the man who didn't seem to be in any hurry to walk again.

As a rodeo cowboy, competition had undoubtedly come easy for him. So it seemed reasonable to believe that he'd want to do all he could to get back on his feet.

"If I find another place and drive you back and forth, will you go?" she asked.

Matt hesitated, but only for a moment. "I'll think about it."

Good. She'd love to give something back to Granny. And she couldn't think of anything better than a healthier son who would soon get out of that wheelchair and quit feeling sorry for himself.

Still, something niggled at her. A whittling sense of guilt that chipped away at her self-confidence.

And why was that?

Because, a small voice whispered, *in some respects, when it comes to not giving one hundred percent, Matt isn't that different from you.*

Chapter Five

While Tori enjoyed the time she'd spent outdoors with Matt this evening, she hadn't been able to shake a subtle sense of guilt for not practicing what she intended to preach.

She wanted Matt to push himself, yet she was content to sit back and not be the woman she was meant to be.

"But in my case," she argued to herself, "it's a different story."

She was just taking a little breather, a little time off to regain her balance. Besides, there always seemed to be some kind of medical emergency on the ranch, giving her plenty of opportunities to be a nurse while not actually working at a hospital or clinic.

To be honest, though, Tori missed her job in a busy E.R. and having the opportunity to sharpen her medical skills.

However, life on the Rocking C was slow paced, which made it a perfect place for her to heal her own wounds.

Now, as she sat in the guest bedroom that she'd been assigned to use, the muted sounds of Matt's television hummed from the room next door. But she ignored it, instead focusing on what had persuaded her to escape her family in the first place.

As much as she loved her maternal grandparents, she wished they hadn't coddled her younger brother and sister and spoiled them rotten.

Deep inside, Tori knew the elderly couple hadn't meant to cause Sean and Jenna any harm. They'd only tried to make up for the devastating loss of their parents.

But while growing up as orphans was a tough row to hoe, it was, unfortunately, their reality and something they had to learn to deal with.

It would have been better if Gram and Gramps had been loving yet firm. If they had, Sean and Jenna might have grown up stronger and more grounded—at least morally and ethically.

Tori had been in high school when her parents had taken a second honeymoon and died in a fluke helicopter accident on the trip. She'd been devastated, too, but at least her character had already been molded.

So after graduating, she went off to college and eventually became a registered nurse.

Her life had really looked promising and bright.

Then, after Sean had a falling out with some of his loser friends, Gram called and asked Tori if he could move in with her. She agreed, hoping that he'd finally grown up. She got him a job at the hospital, and before long, Jenna came looking for help, too. Soon there were three McKenzies working at Lone Star General.

Okay, so the living and working situation had required an adjustment, but she'd felt good about helping out her brother and sister.

That is, until a significant amount of prescription pain medication turned up missing from the hospital.

Tori had never expected one of the thieves to be her brother.

A criminal investigation uncovered his stash, and Tori had been mortified. His defense attorney managed to get him minimal jail time, a fine and probation. Then, as if the shame hadn't been enough, Tori had been reprimanded by the hospital for her lack of judgment in referring her brother and for missing all the signs of his drug addiction.

Just when she thought things couldn't possibly get worse, she found her sister lip-locked with Dr. James Dawson in one of the supply closets at the hospital. James, an intern at Lone Star General, also happened to be the man Tori was dating. The man who was her first— and only—lover.

Needless to say, Tori was crushed to learn that James wasn't the man she'd hoped he was—that he was a womanizer and couldn't be trusted.

But Jenna was her *sister*. And even though Jenna had only been eighteen and was still a babe in many ways, some kind of sisterly code of honor should have been at play. And it hadn't been.

Feeling betrayed and even more embarrassed than ever, Tori quit her job, broke the lease on her apartment and moved out of town.

All she wanted to do was put some distance between herself and the past. So she'd ended up in Brighton Valley, looking for work and a place to rent. She'd begun to run out of hope and funds when she met Granny Clayton. And that's when her luck finally turned.

Or had it?

Could she ever really escape from the past, the embarrassment or the heartbreak?

Maybe she ought to make that separation from her family permanent.

The guilt that had been hovering over her since talking to Matt about putting out a hundred percent stretched over her like a new rubber band, ready to snap and sting.

She might not want to ever see her brother and sister again, but Gram was another story.

Gramps had died last year—before the family had begun to unravel—and now Gram was alone. No matter how you looked at it, Tori was the only person upon whom the elderly woman could depend.

So, no. While Gram was alive, Tori could never fully sever herself from her siblings.

She reached for her purse, pulled out her cell and dialed Gram's number.

Unfortunately, Jenna answered on the second ring.

Tori's first impulse was to ask, "Have you met any new interns lately? Have you set your sights on someone else's lover?"

Instead she merely asked to speak to Gram.

"You have no idea how sorry I am," Jenna said. "About everything."

Tori tensed. Her little sister had been so used to having

her way that she hadn't cared what effect her choices or her behavior might have on someone else. And quite frankly, there was no reason to even go there; what was done, was done.

"May I please speak to Gram?" Tori asked again.

"Yes. But can you wait a minute? I wanted to tell you that, if it makes you feel better, James and I aren't seeing each other anymore."

"It would have made me *feel* better if you hadn't considered him fair game in the first place."

"I know, but—"

"Listen, Jenna. I only have a minute and I really need to speak to Gram."

Her sister finally got the hint and let the subject go. Moments later, Gram came to the phone. "Tori, honey, where are you?"

"I'm at a ranch near Brighton Valley. I told you, remember?"

"Oh…yes, I suppose you did. When are you coming home?"

"I'll be here for a while," Tori said. "But how are *you* doing, Gram?"

"Okay. The arthritis in my neck has been really bothering me, so Jenna's been doing most of the cooking and the housework. She's been so good to me."

"I'm glad to hear it."

"She also took me to see Sean," Gram added. "He's living with some other young men, and he's doing very well. He's so handsome. He looks a lot like your father did at his age."

Maybe so, but other than a physical resemblance, the

two couldn't be any more different. Still, it's not as though Tori wanted Sean to be doing badly. It's just that Gram believed anything he and Jenna told her:

"My homework is done."

"Yes, there'll be chaperones at the party."

"The school attendance clerk is lying. I was in school yesterday. You can ask my friends."

"Sean and Jenna are snowballing you," Tori used to tell her grandparents. But the older couple had never listened, saying only that Tori should cut her little brother and sister some slack.

Tori had known the younger kids needed a firm hand, so when she'd let them each move in with her, she'd thought she would be a positive influence on their lives.

Instead they'd been negative influences on hers.

But that was muddy water under a rickety bridge.

So she chatted with her grandmother for a while, trying to keep the focus on Gram, her health and her friends.

In the box in the corner, a couple of the kittens began to mew, letting Tori know it was time for their bedtime feeding.

"Listen," she told Gram. "I need to hang up now. But I'll give you a call in a couple of days."

After saying goodbye and disconnecting the line, Tori went to the kitchen to prepare the bottles of formula, where she found Granny seated at the round oak table, drinking a glass of milk and eating one of the gingersnap cookies Connie had made earlier.

"Good evening," Granny said. "Would you like to join me for a bedtime snack?"

"I'm afraid the babies are hungry, so I'd better see about them first."

"Is something wrong?" Granny asked. "When you first came in here, you were frowning."

Tori supposed her family burdens had caused some momentary stress, but she wasn't up to discussing them. Especially right before bed. It wouldn't make for a restful sleep. So she mustered a smile. "Everything's fine."

"How did your little talk with Matthew go this evening?" Granny took a sip of milk, her gaze rooted on Tori. "Was he in a better mood?"

"We had a nice chat. I think it was good for him to get out of the house." Tori pulled the little bottles from the cupboard and the kitten formula from the fridge. "Tomorrow morning I'm going to try and find a physical therapist in the area. He gave me reason to believe that he'd be open to making an appointment."

"Good." Granny fingered the white eyelet trim that adorned the bodice of her nightgown. "I'm glad to hear that. He might not be able to ride in the rodeo again, but at least he should be able to walk. His depression has had us all concerned."

"He must have really loved his fiancée," Tori said.

"I'm sure he was fond of her." Granny pushed back her chair, then got to her feet and shuffled to the cookie jar, where she pulled out a couple of gingersnaps, handing one to Tori. "But...well, she just wasn't quite...his type."

Tori took a bite of the cookie as she tried to decipher just what Granny meant by that.

"Have you ever been in love?" the older woman asked.

The question took Tori by surprise. She'd told Granny about James. And while they'd never discussed marriage, they had cared for each other.

Well, at least, that's what Tori had thought until James and her sister had betrayed her.

As she tried to come up with a truthful answer to Granny's question, all she could say was, "I'm not sure."

She'd had feelings for James. After all, their relationship wouldn't have taken a sexual turn if she hadn't.

But had she loved him?

"If what you'd felt was truly love," Granny said, "you wouldn't have had to think twice. There's a powerful zing in the heart that's impossible to deny."

Then, if that was the case, Tori's relationship with James had been lacking.

"I don't think Matt truly loved Cindy, either," Granny added. "But don't get me wrong. Cindy was a nice gal, and I'm sure Matt really liked her. It's just that I never thought they were suited for each other."

Matt must have thought so, Tori decided.

Why else would he have asked Cindy to marry him?

"Well," Granny said. "I'd better get some sleep. Morning will be here before we know it."

"Did you take your pills?" Tori asked.

Granny patted Tori on the arm. "Yes, I did. Thanks for the reminder. I haven't been forgetting to take them anymore. That little, plastic, seven-day container you gave me to use really helps."

As the older woman left the room, Tori cleaned up what little mess she'd made, then carried the bottles back to her bedroom.

She couldn't help thinking about what Granny had said regarding Matt's feelings for Cindy.

And she couldn't help disagreeing.

The man was a competitor by nature. After all, look at his chosen career. To ride wild, bucking broncos, he'd have to be a fighter.

He was also a survivor. She was reminded of the story he'd told her about living with his abusive uncle. She also thought about how feisty he'd been when he'd arrived at the Rocking C as a boy, but how he'd eventually made a place for himself.

Didn't it make more sense that, after a debilitating injury, he'd fight to get back what he'd lost? That he'd be determined to walk—if not ride—again?

No, the depression had to have been caused by grief over Cindy's death.

Granny had said they weren't suited. But what about the old adage that insisted opposites attract?

There was a lot that mothers and others who were sitting on the sidelines had no way of knowing.

Matt must have loved Cindy…a lot.

And Tori couldn't help being just a wee bit envious.

When she'd told James their relationship was over, he'd apologized about kissing Jenna, but he hadn't tried to talk Tori into giving him another chance. Not that she would have given him one. He'd shown his true colors.

But if Tori ever got involved with another man again, it would be with someone who loved her.

Someone who would at least grieve when she was gone.

The next day Tori located a physical therapist in Wexler, a town twenty miles north of Brighton Valley. She informed Matt and was relieved when he agreed to let her make an appointment for him.

So, on Thursday morning, the first available opening the therapist had, Tori woke up bright and early and gave the kittens their first feeding. As she did so, she took care to look over Tippy.

He seemed to be growing stronger, although he was still significantly smaller than the others. She was glad Matt had suggested they use an eyedropper to give him those initial feedings. It had made all the difference in the world.

In a sense, she thought of her and Matt as a team—at least when it came to the kittens. She just hoped that teamwork carried over to his therapy. It was important that she do whatever she could to get him back on his feet again. She owed that much to Granny.

She just hoped she hadn't met her match in the stubborn cowboy, especially when she feared he might never get over the loss of the woman he'd loved.

At nine o'clock she took Matt outside and tried to help him climb into the passenger side of the old ranch pickup.

"I can do it," he said.

She supposed, if he'd been taking showers, that he was managing on his own, but she wasn't sure if he was ready to put weight on his legs. Either way, she couldn't very well force him to accept her assistance.

Not when there was an issue of male pride.

As Matt struggled to get out of the chair and into the truck, his steps were unsteady, and his expression contorted in pain.

It was impossible to squelch the nurse in her. "Are you—"

"I'm *fine.*" He reached for the door, as well as the hood of the pickup. "I'm not an invalid."

She waited for him to get his entire body inside and close the door. Then she collapsed the wheelchair and placed it in back.

Moments later she climbed behind the wheel of the ten-year-old dual-wheeled Ford and began the forty-minute drive to Wexler.

A grimace continued to stretch across Matt's face, and she wasn't sure if it was because of pain or her interference. Maybe it was merely frustration because of how slow his recovery had been. Either way, she decided to bite her tongue until his mood improved.

So she focused on the smile that Granny wore this morning when she realized Matt was really going to finally start the physical therapy. It must be a big relief to know her youngest son was finally on a wellness track.

Just as Tori pulled onto the paved road that ran along the west side of the ranch, Matt reached for the radio knob, turned on the power and chose an FM station.

Tori had never been a huge fan of country-western music, but she couldn't help following the upbeat rhythm of the song that filled the inside of the cab. She was drawn to the words, to the romantic ballad about a love that was lost and rediscovered just before it was too late.

When the tune was over, the deejay, who referred to himself as "Shotgun" Bob Bridger, announced that he'd been playing the latest hit by Greg Clayton, a local boy who'd become one of the most promising performers in the business.

So that was the Clayton brother Tori had seen pictures of but hadn't met. The handsome, dark-haired entertainer whose musical talent was making him famous.

As she listened to the words and the melody, she could certainly understand why his fame was growing. There was something both soothing and alluring about Greg's voice, and it would have drawn her interest and attention even if he hadn't been one of Granny's boys.

"I really liked that song," she admitted. "Greg's musical ability shines. You must be proud of him."

"Yep. He's always had talent and been a showman. His success hasn't surprised anyone who knew him as a kid."

They made small talk as they traveled, but Matt continued to gaze out the window, his attention obviously elsewhere.

Tori wondered what he was thinking about but hated to pry. So she focused on the road as she followed the directions she'd gotten from MapQuest. She had a pretty good idea of where she was going, but when she pulled into the driveway of the medical building she'd been looking for, a white BMW came flying out of nowhere, and she had to slam on her brakes to avoid a collision.

The screeching halt caused them both to lurch forward against the shoulder straps of their seat belts. The blonde driving the Beemer merely mouthed an "Oops" and gave a toodle-dee-doo wave of her fingers before proceeding onto the street.

"Damn," Matt said. "Didn't you see her?"

"No, I didn't."

He mumbled something about women drivers, and she hoped he was commenting about the blond chick driving the BMW.

If he'd been lumping both of them together, she wanted to defend herself. She'd avoided a crash, hadn't she?

She opened her mouth to launch a retort, then thought better of it and clamped her lips shut. Matt didn't need to think about car accidents, especially when he was still recovering from the fatal collision he'd had.

"Do you see an empty parking space?" she asked.

"Nope. Not in front."

There was, however, a spot with a handicap sign. She wouldn't actually shut off the engine, since she didn't have the official decals or plates, but she couldn't imagine anyone complaining once they saw Matt get into the wheelchair.

"I'll let you out right here," she said. "Then I'll meet you inside. That is, unless you need some help with the door."

"I can get it."

While the truck idled, she slid out of the driver's seat and removed the chair from the back. In the meantime, Matt swung his legs around and proceeded to get out of the pickup.

Tori waited for him to settle into the seat, then asked, "Do you want me to push you into the lobby?"

"No." He shot her a frown. "In case you haven't figured it out, I don't like being pushed."

Something told her he was talking about more than having her assistance while he was in the chair. And she supposed she had been pushing him a bit as it was.

She blew out a little sigh, telling herself that she'd at least gotten him to Wexler and to his first physical therapy appointment.

And she'd done so *safely,* even if he didn't quite agree.

"After I park, I'll meet you inside," she said again, ready to circle back to the driver's seat.

"Nope. I'm going in alone." He nodded to a grassy area

near the front of the building, where a bench sat in the shade of a tree. "You can wait over there or in the pickup. Or run some errands and come back for me."

"Okay, but I thought it might help if I… Well, if I went inside and talked to them, they could show me what exercises you need to work on, and we could do them at home."

"I'm a big boy, Tori." The gentle blue of his eyes mocked the gruffness in his tone. "I don't need a personal nurse, whether you think I do or not."

He was right, of course. So why did she feel compelled to continue offering her services?

She told herself it was out of consideration for his mother. But she feared it might be more than that.

As Matt wheeled himself toward the smoked-glass lobby door, she stood beside the idling pickup and watched the ex-rodeo cowboy go.

A part of her sympathized, yet another part actually admired him.

The sun glistened off the glossy gold strands of his hair, as the well-developed muscles in his upper shoulders and arms worked to propel him to the entrance. He stopped long enough to push the square metallic button that swung open the automatic doors.

As she continued to watch him go, a shiver of heat ran through her blood and an unwelcome jolt of attraction struck low in her belly. She tried her best to shake it off.

It was too soon for her to have those kinds of feelings and thoughts again. Wasn't it? Only six months had passed since she'd suffered that ugly breakup, thanks to her younger sister.

Okay, so it had been James's fault, too.

And maybe she would have come to the conclusion that their relationship hadn't been made in heaven, that it hadn't been destined to last.

That wasn't the point.

Still, she needed time to heal and recover without complications. So, finding herself attracted to Matt Clayton was just an indication that she was on the rebound. Why, any man would look good to her now.

Of course, she had to admit that no one else had looked the least bit interesting to her before this wounded cowboy.

Chapter Six

Matt hadn't meant to be rude by shutting Tori out when she obviously had only wanted to be helpful. But before going into physical therapy, he hadn't been sure what he was up against.

He also wanted to hear what the therapist had to say and to be able to ponder without an audience any orders the doctor had given.

So he'd chosen to go inside alone, and now he had the option to decide what—if anything—he wanted to share with Tori.

As it was, he was glad she hadn't been with him.

After assessing Matt's balance, strength and range of motion, the therapist had worked him over thoroughly, and the process had been torturous. But Matt pushed himself hard, and as a result his hips, legs and ankles hurt like hell. In fact, he felt as though he'd been trampled under the hooves of an unbroken stallion.

"It might be best to take some pain medication before your next appointment," Stan Granger, the therapist, had said.

Matt said he would, yet a part of him felt as though he deserved the ache and discomfort, as though that might somehow be fitting and just.

"You can start putting some weight on your legs now," Stan said, "but only for short periods of time each day. And when you do, you'll need to use a walker."

The idea, Stan explained, was to gradually build up Matt's strength and balance.

Now, as Matt wheeled himself out of the lobby and into the natural light of day, he scanned the grassy area, looking for Tori.

He spotted her seated sideways on a bench, reading a book. She looked pretty sitting there, her legs stretched out along the seat, one knee bent. She'd tucked her hair behind an ear, giving him a glimpse of her profile, and he couldn't help slowing himself to a stop so he could watch her for a moment or two.

Her brow was furrowed, and she nibbled on her bottom lip. The words on the pages obviously held some kind of fascination for her, and he suddenly wished he was standing behind her, reading over her shoulder to see what had caught her interest.

Instead he began the slow process of wheeling toward her. If she offered to push him this time, he just might let her.

Of course he'd never ask.

He maneuvered the chair toward the place where the sidewalk met the grass, just steps away from the bench on which she sat.

At the sound of his approach, she glanced up and smiled. She lifted her hand to shade the sun from her eyes. "How did it go?"

"All right."

She studied him as though trying to determine whether he was being truthful, but he figured his sweat-dampened hair and the perspiration on his shirt ought to be pretty convincing.

"It looks to me like someone gave you quite a workout," she said.

"You've got that right." He blew out a raspy sigh. "But if it helps me get out of this damn chair, then it was well worth the effort."

"I'm glad to hear you say that."

He nodded toward the open paperback novel that rested in her lap. "What are you reading?"

Her cheeks had taken on a rosy hue, either from the sun or embarrassment; he couldn't be sure.

She smiled shyly. "I found a book lying on the grass. Someone must have left it. And I…"

Matt looked at the front cover that sported a bare-chested male, his biceps bulging. The top button of his jeans was undone.

A grin tugged at Matt's lips. He suspected that the flush on Tori's cheeks wasn't from the sun after all, but rather from the sexy novel she'd been caught reading.

"Did they give you exercises to do at home?" she asked, getting to her feet.

She placed the book in her purse.

Not back on the grass where she'd found it?

A grin stole across his face. Obviously, she was enjoying the sexy story and meant to finish it at home.

"Yep."

"Lord knows I'd never want to push a man who hates to be pushed," she said with a smile, drawing him away from his erotic musings. "But the offer still stands. If you'd like me to work with you, all you have to do is ask."

Actually, now that he'd met with Stan and realized how tough physical therapy was going to be, how hard he'd have to work at home…

But Matt was never one to admit needing help.

"When is your next appointment?" she asked.

"A week from today."

They started toward the pickup, and her steps slowed as though she wanted to offer to get behind his chair and help again, but she must have thought better of it.

It would have been nice to kick back and rest his aching muscles, though. And for a moment he was almost sorry that she'd reconsidered.

"Do you need to get back to the ranch right away?" he asked.

"No. Why?"

Matt would have preferred to go straight home, but it had seemed like forever since he'd had a decent meal. And even the abundance of sweets was getting old.

He wanted a big, juicy steak, a double helping of French fries and… Heck, he'd even settle for a helping of vegetables, which had never been something he particularly liked. But if they were cooked properly…

"Let's stop in Brighton Valley at Caroline's," he said. "If you don't mind taking our time getting home, I'll treat you to lunch."

"You've got a deal." She tossed him a pretty smile, then waited for him to slide into the passenger side.

It hadn't been easy getting into the vehicle the first time, when they'd been back at the ranch and just starting out. But after that workout, Matt's legs felt as though they were going to buckle at any moment.

And as luck would have it, they damn near did.

Tori, who'd pushed the chair out of the way, stood between him and the door. Apparently sensing a catastrophe ready to happen, she grabbed him just in the nick of time, providing some extra support.

She was stronger than he'd given her credit for.

Softer and warmer, too.

The scent of her shampoo and body lotion, something tropical, snaked around him like a serpent in paradise. And if he didn't have that god-awful pain shooting through his legs, he might have actually enjoyed the awkward yet sensual embrace.

"Are you okay?" she asked.

"Yeah," he said through gritted teeth. "Thanks."

He hated to admit it—Matt Clayton didn't *need* anyone—but if it hadn't been for her quick response, he would have fallen down. And then he might have been in one hell of a fix.

Of course, he was in a different kind of "fix" right now.

Her breasts pressed tauntingly against his side, and as her arms tightened around his waist, a jolt of heat rushed through his blood.

Great.

This was neither the time nor the place for sexual awareness, especially since he wasn't comfortable with his current vulnerability, so he tried to laugh it off.

"I'd like it a whole lot better if I weren't temporarily incapacitated," he said. "I might have copped a feel."

Those cheeks flushed again, a deep telltale shade of pink. And he couldn't tell whether she was flattered or un-comfortable because of his remark.

Flattered, he hoped. Because for the first time in what seemed like forever, he was thinking about something and someone other than Cindy and how he'd failed her.

And interestingly enough, the thought of a sexual romp with Tori promised to work a hell of a lot better than the pain meds or Jack Daniels ever had.

Ten minutes later Tori pulled the pickup in front of Caroline's Diner and parked in the shade of one of the elm trees that lined the street.

Other than the music playing on the radio, the fifteen-minute drive to Brighton Valley had been quiet and uneventful. She suspected it was because things had gotten a little...awkward after Matt had almost fallen while getting into the truck.

Thank goodness she'd been standing beside him when it happened.

As a nurse, she'd always had to be on her toes, so instinct had kicked in.

Of course, it was a different kind of instinct taking the lead when she had her arms wrapped around him.

Being so close, only a breath and a heartbeat away,

she'd caught the hint of fresh perspiration that mingled with the woodsy scent of his cologne. Something primal and distinctly feminine had sparked inside her, and when he'd joked about copping a feel, she'd actually found the idea intriguing. Exciting.

So what was with that?

It was enough to force her to keep her eyes on the road ahead as she drove to the diner, yet she couldn't help stealing glances across the seat at Matt, who repeatedly stroked his thighs.

She suspected he was still feeling the stretch and burn from therapy and wanted to comment about it. But she kept her mouth shut.

If she'd learned anything about him it was that he resented her help and interference. So she'd have to be content to know that he was at least making strides in the right direction, that he was finally doing his part to recover.

"We're lucky the lunch crowd already came and went," Matt said, as he scanned the front of the diner and seemed to note a few empty parking spaces. "There's usually a wait."

"That must mean that the food is every bit as good as you said it was. What kind of things are on the menu?"

"Baked chicken, pork chops, country-fried steak. You name it. And Caroline's mashed potatoes are just the way Granny used to make them. The desserts are good, too."

"Sounds wonderful."

"It is. And you can't beat the price. If you want a real treat and a bargain to boot, read the chalkboard that's set up by the cash register."

"Is that where she advertises the special of the day?"

"Yep. But it always says, 'What the sheriff ate.'"

"I don't get it," Tori said.

Matt chuckled. "The sheriff is Caroline's husband."

Tori got out of the truck. When she had the wheelchair set up, she pushed it to the passenger side.

"I'm willing to help you out if you want me to," she said, trying to make light of the fact that he'd pushed his legs to the limit already today. "But you'll have to promise not to cop a feel."

"No way." Matt lobbed her a grin that matched the one she was wearing. "I don't make promises I don't plan to keep."

A flood of warmth spread across her cheeks, and the thought of him touching her, caressing her, shot a jolt of heat to her core.

He was joking, of course.

Wasn't he?

She opened the door for him and waited as he maneuvered the chair inside. It was fortunate that Caroline's Diner provided handicap access. Tori hadn't been there since the day she'd met Granny, and it was almost like seeing it for the first time. Maybe because she was seeing it through Matt's eyes.

She scanned the small restaurant with its pale-yellow walls and white eyelet café window coverings. Tables dotted the center of the room, and brown vinyl booths lined the perimeter. An old-fashioned counter with swivel seats faced the kitchen.

The chalkboard Matt had told her about stood near the register and was hard to miss. Sure enough, in a feminine script, it was noted what the sheriff had eaten: meat loaf;

country-mashed potatoes; buttered, garden-fresh green beans; and peach cobbler. The price listed was $6.99.

"I'm going to start with the special," Matt said. "Then I'm going to order something else."

Tori arched a brow in question.

"Hey, I'm dying for a decent meal. And God only knows when I'll get another chance to fill up again."

A blond matronly woman at the back of the diner was handing a bill to an elderly man seated at one of the booths, his back to the entrance. As the waitress glanced up at Matt and Tori, she swept her arm in Vanna-White-style. "Feel free to sit anywhere, folks."

"How's this?" Tori pointed to the first table they came to.

"Perfect."

She removed a chair so Matt could wheel in close.

"Well, as I live and breathe," a salt-and-pepper-haired woman said from the kitchen. "Matthew Clayton. You're a sight for sore eyes."

"Hey, Caroline." Matt flashed the woman a grin. "I hope those local boys didn't eat all that peach cobbler."

"I've got just enough left for a couple of helpings." The proprietor's friendly smile faded to sympathy and concern. "How ya doin', hon?"

Matt's grin faltered a bit. "Don't worry about me. I'll be back to fighting weight before you know it."

"That's good," Caroline said. "What can I get you?"

"Do you want the special, too?" he asked Tori.

Actually, she hadn't eaten a good meat loaf in ages. "Sure."

"We'll start by having what the sheriff ate," he told Caroline.

About that time, the silver-haired gentleman who'd been seated at the booth in the rear slowly got to his feet and made his way to their table.

It was Dr. Graham.

He walked a bit stooped, but his eyes and smile were bright as he extended a liver-spotted hand to Matt. "It's good to see you out and about, son."

"Hey, Doc." Matt greeted the man, then introduced him to Tori.

"We've already met," Dr. Graham said, turning his attention to Tori. "How's Joey doing?"

"Sabrina said he's improving every day."

"Glad to hear it." Dr. Graham crossed his arms and gave Tori a once-over. "You know, I was talking to Edna the other day and told her that she ought to encourage you to go back to school and get a medical degree. You'd make one heck of a doctor."

"Thanks. That's quite a compliment and it's certainly an idea to consider." But even if Tori had already put enough distance between her and the past, it was out of the question. She didn't have the time or the money to pursue medical school.

"I'm not going to be around forever," Dr. Graham said. "And when I finally take down my shingle, I'd like to know that folks around here have another physician to keep them healthy."

Matt seemed to sit back and take it all in. "But then we'd lose our personal nurse at the Rocking C."

"Well, now, that's a point I hadn't thought about. You need your own private nurse, Matthew Clayton." Dr.

Graham chuckled. "And I said as much to your mother years ago."

"Why is that?" Tori asked, glad to steer the subject to something she'd rather discuss.

"Edna had to drag Matt into my office for one injury or another. He was always risking his neck doing some fool thing—often on a dare or a bet. As a boy, he was determined to make a place for himself on the ranch and made a habit of trying to prove himself as the fastest and the strongest of the Clayton boys." A slow grin stretched across the old doctor's craggy face, and his gray eyes glimmered. "How many stitches did you end up getting after that that crazy piebald mare threw you into the fence?"

"Only twelve."

Doc grinned. "You know, I told you while I cleaned your scalp that you'd better stay away from unbroken horses. And I swear, that must have been the wrong thing to say to a boy who never backed down from a challenge. Your mother said from that day forward you dug in your heels and swore up and down you'd be a rodeo cowboy. I never did know a young person to be so cantankerous and dead set on proving himself."

"So let me get this right." Tori placed her arms on the table and leaned toward Matt. "You chose a career based on someone telling you that you couldn't or shouldn't do it?"

Before Matt could respond, Doc said, "I wouldn't go that far. Matthew always was a natural-born horseman, and when he became a champion bronc rider, it was no surprise to anyone. But he's got a stubborn streak, that's for sure."

"I've seen it." Tori's gaze snagged Matt's, and something warm and fluid pooled between them, something she feared she might drown in if she wasn't careful.

Fortunately, Doc offered her what amounted to a flotation device. "Did Matt ever tell you why he always jumped at the chance to drive into town to pick up the ranch supplies?"

"No," Tori said. "Why?"

"Apparently, late at night while everyone slept, he rebuilt the engine on one of the old ranch pickups. It wasn't long before he became a teenage legend in these parts by giving every hotrod in town a run for its money. And if he couldn't find any competitors to eat his dust along the county road, he'd play chicken with the freight train that passed through each day."

"That sounds pretty reckless," she said.

"Maybe so," Matt admitted. "But I always had a handle on my limitations."

As his words hovered in the air, she could see him withdraw and grow solemn. Distant.

She assumed he was thinking about his injuries, about his inability to ever ride bucking broncos again. If she were his wife or lover, she'd be a little bit glad about that.

Yet she'd be sad, too.

Banning a man like Matt from the rodeo, from the thing he loved most in the world, would be like hobbling a wild stallion.

And in that sense, she supposed he had a lot in common with her.

So she opted to change the subject—for both of them.

"By the way, Dr. Graham, Matt and I are having a surprise birthday party for Granny in a couple of weeks.

You'll be getting an invitation soon, but I hope you'll help us keep it a secret. She's pretty sharp."

Doc laughed. "You can say that again. I've known Edna for nigh on sixty years, give or take a few. And that woman catches more in the air than most folks do with both feet on the ground. Sometimes I swear she's got an extra set of eyes in the back of her head."

Moments later, Caroline personally brought out their meals, and Doc excused himself, saying he had to get back to his office. He had a full schedule of patients this afternoon.

Two of the first things Tori had noted about the elderly doctor had been his dedication and his stamina. And each time she was around him and watched him work, she was impressed with the skill he'd amassed over the past half century by treating those in the community. And she couldn't help admiring him.

The people in and around Brighton Valley were sure going to miss him when he retired.

As she took the first bite of her lunch, she closed her eyes and savored the mouthwatering flavor of homemade meat loaf. Her mother used to cook meals like this— down home and from scratch—but it had been a long time since Tori had tasted the like. Her grandmother had never been as gifted. Of maybe she had, but she'd just grown tired of slaving away in the kitchen when the younger kids insisted upon fast food and pizza.

"You were right," Tori told Matt. "This food is divine."

When they'd both finished eating, Matt paid the bill. Then they went through the extra motions and effort it took to get Matt out of the chair and into the pickup.

Before Tori could start the engine, she noticed an office supply store that was just two doors down from the diner.

"Do you mind if I run inside and pick up some printed paper and matching envelopes to use for the invitations?"

"No. Go ahead."

Ten minutes later, they were on the open road and driving toward the ranch.

Another Greg Clayton song came over the airwaves, and Tori found herself falling easily into the beat. No wonder he was gaining fans right and left. Soon she would have to count herself as one of them.

"Do you think Greg will be able to make it to the party?" she asked. "I imagine he's pretty busy."

"I'll give him a call. He loves Granny as much as Jared and I do, so I'm sure he'll do his best to at least make a showing."

"Good."

When they arrived at the ranch, Tori parked the pickup where she'd found it, then shut off the ignition.

She was torn between offering to help Matt get out and respecting his pride. Either way, she had to get the wheelchair for him.

Thank goodness he'd be able to use a walker soon.

After unfolding the chair and pushing it to the passenger door, she waited as Matt slid out of the seat and got to his feet.

He grimaced, and she decided to heck with his pride. There was no way she wanted to risk having him fall after such a full and undoubtedly tiring day.

So she reached for him, then hesitated.

He turned slightly, his gaze zeroing in on hers provid-

ing her a glimpse of the man inside. The man who refused
to be beaten by anyone or anything.

A man who could take a woman's breath away with a
smile.

She expected him to settle into the chair, but instead, he
released his grip on the top of the vehicle door and ran the
knuckles of one hand along her cheek in a sensual caress.

A whisper of goose bumps ran up and down her arms,
and her lips parted.

As she sucked in a breath she'd forgotten to take, his
hand slowly dropped, skimming along her neck, down her
chest and nearly grazing one of her breasts.

Still, her nipple contracted, her pulse spiked, and her
breath caught again.

A rebellious grin tugged at his lips and his gaze slid
into the very heart of her.

Then he lowered his butt into the chair and began to
maneuver himself to the back of the house, where the
ramp would allow him entrance.

But Tori remained rooted to the spot, caught up in his
sensual gaze and in the flutter of pheromones he'd set
off overhead.

She'd thought he'd been kidding about copping a feel.
And she supposed he had been playing around. Taunting
her.

Yet she couldn't help wondering if he'd actually touch
her one day…

And hoping that he would.

Chapter Seven

The next day, a hospital supply company stopped by the ranch and dropped off a rental walker for Matt to use.

Stan had suggested that Matt slowly build up his strength, venturing from the wheelchair for a few minutes each day, but Matt decided to push harder than that and used the aluminum-framed walker as often as his bones and muscles could stand.

He knew he was doing more than the therapist had wanted him to, but he couldn't help it. When he set his mind on something, he went after it—just as he had when he'd overstepped his bounds with Tori and pretended to cop a feel.

Under the circumstances, with their relationship being what it was—platonic—it had been inappropriate.

It had started out as a joke, but as his knuckles stroked

the silk of her skin and her breath caught in a sensual response, her gaze had locked on his and turned the entire world inside out.

At that very moment, touching her had seemed like the most natural thing in the world to do.

Not that he needed to get involved in another relationship again. He'd gradually come to the conclusion that the last one had been a mistake from the get-go—and for a multitude of reasons. But that wasn't something he'd ever admit.

Because, if he did, it would make the unnecessary deaths of Cindy and her son even tougher for him to bear, and the guilt he carried even more crippling.

So Matt and Tori had just gone about their lives as though nothing had happened, as though nothing had changed.

"Do you want to take a walk?" she'd asked him during dinner.

He couldn't see why not. There was no reason to remain cooped up inside the house any longer. "Sure."

"You probably should use the wheelchair," she'd added. "That might be easier for you."

Now that he'd started therapy, he wasn't so sure he wanted to opt for easy. Not if it slowed down the recovery period. But he wasn't sure how far he could go outdoors, especially in the dark.

"Whatever," he'd said, unwilling to admit his weakness.

So after dinner, Tori took the wicker rocker, the table and the citronella candle from the front porch and set them up near the barn, obviously thinking that she and Matt would chat as they had last time.

And that was okay with him. To be honest, he'd

begun to enjoy her company. So after he maneuvered the chair down the ramp at the back door, they started their walk.

The moon wasn't as bright as it had been the other night, but the sights and smells of the ranch had the same, invigorating effect on Matt.

"I'd like to send out the party invitations tomorrow," Tori said. "Did you get a guest list made?"

"Yes. And I talked to Greg. He's on tour this month, but he'll be able to fly in for the day. He'll have to leave that night, though. I also called Jared, who asked if there was anything he could do. So I told him to come early and be prepared to work. There'll be a lot to set up in the barn—assuming you're still dead set on having it there."

She'd changed her mind a half-dozen times, unable to decide on the best setting. But she'd finally settled on the area just outside the back of the barn because it was closer to the house and the bathroom.

"The barn will also give us a place to hide everything. After Granny leaves the ranch for church, we can open up the back doors and set out the tables under that big sycamore."

"All right." Matt glanced up at the moon, saw that it was starting to wane. "By the way, I also made a couple of calls, and Red Filkins, a rancher who lives about five miles south of here, has a buckboard he'll let us use. Since you want to make this party a complete surprise, we'll need to ask people to park away from the house. So I figure it'll still come in handy as a shuttle."

"Good."

As they continued their walk, he wished that he was

strolling along beside her, that he could brush his shoulder against hers and risk touching her again.

But that was a fool idea.

He supposed it was best that his grip was on the wheels of the chair. God knew he didn't need to get any more touchy-feely with one of his mother's employees, no matter how pretty she was.

"What about food?" Tori asked. "With a western theme, it would be nice to have barbecue or something Tex-Mex."

"Either way, we'll need to get a caterer," Matt said. "There's no way we can have Connie fix the food."

Tori furrowed her brow and bit down on her bottom lip.

She was probably worried about hurting the cook's feelings, but there was no way Matt would invite his mother's friends to a party and feed them crappy food.

"Connie is a really nice person," Tori said. "And she's got enough to worry about with a baby on the way and no husband or any family support."

Matt slowed the pace and stopped. "I would be tactful when telling her. We'll just say that we don't want to burden her with all that work, especially since she's expecting. Maybe we can ask her to whip up a couple of cakes instead."

Tori brightened. "That's a wonderful idea. Then she'd feel as though she was contributing something."

"Why don't you talk to her, then. And suggest that she bake about ten or twelve of those Texas chocolate cakes she made last week."

"Ten or twelve?" Tori turned to face him. "How many people are you planning to invite?"

"I don't know. Fifty, I guess. But I want to make sure there's plenty to eat."

"With that many people, we'll have to rent tables and chairs. And since we'll need a caterer, do you have any idea who we should contact?"

"I'm going to call Chuck's Wagon."

"Who?"

"It's a guy who has this traveling barbecue setup," Matt explained. "He'll provide chicken and beef, coleslaw, beans, potato salad, corn on the cob. It'll be perfect. You'll see."

"All right. But you might want to contact him tomorrow. He might be busy already."

"Will do." Matt started down the road again, but his wheels hit a soft spot of dirt. "Dammit."

"Do you need help?" she asked.

"No, I'll…" It was more of a struggle than he'd anticipated, but he'd be darned if he was going to ask for help.

Nevertheless, she got behind him and pushed.

"Why don't we turn around," he said. "There are probably more soft spots up ahead."

This time she let him maneuver the chair by himself.

He hated being wheelchair-bound, hated being dependent. Of course, what he hated most of all was the thought that he'd never be able to ride in the rodeo again.

He shot a glance at Tori, wondering if she understood why it was so important for him to do things on his own.

Maybe.

"Do you miss it?" he asked.

She turned to him, brows furrowed. "Miss what?"

"Nursing."

Her lips parted. "I…well, I…Yes, I do. Why do you ask?"

"No real reason, I suppose." They continued to move

toward the table and chair she'd set up when they first began their walk. "It seems pretty clear to everyone who's met you that you were cut out for the medical field."

Just as Matt had been born to ride broncs, he supposed.

She seemed to think on his assumption for a while, then said, "Like I told you before, I needed a break. That's all. I'll go back someday."

"Something tells me that it wasn't a matter of burnout or boredom that sent you to Brighton Valley."

She didn't respond, but that didn't stop him from speculating.

Maybe she felt responsible for someone's death. Maybe she lay awake each night and wondered what she could have done differently.

And kicked herself because she hadn't.

If that were the case, she and Matt had a lot more in common than he'd realized.

Two weeks later, the day of the surprise party dawned sunny and bright. As far as Matt could tell, Granny didn't have a clue that a celebration had been planned in her honor.

For one reason, her actual birthday was still a week away.

Today he sat on the front porch, the walker parked near the wicker chair on which he rocked in a carefree manner. Once Granny was gone, he suspected the party preparations would kick into high gear. Tori had created a list of who was to do what and at what time. He'd never seen a woman so organized.

As he heard the drone of an engine coming down the drive, he glanced at his wristwatch—9:45 and right on time.

It was Sunday, and as had become the weekly routine

for almost as long as Matt could remember, Hilda Detweiler, a friend of Granny's, came by the ranch in her red '86 Cadillac Seville.

Hilda used to own and operate the Pampered Lady Beauty Parlor in Brighton Valley, which she sold when she retired. But she still continued to work part-time out of her home, where she cut and styled the hair of some of her oldest and best customers.

Granny was one of them.

Ever since Granny's husband, Everett, had died, Hilda made it a point to stop by and take Granny to church. Unless something came up that required one of them to go home early, the two friends usually made a day of it by eating lunch at Caroline's Diner and then driving into Wexler for a shopping trip or to see a movie.

Today, Hilda was going to feign a headache after lunch.

As the red Caddy pulled to a stop just steps away from the front porch, the perfectly coiffed silver-haired lady tapped her horn twice to announce her arrival to Granny. Then she rolled down the window of her car. "Hello, Matthew."

"Hey, Hilda. How's it going?"

"Not bad for an old woman. Edna told me you've been getting out of that wheelchair some. I was happy to hear it."

Before Matt could respond, the screen door swung open and Granny started down the steps, the handle of her white handbag draped over her forearm.

"You're welcome to come with us, Matt," his mother said on her way to Hilda's car. "We've got a visiting minister speaking, and he's supposed to be entertaining as well as informative."

"Thanks, but I'll pass. I never was able to sit through a complete sermon." Every time his mother would drag him and his brothers to church, he'd have a million reasons to get up.

Granny chuckled. "That's for sure."

"Have fun," Matt said. "What movie are you going to see?"

"Probably that new one with Ben Stiller. We both like him."

"Let me know what you ladies think of it," Matt said. "I just might catch a ride into town and see it myself."

Granny paused beside the open passenger door of Hilda's car. "You know, I never could figure why you could sit through a two-hour movie but couldn't handle a thirty-minute sermon."

Matt winked at Hilda. "The trick is to stuff me full of popcorn."

Both women shook their heads and chuckled as Granny climbed into the passenger seat. Moments later, the red Cadillac was kicking up dust and gravel along the drive while the silver-haired duo headed for Brighton Valley.

"Is it safe now?" Tori asked, as she poked her head out the screen door and stepped onto the porch.

"Yep. They're gone."

In a matter of minutes, Tori had everyone on the ranch rounded up and assigned their respective jobs.

Connie brought out the bags of party supplies the women had hidden in one of the closets, and soon the ranch was buzzing with activity as they all readied for the arrival of the guests.

Everyone except Matt.

He wasn't able to do much and, as a result, felt about as worthless as a three-dollar bill. So, for that reason, he remained on the porch and watched the others turn the barn into a reception area for Granny's neighbors and friends.

Less than twenty minutes later, a white truck from the party-rental place brought the tables and chairs Matt had ordered. The heavy-set, straw-haired guy who'd been driving said, "I'm looking for Mr. Clayton."

"You found him."

"Good. I'm going to need a signature." The driver carried a clipboard up the steps and handed the paperwork to Matt, who scanned the figures to make sure they'd brought what he'd ordered and at the quoted price.

Satisfied that everything was right, Matt signed his name.

Before long, the tables and chairs were set up behind the barn, and the truck was on its way back to town.

Connie, who'd been outside helping Tori with the decorations, crossed the yard and climbed the steps onto the porch. "I'm going inside. Can I bring you something, Matt? Iced tea, maybe?"

He supposed it was nice of her to offer. And while he'd rather throw back something stronger than tea, something to numb the dark mood he'd begun to slip into as he watched the action going on around him, he wouldn't risk morphing into a jerk and ruining Granny's celebration. "Sure, Connie. Thanks. Tea sounds good. Would you mind putting some sugar in it?"

"Not at all." She went into the house, letting the screen shut behind her, just as the engine of an approaching car sounded.

Matt turned to see a black sedan coming down the

drive. He didn't recognize the vehicle, but when it pulled to a stop, he immediately spotted the driver and his mood suddenly lifted.

It was his brother behind the wheel. Joe Riley, Greg's buddy and the band's drummer, sat in the passenger seat.

Greg parked, then got out of the car wearing dark glasses, a black shirt, faded jeans and designer western boots. The moment he laid eyes on Matt, a million-dollar smile busted over his face.

He climbed the stairs and stuck out an arm. "Hey, little brother. How you doin'?"

Matt glanced down at the chair in which he was stuck. "I've been better. But let's talk about you. They're playing your latest release almost hourly on the radio. So my guess is that things are going pretty damn well."

"I can't complain."

"Are you sure you'll still need to leave tonight?"

"Yeah. I flew in from Louisville at eleven o'clock, rented the car and drove out here. I've arranged to meet the tour bus in Nashville in the morning. So I've got to head back to Houston tonight. I want to be close to the airport for an early flight out tomorrow."

"I'm glad you were able to work this out. Granny's going to be happy to see you." Matt leaned back in his seat, wishing he could stand and give his brother a welcoming hug. As it was, he'd feel funny doing so in this position. While he and his brothers were growing up they always seemed to be competing with each other about one thing or another and trying to prove who was top dog. And right now Matt felt as though he'd rolled over and taken the submissive, belly-up position.

Not that Greg or Jared lorded over him anymore. But as a kid it was important to him to be respected. To be looked up to.

Hell, he guessed it still was.

"I'm not going to be able to stay very long." Greg removed his sunglasses and lowered his gaze to meet Matt's. "Just long enough to wish Granny a happy birthday and sing a couple of songs."

"Great. Where's your guitar?"

"In the back seat of the car."

Joe, who was making his way from the parked sedan to the porch, laughed. "Greg doesn't go many places without that thing. I told him he ought to insure it with Lloyd's of London."

"Very funny." Greg glanced through the screen door. "Where's Jared?"

"He should be here any minute. By the way, our big brother, the one who swore never to get serious about a woman again, has fallen head over heart for Granny's bookkeeper."

"No kidding?" Greg tossed Matt a crooked grin. "That's great."

"Her name is Sabrina."

Before Matt could continue, the screen door swung open, and Connie stepped out carrying a glass of iced tea. She seemed to balk, then continued the motions she'd started.

"Greg," Matt said, "this is Connie, the new cook."

"Nice to meet you." Greg's gaze zeroed in on the petite, shapely woman, but she seemed to take it in stride.

She managed a casual nod and a slight smile. "How do you do."

Weird, Matt thought. Most women fell all over themselves when meeting Greg, especially if they sensed that he had any interest in them at all.

Connie had all but averted her eyes from him during the introductions. Then she excused herself and went back into the house.

"Is she married or something?" Greg asked, apparently getting the same vibe Matt had gotten.

Actually, Matt wasn't sure of her marital status, although he knew she was pregnant, which might explain her lack of interest.

If Matt thought his brother was actually interested in Connie, he would have shared that tidbit of information. But Greg had his choice of women, even if you didn't count the groupies.

"Maybe she hates country-western music," Joe said, crossing his arms and shifting his weight to one hip. "She probably doesn't even know who you are."

No, Matt thought. That couldn't be it. Granny didn't make any secret about how proud she was of her sons, pointing out that Jared ran an impressive spread up north, that Matt was a champion bronc rider and Greg's latest song had hit the top of the charts.

Of course, Connie always kept a low profile around the ranch. Maybe she was just shy.

"It doesn't matter," Greg said. "Besides, it's kind of nice to be able to check out an attractive woman and not have her throw herself at me."

"Speaking of attractive women—" Joe blew out a whistle "—this place is jumping with 'em."

Matt followed Joe's gaze to Tori, who was striding

toward them, wisps of her curly red hair falling from the bun in which she'd secured it. A flush on her cheeks told him she'd been rushing around trying to get everything just so.

As she approached, she wiped her hands against her hips. "We're trying to keep the vehicles parked along the dirt road that goes to the fishing pond so Granny won't immediately see them when she returns. Would you mind moving your car?"

"No problem." Joe flashed her a grin that suggested he'd do anything she asked.

"Tori," Matt said, "this is my brother Greg and his friend Joe."

She reached out a hand, and blessed Greg with the warmth Connie hadn't been able to muster. "It's nice to finally meet you, Greg. Your mom is so proud of you. Actually, she's proud of all her boys."

Matt wondered how his mother was going to be able to boast about him now that he was no longer able to compete. A slow ache settled in his chest.

Almost as if homing in on his discomfort, Tori turned to him. "Are you going to change your clothes, Matt?"

He glanced down at what he was wearing—faded jeans and a white cotton shirt—then back at her. "What's wrong with what I have on?"

"Nothing. I just thought that I would head inside, take a shower and get dressed. And if you wanted to do the same thing, I was going to offer my help."

"I'll stick with what I have on."

"All right." She tossed Joe and Greg a pretty smile. "It was nice meeting you both. I'll see you in a bit."

She headed into the house. As the door shut behind her, Joe uttered, "Damn, Matt. You're slipping."

Greg chuckled. "It sounded as though she was offering to undress you, invite you into her shower and scrub your back."

Matt chuffed. "She meant she'd reach the hangers in the closet or the drawers in the chest."

"I don't know about *that…*" Joe laughed.

"You guys are crazy." Still, Matt thought about the image of Tori removing his clothes, taking him by the hand and leading him into a hot, steamy shower. Of water sluicing down their naked bodies, soap sliding along each and every curve…

Damn. If he wasn't careful, he was going to need a shower all right—a cold one.

"No wonder you came back to stay at the Rocking C rather than with Jared," Greg said.

Actually, Jared had taken Sabrina and Joey back to his ranch and left Matt with Granny. There hadn't been any options. Jared had told Matt to take over Granny's books until Sabrina was able to return.

"Well," Joe said, "we'd better move that car before she comes back. You know what they say about redheads and their fiery tempers."

Ten minutes later the sedan had been moved, and Greg had made his way to the barn, his trademark guitar strapped over his shoulder.

Matt wondered if he ought to go back into the house so he could wheel himself down the ramp in back and head into the yard. People would be arriving soon, and he didn't want to be seated on the porch like an invalid.

As he maneuvered the chair around, he could hear Greg strumming his guitar, and a Texas two-step harmony floated through the air from the barn to the house. It was the kind of song that had a foot-tapping beat and compelled a man to grab a special lady by the hand and head out to the dance floor.

Just as Matt reached for the doorknob, Tori beat him to it, swinging open the screen. She was wearing a light-yellow sundress that reminded him of a field of daffodils. She wore a pretty shade of lipstick, and her curly hair had been pulled into a neat twist.

They stood at a sensual impasse.

At least, that's what it felt like to Matt. He didn't want to move, didn't want to let her out the door.

"Can I have this dance?" she asked, a laugh in her voice.

He suspected that she was joking about them coming face-to-face in the doorway. Or, rather, his gaze to her face.

But for a moment Matt wished that he'd been standing on his own two feet, in full control of his movements.

Because if he had been, he just might have swept her into his arms, danced her back into the house and told her how damn pretty she was.

As it was, maybe it was for the best that he was dumbstruck and unable to say or do something he might regret later.

Chapter Eight

Tori had just left the house and stepped off the front porch when Jared Clayton's dual-wheeled pickup drove into the yard.

Good, she thought. Now all of Granny's sons had arrived. And so had Sabrina, the Rocking C bookkeeper, whose nephew, Joey, was recovering nicely from heart surgery on Jared's ranch.

Since Tori hadn't seen any of them after Joey's discharge from the hospital, she was eager to greet them and catch up on everything.

Jared rolled down his window, and Tori approached the door. As she peered inside the idling vehicle, she saw the six-year-old boy sitting between the adults.

"You're looking great," Tori told Joey. "How are you feeling?"

"I'm good." He grinned. "It was hurting before. But not anymore."

"I'm glad to hear that."

"How is Smokey doing?" the boy asked. "I'll bet he misses me."

Before the surgery, when they'd all been staying on the Rocking C, it hadn't been any secret that the boy loved horses and cowboys. So Jared had asked Joey to look after an old black gelding on his ranch. The child had been thrilled to be granted such a wonderful chore and had taken his job seriously.

"Smokey is doing just fine," Tori told him, "and I'm sure he'll be happy to see you."

"How are the kittens?" the boy asked. "Are they still little?"

"They're doing very well, too." She hated to tell him that the mother cat had died. It hadn't been that long ago when Joey had lost his own mother, and he didn't need the reminder. So if he didn't ask, she wouldn't offer that bit of news. "They were just newborns when you left, so they're bigger now. Matt thinks they're about one month old. Their eyes are open, and they're able to walk around."

"Cool." The boy grinned. "I can't wait to see them."

Tori's gaze shifted to Jared. "Would you mind parking along the road that leads to the pond so Granny won't see your truck when she arrives?"

"No, not at all. Do you really think you've managed to keep this thing a surprise?"

"I believe so." A light summer breeze kicked up a stand of her hair and blew it across her face. She tucked it behind her ear. "But it wasn't easy."

Sabrina opened the passenger door, slid off the seat and waited for Joey to get out. Once the door had been shut, Jared turned the vehicle around and headed down the drive to find another parking spot.

Joey, who'd made his way to Tori, wrapped his arms around her waist and gave her a big hug. "I missed you and everybody else. But do you know what? Jared's ranch is just as fun as this one. He's got horses there, too. And as soon as the doctor says I can ride, he's going to give me more lessons."

"I'm glad." Tori caressed the top of the boy's dark head, glad to know his life would soon be back to normal.

"I'd like to see Pumpkin and Fur Ball," he said. "Are the kitties still in the barn? In the same place?"

"No," Tori said. "They're in a box in my bedroom, next to the dresser. If it's okay with Sabrina, you can go into the house and look at them."

"Can I?" he asked his aunt, eyes wide and hopeful.

Sabrina smiled. "Sure, honey. But just for a minute or two. Granny will be coming soon, and we need to find out where we're supposed to wait so we can surprise her."

"Okay." He spun around and strode toward the house as if he'd never had a heart problem, as if he hadn't had surgery to correct a defective valve a little more than three weeks ago.

"It's great to see him happy and well again," Tori said.

"It sure is."

Tori studied the pretty, dark-haired bookkeeper who had become a friend over the past few months. "You're looking good, too, Sabrina."

"Thanks. I've never been happier." Sabrina slipped an

arm around Tori and gave her a quick hug. "I'm afraid I'm going to have to give Granny my notice, though. I've been offered a better position."

"Are you going to work for Jared?" It had been an easy assumption to make.

Sabrina lifted her left hand, where a shiny new diamond sparkled on her ring finger.

Tori's breath caught. "Oh, Sabrina. It's beautiful! I guess that means your new job description includes being a wife."

"We haven't set a date, but Jared surprised me with the ring last night." Sabrina glanced at the front door, then back at Tori. "While Joey's in the house, I want to ask you something. Do you think Granny would mind if Jared and I left Joey here for a few days to a week?"

"I'm sure she wouldn't. She adores him, and Connie and I would be glad to have him around. What's up?"

"My brother, Carlos, Joey's father, is in prison for a crime he didn't commit. Jared and I hired a private investigator and retained an attorney."

Tori hadn't known that. She and Sabrina had become friends while living at the Rocking C, but they hadn't shared everything, which was understandable. After all, Tori had a few secrets of her own.

"Last night we learned that two new witnesses had been found," Sabrina added. "And they can back up his defense. So there's a good possibility that Carlos may be released. It's a long story, but there's going to be a special hearing, and we want to show family support. We also plan to let the judge know that Jared has a job for Carlos and will let him live on the ranch with us."

"I'm sure your efforts will be helpful."

"That's what we're hoping. Anyway, I don't want to take Joey, yet I'm uneasy leaving him behind." She smiled and gave a little shrug. "But I wouldn't worry about him if he stayed here. You know, with you being a nurse and all."

Tori placed a hand on Sabrina's shoulder. "I'll keep a close eye on him."

"I don't know what we would have done if you hadn't been here that day to pick up on the problem. And besides that, your support before, during and after the surgery was a real godsend."

"You're welcome. I'm glad I was able to help."

When Joey came out the door, grinning from ear to ear and chattering about his kittens, the women let the subject of their discussion drop.

"Is there anything I can do to help with the party?" Sabrina asked.

"I've got everything under control. All we have to do is wait for Granny to arrive."

"When is she coming?" Joey asked.

Tori glanced at her wristwatch. "Uh-oh. Anytime. I'd better get everyone rounded up so we can yell surprise."

They'd no more than headed toward the barn when Jared returned from moving his truck. His gaze wandered toward the corral, where Matt had parked his wheelchair away from all the activity and in the shade of a tree. An older couple had just walked away from Matt when Joey approached the cowboy to say hello.

A frown marred Matt's handsome face, suggesting he wasn't all that happy with the attention.

"I hope my brother hasn't been giving you any trouble," Jared said.

Tori chuckled. "I think Trouble is his middle name. But he's making a lot of progress. He started physical therapy last week and has been using a walker more each day, so that's good."

Jared again stole a peek at his brother. "He doesn't look too happy right now."

"He seems to be in a much better mood when he's in the walker or moving around." Tori studied the ex-rodeo cowboy, her heart going out to him. "I've learned that he doesn't like sympathy or offers of assistance. So I suspect that with all the people stopping by to chat and share their compassion, he feels even more imprisoned by that chair."

"You're probably right," Jared said. "If it wasn't Granny's birthday, I suspect he'd be hanging out inside the house."

"Jared!" Doc Graham, who'd arrived earlier, approached and reached out his hand. As the men greeted each other, Tori left them alone so they could talk.

Minutes later, as everyone had been shepherded into the barn to hide until Granny's return, one of the ranch hands who'd been standing guard down the driveway hollered, "Hey, everybody! She's coming!"

"Shh!" someone said. "Quiet!"

A giggle erupted, then another, but the voices quickly stilled as the sound of an approaching engine sounded. According to plan, Hilda was bringing Granny home early from their usual Sunday outing.

After Hilda parked her Cadillac near the front porch, the women got out of the car.

They hadn't made two steps toward the house when Jared pushed against the barn doors, opening them so

Granny's friends and neighbors could rush out and shout, "Surprise!"

Granny's hand flew to her chest, and her mouth gaped open. "Well, I'll be…" She shot a glance at her friend. "Hilda, did you know about this?"

"Yes, I did. And we were all determined to keep this party a secret since we've never been able to surprise you before."

"Well, you certainly pulled it off." A grin lit up Granny's eyes. "I guess that means you don't need those aspirins after all."

Hilda chuckled. "The headache was an excuse to end our day and bring you home."

"Come on," Jared said. "Let's get this celebration underway."

Tori shot a glance at Matt, whose scowl had softened a tad. Still, something told her this was going to be a long, drawn-out day for him.

For a moment their gazes locked and something passed between them. Something with warmth and substance. Something that gripped her heart and wrung out every bit of emotion that lurked inside.

And she wondered what—if anything—she should do about it.

An hour later the party was in full swing as Tori made her rounds, checking the buffet line they'd set up outdoors, at the back of the barn.

The crew from Chuck's Wagon stood on hand to help serve people, and it looked as though there was still plenty to eat.

Granny and Hilda stood next to the salads, surveying the spread.

"I don't know why you took me to lunch after church," Granny said to her friend. "You know how much I love to eat good barbecue."

Hilda snatched a carrot stick from a platter of vegetables. "You've been telling us all how much you wanted a surprise party, but no one has ever been able to pull it off before. So if I hadn't stopped at Caroline's Diner after church like we do every Sunday, you would have been suspicious and wondered if something else had been planned instead."

Tori grinned as she made her way to the beverage table. She noted that they were getting low on lemonade and iced tea, so she headed for the kitchen for more.

There she found Connie seated at the antique walnut table, an open magazine spread before her.

"Why are you hanging out in here?" she asked.

"No reason."

Connie usually spent a lot of time alone, which Tori supposed was okay. Some people were just naturally reserved, although the new cook seemed to take shyness to the extreme.

"I don't want to press you to do something you don't want to do," Tori said. "I realize some people are uncomfortable in crowds."

"I'm okay with that." Connie closed the magazine she'd been perusing and pushed it aside. "It's just that I prefer to keep a low profile these days."

"You mean you haven't always?"

"Not really."

Tori wanted to quiz her further, but thought better of it. She supposed it wasn't right to pry when she'd taken a break from her own life and preferred to keep her reasons for doing so to herself.

When it appeared that Connie wasn't going to be any more forthcoming, Tori said, "You ought to see all the food that Chuck's Wagon prepared. It probably won't last long. Are you hungry?"

"A little."

"Then why don't you come out with me and get a plate? You can always bring it back in here if you'd rather eat where it's quiet."

Connie seemed to consider that option, then scooted her chair back and stood.

"Will you help me carry something outside?" Tori asked. "It'll keep me from making two trips."

"Sure."

Tori handed Connie the plastic container of lemonade, then grabbed the gallon jug of sweetened sun tea from the counter.

Together, they walked through the living room, out the front door and into the yard. Most of the party guests had moved out back to the tables that had been placed under the shade of the trees, where the caterer was setting out food.

"From what I understand," Tori said, "Greg is going to perform a couple of his songs today. Have you ever heard his music?"

"Yes, I have," Connie said. "He's got a lot of talent, and his career seems to have taken off nicely."

They carried the tea and lemonade to the beverage

table. As Tori replenished the empty pitchers, she encouraged Connie to fill a plate while the food was still out.

After finishing the chore she'd set out to accomplish, Tori placed her hands on her hips and scanned the guests who were either sitting at tables or mingling in small groups.

Matt had parked his wheelchair near the corral. He'd been off by himself most of the day.

Tori had suggested that he not use the walker during the party. The ground was soft and uneven in spots, and she'd been afraid that he'd get tired or have trouble maneuvering it through the crowd. She also feared that he might lose his balance and fall.

He hadn't fought her suggestion. But since he'd begun to use the walker, she'd noted that he seemed to be more withdrawn than usual when using the wheelchair. And she suspected that might be the reason for his deep frown today.

Or it might be the hordes of people who continued to stop by and chat with him. Right this minute, Joey was talking to him.

A furrowed brow marred the handsome cowboy's face, and Tori wondered if the boy was annoying him.

There was only one way to find out. She made her way toward them.

She'd been so wrapped up in party preparations and in being a good hostess that now she realized she hadn't been sensitive to Matt, to his needs or his comfort.

As she approached, she heard Joey say, "We're going to have chocolate cake pretty soon, and I can hardly wait."

"Good," Matt replied. "Maybe you ought to go hang out next to it so you can have the first piece."

"But it's Granny's birthday," Joey argued. "She's supposed to get served first."

"Then maybe you can have the next slice," Matt said.

Was he trying to get rid of the sweet little boy?

"Okay," Joey said. "Then I'll wait in line. Do you want me to get you some cake, too? I can bring it back to you."

"No, thanks."

As Joey left, Tori crossed her arms. "Is it my imagination, or did you just run that child off?"

"Hanging out here and badgering me with a million questions isn't going to do him any good."

Was there something in particular Joey had wanted to know? Something that had set Matt off?

"What did he ask you?"

Matt chuffed and gripped the wheels of his chair. "He wanted to know if I'd be able ride in the rodeo again. And he asked how the accident happened. He also wanted to know if anyone else had gotten hurt."

No wonder Matt had bristled and grown solemn.

"Did you tell him?" Tori asked.

"No. Those questions hammer at me constantly, and I have a hard enough time pondering the answers myself."

Tori wanted to wrap her arms around him, to offer him comfort. Understanding. Compassion.

But she didn't dare. For all she knew, he might slip right back into his old frame of mind and recoil from her touch.

Still, there had to be something else she could do to help, something she could say.

"Joey said he's going to stay here for a few days," Matt said, interrupting her thoughts.

"That's right." Tori was already looking forward to

having the little boy around. He loved the ranch, and everything was a new discovery.

But when she glanced down at Matt, when she saw his terse lips, she realized he probably didn't feel the same way she did.

"What's the matter?" she asked.

"Nothing."

Tori didn't buy that for a minute. Joey loved cowboys and idolized Matt because of his rodeo accomplishments. So she would have thought that he would be flattered by the attention of a little hero worship. Yet he clearly wasn't.

"I don't believe you," she said.

Matt shrugged. "It's not the kid. Not really. With everyone feeling obligated to stop and offer their sympathy and everything, I'd like to disappear with a bottle of Jack Daniel's."

"But you haven't done that," Tori said.

"Apparently, I can be a jerk when I drink to excess. And this feels like it could definitely be one of those days. So I'll suffer through all the condolences."

"I'm sorry this afternoon has been a pain for you."

He shrugged. "I owe it to Granny."

If one considered outward appearances, it would seem that Matt was self-centered and simply feeling sorry for himself. But Tori knew that wasn't the case. So she was determined to help, to do something to ease his emotional discomfort. And she was determined to do whatever it took to ease his pain.

"I need to make the rounds again and see that everyone has what they need," she said to excuse herself. "I'll be back."

Then she returned to the center of the party, hoping to come up with an idea that would help Matt feel like a vibrant man again, and convinced that was exactly what he needed.

As Tori continued her job as hostess, she scanned the guests, spotting Jared near the punch table. Since he wasn't chatting with anyone, she decided it was a perfect time to approach him.

"Have you got a minute?" she asked the rancher.

"Sure. What's up?"

Tori nibbled on her bottom lip as she pondered the best way to ask Jared what Joey had wanted to know, a question she had, too. "Will you tell me about Matt's accident? How did it happen?"

Jared lifted his Stetson and raked a hand through his hair, then he adjusted the hat back on his head. "Matt, his fiancée and her four-year-old son had been at a family reunion. On the way home, a couple of drag racers came barreling down the road. Matt veered to the left to avoid them, but he lost control of the vehicle. He blames himself, although the police report said it wasn't his fault."

"That's too bad," Tori said. "He must have loved Cindy a lot."

"I suppose."

Tori picked up on an odd vibe in Jared's answer. "What does that mean?"

"I only met her a time or two, and she seemed nice. But I'm not sure that she was Matt's type."

That was interesting, Tori thought. Jared had made the same comment as Granny had about the woman. "What makes you say that?"

"Matt's strong-willed. And I think he needs a woman

who will stand up to him. Challenge him. And Cindy was pretty soft-spoken and compliant. But that's all water under the bridge now."

"Still, he wouldn't have been engaged to marry her if he hadn't loved her. Sometimes opposites attract."

"I suppose they do."

Jared turned to Tori, his eyes sweeping the length of her. "Actually, Cindy looked a lot like you. Same fair complexion, same hair color. She was a bit taller than you, though. And she wasn't quite as pretty."

For a moment Tori felt inclined to thank him for the compliment, but the fact that she resembled Matt's deceased fiancée made her feel a little uneasy. Surely Matt had noticed, too.

Did that mean it bothered Matt to be around Tori, just as it apparently bothered him to be around Joey?

He and Tori certainly hadn't hit it off at first.

Of course, they'd had some nice moments, especially on those evening walks that had become a habit.

Her thoughts drifted to the trip to Wexler they'd taken for his physical therapy appointment. The day he'd joked about copping a feel.

At that very moment, as he'd caressed her cheek, then slowly allowed his hand to skim her throat and chest, their eyes had locked on each other. And, joke or no joke, something heated had passed through them. Something that made her feel vibrant and alive.

Like a woman who was lovable and deserved to be loved. And for a moment she forgot all about James and her sister.

Maybe there was something therapeutic about facing one's fears, about getting back in the saddle of life again.

"Thanks for your insight," she told Jared. "It helps me understand him better."

"Good luck. Whatever you're doing seems to be working. At least you got him into physical therapy."

Yes, she'd managed to do that.

She started to turn and leave, but caught herself and spun back around. "Oh! Congratulations on your engagement."

"Thanks." A grin lit up his face, reflecting his happiness.

It was uplifting to know that Sabrina and Jared had fallen in love, yet Tori couldn't help wondering if she would ever be that fortunate.

She'd been hopeful once, when she and James had been lovers. But the charming intern and her sister had put an end to that dream, leaving her feeling as though she was lacking what it took to keep a man satisfied.

As she returned to Matt, she realized that they'd both lost a lover, although the circumstances had been different. Still, they were each alone and hurting in their own ways.

He watched her approach, and she couldn't help gazing at him. He was a handsome man—too handsome to spend the rest of his life in solitude, feeling sorry for himself.

"I take it everything is going well and on schedule," he said.

"Yes, just like clockwork."

But some things weren't right. And she felt a growing compulsion to do something about it, although she didn't know what.

Perhaps a heart-to-heart with Matt would help.

More often than not in the past, he'd shrugged off her

attempts to help, even when doing so meant he risked collapsing into a heap on the ground and hurting himself.

Like he'd nearly done after that first physical therapy appointment in Wexler.

Again her mind drifted to the day they'd embraced, hearts beating. The whisper of a touch. The catch of her breath. The heat of his gaze as it locked on hers.

And again she shook it off.

Still, she couldn't let him sit here any longer, punishing himself and feeling miserable.

Should she try to take him aside and talk to him? Over the last week or so, they'd seemed to have forged a friendship of sorts. And he was always more forthcoming when they were alone.

Maybe, if she could walk that fine line between sympathy and understanding, she might be able to pull him out of the doldrums.

Of course, he probably wouldn't agree to it.

But what had Jared said?

Matt's strong-willed. And I think he needs a woman who will stand up to him. Challenge him.

Well, Tori certainly had no problem doing that. So she got behind his wheelchair and began to push.

"Where the hell do you think you're going?" he asked.

"I figured you wouldn't mind if we slipped away from the party for a while."

He didn't respond, so she figured he was game.

Trouble was, she didn't really know what she was going to say to him when she got him alone.

It would come to her, she supposed.

For a moment, as she pushed him around the barn and

toward the side of the house, she had second thoughts about being so assertive, especially without any real game plan. But she pressed on.

When they were alone at the side of the house and there was no chance anyone would come upon them, she slowed his wheelchair to a stop. Then she walked around to the front of the chair.

His brow furrowed and his lips tensed as he waited for her to speak.

It wasn't too late, she reminded herself. She could give him one of those it's-time-to-straighten-up-and-fly-right talks.

His chin lifted, and his hands gripped the sides of his chair, as though he was sorely tempted to stand up and face her challenge—whatever it might be. "Have you got a burr under your saddle?"

"No. Not really." She couldn't blame him for thinking she'd planned a big confrontation. After all, she'd whisked him away from the crowd as though she did. But actually, she'd known how badly he disliked being confined to that chair and at the mercy of those around him.

So now, with no great plan coming to her, she had to think of a way to backpedal.

He eyed her intently as though he was trying to get to the root of her action, and God only knew what he'd uncovered.

Then he sank back in his seat and crossed his arms. "What's on your mind?"

She'd be darned if she even had a suspicion any longer. Not when she was mesmerized by whatever was simmering in his eyes—dark and dangerous. Alluring and arousing.

She recognized it, though. It was the same heated

something that had sent her senses reeling when they'd been in Wexler, when she'd stepped in to help him from falling when he was climbing back into the truck.

And it was doing it to her again, snaking around her heart and threatening to draw her deep inside of him.

Her brains must have just turned to mush, because for the life of her, it seemed as though someone else said, "There's life after grief, Matt."

"What's that supposed to mean?"

Darned if she knew.

"Why'd you drag me away from the barn?" he asked.

"I'm not sure." A whimsical smile settled on her face as she tried to make light of what she'd done, as well as the adolescent urges zinging through her. "Maybe I'd like to cop a feel of my own."

Oh, dear God. Had she said that?

She'd meant it as a joke, as a bridge to span two awkward pauses in the conversation. But the look in his eyes told her he didn't find it the least bit funny.

And that he might even want to hold her to it.

Chapter Nine

Maybe I'd like to cop a feel of my own.

What in the hell had provoked her to say something like that?

And what, exactly, was going on in that pretty little head of hers?

Matt sat back in his chair, rocked to the core—and tempted beyond belief.

Had she been serious?

Either way, she had him intrigued.

Her hair had come loose from its bun, and the breeze whipped a long, curly red tendril across her face. She brushed it away.

Usually he couldn't stand being looked down upon, which was one reason he hated sitting in this chair. Being the only one seated often stirred up images of his drunken uncle standing over him, with his fist and his voice raised. And so that particular position usually made Matt want to lash out, to fight back.

But right this minute, looking up at Tori didn't have the same effect.

As if reading his mind and knowing his secret peeve, she knelt before him and placed a hand on his thigh. "I'm sorry, Matt. That came out badly."

"Actually, it didn't sound so bad to me." He wasn't really sure what she'd been getting at, and although he'd easily made the leap to sex, he didn't want to make any false assumptions.

"I guess I was just trying to lighten things up."

"Well, it worked. And I don't think you were joking. Not completely."

"Okay," she said. "I'll admit it. I find you attractive. And it's been a long time since…"

"Since you've had sex?"

Her cheeks flushed a deep shade of red. "Okay. So I made a joke that could be taken…"

"Seriously?" he asked. Because he could certainly take it that way.

"Stop trying to put words in my mouth."

"You started it."

"No, you did. That day in Wexler." She blew out a sigh. "The one and only guy I ever got involved with found someone he liked better than me. So I decided to steer clear of men for a while."

"Then maybe it's time you got back in the saddle again."

"You might be right." The hint of a smile—one part shy, two parts naughty—sparked a glimmer in her eyes.

There had to be a hundred reasons why Matt and Tori shouldn't get physically involved—if that's what they were tiptoeing around—yet he'd be damned if he could think of a single one.

Instead he imagined the two of them lying naked in bed, hands touching, exploring. Caressing each other.

Just the thought was enough to chase away the reverberating sounds of clucking tongues and the condolences Granny's friends and neighbors had been drowning him with for the past couple of hours or so.

Their well-intentioned sympathy had only served to stir up his frustration and the guilt he'd been carrying since the accident, but he no longer cared about that now.

Tori touched his cheek, and he found the press of her fingers to be a balm—and far more of one than the compassion he'd been bathed in earlier today.

"You had a tough break, Matt. But your life isn't over. And neither is mine."

As much as he'd wanted to hear her voice the words, he made the leap for them both. "Are we skating around the idea of making love, or are we ready to jump right in?"

She swallowed, a shy smile chasing away all signs of the naughty one. "I don't know. I guess it depends."

"On what?"

"On whether you're interested or not."

He shouldn't be.

But he was.

He placed his hand along the side of her throat, his fingers sliding under a cascade of curls. He used his thumb to caress her cheek. "I'm definitely interested.

And for the record, my legs are the only things giving me any trouble. So if you'd like to give the rest of me a workout, I'm game."

"I really didn't have a motive for coming out here with you—other than to offer you a bit of an escape and to…" She gave a little shrug. "Oh, I don't know."

"Maybe, deep inside, you *do*."

He released his hold, letting his knuckles brush along her throat and down her chest.

But this time, his hand skimmed over her breast, then lingered. He felt the fullness, the softness, the warmth. His thumb grazed her nipple, which hardened in response.

Her breath caught, and her lips parted. When she finally spoke, her voice came out husky and whisper soft. "I've got to put candles on the cake."

She was certainly the right person for that job. She'd just lit a fire under him.

Before she could stand and get behind his wheelchair, Joey came around the corner. "Oh, there you are, Tori. I've been looking all over for you. What are you doing way over here?"

"I was just…talking to Matt."

"But all the fun is over near the barn."

"It was kind of fun over here." Matt's gaze lit on Tori, and he tossed her a grin.

He hoped they weren't tiptoeing on something they shouldn't be messing with.

Things could get…sticky, if they weren't careful.

But Matt had always been up for a challenge.

* * *

The conversation he'd had with Tori at the side of the house continued to replay itself over and over in Matt's mind, even after they'd returned to the party.

Were they really skating around the idea of an affair?

The more he thought about it, the more appealing the idea was.

Trouble was, with a house full of people, it was going to be tough finding some privacy. But Matt had always been innovative—when he'd had reason to be.

As he sat parked in the shade of the sycamore, he watched as Tori called everyone to the dessert table. Then she placed eight candles on the birthday cake—one for each decade of Granny's life—and lit them.

After Greg led a round of "Happy Birthday," Granny made a wish and blew out the candles amidst the cheers and the applause of her friends.

"It's time to open presents," Tori said, as she pulled out a chair for Granny and stacked the gifts next to her.

As Granny oohed and ahhed over each item she'd been given—a box of chocolates, a basket of soap and lotions, a new sweater, a pair of slippers and more, Matt's gaze again drifted to Tori, where she stood near the table that held one of the cakes Connie had baked. She was cutting slices and placing them on small paper plates.

Each time she glanced up from her work, their eyes met, letting him know that she'd been thinking about him, too.

Was she having second thoughts?

A blush on her cheeks suggested she might be.

As Greg began to strum the chords of his guitar, Matt turned his attention to his brother and listened as the singer launched into several of his biggest hits, much to the delight of all the guests.

Even Connie swayed to the music, although she stood off by herself—much like Matt tried to do these days.

One nice thing was that the party was almost over, and they'd both soon be free to go about their business.

After everyone had been served cake, Tori brought Matt a slice, along with a fork and paper napkin.

He took it from her, noting she'd given him an extra large piece. "Thanks. I hope we still have some of that chocolate cake left."

"There ought to be plenty leftover." She crossed her arms and shifted her weight to one hip.

"You've got to be tired," he said. "I haven't seen you stop all day."

Except, of course, when she'd taken him to the side of the house and knelt in front of him.

She blew out a weary sigh. "To be honest, I'm looking forward to putting my feet up."

"Have you had a chance to eat yet?" he asked.

"Cake?"

"I was thinking about lunch. You've been trying so hard to take care of everyone else that I'm afraid you might not have taken time for yourself."

Her lips parted, and a whisper of surprise crossed her face. "Actually, I planned to eat later. After everyone else…"

Matt reached for her hand. His thumb grazed her wrist, where her pulse throbbed. He could swear it was going haywire. "Is that the nurse in you talking?"

"I'm not sure I know what you mean."

He slowly released her wrist. "You've been fussing

about everyone but yourself. And I have a feeling that's the norm for you."

"You're the first one who's ever called me on that."

That was too bad. It should have been clear to anyone who knew her. "Why don't you go fix yourself a plate? I'll have Lester ask some of the hands to clean up whatever the caterer leaves behind."

"Thanks. I'd appreciate that." She blew out a breath. "I'll be glad when this party winds down."

So would Matt. He was eager to slip away and find some peace and quiet—hopefully with Tori. That way, they could finish that little talk they'd started, the one Joey had interrupted.

Of course, even after everyone went home, he and Tori would be hard-pressed to find any privacy.

There was always Clem's cabin, he supposed. When Sabrina had been here, she'd planned to move into it and had cleaned it up. But after talking to Jared today, Matt had realized that Sabrina wouldn't be coming back to the Rocking C to live.

That wouldn't leave Granny in a lurch, though. Jared had asked Matt to continue doing the bookwork until Granny was able to hire someone else.

Still, that was quite a trek to the little cabin on the knoll. And at this point, neither the wheelchair nor the walker was likely to make it.

Damn. He'd have to figure out something else. He drummed his fingers on the sidebar of the wheelchair as he considered other options.

Once, when he'd been a teenager, he'd sneaked

Bonnie Sue Riley into the hay loft. But since his legs were still healing, he wasn't going to be able to make that climb right now.

"Well, look here," Granny said, as she approached. "Just the two I wanted to see."

"Do you need something?" Tori asked.

"Nope." Granny grinned. "I just wanted to thank you both for planning this wonderful party. You have no idea how touched I am."

"Tori's the one who did all the work," Matt said.

Before either Tori or Granny could respond, Greg joined them. "I've got to be taking off, Granny."

"I understand," their mother said. "I'm thrilled that you were able to make it, especially when you've been so busy."

"I wouldn't have missed it." Greg glanced down at the plate Matt held. "Hey, eat up, brother. That chocolate cake was the best I've ever eaten."

Granny smiled proudly. "Connie made it. She's my new cook."

"Lucky you," Greg said. "I get stuck eating most of my meals out."

Matt nearly choked, but he held his tongue. He supposed there wasn't any need to complain about the crummy meals Connie fixed.

"Joe's waiting in the car for me, so I better go." Greg gave their mother a big hug, holding her a bit longer than usual.

But Matt understood why. His brother loved Granny every bit as much as he and Jared did.

When the embrace finally ended, Greg added, "I'm

going to be traveling a lot in the next few months, so I'm not sure when I'll get to see you again. But I'll definitely be home for Thanksgiving. I told my manager not to book anything until after the new year."

"That's wonderful." Granny clapped her hands. "How long can you stay?"

"At least a month. Maybe longer."

"That's the best news I've had in ages. I'll have all my boys home for the holidays." Granny's happiness lit up her face and made her look ten years younger.

"Now, don't go to any extra work for me," Greg said, his voice growing stern. "I don't want you worrying about cooking or baking. I'd rather you relaxed and enjoyed our time together."

"Don't worry," Granny said. "I won't do too much. I've got a cook, remember? So there'll be plenty in the way of food. Maybe we can even fatten you up while you're here. All that traveling from city to city is taking a toll on you. You're too skinny, son."

"Maybe so." Greg chuckled. "But if Connie's cooking is as good as her baking, I'm sure I'll be as plump as a Christmas goose by New Year's Eve."

Uh-oh, Matt thought. If his younger brother was looking forward to Connie's meals, he was going to be in for a big surprise. Of course, maybe Connie would learn to cook by then. Otherwise, Matt was going to suggest that Tori prepare the holiday meals—or at least take an active part.

Greg, with the strap of his guitar slung over his shoulder, said goodbye and took off to meet Joe in the car.

"By the way," Granny said. "I'm going to look after Joey for a few days. Isn't that nice?"

"Yep." Matt tried to feign a little enthusiasm.

To be honest, he hadn't been happy to hear that the six-year-old would be staying at the ranch for a while. But not because he didn't like kids. Or even *that* particular kid.

It's just that Tommy used to look at him with those same soulful brown eyes. Eyes that suggested Matt could do no wrong. And Matt knew better than to be swept away by undeserved hero worship. So he would just try to keep his distance, although that might be a lot easier said than done. For some reason, Joey seemed to gravitate toward him.

"You know," Granny said to Tori. "I think I'll take Joey shopping in Houston tomorrow. Sabrina said that he'll be starting first grade soon, so I figure he'll need some new clothes, a backpack and other supplies. I used to enjoy getting ready for each new school year. It'll be a nice outing. In fact, maybe we'll pack a suitcase and make it an overnight trip."

"Do you want me to go with you?" Tori asked.

"No, someone needs to stay and cook for the men. And since Connie's pants are getting snug in the waist, I'll take her with me. I'd like to surprise her with some maternity clothes."

"I'm sure Joey will do fine," Tori said, "but maybe you ought to run that by Sabrina first."

"I will. But I'll remind her that we'll be close to the hospital and his doctors in Houston, just in case something happens."

"I'm sure you won't have to worry about that," Tori said.

Perfect, Matt thought. If Granny, Joey and Connie were leaving for an overnight shopping trip, then he and Tori would be left alone at the house.

He settled back into his chair and grinned.

Finding some privacy wasn't going to be as hard as he'd thought.

After the party Tori had been tired, but she hadn't realized just how much.

Once back in the house she'd fed the kittens, then kicked off her shoes, slipped off her dress and had lain down on the top of the bed for a little nap. The next thing she knew it was morning.

As she readied for the day, she thought about the sexually charged conversation she'd had with Matt yesterday. She hadn't meant to agree to have an affair, but they'd certainly touched on the subject.

Touched.

When Matt's hand had grazed her breast, her nipple contracted in response to the intimate caress, flooding her with desire. And her body—deep within her feminine core—had reawakened.

For the first time since she'd told James to get out of her life, she'd felt desirable again. And she'd wondered if there was a chance that making love would do both her and Matt some good.

But could she go through with it? Could she have a no-strings-attached affair?

She wasn't sure.

Tori kept busy until after ten, when Granny rounded up Joey and Connie and herded them out to one of the ranch vehicles. Connie had been reluctant to go into town, but she got behind the wheel. Minutes later they were gone.

Earlier, Matt had disappeared into the office, so Tori prepared lunch for the men—leftovers from yesterday.

It wasn't until late afternoon when Matt came into the kitchen and fixed himself a barbecue beef sandwich. "What's for dinner tonight?"

"I thought I'd make pork chops. Is that all right with you?"

"Sure."

Several minutes of silence followed, and when Tori couldn't stand it any longer, she asked, "Are we going to talk about yesterday?"

"You mean the party?"

Did she have to spell it out for him?

"No, I was thinking that we might want to discuss that little chat we had." And the intimate way he'd touched her. The unspoken words that had passed between them. The urges he'd stirred up inside of her.

"You're not backing out, are you?"

Her pulse stopped, then spiked. "Backing out of what? We didn't exactly decide to move forward on anything."

"Didn't we?"

She stole a glance at him, watched him studying her in a way that made her feel as though she'd left the house half dressed. "I wasn't suggesting that we…you know."

"Sleep together?" he asked.

"I mean, if you don't want to—"

"Hey. When a beautiful woman suggests sex, a man would have to be crazy to not be interested."

"I'm not that kind of woman."

"You mean, beautiful?"

She slapped her hands on her hips. "That's not what I

meant. But no, I don't see myself as beautiful. And I don't believe in sex without a commitment. But in this case, I thought…"

"You thought what?" His brow furrowed, yet his lips quirked in a smile.

Darn. The man was infuriating. She suspected he was playing with her—and enjoying it.

"I agreed that I was…thrown from a horse—so to speak."

"Are we still talking about sex?"

She knit her brow and shot him a look of exasperation. *"Yes."*

He wore a cocky grin. Or maybe it was just one of those I-was-funnin'-with-you looks; she couldn't be sure. Either way, the subject seemed to appeal to him.

She was afraid to steal another peek at him, so she got up and reached into the cupboard for a glass. "Anyway, I though it might be good to…you know, get back in the saddle."

There. She'd said it, utilizing the cowboy analogy he'd used yesterday.

"What are you suggesting?" he asked.

"I'm not exactly sure." She poured herself a glass of lemonade. "Remember how I told you that I dated a guy who cheated on me?"

"Yeah. And between you, me and the fence post, the guy didn't deserve a woman like you."

"Maybe not." She worried her bottom lip. "But there's a part of me that wonders if… Well, if maybe it was my fault. If maybe…"

"Don't blame yourself, Tori. Some men are immature jerks when it comes to that sort of thing. When I first started out on the circuit, I used to date several women at the same time. But it wasn't a secret. I was always up front with them, and they had the option of seeing me under those terms."

She supposed it was only fair, although if Matt was seeing someone else, she wouldn't get involved with him.

But this was different, wasn't it?

He wasn't engaged any longer. And he certainly wasn't dating anyone else. They were both adults and able to have a brief, therapeutic sexual fling if they wanted to.

"I realize this wouldn't be anything long-term," she said.

"Good."

She took a sip of lemonade, felt the cool, bittersweet taste as it filled her mouth and tried to wrap her mind around the sexual business deal taking place. "Then I guess we're on the same page."

"Looks like it." He got up from the table. Reaching for the cane he'd leaned against one of the chairs, he got to his feet. "I'm going back into the office. Let me know when dinner's ready."

And that was that.

When Matt left the room, she breaded pork chops and put them in the oven to bake. Then she peeled the potatoes. While she waited for them to come to a boil, she prepared a tossed salad.

Dessert would be something light and easy—ice cream.

But then what? she asked herself.

She'd only had one other sexual partner, and at the time, she'd thought that they'd had something special. That they'd had a future together.

Could she enter a casual sexual relationship with Matt?

Sex always changed things between a couple.

You're not backing out, are you? The question Matt had asked her earlier hung in the air.

She tried to tell herself that she was a nurse, a professional. And that she could be clinical and objective about all of this. Making love with Matt just might right both of their worlds again.

But she couldn't deny that she was having second thoughts. She firmly believed sex wasn't something she could enter into lightly. She'd have to care about the man she slept with.

She had, of course, grown to care about Matt.

Maybe she'd just have to take it one sweet touch at a time.

Chapter Ten

That evening, after Tori called the ranch hands into the kitchen and laid the food she'd fixed on the table, they all raved about the taste of the pork chops, salad, green beans, mashed potatoes and gravy.

And Matt had to agree with them.

"You're one heck of a cook," Lester told Tori.

"That's right," one of the other hands said. "We're lucky to have two great meals in a row."

"Thank you." A light flush tinged Tori's cheeks, making her look especially pretty tonight, even wearing an apron over a pair of jeans and a plain cotton blouse.

"Yeah," Earl, one of the older, weathered cowboys added. "We don't know why Connie's doing all the cooking and you're not."

"I'm sure Granny has her reasons," Tori said. "Besides,

Connie tries hard. And when it comes to whipping up desserts, I can't hold a candle to her."

"That don't matter," Lester said. "Ice cream is fine with us."

Matt figured the men had all been doubling up on dessert for so long that the sweets had lost some of their appeal, but he held his tongue.

Well, at least he kept quiet until the men went back to the bunkhouse and finally left him and Tori alone.

"How are the kittens doing?" he asked.

She turned away from the sink, a damp dishcloth dangling from her hand, and flashed him a smile. "They're doing really well. Even Tippy. I fed them earlier, and I was going to ask if you thought I should start them on a little solid food."

"It probably wouldn't hurt," he said, watching as she went back to rinsing the plates and stacking them in the dishwasher.

He wished he could offer to help her clean up the after-dinner mess in the kitchen, but he wasn't very steady on his feet these days and would probably just get in the way.

More than ever, he was determined to heal and get his body back, even if he wouldn't ever be able to ride competitively again. He figured he'd stewed in his sorrow long enough. What's done was done. It was time to put the past aside—if he could.

He watched as Tori spooned the leftovers into plastic containers then placed them in the refrigerator.

Next, she wiped down the table, the stove and the counters. If he couldn't help, he should at least keep her company.

"Are you up for a walk tonight?" He hoped she'd say yes. He'd actually been looking forward to their time together in the evenings. There'd been something comforting about being alone with her in the moonlight and under a scatter of stars. Something special.

"Sure." She glanced over her shoulder and blessed him with another dimpled smile. "I've just about got the kitchen back in order."

"Good. I want to try this out tonight."

She turned completely, facing him, and leaned her hip against the countertop. Her brow furrowed, and she tucked a long, curly strand of hair behind her ear. "Try out what?"

He lifted the cane he'd found while searching for something else in the office closet. "This used to belong to Everett. I hadn't seen it since the time Granny suggested Greg use it as part of his Halloween costume."

"Who's Everett?" she asked.

"Granny's late husband. He passed away before my brothers and I moved in, so we never got a chance to meet him. I heard he was a true cowboy, the last of a dying breed."

"Why did he need the cane?"

"He had a couple of strokes before suffering a massive heart attack that killed him. So he'd had a bum leg for a while."

Tori rinsed the dishcloth and wrung it out. Then she carefully draped it over the faucet and turned to face him. "I'm really proud of you, Matt."

For a moment, something warm and tingly swelled inside of him, but he shoved it aside as quickly as it surfaced. He hadn't done squat to make anyone proud lately.

"Why would you say that?" he asked.

"Because you're trying so hard."

To walk?

To heal?

To have a better attitude?

Again, he tried to shrug off her comment. "Once I make my mind up to do something, I always try hard. It's the competitor in me."

Still, the sincerity in her tone and her expression—whether deserved or not—touched him in a nice yet unexpected way.

Other than Granny and her old foreman, Clem Bixby, no one had ever told Matt they were proud of him. So he supposed he was a real sucker when it came to hearing the words.

Especially from her.

There was something about Tori that appealed to him. Something none of the other women he'd dated had. Hell, not even Cindy.

He wouldn't ponder what it was, though. Or why it seemed to matter.

Not tonight.

Tori bent to reach for the box of soap that was under the sink, flashing him a lovely view of her perfectly shaped…derriere. For some reason referring to it as an ass seemed crude, even to a man who'd used that term in the past.

Damn. What kind of spell had she cast on him?

Or was it merely the vulnerable position he'd found himself in following the accident?

After she started the washer, she rinsed her hands and reached for a paper towel.

"Are you ready?" she asked, dropping the disposable towel into the trash.

"Yep." He stood and grabbed the cane.

Minutes later they'd made their way outside and were striding toward the barn, slowly but surely. He suspected this walk would end sooner than the rest of them had. He'd probably jumped the gun by choosing to walk with a cane rather than the walker. But what the hell. When he got too sore or tired of walking, he would just suggest that they head back to the porch and sit for a while.

As he leaned upon the cane to move forward step by step, he glanced up at the sky, which was especially clear tonight. The moon was waxing and would soon be full again.

In the corral close to the barn, the chestnut broodmare whinnied, then plodded toward the railing as if she was lonely and in need of a friend.

"What's the matter?" he asked the horse as he started toward the fence. "Do you want some attention?"

Tori followed beside him. "She's a pretty horse. What's her name?"

"Aquila. She was bred to one of the top cutting horses in the state, so we're all excited about her foal." Matt leaned his cane against the fence post, then stroked the mare's neck.

"When is she due?"

"I'm not sure. In a couple of weeks, I think."

Aquila jerked up her head, bumping Matt and knocking him off balance.

Damn. He reached for the railing, just as Tori reached for him.

"Are you okay?" she asked.

"Yeah." At least, he had been until she wrapped her arms around him, until her breasts pressed against his diaphragm. Until her soft floral scent snaked around him, shooting off a surge of testosterone and sending his blood pumping.

As their gazes locked, Matt lost all conscious thought and succumbed to temptation, lowering his mouth for a kiss.

His lips brushed hers once, twice, and he was soon caught up in a swirl of heat and desire.

The kiss intensified, and he leaned against the fence, hoping he wouldn't lose his balance, hoping his aching legs wouldn't buckle. As their tongues caressed, their breaths mingled until they were both consumed by the lust-charged air between them.

Matt couldn't seem to get enough of her, and he lost himself in her wet, velvety mouth. As the kiss deepened, as she tightened her arms around him and pressed her hips against his erection, a shiver of heat slid through his bloodstream, rocking him to the core.

This wasn't going to work. Not here. And not for very much longer.

They would need to move into the privacy of the house, where he could stretch out beside her on a bed and not be hampered by legs that couldn't do all he demanded of them.

He broke the kiss long enough to catch his breath, yet he didn't let go of her; he couldn't.

"As much as I like being outside with you, Tori, I'm going to like being behind closed doors a whole lot more."

"I think I'd like that, too." The arm that she'd wrapped around his waist loosened, and the one that had been around his neck dropped to his chest, her fingers undoubtedly picking up the steady, pounding beat of his heart.

"Do you need help?" she asked. "Should I get the wheelchair?"

"No. It's important for me to make it back to the house on my own."

"But what if you fall?"

It didn't matter.

Sometimes all a man had left was his pride.

Tori had thought long and hard about making love with Matt and had actually decided to go ahead and give it a whirl. But that was before she'd realized how strong her physical response to his kiss had been and how badly she wanted to let herself go. So the closer she got to the house, the more she began to backpedal on that decision.

There was still a big-part of her that believed in true love, that clung to an old-fashioned sense of values that insisted sex was something special, something that bound a couple together forever.

And even though she'd come to the conclusion that she had feelings for Matt, she wasn't sure what they were.

What if she actually fell in love with him?

Getting sexually involved with a man who still loved his deceased fiancée wasn't a good idea. Not if Tori wanted to keep her heart intact.

Once they'd returned to the house, Tori led the way to the family room, where she grabbed the television remote and turned on the power. Then she searched the cabinet that held movies until she found the DVD she'd been looking for. She needed time to think before things went further.

"You want to watch TV?" he asked, setting the cane

against the lamp table and plopping down on the sofa. "Forgive me for not sharing your enthusiasm when we could be doing something a lot more fun."

"Believe it or not, there are parts of me that are complaining, too." She held up the movie Sabrina had said was exceptionally good. "But this is a comedy, so it'll be fun."

"It's a chick flick."

"You say that like it's a bad thing." She placed her hands on her hips. "Would you like me to choose a film in which someone dies?"

Matt stiffened, obviously thinking about Cindy and her son.

Oh, God. Why was it such a struggle to say the right thing around him?

"I'm sorry, Matt." She sat next to him on the sofa. "That just slipped out."

He turned to his right, his knee brushing hers. He lifted his hand and trailed his knuckles along her cheek. "I know. Don't worry about it. There's life after grief, remember?"

Yes, she'd told him that. And she desperately wanted to believe it—at least for his sake.

Her heart surged with compassion—or was it something else? She couldn't be sure, but whatever it was filled her chest to the brim.

Their gazes met and locked.

Matt reached for the back of her head and slowly pulled her mouth toward his.

Oh, God. He was going to kiss her again.

Every bit of sense she'd ever had told her to pull back, to put a stop to what would surely be an arousing assault of her senses.

No, her conscience tried to say, yet it didn't do any good. Tori couldn't stop herself.

The kiss began softly, tentatively, just as the last one had.

Her lips parted of their own accord, and his tongue swept inside her mouth as though it belonged there, as though it had come home to stay. Kissing Matt felt good—and right—sparking something deep inside her and triggering thoughts of white lace and forever.

As they necked on the sofa like a couple of teenagers with their hormones raging, she couldn't help wondering if she'd found someone she'd always been looking for, that special something she'd never had.

The idea was both frightening and thrilling.

Yet she couldn't put a stop to the heated assault on her senses. Nor could she keep from leaning into him as he stretched further back against the armrest of the sofa, drawing her to him.

Their hands groped and stroked and touched as though they could somehow get a grip on the desire that raged between them. But control was beyond reach. The need that had been building inside of her exploded, causing an aching emptiness deep in the most feminine part of her.

An emptiness only Matt could fill.

Any thoughts of slowing down had vanished within the inferno of their kisses, but she stopped long enough to catch her breath and say, "Let's go into the bedroom."

"Good idea."

Had she actually suggested that? And would she really be able to go through with it?

Apparently so, because she led him down the hall toward the room she slept in.

Was she somehow overstepping her boundaries as a nurse by having sex with a patient?

No. Matt Clayton was a man, not her patient.

And there was nothing clinical about any of this.

If her heart became involved, as she feared it might—as she feared it actually had—she'd deal with it in the morning. When she'd had her fill of the rugged cowboy.

He pulled on her hand, slowing her steps to a stop.

Was *he* having second thoughts?

She could certainly see the wisdom in refraining from sex and would probably thank him for his foresight later, but she couldn't stop the disappointment from raining down on her.

"I've got some condoms in my room," he said. "Maybe we ought to use that bed."

At this point, with her desire for him raging, she wouldn't complain if they stopped right here and made love on the hall floor, so she allowed him to lead the way.

Once inside his bedroom, she scanned the decor, the oak furniture, the queen-size bed, the blue plaid comforter. She'd cleaned this room many times, yet right now she'd never been more aware of Matt's scent, of his presence.

He took a seat on the edge of the mattress, resting his legs, no doubt. "Come here."

She couldn't have remained in the doorway if she'd wanted to. So she closed the gap between them.

As she neared the bed, he spread his legs so she could get as close to him as possible. As she stood before him, the outsides of her legs touching the insides of his, he reached up and pulled one of her curls, watching as it lengthened then sprang back in place.

"I like your hair. The color, the style."

"Thanks."

Did he like *her,* too? Was there something he saw within her that was different from Cindy? Something that gave Tori a unique place in his... Well, maybe his heart was too much to ask for. But certainly in his thoughts. Was it too much to hope for?

For a moment she wanted to pull away. To insist that he should care for her, too. That whatever she was beginning to feel for him should be mutual.

But she feared they'd moved beyond that now.

So in spite of a momentary hesitation, she chose to not dwell on it.

He placed his hand upon her jaw and drew her lips to his. Within a heartbeat, they were kissing again, deeply, mindlessly. Desperately.

His hands caressed her back, her sides. Up, down and back up again until he sought her breasts and found them ready and practically begging for his touch.

As his thumbs stroked her nipples through the cotton of her shirt and the satin of her bra, her whimper burst forth in his mouth.

Had anything ever felt so good, so arousing?

She wanted to remove her clothes, to feel his skin against hers.

And she wasn't able to wait a minute more.

So she drew back from him long enough to remove her blouse. And as she did so, her eyes locked on his, awaiting his reaction. His response.

She'd give anything to know what he was thinking, what he was feeling.

* * *

Matt watched in awe as Tori lifted her shirt over her head, then dropped it onto the floor. His hormones raged as she unhooked her bra and freed two perfect breasts with their dusky pink nipples contracted in response to their recent foreplay.

A flush blazed across her throat and chest, telling him that her desire for him was every bit as strong as his was for her.

For some reason he suspected that Tori was different from any of the other women he'd known. But he'd be damned if he knew why.

He cupped her face, brushed a thumb across the silky texture of her cheek, saw the glaze of passion in those pretty green eyes. "I'm going to make this special for you, honey."

Oops. Matt didn't use terms of endearments when talking to women, so he wasn't sure where the "honey" had come from. But it no longer seemed to matter when she unbuttoned her pants and pulled down on the zipper. Then she peeled the denim over her hips and stepped out of her jeans altogether.

As he watched her remove her panties—a skimpy white pair—he wanted to shed his clothes, as well. But he was afraid to take his eyes off her, afraid he'd miss the pleasure of all she was offering him.

When she stood before him in naked beauty, he couldn't stand it any longer and peeled off his shirt. Then he drew her into his embrace, relishing the way her breasts splayed against his chest.

Damn, she felt good in his arms.

"I want to make love with you, Matt." Then she pressed

her mouth to his, kissing him senseless and stoking a blaze deep within.

He'd never completely allowed himself to succumb to a woman's allure before, never expected to. And he had the urgent need to bury himself deep inside of Tori, to make her his, if only for tonight.

So he stopped kissing her long enough to shuck off his pants and boxers, then he stretched out on the bed and waited as she joined him.

As they lay side by side, hands seeking and exploring, they made out like a couple who'd saved themselves for each other. A couple who'd never experienced anything like this before.

Odd, he though, shaking off the romantic notion and clinging to the lust that drew him to her.

As their kisses deepened, he was completely swept away. His legs wouldn't allow him to get up on his knees, but it didn't seem to matter. As their lovemaking progressed, he was surprised to find out just how adaptable he was.

Even the occasional ache or pain didn't bother him. And before long, the only thing he was aware of was the heat of her touch, the sweet taste of her mouth, the seductive swirl of her floral scent.

Be careful, a small voice whispered. *Don't get too involved.*

The warning held merit, but right now he didn't care about tomorrow. He just wanted to be deep inside of her, thrusting in and out, taking and giving. Showing her all that making love could be.

He might be sorry later, but he wouldn't worry about

that now. Not when the only thing he could think of doing was to make her writhe with need.

A need only he could fulfill.

As he rolled to the side, taking her with him, she pressed her body against him. Fully aroused, she began to move against his demanding erection, dipping and rubbing and grinding until he thought he'd explode.

"Damn," he said, as he realized that she was the one driving him wild, rather than the other way around.

"Am I hurting you?" she asked, slowing her movements.

Not in the way she thought. But the ache in his loins was begging for release. "I've never been better. And the only thing that's going to hurt me is if you stop doing that."

She smiled, basking in her feminine power, it seemed. Then she proceeded to kiss his jaw, his neck, his chest, his abs, his belly, his…

Good grief, the woman was going to drive him insane.

Before long, they were stroking and caressing and tasting each other, caught up in a fire that might never burn out.

He fumbled for his shaving kit, which rested on the nightstand near the bed and nearly knocked it to the floor. Moments later he came up with a condom. She waited as he ripped into the packet and protected them both.

Finally.

Yet he was torn between wanting to end the sweet aching ecstasy and making it last.

"Would it be better if I got on top?" she asked.

"I don't know about *better*. But it certainly sounds appealing to me." He shot her a grin, thinking it might be nice to let her take the lead.

As he rolled onto his back, she positioned herself over

him. Then, with one knee on each side of his hips, she controlled their initial joining. As she lowered herself, he arched up, and they were soon lost in a lover's frenzy of lust and passion.

Their positions changed several times, and when they peaked, she cried out in pleasure. A powerful climax, the likes of which he'd never had before, damn near turned him inside out, shaking him to the core.

Tori gripped Matt's shoulders and held on tight as she rode each wave of rapture, afraid to open her eyes or breathe.

Their joining had been sweeter and better than she could have imagined, and that left her a bit uneasy.

She'd wanted to make love for the sake of having sex, but she feared it had been so much more than that. At least, it had been to her. She had no idea what to expect when they both came to their senses, but for the time being, she would hold Matt until the last wave of sexual bliss ebbed.

Yet even then she was reluctant to release him, to risk losing what they'd just shared.

Because maybe, if she lay with him long enough, she'd understand why she so desperately wanted to say, "I love you."

It was only sex, she reminded herself. And the overwhelming urge to put a name on what she was feeling and share that emotion with him was merely biological. An innate need to bond.

But she couldn't shake the fear that whatever Matt had stirred up inside her was more than chemistry, more than hormones.

Heaven help her, but somewhere between that first

kiss and the last, she feared that she might have fallen in love with Matt Clayton.

And she wasn't sure what that meant. Because if it was love, she feared it would lead to heartbreak.

After all, there was no way Tori could—or would—compete with a ghost.

Chapter Eleven

The next morning, while Matt sat in the office and went over a bid to repair the roof on one of the outbuildings, his mind kept drifting back to last night. As he relived the pleasures he and Tori had shared in bed, he realized that he finally felt alive again.

He and Tori had made love several times during the night, and at dawn they'd awakened in each other's arms. When Tori glanced at the clock on the bureau and saw the time, she'd quickly excused herself to shower and to make breakfast for the ranch hands.

And, oddly enough, when she'd left Matt in bed, he'd felt a bit…unbalanced.

They'd both known that their affair wouldn't be long-term—which, by the way, was okay with him. But as he lay alone in bed, as he heard the water in the shower turn on, he had to admit that he wasn't ready for it to end. At least, not yet.

He didn't say anything, though.

How could he when they'd both agreed that all they wanted was the physical release that came with sex?

Besides, he wasn't sure what more he wanted from her anyway.

In the past—before Cindy—he hadn't wanted a lasting relationship with anyone.

And after Cindy? Well, he hadn't thought that he would ever want to make that kind of commitment with anyone else again.

But last night, after each heart-spinning climax, when he'd actually had a legitimate reason to roll over and go to sleep, he hadn't. Instead he'd succumbed to the over-whelming compulsion to hold Tori close, to nuzzle her shoulder, to savor the scent of her shampoo.

So what was with that?

For some crazy reason, he hadn't been able to call it a night.

And he still wouldn't.

He blamed that unsettling fact on the accident, on his need to feel whole again. After all, he didn't have anything to offer a woman. Hell, he hadn't even had anything to offer Cindy. He suspected that their relationship had been…

Damn.

He raked his hand through his hair. Whenever his thoughts strayed in that direction, whenever he stirred up the guilt he'd been harboring, his mood floundered.

On the upside, that bit of reality would allow him to roll over and call it a night—figuratively speaking, of course.

So after a morning shower, he'd joined the ranch hands in the kitchen for a breakfast of scrambled eggs, bacon and fried potatoes.

The men had all clucked and fussed over Tori and her cooking skills like little speckled hens, but Matt continued to hold his coffee mug with two hands and pretended to enjoy the flavor of the fresh brew. He'd be damned if he wanted any of those cowboys to suspect what he and Tori had done last night.

As Lester and the others headed outside to start the day, Matt went into the office and got to work.

There was no need to hang around Tori this morning like a lovesick puppy. Besides, he didn't want to lay himself open for one of those awkward, after-the-loving chats, although they'd both been up-front with each other and clear about their expectations. Or, rather, their lack thereof.

Still, making love with her wasn't something he'd easily forget. In fact, just thinking about it slapped a goofy grin on his face.

At just after ten o'clock, a knock sounded on the office door.

"Come on in." He figured it was Tori, but he glanced up to see Lester instead.

Surprisingly, he had to bite back a sense of disappointment.

Lester carried in a stack of envelopes and set them on the desk. "I was at the feed store earlier today, so I stopped by the post office box and picked this up."

"Thanks."

As the ranch foreman left the office, Matt thumbed through the mail, sorting it.

Earl, one of the cowboys who'd worked on the ranch for ages, had gotten a letter from his son in Arkansas.

The bank statement came, as well as the power bill. And Granny had received two birthday cards from friends who hadn't been able to attend the party.

As he neared the bottom of the stack, he spotted another envelope for Tori. And just like the last one, it was from her brother, Sean, who was still at St. Sebastian, the rehab facility.

Apparently, her lack of response to the first letter hadn't stopped Sean from trying to reach her again.

For some crazy reason, Matt felt sorry for the guy. He still remembered the day he'd tried to apologize to Dave, Cindy's ex-husband. Matt hadn't been able to go to the funeral they'd held for both Cindy and Tommy, but he'd called Dave, tried to apologize for...

God, he couldn't even say what he'd actually been sorry for. His competitive spirit? The need to win at all costs?

But Dave had lashed out at him in a fury of grief and pain, leaving Matt to choke on his remorse.

Matt glanced back at the letter and tapped the corner on his open palm.

What had Tori's brother done? Had it been so bad that she couldn't forgive him?

If there was something Matt understood, it was being sorry and not being granted the forgiveness he desperately needed.

The fact that Sean was in rehab told Matt that he was at least trying to make some changes in his life. And that it was likely his drug or alcohol addiction that had been a contributing factor.

With his curiosity mounting, Matt pushed the chair away from the desk and carried the letter out of the office.

"Tori?" he called.

"I'm in the family room."

He took the letter to her, where she was dusting the bookshelf. She watched him enter, then blessed him with a pretty smile. For a moment he thought about backpedaling and not pressing her about the letter. But maybe if he knew what her brother had done he would understand.

So he held up the envelope. "Lester brought the mail. This came for you."

She stiffened, the dust cloth dangling in her hand.

When he gave her the letter, she scanned it briefly, then shoved it into her apron pocket.

"Aren't you going to read it?" he asked.

She studied him for a moment, as though she meant to tell him he was butting into something that didn't concern him. And he would have understood if she'd actually said that. Instead, she said, "Not now. Maybe later."

"Why do I get the feeling that you might never read it?"

She shrugged.

About the time he thought she might not provide him any more answer than that, she placed the dust rag on the shelf, then climbed down from the stool on which she was standing and made her way to the sofa, where she took a seat.

Matt recognized the cue and took a seat beside her, close enough to touch, yet keeping his distance.

"My brother had a drug problem," she said, "but no one told me. I guess they thought it would just magically go away if he left town. So, one day he called and asked if he could move in with me for a while. I figured if he got away from my grandmother, he'd grow up and become more responsible than he'd been in the past. So I said okay."

Matt continued to sit, to listen.

"Not only did I provide him with a place to live," Tori said, "but I also got him a job at the hospital where I worked."

Matt would have done the same thing for either Jared or Greg. "What happened?"

She blew out a sigh. "He got involved in drugs again and stole some pain medication from the hospital. The police were called, and an investigation led to him. They got a warrant and searched my house from top to bottom, finding his stash in his bedroom."

"That must have been tough for you."

"I was devastated and embarrassed. Plus it took a while for me to convince everyone that I didn't have anything to do with the theft."

"Is that why you left the hospital?"

"It was part of the reason." She blew out another sigh, yet kept those other reasons to herself. "I'll probably forgive him someday. But I'm not ready to do that yet. Not until I know that his efforts to clean up and be a responsible citizen are sincere."

"He's in rehab," Matt said.

"I hope that helps, but I know for a fact that he's got a long road ahead of him."

"Would it hurt to answer his letter?" Matt asked.

"Yes," she said. "It hurts whenever I think about the police rummaging through my house, my drawers. And it still tears me up inside when I think about sitting on the sofa of my living room, cuffed like a common criminal because they came to search *my* house because of my brother's drug addiction and theft. Then I was called into work and officially reprimanded for not seeing the signs of his addiction. I nearly lost my job over it all, so I'm not eager to set myself up as one of his enablers again."

Matt could understand that.

But he also knew how it felt to be on the other end, to be the guy wanting to be forgiven.

"My younger brother and sister were spoiled rotten by my grandparents," she added. "They've been allowed to believe that only their wants and desires count. That no one else matters. In the past six months both Sean and Jenna betrayed me one way or another. And I would have never done to them what they did to me."

As the tears welled up in her eyes, Matt reached for her, drawing her close and holding her while she cried.

His heart went out to Tori for what her brother had put her through, but he couldn't help believing that some people ought to get a second chance.

Matt certainly wanted one.

Whether he deserved it or not.

Tori had just finished washing the dishes after the noon meal when Granny and her entourage returned from the city. They entered the house through the back door, loaded down with bags.

Even Connie, who brought up the rear, had her hands full.

"That was fun," Granny said, as she pulled out a kitchen chair and sat down. "Do you want to see all the stuff we bought?"

"Sure." Tori folded the dish towel she'd been using and set it on the counter. Then she watched as the smiling trio spread their purchases across the antique tabletop, displaying school clothes and supplies for Joey, a couple of toys and some pants and tops for Connie.

"Look at my cool backpack." Joey's eyes lit up as he showed her how each zippered pouch worked.

"That's really neat," Tori told him.

Granny furrowed her brow and scanned the doorway that led to the rest of the house. "Where's Matt?"

"He's been working in the office," Tori said.

Granny seemed relieved. "Did you two enjoy having some peace and quiet while we were gone?"

Tori's cheeks warmed, and she hoped she wasn't blushing. "It was all right."

When Joey went to put his things away in the bedroom he'd once shared with Sabrina, Granny excused herself to go to the office and talk to Matt, leaving Tori and Connie alone.

"I really wish Granny hadn't insisted upon buying me those maternity clothes," Connie said.

"From the look on her face, I'm sure she enjoyed being able to do that for you."

"It just seems weird for an employer to be so kind and generous to her employees."

Tori smiled. "Granny isn't like anyone I've ever met."

"I agree. And although I haven't had much experience in the workforce, this job has been a real godsend."

Tori glanced at Connie's tummy, at the pooch that had begun to form. She suspected Connie's options had been somewhat limited with a baby on the way. "When are you due?"

"Around Thanksgiving."

Tori and Connie had been chatting more lately, and it seemed only natural to ask some of the questions she'd had. She was curious about Connie's history and couldn't help envisioning how much fun it would be to have a newborn during the holiday season. "Is your family nearby? With the baby coming, I'm sure that time of the year will be even more special."

Connie placed an elbow on the table and propped up her chin as though trying to decide whether or not she could trust Tori with the details of her past. "They don't know I'm pregnant, and I'm not planning to tell them."

"Ever?" Tori asked, thinking Connie would have to either give up the baby or never see her family again. A child didn't seem like the kind of thing that would be easy to hide indefinitely.

"Well, I'm not going to tell them for a while. The baby wasn't the only reason I left home. My mom…well, let's just say she's ultraconservative and has a high-profile job. Having an unwed, pregnant daughter would be a huge embarrassment for her."

Too bad Tori's brother and sister hadn't given any thought to the embarrassment their choices and behaviors would have on her.

Rather than say anything, Tori studied the attractive, quiet-spoken cook. She'd had her hair cut while in the city. Had she wanted to get rid of the blond highlights that had been growing out?

Or did she just like short hair?

Either way, there had to be a whole lot more to Connie's story than she'd let on, because Tori thought that most pregnant women would want to be close to their mothers and their families at a time like this.

"It's not unusual for a single mom to raise a child on her own these days," Connie said. "And it's really not so frowned upon in our society anymore. But I wasn't supposed to let this happen to me."

"So you're sure your family won't be supportive?" Tori asked.

"No. I'm afraid they would only be disappointed if they knew. So I left them a note about needing to find myself and left town."

It didn't sit right with Tori to think that Connie would have to go through labor and delivery alone.

"How long can you keep the baby a secret from your parents and your immediate family?" Tori asked.

"My family and their disappointment weren't the only reasons I left." Connie combed a hand through the spiky strands of her hair as though she was trying to get used to the shorter length. "I'd rather not go into the rest of it, but let's just say that I learned a very painful lesson about letting my hormones rule my head."

She was talking about the baby's father, Tori realized. "Does he know you're pregnant?"

"No. And I don't intend for him to find out—ever."

Tori didn't know what to say. To her it seemed only fair to tell the man about the baby. But she supposed that was Connie's decision to make.

Still, there was also a practical consideration Connie

should keep in mind. "I guess that means he won't be sending you child support."

"No, the baby and I are on our own." Connie sighed. "But I'm sure everything will turn out okay."

"You don't sound completely convinced."

"I'm sure it will be tough financially." Connie gathered up the bags she'd carried inside. "But the baby's father had a violent streak that I hadn't known about. And I won't live like that. I want to raise my child in a loving, peaceful environment."

Tori could certainly understand that. She'd seen women who'd come into the E.R. battered and bruised by the men who'd sworn to love, honor and cherish them. And she admired Connie for getting out of an abusive relationship before it worsened.

"Have you ever gotten involved with a man before you got a chance to really know him?" Connie asked.

Matt came to mind.

Tori had certainly gotten to know him. And she doubted he had an abusive bone in his body. But she had to admit she'd jumped into a sexual relationship. Especially when she suspected she was feeling more for Matt than he was for her.

A lot more.

"I can certainly see how it could happen," Tori said.

"Hindsight is wonderful, isn't it?" Connie smiled wryly. "If you'll excuse me, I'm going to put these things away, then get started on dinner."

Alone in the kitchen, Tori's thoughts returned to Matt, to all they'd shared last night.

She might have initially made love with him thinking that it was a brief affair, but now she knew differently. She was falling in love with him and wanted their relationship to last.

The problem was, she didn't know how Matt felt about anything long-term. Or about her.

Of course, what did she know about real love anyway? She'd only had one, ill-fated romance in the past.

Matt, by his own admission, was far more experienced than she was. And even if he were open to them having more than an affair, was he the kind of man who could limit himself to one woman? After all, he'd been the kind of man who had dated several women at once.

Sure, he'd been honest with them. But would he revert back to his old ways again once his body had healed?

Was Tori simply part of his healing process?

But what about Cindy? a small voice asked. Matt had made a commitment to her.

Yes, he had. But he'd loved Cindy. And Tori had been a convenient replacement.

She blew out a weary breath. They sure had a lot working against them, not to mention the biggest hurdle of all.

How could Tori compete with the memory of the woman Matt had loved and lost?

Matt was in the office when the call from the title company came in.

Six weeks ago, Granny had sold some property in Las Vegas to Dazzling Desert Ventures, a limited liability corporation owned by some casino bigwigs. From what he understood, the escrow was due to close any day.

The woman introduced herself as Tamara Aguilar and asked to talk to Mrs. Clayton.

"She's not available," Matt said.

"Then is Matthew Clayton there?" the woman asked.

"Speaking." Matt sat back in the desk chair, the springs squeaking.

"Mrs. Clayton gave me permission to discuss this escrow with either you or Jared, so I wanted to let you know that we closed this morning and the funding will take place late this afternoon."

"That's good to hear," Matt said. "Do you have the information needed for an electronic transfer to Mrs. Clayton's bank account?"

"Yes, I do."

Matt thanked her for the call and had no more than hung up when a rap sounded at the door. Before he could invite in whoever had knocked, his mother entered and left the door open.

"Hey," he said, looking up with a grin. "I didn't know you were already home. The title company just called and said the money should be in your account before the end of the day."

"That was quick." Granny took the seat across from him. "I've been talking to Grant Whitaker, my accountant, about the best way to invest that money. I don't suppose you'd mind calling him and letting him give you his thoughts on it."

"Not at all." Matt knew Granny had decided not to reinvest the money in a 1031-exchange by purchasing another piece of property. Instead, she would take the hit and pay the capital gains tax, which would be substantial. But there would still be millions left to invest in other ways.

"I don't know if I told you," Granny said, "but Sabrina won't be coming back to work at the Rocking C. She's going to stay on at Jared's ranch with him."

Matt already knew that after talking to Jared at the party. "I figured you were going to need a new book-keeper. Jared took a hard tumble for Sabrina, and when she was here for your birthday, she seemed just as starry-eyed to me as he was."

Granny winked and pointed her finger at him. "You should be so lucky, Matthew."

He scoffed, yet for some reason he felt a bit hypocriti-cal for his reaction—especially when he'd gotten involved with one of his mother's employees, too.

"Would you mind helping me with the bookkeeping and office work for a while?" Granny asked. "I'd like to have someone I trust. And your math skills have always been good. Besides, you know the ins and outs of ranching."

That was true. And while the offer was both flattering and sound, he struggled with the fact that by accepting the job, he would be accepting his physical limitations and settling. That he'd finally have to come to grips with the fact that he would never ride in another rodeo, never hear the roar of the crowd, never feel the adrenaline rush.

"Sure," he said, trying to muster some enthusiasm in his voice. "I'll help out—at least for the time being."

"I was also thinking," she said, pausing as though wanting to gather her thoughts.

Uh-oh. Granny had a way of orchestrating things to go the way she wanted them to. And while it was known throughout the community that she had a good heart, she also could be cagey when she set her sights on something.

Matt crossed his arms and waited to hear what she had to say.

"Well, Aquila and the foal she's carrying got me thinking. We've always focused on cattle, which is our bread and butter. But I wouldn't mind raising some horses, too. Would you be interested in partnering up with me?"

"You'll be eighty years old next weekend," Matt said. "Why get involved with breeding horses now?"

"Because Everett always wanted to diversify his interests and raise cutting horses. Buying a few good broodmares would be a fitting way to invest some of the money we got from his Las Vegas property investment."

Granny chuckled, then added, "Heck, I might even fancy having a Thoroughbred or two. Can't you just see me hobnobbing with those fancy folks who are involved with horseracing? I sure can."

"Are you kidding?" The word slipped out before Matt could catch them. Was she serious? It wouldn't be the most unpredictable thing she'd ever done.

"It's not a joke. But since you're the one with all the knowledge about horses, I wanted to run the idea past you. I'd also like you to be involved." She slowly got to her feet. "So give it some thought, will you?"

"Sure." As he watched his mother leave the room, he spotted Joey walking down the hall.

The boy paused in midstep, then turned and entered the office. "Hi, Matt. I wish you could have gone with us to Houston. It was really fun."

"I'm glad you had a good time." Matt returned to his work, hoping the kid would think he was too busy to chat.

"Did Sabrina call while we were gone?" Joey asked.

"No, not that I know of."

"Oh." Disappointment seemed to hang on that single utterance.

"What's the matter?" Matt asked, unable to ignore the boy's needs.

"I was hoping that Sabrina would have some good news about my dad."

As much as Matt wanted to cut the conversation short, he couldn't help sympathizing. Joey had lost his mom about six months ago, and his dad was in prison. Matt didn't know many of the details, just that Jared and Sabrina were both convinced of the guy's innocence.

So in spite of his resolve to steer clear of Joey, Matt set aside the invoices he'd been sorting through and gave the boy his attention. "I'm sure she'll call as soon as she knows something definite."

"Yeah. I guess she will." Joey nibbled on his bottom lip, his brow furrowed. "It's just that my dad didn't do anything wrong except try to save a guy's life. And I think he should get a medal or something for that."

"What happened?" Matt asked, wondering what the boy's spin on it was.

"My dad was in his rig when he saw some guys beating up another trucker. So he jumped out to help. And then the men started fighting him. One guy got hurt and died, and my dad got blamed for it."

Matt wasn't sure of all the particulars, but according to what he'd been told, a witness or two who could exonerate Joey's father from any wrongdoing had come forward.

"When my dad gets out, Jared is going to give him a

job on his ranch," the boy added. "So then my dad won't have to drive a truck and be gone all the time."

If there was one thing Matt and his brothers had learned while living with Granny, it was that a guy deserved a second chance.

His thoughts drifted to Tori's brother, a young man who'd definitely made several mistakes. But wasn't the fact that he was in rehab a sign that he wanted to straighten up his life?

What if Matt's uncle had entered rehab? Would Matt's early years have been brighter and more loving?

Kicking an alcohol or drug addiction had to be tough. And Tori's brother was going to need all the help and support he could get.

"Well," Joey said. "I'm going to visit Pumpkin and Fur Ball and the other kittens. See ya later, okay?"

"Yeah. Sure." Matt watched the boy go.

He wondered if he ought to talk to Tori. He didn't want to press her into doing something she wasn't comfortable doing.

But heck. She'd been pretty brutal when it came to pushing him to do the right thing.

In retrospect, he supposed he ought to thank her for that.

And in this case, maybe turnabout was fair play.

Chapter Twelve

That evening, after dinner, Matt grabbed his cane and asked Tori to go outside with him. Apparently, since their nightly strolls had become a habit, no one seemed to give it much mind.

But he'd really begun to look forward to their time together. And he couldn't help wishing they had one more night with the house to themselves.

As they started along the graveled drive, Matt studied the darkened, star-speckled Texas sky, a view in which he'd begun to find comfort. The moon was half its size tonight, only a piece of what it could be.

Just like me, Matt thought, pondering all he'd had to give up over the years.

When he was a kid, he'd lost his biological mother to death and his father to desertion. Then Granny had stepped in, offering him a second chance at love and family.

Maybe that's why he sympathized with Tori's brother, why he thought the guy ought to be given another chance—if he was truly trying to turn his life around.

For some reason, even though Matt didn't know Sean McKenzie from Adam, he felt drawn to the man's cause.

He'd be damned if he knew why it was so important, though.

As Tori walked at Matt's side, he slid a glance her way. Maybe there was more to it than that. Maybe he just needed to know that Tori was the kind of woman who would give a deserving man a second chance.

Since Matt could no longer fall back on his rodeo laurels, he'd have to build another life for himself—a lesser life, one in which his shortcomings would surely come to light.

And if he were involved with a woman…

Again, he stole another peek at Tori.

Hell, he had no idea what was going on between them, but it seemed to be more than just great sex. And if something more serious developed, he needed to know she'd be able to forgive him if he messed up. Because if he couldn't trust her to do that, he wouldn't let things go any further between them. He couldn't.

So in a weird way, Matt had a vested interest in Sean's recovery from addiction.

And that's why he felt compelled to quiz her about her brother, to ask why she wouldn't even read his letters.

It was a touchy subject, though. So he had to think of a way to casually bring it up. While he pondered an opening remark, she beat him to it.

"Tell me about Cindy," she said.

Matt didn't mind talking about his past, but Cindy was the one topic he hadn't wanted to discuss. Yet for some reason—the moon, the summer evening…

Heck, maybe because of the intimacy they'd shared the night before and he hoped they would share again, he decided to answer.

"Cindy was actually the ex-wife of one of the other guys on the circuit."

"Was he a friend?"

"Not exactly. Dave and I were competitors, and while we interacted at various rodeos, we really didn't socialize."

"So how did you meet her?"

"She was visiting a ranch where a buddy of mine had been staying."

She paused before asking, "Were you responsible for their divorce?"

"No. I've got a lot of faults, but dating married women isn't one of them."

Of course, there had been times when Matt had suspected Cindy still felt married to Dave, even after their divorce had been finalized.

"Dave hadn't treated her right," Matt added, more for his own sake than for Tori's. "Cindy hadn't been happy."

"Was Dave abusive?" Tori asked.

"Not physically. But he was gone a lot. And he cheated on her."

Tori seemed to flinch, although he couldn't be sure.

"Some men are weak," Matt said, thinking about the bunkhouse wisdom Clem, the old ranch foreman, had shared with Matt and his brothers.

Listen up, boys. If you marry a woman, then you damn well better honor those vows.

I'd never trust a man who cheated on the person who was supposed to be his life partner and his best friend.

If a man would screw over his wife, what makes you think he'd be any more loyal to you?

"Cindy must have been special," Tori said, drawing Matt from his musing.

"Yes, she was." She'd been quiet, gentle and a good mother. In fact, there'd been something maternal about her that had fed his soul. And he suspected that, deep inside, he knew she'd make a good wife.

"It's funny," he added, "but a lot of people thought we weren't suited. She wasn't like anyone else I'd dated."

"I guess that says a lot," Tori said. "You had plenty of women to compare her to."

She was right about that. Matt had met his share of rodeo groupies—buckle bunnies—who'd wanted to latch on to him because of his fame. Women whose names had blurred with the night like the scenery out the window of a fast-moving train.

Yet for some reason he didn't particularly miss that part of his life. And he'd be damned if he knew why.

Tori continued to walk on his left, the side not depending on the cane. When her arm brushed against his, his hand slipped into hers, and he gave her fingers a gentle squeeze.

It had been an unconscious move, one that felt good and right.

"You must have really loved her," Tori said.

Matt had cared for Cindy. That part was true.

He'd also liked Tommy, a kid who'd thought Matt had hung the moon. Of course, part of that reason was because Matt had filled the daddy-void in his young life.

At least, he had until Dave started coming around and asking for visitation.

To be honest, there was a part of Matt that had actually thrived on winning something one of his competitors had lost.

So, he guessed it was fair to say his and Cindy's relationship had been emotionally complicated.

"A single woman with a child can scare off a lot of men," Tori said.

Matt shrugged. "I guess so."

If truth be told, he'd found the idea of a ready-made family appealing. And although he would have had to work through the shared-parenting thing with Dave, which he had to admit also fed his competitive spirit, he hadn't minded.

So when Cindy had suggested marriage, he'd agreed and they'd become officially engaged. But at times Matt had wondered if wearing his ring had been her way of getting back at Dave, at showing him that he'd lost her to a better man.

But had Matt been the better man?

He'd once thought so.

Now as he looked back upon that last day of Cindy's life, he knew differently.

That fateful Sunday afternoon, her family had shown up at the park for a picnic reunion, which she'd insisted Matt attend with her.

Dave had been an old neighbor of Cindy's and a

friend of her brother's. So when asked to drop by, he had.

But Dave's presence made Matt uneasy and, true to form, Matt had been determined to be one up on the man each chance he got.

Cindy seemed not only uncomfortable with the competition, but annoyed by it. She insisted they leave, and on the ride home, her anger and disappointment permeated the cab of the truck.

As they traveled along the county road near her house, two drag racers came barreling down on them out of nowhere. With only a split second to make a decision, Matt turned the wheel to avoid a head-on collision, opting to run into a ditch. In an attempt to get out of the way, one of the racers turned off, too, and the resulting collision had proved fatal.

Tommy was killed upon impact, and Cindy died while Matt held her hand. She'd asked him to see to it that Tommy was put in his father's care, and he agreed.

He hadn't had the heart to tell her that the boy hadn't made it.

Matt suffered a broken hip and multiple fractures in both legs and ankles. From the beginning, doctors had been unsure as to what extent he would recover, but either way, he would never compete in the rodeo again.

The old Matt would have fought and jumped at the chance for physical therapy and rehab, eager to show them they were all wrong, but the old Matt no longer existed after that horrible day.

While grief and his own guilt had been enough to bog him down, that wasn't even the half of it.

Dave, who was grieving over the loss of his son and ex-wife, stopped by the hospital and lashed out at Matt, blaming him for the accident. "If you hadn't been such a jerk, Cindy wouldn't have insisted on leaving."

The additional guilt was staggering, and Matt had lost—at least, temporarily—the will to push himself, the will to get better.

Why did he have to stir up things with Dave at the picnic? Why hadn't he been more considerate of Cindy?

As Matt's legs began to ache, drawing him from the dark memories, he slid another glance at Tori.

She, too, seemed lost in her thoughts and probably hadn't noticed Matt's lapse into silence.

Tori glanced ahead, noticing that they'd walked farther than usual tonight.

"Are you okay?" she asked. "Do you want to turn around?"

"I'm all right, but I *would* like to head back. I didn't realize we'd walked so far."

Then, obviously his mind had been on something—or rather *someone*—else. And she didn't need a crystal ball to know who that someone was.

He had to have been thinking about Cindy. With a loss that great, that heartbreaking, he'd probably needed some quiet time with her memory.

Still, he continued to hold Tori's hand in a warm and steady grip. Why was that? Had she become a replacement for Cindy?

Of course, she hadn't felt like a replacement last night. In Matt's arms she'd felt like the only woman in the world.

Had she been? Was it possible?

Or had he honed that particular skill after having had his share of lovers?

"You know," he said, "I think your brother and I have something in common."

She tried not to bristle, but she didn't think she'd succeeded. "What makes you think that?"

"I know what it's like to want someone's forgiveness and not receive it."

Was Matt thinking about Cindy again? Did he blame himself for her death?

"Something tells me that Sean may be suffering, too," he said.

"That's the idea. Haven't you ever heard about tough love?"

"Yeah, I've heard about it."

They continued their walk toward the house, the light at the end of the barn illuminating their way.

"Showing Sean tough love might be the right thing to do," Matt said. "But if you've turned your back on him out of anger, it's only going to eat away at you both. And anger can be just as crippling as guilt."

He remained quiet for a while as they walked along the side of the barn.

Tori forced herself to consider Matt's words and try to look at the situation from his point of view. She supposed it was possible that Sean was truly remorseful for what he'd done. After all, he was seeking help for his addiction, since he was still at St. Sebastian's. But it was more complicated than just trying to forgive Sean. She couldn't do that without forgiving her sister. And she just wasn't ready to do that yet.

The intern Tori had been dating—oddly enough, his name didn't come so quickly to mind these days—had represented the future she'd wanted for herself. And so had her job at Lone Star General.

Now, thanks to both of her siblings' selfish acts, along with the public knowledge of them—the whispers and knowing looks—Tori had quit her job and walked away from it all.

Matt gave her hand another light squeeze. "I think we've both had enough serious talk for tonight."

"You're right."

Matt's lips twisted in a little-boy grin, and his mood lifted. "So if you have trouble sleeping in the middle of the night, feel free to sneak into my room. I wouldn't mind having you warm my feet."

"Just your feet?" she asked, trying to play along when she wasn't sure if she actually should.

He slid an arm around her and pulled her close. "Honey, you can warm anything you want."

Matt had lain awake for hours last night, listening for footsteps, for the sound of his doorknob turning. But he'd waited to no avail; Tori hadn't shown up.

Not that she'd promised to, but his invitation and her acceptance had certainly been implied.

Hadn't it?

He supposed there were a hundred reasons she had remained in her room. She could have fallen asleep before the rest of the house had gone to bed.

Or maybe she'd really meant it when she'd said she didn't want a long-term relationship. And she'd suddenly decided that making love two nights in a row was getting in too deep. Or that it might send the wrong message.

Then again, she might have gotten annoyed with him for butting into her business and suggesting that she forgive Sean.

He wished he knew.

But then at breakfast, when she'd asked Matt if he wanted her to drive him to Wexler for his physical therapy appointment this afternoon, he'd figured she couldn't be too angry.

Still, he'd declined her offer.

"I've decided to drive myself this time," he'd said. "But don't worry. I can handle it. Besides, it'll be good for me to venture out on my own."

She'd managed a smile, so he hoped she was okay with him shutting her out, but he had an errand to run today and didn't want her to ride along with him.

So, after grabbing a couple of pieces of toast and a cup of coffee, he'd headed to the office, where he did an Internet search for St. Sebastian's in Houston. Then he studied the Web site, reading up on the rehab center's program, their approach, their success rate.

Yesterday, when contemplating his reasons for being supportive of Sean, he'd neglected to admit one thing that might have been obvious to Jared, who'd had to put up with Matt those first few months after the accident.

While Matt had been recovering at his brother's ranch, he'd hit the booze pretty hard. The only way he'd been able to sleep at night was to drink himself numb. And while his dependence had been circumstantial and he didn't believe he was an alcoholic, he could certainly see how someone who was hurting emotionally could rely upon drugs or alcohol to ease their pain until they were hooked.

So, after finishing all the pending office work, Matt had taken the ranch pickup to Wexler and had another workout with the physical therapist. Then he'd driven to St. Sebastian's in Houston.

It hadn't been as easy to see Tori's brother as he thought it would be, and there'd been a bit of a wait. But eventually, he introduced himself to Sean McKenzie, a young man in his early twenties with short dark hair, green eyes and a ready smile.

Matt mentioned that he was a friend of Tori's, although he hoped that was still true after Tori found out about his visit to meet her brother.

Interestingly, Sean seemed pleased to meet Matt. And he didn't hold back any punches when he talked about the path to his addiction.

"Losing our parents was tough," the younger man said. "And then, six months later, my grandfather was diagnosed with cancer. Tori was in college at the time, and my grandparents didn't want to stress her out, so they kept a lot of that from her. But it got pretty bad. Grampa was really sick with all the chemo they gave him."

"I've heard it can be tough," Matt said.

"You know, it wouldn't have been so bad if there'd been a chance he could have pulled through. But looking back, I think he was trying so hard to live—even if it was a matter of six months or a year—so he could be a dad to us kids. He fought both the disease and the agony of the treatment when most people in his situation would have just accepted that their time had come."

Matt hadn't realized that Tori had dealt with her own share of guilt. She hadn't mentioned anything about the loss of her parents or her grandfather. He was beginning to guess that her way of dealing with grief was to bottle it up inside—just like him.

"I hurt so bad," Sean said, "but I couldn't cry. So no one knew what I was going through. And I couldn't seem to tell anyone that I was dying on the inside. My grandmother tried her best to help, but she was dealing with her own grief. She'd lost both a son and a husband in a very short period of time. So she gave Jenna, my younger sister, and me way more freedom than she should have. I can see that now, even though I couldn't back then."

"When did you start using drugs?" Matt asked.

"At first, I took the leftover pain medication that had been prescribed for my grandfather. But when that was all gone, illegal drugs were easier to get. Because I wasn't using it for recreational purposes, I figured that I would be able to kick the habit when the pain went away."

"But the pain never went away," Matt said. "Did it?"

"No, because I never allowed myself to go through the grieving process."

Sean seemed to be learning a lot about himself, about his addiction. And Matt suspected there was a good chance that his sobriety would last.

"Tori said she got you a job at the hospital where she worked." Matt hated to pry, but he needed to know more about how Sean's decisions and drug use had directly affected Tori.

The younger man nodded. "I swear, Matt. I moved in

with her to try and kick my habit. I figured that if I got out of town and the environment I'd been in, if I met new friends, that it would be easier. And in that sense it was."

"How did you get access to the drugs at the hospital?" Matt asked.

"There was a nurse I'd been dating who had a problem. It's weird how addicts seem to find each other." Sean blew out a sigh. "Anyway, she's the one who had access to the meds, and she got some for me. But I'm afraid I was the one who got caught."

"She didn't?"

"I heard they eventually investigated her, too. But at the time, I thought of her as a friend and didn't want to get her in trouble." Sean raked a hand through his hair. "In retrospect, I should have blown the whistle on her. Her drug problem was risking the lives of the patients she took care of."

"How's the rehab working out for you?" Matt asked.

"Good. *Real* good. In fact, I've decided to go back to school. I want to counsel others when I get out of here. I've really learned a lot."

"Your sister ought to be happy to hear that," Matt said.

"I hope so. I love my sister. She was always good to me. And I'm really sorry about the embarrassment I caused her."

"I'm sure she'll come around," Matt said.

"Me, too. But either way, I'm facing the consequences for the bad choices I made."

The men shook hands, then Matt left the center, climbed into the truck and headed home.

No matter what Tori's decision would be, he was glad

he'd come, glad his decision to support her brother had been validated.

He just hoped that when he told her what he'd done, she'd be okay about his visit to meet Sean and see what he could do to facilitate peace.

Because if she wasn't, if she couldn't see any reason to give her brother a second chance, Matt wasn't sure he could risk laying his heart in her hands.

Tori had gone through the motions today, washing windows and cleaning out closets. She wasn't sure why Matt had wanted to drive to Wexler by himself, and she'd been disappointed when he'd made the announcement.

For a while she wondered if he was angry at her.

She supposed he might have been expecting her to come to his room last night. And she'd actually thought long and hard about slipping into bed with him after the house was quiet.

But while talking to him about Cindy last night and re-alizing how much he'd loved her, she'd actually been jealous.

Jealous of a woman who'd become an angel in Matt's eyes. How was that for pinning her heart on an impos-sible dream?

She couldn't help thinking that Matt's misery had been caused more by the death of the woman he loved than the loss of his rodeo career. So she'd decided it was best not to get any more involved with Matt than she had already.

Glancing at her wristwatch, she realized it was nearly five o'clock. Where was Matt? His physical therapy ap-pointment should have been over hours ago.

She strode to the living room, then pulled back the curtain to peer outside.

There was still no sign of him.

Just as she was about to lean away from the window, she spotted the truck coming down the drive.

Relief rushed her chest. Thank God he was safe. In spite of wanting to remain cool and detached, she went to the door and stepped onto the porch.

As he climbed from the pickup, he spotted her watching him and smiled. Her heart clenched as he grimaced in pain, but she knew better than to fuss over him. He'd been clear about that.

And look how independent he'd been today. He hadn't even wanted her to go with him.

Maybe he was pulling away from her, from what they'd shared.

Yet as much as that possibility hurt, she realized it might be for the best.

"Where have you been?" she asked.

"Were you worried?" His face lit up as though her concern mattered, and for a moment she couldn't help believing that there was actually a chance the two of them could become a couple.

"Yes, I was."

He removed the cane that had been lying across the truck seat, then closed the door and made his way to the porch.

"I don't know how you're going to feel about this," he said.

"Feel about what?" she asked, clearly at a loss.

"I drove into Houston and met your brother."

A knot formed in Tori's gut. "You did what?"

"I went to see Sean." He leaned against the porch railing. "He looks good, Tori. And he seems to have his feet on the ground."

Matt might have thought he was being helpful, but an overwhelming sense of betrayal poured over Tori until she found it hard to breathe. Had Sean told Matt about Jenna and James? Did he know that her sister had made a play for Tori's lover?

"You had no right to interfere," she said.

"You're right. But I did it anyway."

Her hands clenched and unclenched, as her anger heated to the boiling point. "I can't believe this. You didn't want me interfering in your life. So how could you do that to me?"

"I only wanted to help. I had a feeling your brother was remorseful, and I believe he's truly sincere. He's been sober for two months, and he's trying to put his life back in order."

But what about Tori's life? How was she supposed to go back to Lone Star General and ask for her job back? And even if she wanted to work at another hospital, she'd still need to provide a reference from her previous employer.

God only knew what had been written in her file.

"Is it that hard for you to forgive someone?" Matt asked, his brow furrowing, his gaze intense.

His question had the effect of a big index finger jabbing her chest. But instead of recoiling, it made her want to stand tall. To fight back.

It wasn't as though she would never forgive her brother. She just needed some space and time to heal, to sort through her options, to replot her future.

"What's the matter?" Matt asked.

"I don't appreciate your going to see my brother. Are

you planning to go back to the hospital and try to get my job back for me, too?"

"Did they fire you?" he asked.

"No. I quit."

"And instead of being the nurse you were meant to be, you prefer to hide out on a ranch instead."

"So what?" she asked, the Irish blood in her starting to rise, her defense on the alert.

He might claim to be trying to help, but she knew what he was really doing. He was chasing her off, just as he'd tried to do with Joey. She'd gotten too close, and he preferred to grieve for Cindy rather than risk loving again.

"You're running away from your troubles," he said, his expression suggesting he'd had a lightbulb moment. "Just like you accused me of doing."

She was running away?

Right this minute she didn't give a rip whether Matt had a point or not. Instead she was trying to regain her footing and decide how to deal with what he had done, what he'd meant to do.

"My career was taken away from me," he said. "But you just threw yours away."

He was encouraging her to get on with her life so she would get out of his.

Well, maybe she'd just make it easy on him.

"I think we need to put some distance between us," she said, trying to garner her pride. Trying to rein in the love she'd felt for him and to protect her heart from breaking any further.

He just stood there, leaning on his cane, and studied

her as though he had a big decision to make. Finally he slowly nodded. "You might be right."

Then he headed into the house, letting the screen door slam behind him.

Ten minutes later he'd packed an overnight bag, then he limped out the front door and headed toward the pickup.

Tori knew she might be able to stop him.

Instead she let him go.

Chapter Thirteen

Matt drove back to the three-bedroom stucco house he owned on the outskirts of Houston. He hadn't been home since before the accident and it showed.

The five-acre property looked deserted and was in need of a good weeding, something he'd have to hire someone to do tomorrow. He'd also have to get the sprinklers going.

It was time, he decided, to face the past, as well as the future.

Walking away from Tori had been one of the hardest things he'd ever had to do. And it had hurt like hell.

After they'd made love, he'd hoped to be able to cut bait before his heart got involved, but apparently it was too late for that. On the way home, as he'd struggled with his emotions, he'd realized that he'd already fallen in love with her.

Some men might not give a rat's hind end about second chances. But they mattered to Matt.

Not that he planned to do anything that needed to be forgiven, of course. But if he did, he didn't want his errors held over his head.

When he was a kid, his uncle used to do that to him. He'd start by bawling out Matt for some childish indiscretion, like spilled milk or whatever. But then he'd start bringing up past grievances, and a beating would follow.

That's why Granny's kindness had been such a soothing balm. And that was why Matt had needed to know that Tori had a forgiving nature before he could consider making any kind of commitment to her.

He chuffed. A commitment. Funny he should ponder one when she hadn't even implied that she wanted one.

As he unlocked the door and let himself into the house, he was met by a wallop of stale, musty air.

The plant Cindy had given him, once green and lush, still sat on the glass-topped table. But now it was withered and dead, a testament to what he'd once had and lost.

"You need a little life and color around here," Cindy had said two days before the accident, when she'd adorned his living room with the potted plant.

She'd been right, Matt thought, as he scooped up the pot, his motion raining dead leaves onto the table.

Then he carried it into the kitchen and tossed the whole kit and caboodle into the trash.

Next he opened the windows and turned on a couple of fans. With that done, he made a quick scan of the house.

On the dining room table, surrounded by a layer of dust, a pile of mail awaited his attention.

Jared must have stopped by while Matt had been in the hospital and collected it from the mailbox that stood in lonely vigil at the road in front of the house. This stuff had probably arrived before his brother had asked to have Matt's mail forwarded to Jared's ranch.

As Matt thumbed through the stack—a lot of it junk that he would toss—he spotted a letter addressed to him.

It was from Andy Thompson, the kid who'd caused the accident.

Not long ago, the teenager had written to tell Matt how sorry he was. But Matt hadn't responded. How could he forgive the kid, when he couldn't even forgive himself?

This letter must have come first, he realized, as he set it aside—unread.

Then his movements froze. He'd been asking Tori to do something he hadn't been able to do.

His sympathies shifted to the sixteen-year-old kid whose stupid decision proved to be a fatal mistake. And he understood Andy's need for absolution.

Heck, Matt would have given anything to hear Dave say, "I know that the accident wasn't your fault." But Dave had lost his only child and his ex-wife, a woman he'd never stopped loving. And, apparently, it helped to have someone to blame when he was hurting, which was a real bitch, as far as Matt was concerned.

And as far as Andy was concerned, too, he supposed. So he tore open the letter and read the kid's words:

Dear Mr. Clayton,
    You have no idea how sorry I am about that

accident and the loss of your loved ones. I am so sorry that I can't eat or sleep.

My parents and the attorney for our insurance company advised me not to contact you, but I just couldn't help it. Will you please forgive me?

Andrew Thompson

Matt blew out a weary sigh. Then he dug through the cupboard in the hutch until he found a notepad and pen.

He might not be able to convince Dave to forgive him for the part he'd played in the tragic accident, but he didn't have to harbor that same, hard-hearted spirit.

As he began his response to Andy, the emotional millstone that had been tied around his neck began to loosen and lift.

His words were short and right to the punch. "Andy, you're forgiven. Enjoy dinner and sleep well tonight. Matthew Clayton."

Then he addressed the envelope, placed a stamp on it and carried it outside, walking along his own driveway tonight, instead of Granny's.

It was a lonely stroll without Tori at his side. But it was a necessary one to make, because as he placed the letter in the mailbox and lifted the red flag, he felt a hell of a lot better than he had in months.

When he returned to the house, he turned on the radio, hoping the noise would lift his mood and help him to shuck the loneliness that had dogged him while he'd been outside.

As a hit by Toby Keith ended and another song began, Matt recognized Greg's voice. His brother sang a ballad about love lost and found, of second chances and new beginnings, and Matt's eyes grew misty. He swiped at them with the back of his hand.

There was one more apology that needed to be made, as well as one more confession.

And it couldn't wait until morning.

When Connie called the household to dinner that night, Tori passed, thanking her but saying she wasn't hungry.

"Where's Matt?" Connie asked.

"I don't know." Tori's words came out soft and slow, a direct contrast to the ones she'd shared with Matt earlier. But with each minute that he'd been gone, her anger had been dissipating.

"Did he ever get back from physical therapy?" Connie asked.

"Yes, but he left again."

"Will he be coming back tonight?"

"I don't think so." Tori's heart clenched at the thought. But she had no one to blame but herself.

A slice of guilt lanced her chest.

She shouldn't have done that. This was Matt's mother's house. If anyone ought to have gone, it should have been Tori.

Besides, she'd begun to see the truth in Matt's words.

She'd let her emotions cripple her, too. She'd been hanging on to her pain, just as Matt had clung to his wheelchair. And she'd refused to do what she could to get better, to heal. She'd been running, too—and not just from her past. In her efforts to escape, she'd nearly thrown away her future—her career as a nurse.

While the others ate dinner, Tori sat in the living room,

an open book in her lap. Yet she wasn't reading. Instead she was listening for the sound of an approaching car in the driveway.

But not just any car, she realized. The pickup Matt had been driving.

Yet the only noise she heard was the tick-tock-tick made by the antique clock on the mantel, reminding her how much time had passed since Matt had left.

If she could wind back the hands, if she could have that moment of confrontation all over again, she wouldn't have been so quick to anger. So quick to defend herself.

Everything Matt had said about her had been right. She'd run away from her problems, and she'd given up the career she loved.

As shuffled footsteps sounded in the doorway, Tori looked up to see Granny enter the room.

"Oh, there you are," the older woman said. "We missed you at dinner."

"I wasn't hungry."

"That's what Connie said."

Tori set the book aside. "Do you have a home phone number for Dr. Graham?"

"I sure do." Granny furrowed her brow. "What's the matter? Are you sick?"

Yes, she was sick at heart. But there wasn't a pill or an injection that could heal that.

"I'd just like to talk to him," Tori said. "That's all."

After Granny gave her the number, Tori placed the call to the country doctor.

"Hello?" the familiar, aged voice said.

"Dr. Graham, this is Tori McKenzie, Granny Clayton's housekeeper."

"Is everything okay at the Rocking C?" he asked.

"Yes, it's fine. But I wanted to talk to you about something. I'm interested in going back to work as a nurse and wondered if you knew of any job openings in or around Brighton Valley. I'd really like to stay in the area."

"As a matter of fact," Doc said, "I've had several conversations with Betsy Bramblett, the latest of which was this afternoon. Dr. Bramblett is a family practitioner in a medical group located in Wexler, and she's interested in buying my practice."

"Are you going to sell it to her?"

"Yes, because I trust that she'll provide the kind of care my patients have come to expect from me."

"Oh," Tori said, her spirits sagging a bit.

"But don't you worry," Doc added, "I just happen to know that Betsy will need a nurse. So I'd be happy to give you my recommendation."

"Thank you, Doc."

"No problem."

When the line disconnected, she felt as though she'd taken a big step in the right direction, yet there was something else that still needed to be done. But that call would need to be made from the privacy of her bedroom.

After closing the door, she dialed information and asked for the number to St. Sebastian's Rehab Center. She was routed to several different people before her brother finally came on the line.

She made an attempt at stilted small talk before getting

to the meat of the matter. "Sean, I'm sorry for not answering your letters. But I want you to know that I support your efforts to get your life back on track."

"Thanks, Tori. I really appreciate that. And I am so sorry for screwing things up for you at Lone Star General."

"I know," she said. "I should have recognized your drug problem sooner. I guess I bailed out on you, Jenna and Gram."

"Hey, I'm learning all about second chances here. And to take one day at a time. So I'm sure things will only get better for our family."

She hoped he was right.

"For what it's worth," he said, "I'm making progress, and I'm assuming responsibility for the mistakes I made."

That was definitely a step in the right direction.

"You know, yesterday in group, one of the guys told the story of a kid who'd played football with him in high school."

Tori wasn't sure where this story was going, but she listened intently.

"The kid's name was Arnie, and each day, after practice, when the guys would go into the locker room and shower, Arnie would just pack up his gear and leave. Whenever anyone asked why he was leaving, Arnie would say, 'I'm going to shower as soon as I get to my house.' But the next day, one sniff told them that he hadn't. One of the guys said that Arnie probably came from a family that didn't make a big deal out of bathing regularly."

"That's probably true," Tori said.

"Yeah, but then my friend in group shared something

pretty profound. Something that really stuck with him and made a point for all of us."

"What's that?"

"Arnie might have grown up in a home where no one encouraged him to bathe. But by the time he was eighteen, he was old enough to know that he stunk. And the only one who could shoulder the blame at that point was Arnie."

"You're right about that," Tori said. "I guess we can only blame others for our shortcomings for so long."

"For what it's worth," Sean said, "Jenna realizes that she stinks, too. And she's making an attempt to take charge of her life. She's been coming to some of the group meetings we have here for the members of our families."

"I'm glad to hear that," Tori said. She supposed she'd have to make a call to Jenna one of these days, too. Not to apologize, but to open the lines of communication between them.

"And that thing with James?" Sean said. "She swears it was only a kiss. And she's not seeing him."

"She needs to realize that women don't do that to each other," Tori said, still angry at the betrayal.

"You're right, sis. But maybe you could cut her a little slack. She lost her mother, remember? And her big sister moved out of the house to go to college. I'm not sure if you knew this or not, but Jenna didn't have many friends. So she's lacking a few social skills."

Sean had a point. Jenna might have been eighteen when Tori had gotten her the job in the hospital cafeteria, but she'd been a baby in so many ways. And while she was wrong for getting involved with James, the intern had been ten years Jenna's senior and had made a commitment to Tori. So, in that sense, he was more to blame than she was.

"Listen," Sean said. "We've got a group session I need to attend, so I have to hang up. But I appreciate your call. And your support."

After promising to visit him soon, Tori disconnected the line and hung up the phone.

But before she could get to her feet and return to the living room, a knock sounded at her bedroom door.

"Who is it?" she asked.

"It's me. Matt."

Tori's heart threatened to burst from her chest. "Come in."

The door creaked open. "I hate to bother you," he said.

"It's no bother." She continued to sit on her bed, her hands resting on the mattress, her feet on the floor, her eyes on the cowboy who'd stolen her heart.

"I came to tell you I'm sorry," he said. "You were right. The decision to forgive your brother is yours to make. I shouldn't have interfered like I did."

"I have an apology to make, too," she said. "For getting angry when you pointed out that I was running from the past. Once I thought about what you'd said, I realized you were right. In fact, I just got off the phone with my brother, and I think I'm going to visit him next weekend. I also called Dr. Graham. He's going to give me a recommendation when I apply for another nursing position."

Matt's grin turned her heart on end. "I'm glad to hear it."

She glanced at the cane he held in his right hand and patted the mattress beside her. "Why don't you sit down?"

"Are you inviting me to share your bed?" he asked, taking a seat.

"Actually, as much as I'd like to make love with you again, I don't think that's in my best interest."

"Why not?" he asked.

She could hold back her feelings, as she'd been prone to do in the past. But she'd begun to realize that no matter how scary or painful they were, she needed to face them head-on. "Because I wasn't being honest with you or with myself when I suggested that we have sex with no strings attached. There's something sacred and safe within those strings. And I'm not going to be comfortable without them."

"Do you want a commitment from me?" he asked, his voice growing somber.

"I realize that Cindy will always have a special place in your heart that no other woman can fill. But I love you, Matt. And if you can't find a little corner of your heart for me, I won't make love with you anymore. I can't set myself up for heartache."

Matt started to chuckle, and she turned to face him, wanting to throttle him. What in the world had he found funny about her heartfelt confession?

When she did, he turned and caught her cheek in the palm of his hand. His thumb skimmed her cheek. "I didn't just come all the way back to the ranch tonight to tell you that I was sorry for butting into your life. I came to tell you that I want you to be a permanent part of mine."

"But—" Tori blinked, trying to make sense of what he was saying.

"There aren't any buts about it, Tori. I love you. And you can have every inch of my heart. It's yours, honey. Now and forever."

Tears welled up in her eyes, and she studied the man

she'd come to love through a watery blur, the man who'd lost the woman he'd loved. "But what about Cindy?"

"I cared about her. A lot." Matt brushed his thumb under her eye, whisking away her tears. "But I don't think it would have lasted."

"The marriage?" she asked.

"No, the engagement. Dave loved Cindy. And the harder he fought to win her back, the harder I fought to keep her. I convinced myself that I loved her, when now I realize what love really is. My feelings for her couldn't hold a candle to what I feel for you."

"Are you sure?" she asked, unable to wrap her heart around his words.

Matt brushed his lips across her mouth, deepening the kiss and showing her just how sure he was.

When they pulled away long enough to catch their breaths, Matt tugged at one of Tori's curls and smiled. "How about coming back to Houston with me?"

"Tonight?"

"My mother might be a romantic at heart, but I'm not sure how she'd feel about us sharing a bed in her house. And since I plan to sleep with you every night for the rest of our lives, I figured we could start now."

"Are you proposing?" she asked.

"I hope you don't expect me to kneel at your feet. But if you'll give me a rain check, I'll ask you properly as soon as my physical therapist gives me an okay."

Tori wrapped her arms around the man she loved. "Then I accept, Matt."

"Excuse me," Granny's voice said from the doorway. "I hope I'm interrupting something."

They both turned to see Granny grinning from ear to ear.

"I might be hearing things, but it sounded as though I walked in on a marriage proposal."

"As a matter of fact," Matt said, "you did. And I hate to be the one to tell you, but you're going to be losing a maid along with that bookkeeper who just gave you his notice."

Granny brightened and clapped her hands together. "I've never been happier to replace a couple of employees in my life. And off the record, that was my plan all along."

"Have you been matchmaking?" Tori asked, stunned.

The older woman's grin stretched across her face, softening her wrinkles. "Now only one of my sons is still unattached, but I hope to get that corrected by Christmas."

And there was just one single, female employee left, Tori realized—unless, of course, Granny had someone else in mind. How many women would set up their sons with a pregnant woman?

Granny leaned against the door. "Have you given that business deal any thought, Matt?"

"Yes, I have." He slipped his arm around Tori's waist. "If you're sure a horse-breeding venture is something you'd really like to get involved with, I'm game. Besides, with my future wife looking for a nursing position in this neck of the woods, it won't do me much good to be based near Houston."

"Good." Granny straightened and took a step backward. "Then I'll leave you two alone so you can plan the details of your wedding."

As his mother slipped out of the room, Matt got to his feet, reached out his hand and pulled Tori to a standing position. "Come on, honey. Why don't you ask Connie to babysit the kittens for us? Then pack an overnight bag, and let's get out of here."

She couldn't think of anything she'd like to do more, but she tossed him a playful smile. "What about those wedding details you told Granny we were going to discuss? She'll probably quiz us on the way out."

"There's not much to talk about." He placed a hand on her jaw, his thumb drawing slow, sensual circles on her cheek, his gaze warming her from the inside out. "You planned one heck of a birthday party that went on without a hitch, so I know our wedding will be the talk of the town. You can call the matrimonial shots. My only suggestion is that we plan to have it in December."

That was six months away, which meant she'd have to get busy and start planning.

"Christmas weddings can be beautiful," she said.

"Ours will be nice whenever we have it, but Greg will be home for the holidays. And I'd like my entire family to meet yours." He brushed a kiss across her brow. "Are you okay with waiting? Otherwise, we can get married right away and plan a reception in December."

"I can wait. I've always dreamed of having a wedding. Nothing big. Just family and friends."

"Good." The love in his eyes filled her heart to the brim. "We can hammer out the other details later. But right now, my mind is in honeymoon mode. And it's a long drive back to Houston. I just hope we make it without having to pull over and find our own little Lover's Lane."

Tori stood and wrapped her arms around the man she would promise to cherish for the rest of her life. "I love you, Matt Clayton."

"I love you, too." Then he placed his lips on hers, claiming her as his own.

Tori wasn't exactly sure what the future would bring, but with Matt at her side, she knew they would weather any storm.

Happily-ever-after didn't start any better than this.

* * * * *

*Mills & Boon® Special Moments™
brings you a sneak preview.*

In The Inherited Twins, *raising her orphaned niece
and nephew and struggling to keep her Texas ranch
afloat doesn't leave Claire Olander much time for
relationships. Until gorgeous Heath McPherson comes
to Red Sage Ranch with an offer she can't refuse...*

*Turn the page for a peek at this fantastic new story
from Cathy Gillen Thacker, available next month in
Mills & Boon® Special Moments™!*

*Don't forget you can still find all your favourite
Superromance and Special Edition stories
every month in Special Moments™!*

The Inherited Twins
by
Cathy Gillen Thacker

In most situations, twenty-nine-year-old Claire Olander had no problem standing her ground.

The only two Texans who could weaken her resolve ambled to a halt in front of her. In perfect synchronization, the "negotiators" turned their faces upward.

Her niece, Heidi, pushed the halo of short, baby-fine blond curls from her face and tucked her favorite baby doll under her arm, football-style, so the head faced front. "How come we have to clean up our toys now, Aunt Claire?" the preschooler demanded.

Her twin brother, Henry, adjusted his plastic yellow hard hat with one hand, then gave the small wooden bench he was "fixing" another twist with his toy wrench. His amber eyes darkened in protest as he pointed out with customary logic, "It's not dinnertime!"

Claire wished it was. Then the business meeting she had been dreading ever since the bank auditors left to tally their results, six weeks ago, would be history. Aware there was no use worrying her nearly four-year-old charges, she smiled and tidied the stacks of papers on her desk one last time.

Everything was going to be all right. She had to keep

remembering that. Just like her late sister, Liz-Beth, she was more than capable of mothering the twins and managing the family business they'd started. "We are cleaning up early, kiddos, because we have company coming this afternoon," she announced cheerfully. In fact, the Big Bad Wolf should be here at two o'clock.

Heidi sat down cross-legged on the floor, placed her doll, Sissy, carefully across her lap, and began stuffing building blocks ever so slowly into a plastic storage bin. "Who?"

Claire knelt down next to her, and began to help, albeit at a much quicker pace. "A man from the bank."

"Can he hammer stuff?" Henry demanded.

Claire surveyed the two children who were now hers to bring up, and shrugged. "I have no idea."

Heidi paused. "What *can* he do?" she asked, curiously.

"Manage a trust." *Destroy my hopes and dreams...*

Henry carefully fitted his wrench in the tool belt snapped around his waist, and sat down beside Heidi. "What's a trust?"

"The fund that's going to pay for your college education one day."

"Oh." He looked disappointed that it wasn't something he could "repair" with his tools.

"Is he our friend?" Heidi asked.

Claire fastened the lid on the building blocks bin, and put it on the shelf in her office reserved for the twins' playthings. "I've never met him, honey. He just moved here a couple of weeks ago." She'd heard a lot about him, though. The newest member of the Summit, Texas, business community was supposed to be thirty-three years old, to-die-for handsome and single, a fact that had the marriage-minded females in the community buzzing. Fortunately for Claire, she was not one of the group jockeying for attention. She had her hands full with her fledgling business and the twins she had inherited from her late sister and brother-in-law.

"Is he going to have good manners?" Henry, who'd lately become obsessed with what to do and what *not* to do, inquired.

"I'm sure Mr. H. R. McPherson is very polite," Claire said. Most bankers were.

Heidi put Sissy on her shoulder and gently patted her back, as if burping her. Her brow furrowed. "What's H. R. McDonald's?"

"H. R. McPherson, honey, and those are initials that stand for his first and middle names." Claire could not blame him for using them on business correspondence, even if it did make him sound a little like a human-resources department. "Although," she observed wryly, shelving the last of the toy train cars scattered about, "who would name their son Heathcliff *and* Rhett in this day and age, I don't know."

"As it happens," a low male voice drawled from the open doorway behind her, "the hopeless romantic who came up with that idea was my mother."

As the sexy voice filled the room, it was all Claire could do to suppress her embarrassment. Talk about bad timing! She'd just mouthed off about the man she could least afford to insult.

Slowly, she turned to face the interloper.

The ladies in town were right, she noted with an inward sigh. Tall, dark and handsome did not begin to do this man justice. He had to be at least six foot four inches tall, and buff the way guys who worked out regularly were. Nicely dressed, too, in a striking charcoal-gray business suit, navy-and-gray-striped shirt and sophisticated tie.

His midnight-blue eyes glimmering with amusement, he waited for her to say something.

Flushing, Claire flashed a smile. "This is awkward," she said.

"No kidding."

She took in the chiseled features beneath the thick black hair, the straight nose, the eminently kissable lips. "And you're early."

He shrugged and stepped closer, inundating her with the compelling mixture of soap, man and sun-drenched November air. "I wasn't sure how long it would take me to find the ranch." He extended his hand for the obligatory greeting, then assisted her to her feet. A tingle of awareness swept through her.

"I didn't think you'd mind," he added cordially.

Claire probably wouldn't have, had she not been down on the floor with the kids, speculating inappropriately about his lineage, at the exact moment he'd walked in.

Ever so slowly, he released her hand, and she felt her palm slide across the callused warmth of his. She stepped back, aware she was tingling all over from the press of skin to skin.

"You can call me Heath," he told her.

She swallowed nervously. "I'm Claire." Aware of the little ones taking refuge at her sides, she cupped her hands around their shoulders and drew them closer, conveying that they would always be safe with her. "And this is Heidi and Henry, the beneficiaries of the trust."

Heath shook their hands solemnly. "Pleased to meet you, Heidi. Henry, nice to meet you also."

"Pleased ta meet you!" the twins echoed, on cue.

Claire grinned, happy her lessons on manners were sinking in.

"So when do you want to get started?" Heath asked in a more businesslike tone.

"Just as soon as their sitter arrives," Claire declared, glad he was putting them on more solid ground.

SPECIAL MOMENTS™ 2-in-1

Coming next month

THE INHERITED TWINS by Cathy Gillen Thacker

Raising her orphaned niece and nephew and struggling to keep her Texas ranch afloat doesn't leave Claire Olander much time for relationships – until Heath McPherson comes to call.

CHRISTMAS IN KEY WEST by Cynthia Thomason

Abby Vernay's coming home to the man left behind. But if they're going to have a future together, she has to confess the secret she's been keeping...

HER BEST CHRISTMAS EVER by Judy Duarte

Stranded alone with *very* pregnant Connie, superstar Greg Clayton had to deliver her holiday baby! Now he wanted to make all of her Christmas dreams come true...

A MAN WORTH KEEPING by Molly O'Keefe

When Delia Dupuis's past catches up with her, she discovers Max is a man worth trusting with her daughter, her life...and her heart.

IT'S THAT TIME OF YEAR by Christine Wenger

Sam was determined to make Melanie believe in his love for her and her son – in time to give them all the best Christmas gift ever...

MORE THAN A MEMORY by Roz Denny Fox

Garret Logan is still mourning his fiancée's untimely death when, seven years later, she reappears with a new name, claiming not to remember him...

On sale 16th October 2009

Available at WHSmith, Tesco, ASDA, Eason and all good bookshops.
For full Mills & Boon range including eBooks visit
www.millsandboon.co.uk

millsandboon.co.uk Community

Join Us!

The Community is the perfect place to meet and chat to kindred spirits who love books and reading as much as you do, but it's also the place to:

- Get the inside scoop from authors about their latest books
- Learn how to write a romance book with advice from our editors
- Help us to continue publishing the best in women's fiction
- Share your thoughts on the books we publish
- Befriend other users

Forums: Interact with each other as well as authors, editors and a whole host of other users worldwide.

Blogs: Every registered community member has their own blog to tell the world what they're up to and what's on their mind.

Book Challenge: We're aiming to read 5,000 books and have joined forces with The Reading Agency in our inaugural Book Challenge.

Profile Page: Showcase yourself and keep a record of your recent community activity.

Social Networking: We've added buttons at the end of every post to share via digg, Facebook, Google, Yahoo, technorati and de.licio.us.

www.millsandboon.co.uk

2 FREE BOOKS
AND A SURPRISE GIFT

We would like to take this opportunity to thank you for reading this Mills & Boon® book by offering you the chance to take TWO more specially selected books from the Special Moments™ series absolutely FREE! We're also making this offer to introduce you to the benefits of the Mills & Boon® Book Club™—

- **FREE home delivery**
- **FREE gifts and competitions**
- **FREE monthly Newsletter**
- **Exclusive Mills & Boon Book Club offers**
- **Books available before they're in the shops**

Accepting these FREE books and gift places you under no obligation to buy, you may cancel at any time, even after receiving your free books. Simply complete your details below and return the entire page to the address below. You don't even need a stamp!

YES Please send me 2 free Special Moments books and a surprise gift. I understand that unless you hear from me, I will receive 5 superb new stories every month, including a 2-in-1 book priced at £4.99 and three single books priced at £3.19 each, postage and packing free. I am under no obligation to purchase any books and may cancel my subscription at any time. The free books and gift will be mine to keep in any case.

Ms/Mrs/Miss/Mr _____ Initials _____

_____

Surname _____

Address _____

_____

_____ Postcode _____

Send this whole page to: Mills & Boon Book Club, Free Book Offer, FREEPOST NAT 10298, Richmond, TW9 1BR

Offer valid in UK only and is not available to current Mills & Boon Book Club subscribers to this series. Overseas and Eire please write for details.. We reserve the right to refuse an application and applicants must be aged 18 years or over. Only one application per household. Terms and prices subject to change without notice. Offer expires 31st December 2009. As a result of this application, you may receive offers from Harlequin Mills & Boon and other carefully selected companies. If you would prefer not to share in this opportunity please write to The Data Manager, PO Box 676, Richmond, TW9 1WU.

Mills & Boon® is a registered trademark owned by Harlequin Mills & Boon Limited.
Special Moments™ is being used as a trademark.
The Mills & Boon® Book Club™ is being used as a trademark.